Grand Central Publishing
Hachette Book Group
237 Park Avenue
New York, NY 10017

www.HachetteBookGroup.com

Printed in the United States of America

First Edition: May 2010
10  9  8  7  6  5  4  3  2  1

Grand Central Publishing is a division of Hachette Book Group, Inc.
The Grand Central Publishing name and logo is a trademark of Hachette Book Group, Inc.

Library of Congress Cataloging-in-Publication Data
Gomez, Iris D.
  Try to remember / Iris Gomez.—1st ed.
    p. cm.
  ISBN 978-0-446-55619-4
  1. Fathers and daughters—Fiction.   2. Mental illness—Fiction.   3. Immigrants—Fiction.   4. Domestic fiction.   5. Colombians—United States—Fiction.
6. Miami (Fla.)—Fiction.   I. Title.
  PS3607.O49T79 2010
  813'.6—dc22
                                                    2009032519

# PRAISE FOR
# Try to Remember

"This stunning debut offers a fresh and vibrant coming-of-age novel full of universal truths and dazzling particulars. Gabriela is a character you'll root for and grow to love. TRY TO REMEMBER is a book impossible to forget. I adored every single page."

—Mameve Medwed, national bestselling author
of *How Elizabeth Barrett Browning Saved My Life*
and *Of Men and Their Mothers*

# Try to Remember

## IRIS GOMEZ

GIC

**GRAND CENTRAL**
PUBLISHING

NEW YORK   BOSTON

G

*For Javier, Karen, and Mando,*
*with love from your sister*

## Patria

*That tangle of root vegetables*
*called "patria" receded, became more than*
*the place I'd belonged to,*
*and without the words to tell how I knew*
*my country was my father.*

# Try to Remember

## [ ONE ]

THE GREAT MIAMI HURRICANE OF 1971 took its time gathering. Only it wasn't the kind that rode in on distant winds, as if a fierce Caribbean cyclone were aiming its evil eye at us. No, the storm that would end up sweeping me away from my family stirred and blew its first breath right inside our pink Florida house.

My father had become absorbed in furious daily scribbling, his bedroom blinds shut against the piercing equatorial light. From time to time, the walls of our house shook slightly as planes flew overhead like giant robot seagulls. When he emerged from his abyss one afternoon, his black eyes grim, he lugged an old Royal typewriter in one hand and a smattering of *Seminole Sentinel* ads, *Journal of Home Mechanics* magazines, and loose leaf sheets of paper in the other. He tossed all that paper onto the Formica kitchen table in front of me. "¡Necesito estas cartas!"

"Sí, Papi." I shoved my worksheet aside for my father's task while repeating the fifth commandment, *Honor thy father and thy mother*, to myself. If he needed me to type his letters, that was surely what I would do.

The page at the top of his pile beamed whitely. His handwriting was dark with emphatic block letters, the ink trailing off as though the writing had been abandoned in an emergency.

DEAR TO BONIFAY INDUSTRIAL:

PLEASE I INTRODUCE MYSELF WITH RESPECT.
ROBERTO DE LA PAZ. WITH MANY YEARS EN LA
PRODUCCIÓN CRUDA, I PROPOSE TO YOU FOR
PUMP MANAGER POSICIÓN.

Of course, the Spanish words didn't belong—and wasn't Bonifay advertising for a solderer? I checked the classified ad in my
father's pile. I was right. But his letter said pump manager.

"What's that, Papi?" I underlined the words with my finger to
figure out the mistranslation.

"The pump? That's how the oil is recovered."

"Oil?" I reread the ad—nothing about oil—then studied the
rest of his letter dubiously while my father forced the typewriter
out of its ancient charcoal gray box.

IS IMPORTANTE MAINTAIN VALVE PRESSURE
CORRECT. MY EXPERIENCE DRILLING FOR
MEASURE OUTPUT. EN PUTUMAYO RESERVES,
IS NECESSARY INJECT THE WATER.

Apart from the problem that his Spanish didn't fit in, there
was no connection between one sentence and the next. I flipped
through the other equally peculiar letters with growing trepidation. Everything went downhill after the "DEAR SIR." Each letter
offered his services and opinions to product advertisers in *Home
Mechanics*, a peopleless glossy about equipment I'd never heard
of—the subscription gift, I recalled, from a Hialeah repair shop
where he'd been briefly employed after his airport job layoff. But
what did all this have to do with the classifieds?

"Papi," I responded at last, "you have to write for jobs the companies want. In the newspaper ads."

My father blinked. "What?"

"You can't pick any job and just apply for that."

He jumped out of his chair and loomed over me. "Didn't I tell you to type? Type it, ¡carajo!"

As I crouched into my seat, my mother rushed in, sponge rollers askew. "Roberto," she cajoled, "I need Gabrielita for just one minute. She'll be right back." Hands on my shoulders, she marched me out of there toward my room and sat us both down on the bed.

"Do what your father asks, mi'jita," she implored, her voice weighted by the duty of love.

I shook my head. "But those letters don't make sense, Mami."

"Por favor, mi'ja." She brushed a wild brown curl from my forehead. "Can't you make them better?"

I searched Mami's eyes, gold flecks floating in the wells of our family ojeras. Fleetingly, I recalled better times when my father used to tease his pretty wife, Evangelina, about being the baby of her own family. But that was back in the olden days. Before the dark circles beneath her eyes underscored how tired she'd become. "All right," I sighed. "I'll try."

I didn't exactly know *how* to try with this, but helping my parents had often helped me, too, to feel less confused. Assisting with their translations, utility company calls, and similar tasks, I'd earned my middle name, Auxiliadora—the Helper. Bringing in income, however, had been one burden that they alone shouldered—at least, until the layoff.

Now, as I returned to the kitchen, I bravely resolved to set aside my lapse in confidence over this unusual form of job-hunting.

My father patted the chair in front of the typewriter. "Toma, mi'ja."

"Gracias, Papi," I said, cautiously dropping into the chair and leaning forward for a sheet of paper. I rolled it into the Royal. Mami had bought the typewriter at a garage sale during our first cheerful month in Miami. Though she had finer dreams for me, at the very least, she'd told me that day, she would equip me for a decent secretarial position.

I mustered the nerve to inform my father about one of the many grammatical mistakes in his English: not putting "to" in front of verbs that required it, making the sentences look toothless. "You want me to fix that, Papi?"

"Sí, claro, mi'jita." All jolly now, he smiled as I began to edit bits of sense into his odd paragraphs. How futile the letters seemed. Regardless of the corrections, the electric drill company would not appreciate my father's convoluted notions of oil drilling in Colombia. But the word "drill" seemed to have rung a bell in my father's head and he wanted to ring it alongside the bells already there.

He watched patiently as I plodded away. "Gracias, mi'jita," he said once, touching my shoulder in affection.

*A father shouldn't have to depend on a kid to fix his letters,* I thought sadly. *Please, someone, take pity on him. Give him a job.*


For several days in a row, my fingers hunted that forest of keys with my father's breath on my neck, and my mind circling around and around the turn of events that had gotten me and my family so lost in this situation.

I'd never known better than to love them. Whatever might happen, I'd believed in my parents' dream: that Miami would make up for the long lost warmth, balconies, stars, and fishermen of Cartagena de Indias—the small Caribbean port city where I'd been born.

In the beginning, we'd lived like exiles in the Northeast. But after four years, that bitter North Pole of New York fell behind us, skyscrapers tumbling backwards in the rearview mirror of our rented van. We approached the southern horizon again, and our sky grew large. Trees, undaunted by a suffocating heat that passed for air through our windows, held out scrappy limbs, and we were Welcomed To Florida. Across an endless flatness, we zoomed past clumps of orange trees too short to shade cars from the wicked sunlight. Men with baseball caps worked in orchards. We passed gas stations, trailer parks, miles of nothing but heat and grass.

Here at last was cheery Miami: tin motel signs for working people on vacation, houses painted ice cream flavors, swishing palms, and tropical weather that lulled us into forgetting seasons could change.

Change, however, they had. On a bright Father's Day in June 1968, only two months after we'd settled into our new home, my mother announced that my father had lost the job that rescued us—my parents, my brothers Manolo and Pablo, and me—from cold, bitter Queens and reunited us with our large Miami family at last.

That was when I, Gabriela the Helper, got assigned to the *Seminole Sentinel* classified ads. My job was to stalk each issue with a blue Magic Marker for the elusive GRINDER position that my father needed. And then, after I had circled any ads I could find, I began the sad, confusing *Home Mechanics* letters I pecked out of the tired Royal typewriter.

Every day during that week, my father yelled after our postman in angry, rapid-fire Spanish for bringing the mail late, for bringing standardized rejections, or for not bringing anything. My mother and I waited on pins and needles until the poor rattled American mailman had come and gone.

Even before the advent of the *Home Mechanics* letters, I'd believed the underlying reason for my father's difficulty finding work was the English language. Despite a tape he listened to religiously, when the time came to answer in public, such as with a stranger asking for directions, my father clammed up, leaving it to me or someone else to respond. I knew it was embarrassing for him to make mistakes in front of people the way my mother did, not minding. "Ees eesy walk al A&P," she'd say, mixing in Spanish prepositions but forcing the inquiring pedestrian to listen until he got the gist. My father was too proud to expose himself like that. He wanted the world to see the mettle he was made of. But strength, I'd learned, didn't count when it came to learning a language. You had to let yourself be weak.

The letters became my first clue that a greater force was testing my father's mettle, although I didn't fully understand what it was until the day his scribbling blitz halted and Tío Victor and Tío Lucho, my father's brothers, showed up to coach him. I was finishing my summer reading, a surprisingly moving nature book called *The Everglades: River of Grass*, when they arrived. Pretty soon, I'd drifted from the grassy banks of the Everglades toward the decidedly more interesting conversation taking place among the men in the living room. Instead of advising my father to speak up for jobs, my uncles were encouraging him to speak *less*.

"You don't have to tell the world everything," said Tío Victor, taking the lead as usual. The youngest brother, Tío Victor had done well in this country. He'd joined Tío Lucho, the eldest, already working in Miami at a tailor shop, and later started a private lawn care business on the side. With his kind, sloping eyes, my generous Tío Victor was the uncle who, according to my mother, "nunca sufrió"—he'd never suffered. He didn't drop out of high school to support the women in the family the way my father had to when my abuelo died back in The Village of the Swallows, Montería.

"And especially don't discuss things with el jefe," added mild-mannered Tío Lucho, as he nervously lit his cigarette. He was more than a decade older than my father and Tío Victor, and he smoked so much that his skin was nearly as gray as his hair. "It's better," he puffed, "to keep your ideas to yourself."

"Why should I act dishonestly?" my father complained. "I work hard. I don't have anything to hide."

"No, it's not that," Tío Lucho coughed out. "It's just, you know, people don't always see things the same. Jobs are tricky. Why disagree with el jefe and give him excuses to... prefer someone more tranquil?"

"Tranquil?" My father's voice rose.

"Roberto," Tío Victor intervened. "Don't you see we're trying to help you, hombre?"

"Of course I do," my father railed. "But I'm the one with the new house and debts to pay. This isn't helping. Tell me where to look. That will help me."

My uncles fell silent. Finally, Tío Victor agreed to see what he could do.

After they'd gone, Mami and I gathered clothes off the line my father had strung between our mango and the unusually crossed lime/grapefruit trees. Casually I asked, "Mami, why did the tíos want Papi to talk less at job places?" Leaves stirred slightly as I removed an undershirt and tossed the clothespins into a basket.

Mami frowned. "Because of that Hialeah jefe," she replied, shaking the wrinkles out of a pair of slacks and relating the story. An odd conversation had terminated my father's one brief job since the airport layoff. For some reason, he'd tried to convince his boss to buy a giant drill. He even brought in drawings of the ones used in Colombian oil fields, despite the fact that the shop repaired tiny parts that had nothing to do with petroleum. His boss became aggravated when my father wouldn't drop the drill talk, and my hot, offended father quit on the spot. "And that wasn't the first time your father didn't control his temperamento," she added, grimacing as she hoisted the basket of clothes onto her hip to carry inside.

I stayed outside to finish folding the rest. The story gelled together several troubling ways in which my father had been changing over the last few months. There were his new, weird ideas to contend with and his temper, which had undeniably gotten worse. Take the blowup the day before, when he'd pelted my younger brother Manolo's legs with a belt just for letting the hose run for too long. Though my father had always had a short fuse, these recent fits were more extreme, unpredictable. It bothered me, too, that other people like Tío Paco, Mami's brother, had lost a job without becoming so angry and difficult.

As I folded our washed brocade tablecloth under the mango tree, a sentimental longing for how my father used to be composed itself from bits of memory into the picture of faraway Queens. A great, grassy hill had connected our pedestrian bridge to Lucio Antonio Fiorini Highway, and I could see my father laughing at the bottom of that hill, with sunlight in his eyes and wearing a shirt like the sky, while Manolo and I rolled down, yelling at the top of our lungs with as much fear as excitement, until my father caught us and lifted us out of that wild gravity.

The picnic had been his idea; he'd carried the brocade tablecloth, our camera, and lunches in his straw mochila while squeezing each of us in turn through the gated opening he'd discovered walking home from his night job. The breeze was cool, and bright spring grass sloped down on three sides of us so that I imagined we'd climbed a mountain—the first time, maybe the only time, that something in that cold and colorless network of buildings, bridges, and highways that was New York became almost beautiful.

A few minutes later, I carried my folded laundry inside, and the father from the beautiful picnic promptly evaporated, leaving in his stead the black typewriter beside a large stack of papers on the table.

I cast a pained look at my mother, whose eyes flashed in momentary annoyance, but she continued cleaning as if all were right with the world.

Rifling through his papers, I heaved a deep sigh. "It's so much," I said feebly, more to myself than to her. But resigned to my duty, I sank into a chair and began the daunting task before me.

When the sounds of my brothers playing football with new-found friends trickled in from the yard an hour later, the disappointment over everything that Miami was supposed to offer us washed over me like a tsunami. My searching eyes found my mother, blithely tossing onion slices into the sizzling frying pan. Did she secretly believe that these mixed-up letters might help my father find work? My uncles' words of advice—*don't tell the world everything*—crackled ominously in my head. Perhaps my father shouldn't be broadcasting his thoughts on paper any more than in conversations. As I gazed at his inky black handwriting, another possibility darkened there too: Maybe neither of my parents knew what they were doing anymore.

## TWO

IWAS RELIEVED when my father resumed his bus rides in pursuit of *Sentinel* job listings. More glad tidings arrived with my
fat back-to-school packet in the mail. Eagerly carrying the manila
envelope to my room, I hesitated in front of our hallway phone. I
thought of the one friend I'd made here: Lydia. We'd met at the
bus stop in front of her house, a shadowy place with thick brush
and rubbery plants squeezing up against rough-textured walls—
that was back in the spring after my family moved here. Most
Miami houses were spread out wide, exposed to the sun, but hers
seemed to belong to the insular "old Florida" era that our chatty
neighbor Mr. Anderson often described.

Lydia wore lipstick. "Wanna try it?" she'd asked, as I watched
her apply the shimmering white lip color over her mouth. She was
busty and dark-skinned, with shiny black curls she greased into
points at her temples.

I shook my head vigorously.

"¿Qué te pasa, chica?"

I told her what the problem was: "I'm not allowed." I explained
that on my father's moral equivalency charts, waltzing in wearing
lipstick rated right alongside prostitution.

"So what. Take it off before you get home," she suggested.

This girl wasn't too knowledgeable about the fifth command-ment. She had very little notion, it seemed to me, of how a person earned points for Heaven. I felt obligated to fill her in.

"¡Ay chica! We don't go to church," she replied wanly, smiling as if she pitied me because I did. Then we grabbed seats together on the bus and began comparing families. I started off by listing the Miami relatives ahead of those left in Cartagena—saving for last my beloved grandfather Gabriel, who wrote me long, elegant verses praising the waves and light of the Caribbean on each of my birthdays.

"You're lucky," she commented. Lydia, her parents, and her brother Emilio had arrived from Camagüey "to escape Fidel Castro."

I'd heard about Fidel, so I nodded knowingly.

On the day school recessed for the year, Lydia gave me her phone number. All summer long, I couldn't get over my awkward-ness about making the call. But some greater need propelled me to do so now.

"Hi, chica," she answered warmly.

"Hola, Lydia," I replied, losing my shyness. "Hey, did you get your assignment letter?"

"Yeah. I have that witch doctor, el brujo Silber."

I laughed and told her my teacher's name, then asked about meeting at the bus stop like before.

"Gabriela!" my mother called out. "Who are you talking to?"

"Just someone from school!" An uneasy twinge accompanied the recollection of Mami's admonishments against befriending anyone who didn't come from Una Familia Decente. But how was I supposed to know if Lydia's family was decent unless I did befriend her?

Quickly, I finished up my phone conversation and went to see what Mami wanted. I sent a flutter of prayers up toward the Holy

Family in Heaven. *Let Lydia stay my friend. Let her family turn out to
be decent. Please.*


The following day, after I'd typed another oddball letter, my father
went to see about a real job and Mami took me to Little Havana
to get my medical permission slip for gym class. No longer could
a permission slip be accepted without a doctor certifying that he'd
actually examined me. Last spring, after I'd turned my note in,
I'd been assigned to the library with other excused Latinas whose
families had ultraconservative views about female propriety. For
the rest of the term, messengers periodically brought handouts,
such as "The History of Women's Volleyball in Massachusetts"
and "Female Reproduction," and marched The Excused into the
auditorium for tests; but most of the time, I'd read novels galore
from the library stacks.

For my doctor's appointment, Mami insisted I don a dress she'd
made me with a rose cotton print and puffy shoulders that seemed
way too juvenile. Stoically, however, I tied the sash around my
back and uttered not one word of protest as I clipped my unruly
hair into a ponytail. Chibcha hair, my father often teased Mami
whenever the thick, dark locks defied her efforts to tame them. The
reference was to the indígenas of Colombia who seemed to have left
subtler traces in history than the Mayas and Aztecs, who were actually taught about in textbooks. The morning of my appointment,
as I stood in front of the mirror without my mass of hair to hide
behind, my eyes appeared bigger and blacker—as if I were growing
up to be more my father's daughter than Mami's, despite the lonesome Arabic eyes I'd inherited from her side of the family.

Little Havana was an expanding Cuban neighborhood of stucco
houses with Virgin Mary statues and Santería food offerings in
the yards. Not only was the neighborhood larger in size than its

name portended, it had no resemblance whatsoever to the Havana
of postcards I'd seen pasted to Lydia's notebook. That Havana had
breathtaking views of the Atlantic Ocean, majestic Spanish buildings with romantic facades, and prettily coiffed women in dresses
and pumps.

The doctor's office was not even in a hospital or clinic. It was in
a stucco house with the typical Florida door—an aluminum frame
that held rows of windowpanes you cranked open with a lever. Inside
the house, the doctor sat behind a desk in a dark, paneled office. The
dim illumination was a good thing, since Dr. Sanabria was so unattractive. It was hard to decide which feature—his extremely large
size, the loose hair on his scalp, or the big stains on his hands—was
the ugliest. The doctor seemed too tired to get out of his chair,
and my examination consisted of questions directed exclusively to
Mami about my general well-being and character as a person.

"Se diría que es nerviosa." This was stated more as an assertion
than a question.

My mother reflected. "Yes, I would say she's a little nervous."

"Y la menstruación —¿padece de dolores?"

Mami looked down modestly, fiddling with her pocketbook.
"Oh yes," she agreed. Her daughter suffered from menstrual
cramps too.

For five more minutes, Dr. Sanabria continued to suggest symp-
toms of some malady that he seemed sure afflicted me. I felt grateful that there would be no actual physical examination, though
its omission made me suspicious about whether the guy was a real
doctor. In Latin America people with degrees, like lawyers, were
customarily referred to as doctor, but that didn't mean the same
thing here.

At the conclusion of the appointment Dr. Sanabria extracted
a sheet of stationery from his drawer. Slowly and in large, terrible
penmanship, he wrote out the permission slip that was to excuse

me from the Flagler Junior High School Physical Education Curriculum.

When we returned home, Mami told me not to say anything to my father about the note because it would only upset him to hear about these immoral aspects of public education. Of course, I did as I was told.

Passing his silent bedroom cavern, I could only hope he'd found a more constructive way to use his time than the frantic writing that was becoming a burden to me.

In the living room, oblivious to anything else happening in our household, my brothers sat watching TV. As if I didn't have a care in the world either, I ambled in, joining my youngest brother, Pablo, who was comfortably ensconced on the two-seater couch with the orange cushions. Manolo was in a chair by himself. Shortly afterward, Mami came in and started flipping through the channels until she settled on a movie about gladiators and sat down. Sunlight jabbed us through the blinds as we became engrossed in the movie.

Then my father made his entrance. He stood off to the side at first. Mami patted a chair near her, but he continued to stand, and after a while we forgot about him altogether. That is, until the kissing started.

Hercules had untied his hands and managed to extricate himself from a primitive stone torture wheel. Male slaves turned the wheel, and one of the bad guys continually whipped them to turn faster. Earlier on, Hercules had won the slaves over, so they revolted and helped him escape. Now, quickly, he made his way up a winding stone stairway into the gloomy dungeon where his sexy girlfriend was being restrained. Valiantly, he broke in, and the lovebirds embraced with passionate kisses.

"¡Basura!" my father burst out in anger.

Caught up in the drama, we all ignored him. We wanted to

see how Hercules would slip himself and his true love out of the dungeon without getting stabbed by the army of bad guys in the process. But just as Hercules and his lady love untangled from their embrace and the muscular hero unsheathed his knife, my father whacked the TV off with his palm and yelled at us again that it was garbage. As his attack continued, Pablo and I backed up to protect ourselves from his swinging arm.

Mami tried to object. "Pero Roberto—" She didn't finish the sentence, because when my father turned around his face was terrifying.

That was the moment I seized to creep away. With my heart racing, I escaped into the bathroom and pulled in the wall phone to call Lydia—just to hear a normal voice. *Maybe I'll tell her about that questionable Dr Sanabria*, I planned out mentally, but as we began chitchatting, I heard my father screaming his head off about how his mujeres weren't going to be watching any more of that basura!

"What's that noise?" a startled Lydia asked.

"Um, my parents are having a fight," I mumbled apologetically. "I mean, about what our family can watch. My father's kind of strict." Even that minor disclosure felt disloyal.

"My parents let me watch whatever I want," Lydia confided. "They have bad fights too, about worse stuff." She admitted that sometimes her father didn't come home until the wee hours of the morning, and that her mother waited up all night to yell at him and call him names like ¡mentiroso! and ¡mujeriego! "I don't even care if she does get a divorce," Lydia concluded, "as long as my brother and me get to stay in the house with her."

Lydia's shocking but matter-of-fact revelations unnerved me, though a part of me envied her—in her house there was no doubt that her father was the villain. You didn't have to feel sorry for him, even when he was acting unreasonably.

•    •    •

The following Tuesday, while my brothers walked to nearby Rick-enbacker Elementary, I boarded my bus to Flagler Junior High, a pastel complex of one-story buildings that had been augmented with a cluster of aquamarine trailers to accomodate the growing number of Cuban refugees "rescued" by the Americans. No one had saved me, a Colombian immigrant, but I fit right in among them with my homemade wardrobe and old-fashioned parents. Nationality mattered less than the fact that we all ate arroz every day and spoke Spanish. Here, in contrast to my parochial school in Queens, I could speak my native language on the playground, in the halls and cafeteria, and even during class if a teacher wasn't paying attention. All my Spanish broke free of its dams and flowed out of me.

Since I'd moved here so late in the school year, I didn't know many people and was eager to pal up with Lydia. Together, we headed to gym. Lydia didn't have a doctor's note to excuse her from undressing among strangers, and soon I wished I didn't either. The teacher, whose face seemed to be engraved with a permanent scowl, frowned at Dr. Sanabria's permission slip. She tapped her amazingly white sneaker against a stool and announced, "I'm taking this to the principal." Then she pushed a lock and gym suit at me. "Go change."

*What could be wrong with my doctor's note?* I worried as I turned to nervously follow the other girls. If only Phys. Ed. could be an elective like Spanish, I wished forlornly, imagining my father's apoplectic face when he found out the school made us undress. Even my mother had reacted badly when I'd first brought home the gym suit payment request. "Why aren't your own clothes allowed?" she'd demanded, examining the notice suspiciously. "The nuns never made you change your clothing."

"We're supposed to exercise on a field and you sweat a lot," I'd tried to explain patiently. "They want us to shower so we won't smell."

"Shower!" Mami exclaimed.

"Yes! They have a room with showers. And when you come out, the teacher hands you a clean towel."

"You're naked?" she'd asked, incredulous. That had prompted her to spring into action. She got on the phone with relatives until she found out about the mysterious Dr. Sanabria. Though she'd acted as if her own morals were at stake, I knew they were wrapped up with those of the Latin American dictator in charge of our feminine virtue.

Now, as other girls began changing in the locker room, I tried to figure out how to undress as modestly as possible in that very public arena. The truth was, I wasn't looking forward to disrobing and parading around in the nude myself. Hesitantly, I unfolded my gym suit and slowly began putting it on under my jumper. Then I rapidly slipped the jumper off over my head while sliding the gym suit up to cover my bra at the same time. Out of breath by then, I jerked my arms into the suit and quickly snapped it shut over my chest. When I darted anxious glances around the room, no one seemed to be watching. The other girls were too preoccupied with how bad their own suits looked on them to judge me. I studied myself in the nearest mirror. The gym suit was made out of a white canvas material you couldn't see through. The top half was okay, but the bottom resembled a diaper that bunched up over your rear. This totally accentuated the thighs, and mine suddenly felt more naked than they ever had before.

Alina, a friend of Lydia's who'd been assigned a locker next to mine, complained bitterly. "At least you have long legs," she pointed out. "Look at these fat drumsticks."

I shook my head in empathy as we headed outside. Since I hadn't brought in sneakers, I was forced to wear my flats, making my long, exposed legs stand out even more. How immoral I felt wearing that outfit!

Soon, however, our activities made me forget about appearances and morality.

First, we were ordered to jog around the field. It was toasty out—not a lick of dew left in the grass. I teamed up with Lydia and Alina as we seemed to be the slowest of the bunch. Other girls whizzed by, making fun of us, and Alina whistled back in defiance. By the time we reached Miss Michaels and her stopwatch, my feet ached from running in flats and I was completely drenched in sweat. Alina gave me a high-five for being the last one in with her. At least I was making friends.

Miss Michaels glared. "Ladies," she said coldly, "we need to work toward an eleven-minute mile." Then she shooed us over to the other side of the field, where a plucky girl named Connie McGill was supervising other girls on various exercise contraptions. The most intimidating of these was The Horse, a wooden podium topped with a vinyl pad that we were expected to run toward and then leap over, splitting our legs apart, to land harmlessly and gracefully on our feet. In Alina's group, shrieks of joy rang out when somebody actually made it across safely. Miss Michaels ordered those who'd completed a successful jump to the tennis nets, then stood before the rest of us with her arms crossed. "This is not a joke. I expect each of you to perform this jump. Do you understand me?"

Doubtful nods followed.

Lydia strolled diffidently to the front and managed to get across with a slight push from the spotter. Her fans applauded and cheered. Next, there were two failed attempts by a big girl, Margarita Dominguez, and her friend Carmen. No one laughed this time. Miss Michaels wiped her forehead with a towel. By the time my turn came, I had a terrible case of jitters. Plus, the podium was like distant Pluto. How would I ever reach it?

"You don't have to start so far back," Miss Michaels yelled at me. But I didn't trust her. I backed up a few more steps, closed my eyes, willed the nervousness out of me, and ran as fast as humanly possible. At some point, I heard Miss Michaels yell "Jump!" and leapt at her command—succeeding in grabbing the vinyl covering before my shoulders inexplicably hit wood. I'd entirely forgotten to shoot out my legs and somersaulted over, landing on the damp grass beyond the podium. Flat on my back, I thought of my family—my mother, aunts, uncles, and especially my Jehovah-like father—hovering above my hospital bed while I lay comatose and awaiting final Judgment in that awful, skimpy white gym suit. When a pair of helping hands pulled me to a sitting position, my life returned, and I was surprised to find that despite a burning sensation in my neck nothing was even broken. I scrambled to my feet.

Without a word of contempt, Miss Michaels pointed her pencil toward the tennis nets.

After that nerve-wracking experience, I slid thankfully into a seat in an ordinary class. There, amid the whirring fans, I was delighted to discover that everyone around me was Latino. For the first time, I'd actually been allowed to study Spanish at school. Señora Rubio, a petite Cuban matron in an ivory blouse and skirt, began the class as if she were an agent sent there by all Latino parenthood: "¿Qué es familia?" she inquired.

Only one person—a quirky, dark-haired boy named Claudio Sotomayor—raised his hand. From the back, he murmured something about family meaning heritage and human history. His serious voice made me turn around in order to hear better, but he spoke in abstractions that floated as if on parallelograms of light across the room. In the warmth of the trailer where our class was held, I began to drift dreamily with the rhythm of the sounds until the meaning of familia slipped away.

Lydia invited me to her house after school. Eager to postpone

*Sentinel* searches and typing, I called Mami for permission to do my homework there and hung up afterward with only a small twinge of guilt. She wouldn't have been so agreeable had she known the scandal that was unfolding at Lydia's house. Still, it was only Lydia's father who was indecent, I reassured myself, not her whole family.

As she and I stepped off the bus, we were greeted by her older brother, who was sprawled, hairy and shirtless, across their front steps. Let me just say that Emilio's morals were nothing my parents would approve of either. His magazines were spread out so that we could clearly see naked women in them, and he was leaning back on his elbows to observe our reactions. I hesitated at the bottom of the stoop.

"Emilio, you're a jerk," said Lydia, kicking his dirty magazines as she flounced up the steps. "Come on, Gabi."

"Maybe she likes them." He raised one thick eyebrow at me.

I shook my head in vehement denial and raced into the house behind Lydia.

When we reached her bedroom, I sat in a chair and got out my math problems while she went rummaging for her mother's foto-novelas. The sexy photograph-filled comics, with their compli-cated sagas of forlorn ex-wives or bitter mothers-in-law conspiring to lure sons back from the clutches of an evil woman, were wildly popular in Miami. Even Mami devoured them when Tía Rita or her new Colombian friend Camila occasionally passed one on, although Lydia's mother seemed to be a real fotonovela junkie.

"Here," said Lydia, offering me a whole stack. "Take these home if you want."

"Wow. Thanks a lot." I'd only been able to read my mother's occasional fotonovela in secrecy, and sometimes skimmed one of Lydia's on the morning bus ride before she traded it away at school.

An hour later, I was heading home.

Kissing my mother's cheek, I went to briefly greet my father before darting back to the kitchen. As I sat down to complete emergency contact and medical forms, I wondered again how I could prepare my mother for this gym class situation.

"Mami," I queried tentatively, twirling the pencil between two fingers. "Should I put Dr. Sanabria down as my doctor?"

"Oh no. Put the hospital."

"Jackson Memorial? That's strange, Mami. You can't write the name of a hospital. It has to be a doctor."

"¡Ay, mi'ja! Don't put anything then."

*Was he not a real doctor then?* I worried, imagining the school's investigation.

In the end, I scribbled "Not Applicable." I would have to wait and see what Miss Michaels did before I discussed any gym matters with Mami.

After dinner, while my brothers watched television, I snuck into bed with one of Lydia's fotonovelas disguised behind a textbook. In the distance, I could almost hear the ghostly echo of my puritanical father yelling at the mujeres sucias who flaunted their sexy wiles on the TV screen and in the pages of my magazine. I got up and went to make sure my father wasn't actually nearby. It was only my nerves acting up, so I climbed back into bed and resumed the illicit reading. My heart kept beating rapidly in fear that he might appear. Frustrated, I ducked into the bathroom and locked the door to finish reading in peace there.

The next morning—with sneakers in hand—I bravely reported for gym class. To my surprise, Miss Michaels beckoned me toward her office. She opened a folding chair for me. "Sit down. I want to talk to you about your health."

An alarm went off in my head. *Would she quiz me?* Quickly, I made a mental review of what Dr. Sanabria had written about my condition that "contraindicated sports."

"Girls your age need to exercise regularly," Miss Michaels began. "Your heart needs it. Your mind too."

Was she going to make me do an alternative exercise? Calisthenics? Yoga? That would be okay if I didn't have to change clothes.

"Gabriela." She leaned forward and looked me squarely in the eye. "I know what's going on with those notes. You know very well why we have Phys Ed. It's not a punishment, for God's sake."

With her eyes probing me, I pretended to fiddle with the combination lock I held in my lap. She'd practically accused me of cheating. I'd never cheated. Ever. That stupid permission slip hadn't been my idea, though now I felt responsible for it.

"I'm so sorry, Miss Michaels," I offered humbly. "I know Phys. Ed. is good for you." I wanted to go on and explain the note, but a nightmarish vision of my father storming the girls' locker room and ripping up gym suits while calling everyone prostitutes stopped me. How could I explain the very unusual world of home? Still, I felt obligated to try. "Miss Michaels, it's just that—" I took a deep breath. "My family's different." But as soon as those words left my lips, I felt I'd betrayed my entire familia.

"Everybody's family is different, Gabriela. Not all Cuban students excuse themselves from gym."

"We're Colombian."

"Whatever. You know what I mean."

I took a good look around at the Presidential Medals, Certificates of Achievement, and team pictures of blonde girls in tennis skirts. Things for Americans were awfully black and white. Not much room for my complications. Why, oh, why couldn't I have been good in all the ways people expected me to be—a gym star as well as honorable to my family? I sighed in frustration, and then

I sighed in defeat. The difference between my parents' world and this one was so great that the ball—me—would never get across the net.

Miss Michaels waited, trying not to tap her sneaker, for me to say something more.

"I'm sorry, Miss Michaels," I repeated feebly.

"Okay." She slapped her hands on her thighs and stood up straight. "Why don't you go down to the library?"

Silently and without looking her in the eye, I handed back the lock that I no longer needed. She folded up the chair, her silver whistle tinkling.

## THREE

Tío VICTOR FINALLY PUT my father in contact with a
Cuban contractor his lawn care business partner knew. For
several nights in a row, my father patiently called the contractor to check on his roofing schedule. But after getting the fourth
"call tomorrow" spiel, my father stormed into the living room
where the rest of us were quietly watching a movie. For a while
he stood silently, testily shifting position. Then the inevitable lov-
ers' embrace unfolded on the screen. Immediately, he went on a
rampage, kicking the defenseless TV while struggling not to trip
on his long pants. The TV wobbled, and I raced fearfully to my
room.

This fit, unlike the last, had been sparked by an embrace
between married characters. Wasn't that normal, married people
kissing? What did he find so offensive about that? In the calm of
my room, I tried to reason logically. He and Mami had once held
hands, after all, when they went walking. But maybe that was
too long ago, back when he wasn't going bananas over every tiny
thing. Maybe Mami didn't love him as much anymore. Maybe
watching romantic TV embraces reminded him that he was missing something.

I tried to stifle my preoccupation with these incidents by

reading, but my troubled mind kept returning to when my father had been predictable and behaved like a normal person, instead of a scary one who chased people out of rooms. The last happy day I could remember was in the summertime, when he'd gotten our dining room table out of layaway. To celebrate, Mami had prepared his favorite dessert, dulce de leche, the old-fashioned way, stirring the milk and sugar on the hot stove with her wooden spoon. Surely, she'd loved him then. After dinner, my father had eaten several helpings and the dessert disappeared from our yellow serving bowl. He'd tried to convince my brothers to surrender some, teasing them, "You boys are one-fourth my size. I should get four times as much." But Manolo and Pablo had only answered by wolfing down their dessert, while my father watched longingly.

"Toma, Papi," I'd said then, willingly passing him my plate.

How gratefully he'd smiled over that little portion of dulce de leche. "Gabrielita, you're the one who really loves me."

As nice as the memory was, I forced myself to shake it off and focus on my assigned pages of *The Heart Is a Lonely Hunter*. After a while, I had to stop and rest my own heart. Sometimes the girl in that book made it painful to read.

Perhaps the Cuban contractor had a heart too, since he ended up giving my father a roofing job a couple of days later—and it was like the windows of our house flew open.

Construction work was dependent, however, on how many men the boss had already lined up for each project. Often, my father didn't know until late at night whether he would be needed the following dawn. Mami hardly slept, waiting for the call and rising early to prepare his breakfast when he got asked to work. My father went roofing and came home filthy and sunburned. Though the grueling hours of physical labor wore him out, they put a fortunate end to his frightening outbursts over the TV embraces, our incoming mail, and the simple incidents of everyday life.

The week he started roofing, I started traipsing off happily with Lydia to the Chekika public library every day after school. Outside the sleek white building, she taught me the art of smoking cigarettes, and then we went in for our books. Lydia wasn't exactly a model student, but she loved reading Gothic novels. For me, they offered a superior advantage over fotonovelas: The darkish landscape covers were a perfect smoke screen for the passionate romances my father would have deemed trashy, opening up the possibility of anxiety-free reading in the comfort of my own room instead of the unpleasant bathroom. I immediately became addicted to the Gothics as well, even begging Mami to let me stay home one night when we were expected at Tía Rita's. Mami flatly refused, saying she wouldn't allow me to turn into a montuna—a simple country girl lacking in all social graces.

Passion, I quickly discovered, also dominated the revelatory notas that girls in Lydia's clique exchanged at school along with their fotonovelas. Unfortunately for me, unlike Lydia who obsessed over a flirtatious lover-boy at the gas station near the library, I didn't "like" anyone. My father's TV fits were giving me a complex about real-life kissing, and I hoped to avoid the boy thing altogether. Still, I wanted to fit in with the gang, so I searched for someone safe to pretend to moon over and ended up choosing a green-eyed Cuban boy who had a girlfriend and, thankfully, no idea that I existed. In my own notas to the girls about him, I aimed to emulate Gothic novels, but it was more difficult to compare El Gringo, our secret alias for him, to my metropolitan landscape than a Gothic hero to the wild English moors. My creativity was squelched by Miami's cement and glitter, the condominiums and corner malls under perpetual construction all the way out to the unincorporated lands beyond the city. For beauty, I had to stick to Biscayne Bay. My pals had hearty laughs over "the salty waves of El Gringo's stormy eyes," but the fictional romance of notas,

Gothic novels, and fotonovelas let me rise above my own drab and disappointing life for once, like those Frenchmen over Paris in the first hot air balloon.

Then one night at home, the little bubble of optimism burst. The contractor called to say that my father's roofing job was no more.

The next morning, Saturday, I was forced awake early by the sounds of Mami clobbering around the house while reciting her trials and tribulations. With my eyes closed, I listened for a lament over the untimely demise of my father's roofing job, but the only new woe I heard in the litany was that the washing machine had given out.

My father devoured his breakfast in seemingly peaceful oblivion. Putting aside the *Sentinel* ads I'd marked up at my mother's command, he escorted my brother Manolo and me to the nearby Laundromat with our hampers of dirty clothing. While I loaded washers, my father chatted with the Cuban owner whose friendly demeanor seemed false to me, but at least the guy didn't appear to mind my father's conversational eccentricities. After a while, my father left me with my twelve-year-old brother to chaperone. Manolo didn't want to stay, but my father reminded him that he was the man of the family in his father's absence and pathetic Manolo believed him. When our clothes were fully dry, I was supposed to send Manolo to fetch my father. Why I required a paternal escort back and forth if I was left to my own devices in between was another unsolved mystery in my father's moral code.

Arnoldo, the owner, was a balding guy with gold teeth he flashed while offering Manolo and me free Cokes. When Manolo went to sit by the chairs, Arnoldo walked over to hand me my soda. I thanked him, popped the can open, and then lifted it to my lips, but suddenly Arnoldo came around behind me and his grubby hands began rubbing my breasts. In shock, I choked, dropping the Coke.

Laughing evilly, Arnoldo let go of me. "I'll get you another one."

"No, thanks." I dashed to the chairs, plopped myself next to Manolo, and placed our laundry basket on the other side, my arm on top so that the sicko couldn't sit there.

After our clothes dried, I went for my father instead of sending Manolo.

I was terrified of telling my father what had happened. What if he blamed me? The outfit I'd worn consisted of a baggy T-shirt and shorts that camouflaged my developing body. But still, what if he didn't believe that I hadn't invited the guy's lewd advances?

When we returned home later with all our clothes done, I thought I would go tell Mami about it and found her outside, gardening. Before I could find the words to explain, I saw her kneeling beside the níspero seedling our elderly neighbor, Mr. Krantz, had given her. A confusing shame overcame me and I quashed the impulse to confide. Turning around, I went back inside to put away the clean clothes.

When I'd returned to help plant, someone called my name from across the street. It was Lydia, waving and coming toward us.

Awkwardly, I introduced Mami and Lydia to each other.

Lydia smiled and commented on how nice it was that my mother was growing her own tree. "I wish my mother would try that. We only have bushes by our house."

"We'll have to see if it grows," Mami replied with a shy smile. "Si Dios quiere." Despite giving God the credit, she seemed pleased that Lydia had recognized her contribution to the process.

Lydia asked if I wanted to go the library, but after that awful Arnoldo episode, I wasn't in the mood, so I told her I wasn't feeling well.

She turned to Mami. "Do you need anything from the 7-Eleven, señora? I have to stop on my way back."

Mami declined the offer politely and Lydia took off.

"That girl has good modales," Mami concluded, as she knelt back down in the dirt, pleased I'd found a friend with such good manners.

Off and on for the rest of the week, the Laundromat lecher slipped into my thoughts uninvited. Somehow, in the frenzy of typing my unemployed father's perplexing letters, I managed to forget about it until Manolo jostled me awake on Saturday morning with the news that our washer was beyond repair.

Thunder cracked out my window. Clouds drifted rapidly across the sky, the way one would expect them to on Judgment Day if God were really as mean as in the images from my old catechism text. Maybe, if luck were with me, it would rain. *Deliver us from Laundry Duty,* I prayed.

But the skies didn't deliver a single drop of rain, and off we went. I was greatly relieved to see a noisy family also doing their laundry this time. After my father had gone, I hung around near the mother while her kids were off pushing metal carts against one another and keeping Arnoldo busy pulling the carts away. He tried to chastise the kids without offending their pudgy mother, a lady in pink rollers and painted-on eyebrows who appeared to be a graduate of the Ay Bendito school of mothering—throwing her hands up in the air and uttering "¡Ay bendito!" each time one of her children did something bad. Arnoldo kept giving her his fake laugh.

When my clothes dried, I stationed myself at the folding area next to her. Feeling safe, I sent Manolo home for my father. I didn't count on them taking so long to come pick me up, though. When the lady finished and wheeled her cart away, I threw my unfolded clothes into a cart in alarm and wheeled after her, but Arnoldo was faster. He caught me in both arms and started the horrible rubbing thing. Somehow, he pinned me between himself and the table and went straight for my crotch. I nearly hyperventilated out of panic. A nauseating odor of cumin mixed with sweat, as if he'd used spices for deodorant, overwhelmed me as I tried to wriggle out of his grip. Only when one of the lady's kids began shaking the Coke machine on the other side of the Laundromat and quarters started popping out did Arnoldo finally release me to attend to that.

Seizing the moment, I grabbed my clothes basket and made a mad dash for home. Cars swished past me down Calle Ocho at a dizzying speed with other lecherous Arnoldos beeping out of them at me. When my father and brother came into view, I ran to meet them, handed over the basket, and sped homeward.

Mami complained about the wrinkled clothes. "See what happens when you don't fold first," she said, showing me a crumpled shirt.

"I'll iron it," I offered wearily, knowing then that I would never tell her.

The next morning, I went to the early services at St. Stephens. It was a contemporary church with pale pastel windows, as if Florida had drained them of their original color. My mother attended Mass there sporadically; my father and brothers, not at all. I'd become the family emissary, my prayers very weighted. But without the Benedictine sisters around to guide me, I felt lost in the echoing vastness of this Miami church where a person was utterly exposed. How I missed my small, dark church in Queens!

I'd always been afraid of God and avoided praying directly to Him. Instead, I prayed to the Holy Family—Baby Jesus, the Virgin Mary and gentle Joseph—with God the Father merely hovering nearby. This time, I prayed to them all from the heart. I asked for the Laundromat sicko to leave me alone; for a miracle job for my difficult, desperate father; for relief for me and the entire family from his horrible temper; and for Mami to lay down her worries once and for all. Most and hardest of all, I prayed for a stronger faith in both my parents.

Like a sign from Heaven, a tiny path was illuminated through the quagmire of my father's moral doctrine by the *TV Guide*. "Look," I exclaimed to Mami that afternoon as we stood at the A&P checkout counter and I pointed out movie descriptions. "I can try to figure out which ones Papi will like, so he won't get mad."

She brightened at the prospect of relaxed TV viewing too. "All right, mi'ja," she said, adding the digest to our cart.

When we got home, I read the whole week's worth of *TV Guide* listings and highlighted the programming that seemed unlikely to spike my father's temper. *The Wizard of Oz*, game shows like *You Don't Say!*, and cartoons seemed like good choices. I picked out a couple of horror movies too.

Later that night, as we all sat watching complacently, a scene in the horror movie nevertheless managed to incite my father's wrath. Mami tried to defend the vampire, who wasn't kissing the girl, he only wanted to suck her blood. But when my father was on a moral rampage, you couldn't sit around and discuss the subtleties of a movie. My brothers and I fled.

Hours later, I ventured out of my room and noticed that Mami was still sitting alone and quiet, with her arms folded over herself, in front of the dark television set. Watching her, I began to worry whether any job existed that would work out for my father, if no one could tame his terrible temper.

Tío Victor and Tío Lucho arrived the following Saturday in response to Mami's call for help. While my father was taking a shower, the uncles sipped tintos and Mami planted herself across from them to plead for a job, any job my uncles could think of, that my father might perform at their tailor shop. The problem was, my uncles were only employees, though both had worked at Sal's a long time. Tío Lucho had been employed there eleven years. Marrying early, after his father died, he'd become the first to immigrate here. I had trouble understanding how Mami could expect my uncles to rescue us from the entire problem of my father; but it was as if she refused to accept that perhaps there were some things in life from which no one could rescue you.

"We'll do what we can," said Tío Lucho wearily. "Maybe we can use another sweeper, eh Victor?"

Tío Victor cocked his head doubtfully. "Maybe."

After the uncles had gone, I washed out the coffee cups and returned to my room while mulling over the jobs my father had held since his airport layoff. How abruptly they'd all ended. My parents hadn't really explained why that contractor stopped calling my father for work either. The story of the Hialeah jefe and the drill nagged at me.

"Mami," I inquired when she came in, "what if Papi says or does something that turns into a problem for the uncles? What if they end up losing their jobs?"

"Don't be disrespectful," she retorted. "I've told you a thousand times. Your father is a hard worker. Where did those nice things in your room come from?" She gestured toward my pink and white décor. "Your father's sweat, mi'ja. Your father's sweat."

But I saw trouble in her eyes.


That afternoon I grimly rescued myself from my private struggle by making Manolo stick with me through all stages of Laundromat washing and drying. No way was I going to be left alone with that pervert anymore. Manolo gave Arnoldo his ignorant, goofy-tooth smile and sat down to drink his free Coke, and I quickly nabbed a vacant seat between my brother and another kid. I refused Arnoldo's complimentary drink offer.

"I don't like Coke," I told Manolo, who looked at me puzzled.

"But there's Oranhina," Arnoldo replied, pronouncing it the Latin way—*h* instead of *g.*

"I don't like any sodas," I insisted, staring into my novel.

Arnoldo returned a wicked chuckle.

Only when I got home to my room did I give in to feeling sorry for myself. My gaze fell on the photograph of my grandfather from my little kid days. He was wearing a white guayabera and smiled out of those slow eyes I'd inherited. Back then, either my grandfather or Mami would grab my hand the second we walked out the door and hold on tightly until I'd been safely delivered to wherever I was supposed to be. In my mind, I knew I was too old for that silly hand-holding stuff, but the little girl still inside tried to push out of me, only she got stuck, leaving a huge, terrible clump in my throat.

Later, I sat cautiously in front of the TV after my parents had gone outside to meet a new Cuban neighbor. I flicked the channel to one of the movies I'd screened as "safe" and watched curiously for a while. My brothers soon joined me. When the fairy-tale ending neared with its inevitable kiss, my heart began to flutter and a discomforting shame overtook me, though my father was nowhere in sight. I stood up in despair, abruptly telling my brothers that I didn't like movies anymore and, grabbing the *TV Guide,* returned to my room. Manolo promptly switched the channel to an unscreened movie. "I'll take my chances," he called after me, as if he'd figured out that my father's screaming moral patrols were for my benefit and not his.

I read the *TV Guide* quietly in my room. From time to time,

I closed my eyes and imagined a movie into action. Effortlessly, I became the big-hearted cowboy, the charming reporter, an English doctor curing heathens on the Dark Continent. Never a confused teenager with a furious father on the loose. In my private movies, I could kiss any hero if I wanted to in the grand finale.

## FOUR

MY FATHER'S ONE-WEEK SWEEPING JOB at the tailor shop was un gran desastre.

We were summoned to Tío Victor's. Mami and my aunt retreated with their drink glasses into my aunt's bedroom after dinner to speak privately. My cousin Raquel and I followed, sneaking outside to the wrought-iron patio bench where we could kneel and peek in through the bars of the bedroom window.

Our mothers were perched on the edge of Tía Rita's bed. "The dress was ordinary," we heard her say. I could barely make out my aunt pulling on her tight skirt with one hand while balancing her drink with the other. "Aida told me it *was* a little short," she continued. "Still, as long as the girl's mother didn't object, why should anyone else?" My aunt stopped to sip her whiskey, and Mami joined in with her own drink.

Raquel and I lifted our heads higher for a better view.

"Well, imagine," my aunt continued, "when that girl tried it on, Roberto came out raging like a maniac and attacked that poor customer as if she'd sold her daughter into prostitution. ¡Desgraciada! ¡Inmorales! Who knows what other insults he humiliated her with? And imagine that child standing there in her bare feet—horrified! Aida told me that she practically swallowed her pins. Roberto created such a scandal!"

"Qué vergüenza, Rita," said my mother in a timid voice. She looked down at her drink as if it might be poisoned.

My aunt rushed to finish Mami off. "Victor and el italiano— you know, the son of the owner—dragged Roberto out of there to calm him down, all the while protesting of course about going back to work. What a fiasco!"

I ducked when Tía Rita glanced out the window, but when she turned back toward Mami, I bobbed up again.

"Evi. I'm not burdening you with these details to mortify you. I'm only telling you because you have to understand that Victor can't have him there. It's impossible." She paused. "Can you imagine if he'd actually hit someone?"

"¡Rita!" my mother protested. "¡Roberto no es un delincuente!"

"No." My aunt shook the remaining alcohol out of her ice, her Lucite bracelets jangling. She raised the glass to her mouth and swallowed. "But he's not the man he used to be."

"He hasn't changed that way, Rita," my mother insisted. "Roberto would never dishonor us."

In silence, they both stared into their glasses.

"If only he could go back to a regular job," Mami said wistfully, "I'm sure he could recuperate himself."

"Gabrielita." Tío Victor had come out to the patio. "What are you two doing there?"

Startled, Raquel and I climbed down.

"Come on," my uncle said. "I have to drive you back. Everybody has to work tomorrow."

"Not everybody," I answered softly.

As I went to grab my things off Raquel's bed, my cousin watched me. "How come your dad gets so mad, Gabi?" she asked quietly.

I looked away. "I don't know." On Raquel's dresser was a porcelain ballerina balanced on one tiny toe. "It's just his temper," I offered by way of apology. "Everybody gets mad sometimes." Raquel shook her head. "Not like that. Not my father." "Well, a lot of people do," I said, defending my father. His temper just *happened*. It wasn't a matter of fault.

That night at home, though, the house seemed too quiet and I had trouble falling asleep.

No one sent Manolo to buy the *Seminole Sentinel* the next morning. Mami seemed to be upset with the entire family and pretended not to be home when Tía Rita called. She played that game until Tío Victor finally got through the following night and informed her that he was buying Tía Rita a new washing machine and giving us their old one. I could barely contain my joy when I heard the news. Even if my father never worked another day in his life, I swore, no matter what else my parents demanded of me, I would forevermore *love* washing clothes.

All cheer evaporated, though, when we learned that the tailor shop customer had filed a criminal complaint against my father.

"Oh my God," I gasped to Mami while my distraught father was on the phone with Tío Victor. "Could they put Papi in jail?"

"¡Mi'ja! Why do you always think the worst?" My mother rubbed her temples. "Victor will find us a lawyer."

Sure enough, later that week, my parents and I took the downtown bus to meet a lawyer my uncle found. The building was near the Parque de las Palomas on Biscayne Bay, where so many pigeons had congregated along the wall that you couldn't help but be reminded of that disquieting Hitchcock movie *The Birds*.

A rickety elevator took us to the sixth floor. I gave my father's name to a lanky African-American guy wearing thick editor's glasses who seemed to be the receptionist. "Mr. Korematsu's not back from court yet," he disclosed.

My mother returned a faint smile.

Luckily, both my uncles made it there on their breaks before the young lawyer appeared, laden with folders. He was wearing a proper suit but sported a haircut from which shiny black strays stuck up, defying maturity. Smiling breezily, he rushed into his cubicle of an office and kicked the door shut behind him.

My father turned to Tío Victor with a puzzled look. "¿Es chino?" he inquired.

My uncle shrugged.

"Hawaiian," volunteered the receptionist guy, who'd evidently understood, in English.

When the lawyer's door finally popped open, the receptionist guy, Arthur, offered him a file. The youthful Hawaiian lawyer took it with a cheery smile and walked toward us. In deliberated, accented Spanish, he inquired who Mr. De la Paz was. When my father and both uncles stood, the lawyer laughed, saying, "No, no, perdón. I mean el cliente."

Tío Lucho promptly dropped to the couch while Tío Victor remained on his feet. At my mother's nudging, I stood too. "Excuse me," I said. "It's just that my uncles can explain things better. My father doesn't speak English that well. So my mother was thinking maybe we could all—"

"I'll have to talk to your dad alone first," he told me in an earnest tone. "Then we'll bring you guys in, okay?" He translated the same thing more or less to my mother and uncles, who acquiesced with nods.

As my father headed for the cubicle office, Tío Victor tapped his shoulder and reminded him, "Don't forget to explain about the green card problem."

"Claro," my father agreed.

I waited until we were sitting to ask, "What green card problem, Tío?"

"Who knows if it's a problem yet," Tío Lucho cautioned.

"I know it takes two crimes," countered Tío Victor, holding up two fingers for emphasis. Turning toward me, he added, "You should learn about these things too, Gabrielita. Your green card can be taken away if you get into any trouble with the law."

"Not *any* trouble," Tío Lucho clarified.

"Why do we have to worry about that?" I asked. "I thought we were allowed to live here permanently."

"Well, your father had one problemita in New York," Tío Victor informed me. "This is number two."

"He did?" I looked at Mami.

"Oh, that was a misunderstanding," she responded quickly, swatting at the air as if there were a fly. She went on to explain that my father had been shopping in a big store on one floor and then taken an escalator to another floor without realizing that they were two different establishments. "He hadn't paid," she clarified, "but that's not stealing. He tried to get that horrible man, that security guard, to understand. But he didn't have the facility with the language."

"How come you didn't help?" I asked in surprise.

"I wasn't there," she admitted, then she described how my frustrated father had lost his temper so that, in the end, "Nobody believed him and we had to pay the fine."

Tío Lucho, less familiar with these details than Tío Victor, quizzed her about what had happened to the case after my father's arrest, while I tried to take in the fact that it had happened at all. *My father—arrested as a thief?*

When the lawyer's door finally reopened, he called out to Arthur to send the family in.

We filed into the cubicle office and sat among piles of files. Mr. Korematsu posed questions to my uncles, in a mixture of English and bad Spanish, about what had happened at the tailor shop that day. When they'd finished, he pronounced that everything "was

consistent with the police report and the victim's story." Mami
flinched at the word "victim" and my father began to argue about
whether there had been such a thing, but the lawyer fended them
both off by reading "allegations" from the report until they both
backed down in alarm.

"So here's the recommendation I've made to Mr. De la Paz
about how to handle these charges," he explained, turning to my
mother. Whereupon he set sail on a sea of legal discourse until his
ship floundered on the shoals of translation and he gave us a wob-
bly smile. "In English it's known as an 'Admission to Sufficient
Facts,'" he stated after a pause. "Similar to a guilty plea, except
that you're not actually found guilty. The disposition gets deferred.
The idea is, if Mr. De la Paz doesn't get into any more legal problems for the period in question, the charge will be dismissed. If
we take care of the Disorderly Conduct count that way, I'm pretty
sure we can dismiss the more serious Assault on a Minor without
any admission or finding of guilt."

Had my father assaulted *a kid*? As I recoiled, my baffled mother
asked, "When do we go to the court?"

"Tuesday," the lawyer informed her. "We'll resolve everything
right at arraignment."

"What about his green card?" Tío Victor demanded. "Did he
tell—"

"That's the whole point of the deferred disposition," the lawyer
answered smoothly. "If Mr. De la Paz keeps his nose clean for the
entire period—think of it as a kind of probation—the whole thing
goes away and there won't be any adverse immigration impact."

"Gracias a Dios," Mami said, sighing with relief as my father
stroked her hand and smiled benevolently.

"But"—Tío Lucho threw a dubious glance in their direction—
"what if we did have another problemita?"

The lawyer held up both hands as if surrendering to the entire

De la Paz family. "Then the disposition doesn't work, right? If he's arrested, he can be convicted on both of the outstanding charges. Plus, he could be convicted on any new ones," he noted. "Unless we had some reason to think we could go to trial and succeed."

"That would mean losing his green card," Tío Victor stated soberly.

"Based on what he's told me, yes—if there's moral turpitude involved." The Hawaiian turned toward my father. "But I'd have to see your out-of-state conviction records to be sure," he qualified. "Hypothetically, though, the larceny plus any kind of enhanced assault could certainly lead to deportation. I would probably refer you to an immigration lawyer."

"Deportation?" I echoed. Visions of border guards danced in my head.

The lawyer shot me a reassuring smile. "Let's hope it won't come to that."


On the morning of the arraignment, Tío Victor took off from work to drive my parents to court, where they were supposed to meet up with El Chino, as all of them were now referring to my father's lawyer, even though we'd been told he was from Hawaii, not China. Korematsu wasn't even a difficult name to pronounce, but maybe the nickname helped them trust him more. He became an immigrant, one of us.

When my parents got home, Mami was palpably relieved that everything had gone according to El Chino's plan. My father, she informed me proudly, wouldn't even have to return to "the court" at all until his probation period—or whatever it was supposed to be—expired.

"Two years seems so long, though," I observed with concern. Could my father really keep his temper under wraps all that time?

"The best thing," Mami replied, ignoring my concern, "will be for your father to go back to a decent job once and for all. And that's where you come in, muchachita," she added, poking my shoulder with her finger.

Obviously, she had the classified ads in mind. But her hope that my father, shaken by his legal crisis, would get promptly on the right track was thwarted when he buried his face in his magazines again.

Her own brother was the culprit who really upset her applecart of family order, however. Having quit a job at Pan Am that he'd gotten after his own airport layoff, Tío Paco located a shoe factory that he said had lots of openings, even one for my father. The only problem was, it happened to be located hundreds of miles away in Lynn, Massachusetts—a detail he revealed ten days before the work was to start.

"¿Cómo se te ocurre, Roberto?" Mami exclaimed at the prospect. How could my father possibly think of leaving her alone with the kids?

My brothers and I, bent over a game of Trouble at the kitchen table, perked right up.

"¿Y cómo me quedo en esta situación?" my father bellowed back.

Yes, how could she expect him to stay, Tío Paco agreed, adding, "Roberto can't very well return to the tailor shop now, can he?"

That silenced everyone.

Eventually, he spoke again. "Evangelina," he said thoughtfully, rolling his mustache hairs between his thumb and forefinger, "it's only for a short time. Until the situation improves."

Mami didn't respond. Obviously, she was scared to be left behind, though my father couldn't see it through his own desperation. The youngest of nine children, she'd often seemed overwhelmed to me, and this new development had definitely caught her off guard.

"There's only one room," my uncle added apologetically. Sharing one room in his Puerto Rican friend's apartment would keep costs down, Tío Paco reasoned, allowing my father to send us more of the money he earned.

As my mother's arguments thinned out, my uncle suggested trying it out for a year. By then, the situation in Miami would surely have improved. "I can keep an eye on things too," Tío Paco offered obliquely—meaning my father's temper, I presumed.

Mami fell silent, her shoulders slumping with resignation.

Eventually, I was assigned to escort my uncle to the ticket office.

"Tío knows enough English to buy a ticket," I protested.

But my uncle objected, "What if they ask me things I can't answer?"

I rolled my eyes at that remark, but I knew I could never win with the "what ifs," so I kept my mouth shut and headed off with him.

It panned out to be an unpleasant, hour-long bus trip all the way downtown, the chemical smell of air-conditioning combining with the body odor of men on the bus. On top of that, Tío Paco wasn't easy to be with. His height and oversized mustache distanced him from other people, and he didn't converse much. When he did, his jokes were sarcastic. A brief marriage to a gringa had resulted in her leaving him, and since then he was always moving. My mother collected mail for him when he was trying out places. "Some men have trouble finding their hearts again, mi'jita," she'd told me once, assuring me that once upon a time my uncle had been a sweet boy. "Suffering can make a person hard," she'd foreshadowed wearily.

As I stood in the Greyhound line, I had trouble enough picturing my uncle suffering amicably with my father in their Massachusetts room, let alone successfully managing my father's temper. When my turn at the ticket counter came, my uncle shoved money into my hand and I purchased the tickets without having to say much; all in all, it was a simple transaction, and I rode home feeling disheartened by the never-ending helplessness of my family.

Back home, I roamed the house to let the idea of my father leaving sink in. He spent most of his time in his dark bedroom these days, but a sense of him radiated throughout the entire house. Would he really go?

Only when Tío Victor and Tía Rita hosted a good luck party a few nights later was I truly convinced that he was leaving us.

The party lifted everyone's spirits except Mami's. She finally cheered up with the arrival of Fernandita, her niece and only other relative in the U.S. besides Tío Paco, who was now abandoning her like my father. Fernandita had always been good to Mami; she even ordered her wild boyfriend, El Loco, to provide needed rides if the uncles weren't available. After Fernandita brought her a glass of wine, Mami began to relax at last and enjoy the antics of Tía Rita, who'd teased her blue-black hair into a bob and kept gossiping about Jackie Kennedy and Liz Taylor—her favorite heroines—in between playing a Petula Clark record over and over and chiming in for the one-word chorus.

The party seemed to confirm the truth in the toast Tío Victor made after dinner. Putting his arm around my father's shoulders, he raised his glass on behalf of every relative present that night and announced, "A family is much more than a man, his wife, and his children." Everyone smiled, nodded, and, as if further illustrating his point, began to dance around the living room before the dishes had been cleared. Even Tía Rita's tiny elderly aunt was able to hang on by her chinny chin chin to my cousin Luchito, who was exactly her height, as they made their turns.

"Why don't you marineras get up?" Tío Victor teased Raquel and me as he twirled Tía Rita through the room. He'd only called us sailor girls because of the identical red-and-white dresses my mother had sewn for us.

"That's for old people," Raquel called back, her sloping brown eyes smiling.

"Bah! Don't be tonta."

Raquel and I looked at each other, shrugged, and got up. We mixed cumbia steps with American dances like the Fish, but when a slow vallenato came on, immediately took our seats. Tío Victor joined us and put his arm across Raquel's shoulders. With interest, we watched my parents waltz, my father's crystal whiskey glass jiggling at the small of my mother's back and her hand resting on his arm. For a moment, my father seemed really happy, the way he used to be on holidays in New York when he wasn't working so hard to prove himself worthy of my mother.

I was happy too. At last, our family seemed to be headed in the right direction. Leaning my head back on the couch, I listened to the music. "What a funny love song," I said to Raquel and Tío Victor. It spoke of love as a soldier's loyalty, of a grito de independencia—they were words for an anthem, really.

"Ah, but the accordions are fantastic," Tío Victor pointed out with his finger in the air as he stumbled up for a refill.

"My father's drunk," Raquel observed. "And look at my mother." Tía Rita was dancing a salsa caleña with paunchy but fleet-footed Tío Lucho. "Pretty soon, she'll be coming over to tell us how much she loves us," Raquel predicted with a tolerant smile.

My parents never did that, even when drunk. I knew they loved me by their gestures. The gallant way my father pushed a chair in for me when I had to study; the battles my mother waged against my impudent hair to make it beautiful. Everyone loved in a different way, didn't they?

Two days later, my father's travel date arrived. He came into the kitchen on the eve of his departure and stood silently watching my brothers and me for no ostensible reason as we did homework.

By dawn, he was gone. Mami confided afterwards that he'd come to our rooms to kiss us good-bye when it was still dark.

That morning over breakfast I relaxed, glad to be done with worrying about my father and all our family problems. As the day progressed, though, his absence grew into a shadow that trailed me through the house. An impression of something I'd once experienced when trying to learn to float came back like déjà vu. It was the moment Tío Victor had taken his hand away and ocean water had unexpectedly lapped my face. That had scared me, making me flail in panic. My uncle had laughed with his Pall Mall cigarette between his teeth and reassured me, "Relax, nena, no one's trying to drown you." But a dread of the things you couldn't count on stayed beneath the surface of the words and their comfort.

[ FIVE ]

WITHOUT MY FATHER AROUND, Mami loosened the reins. On Saturday, I got permission to spend the day at Alina's apartment on the other side of Flagler Street. With the swamp-cooler on, Alina, Lydia, and I tried on glittery ball gowns and strutted around smoking cigarettes. The next day, we crashed a swimming party at the elementary school, this time pretending to be younger instead of older than we were.

Suddenly I was happy about everything! And Mami seemed happier too. Her friend Camila walked over on Sunday night with a bottle of jerez that they nearly emptied over a marathon of bizarre stories and gossip, which took their minds off their own troubles. Like my mother, Camila had had her fair share of them— her husband suffered from leukemia.

When a money order from my father arrived a week later, Mami wasted no time paying bills and buying lots of groceries. "I'm cooking you kids sancocho tonight," she announced gaily. While the substitute Man-of-the-House Manolo cut our grass, Pablo and I helped her chop yuca. After dinner she put on a movie in which Cary Grant did somersaults with Katharine Hepburn and engaged in witty repartee that Mami didn't understand but smiled at anyway. She sat cheerfully sandwiched between Pablo and Manolo on the two-seater couch. It was like those nights back in Queens when my father used to work and when, for simple entertainment since we didn't own a TV, the three of us would snuggle together in bed with her and watch the searchlights sweep the city. All in all, I couldn't decide if it was better to be small and loved or to live a glittering, grown-up life.

Without paternal obligations to fulfill, I had more time on my hands, and the southern horizon itself became interesting. In social studies class, I discovered that Florida had once been "old agriculture," but now it was a kind of new land of opportunity. Mr. Lanham's grainy slides of the old Florida showed us swamps, palmetto groves, and tiny fishing towns. They led to slides of the "new" Florida: Dixie Highway, Miami Beach hotels, the Cape Canaveral Space Center, I-95, and cluttered images of downtown with its tall, centrally air-conditioned department stores and noisy buses that crossed the Miami River north, south, east, and west.

Miami was a unique mix of big city and hick town. Some hick parts were like my neighborhood—houses looked nice enough, but were built on streets that dead-ended unexpectedly into canals lined with sharp, weedy grass. The canals often went on for miles, piercing the distant Everglades, including the tourist section in which fearsome-sounding airboats cut through the saw grass clogging the water but never disturbed the alligators.

After seeing Mr. Lanham's slides I began to walk around and explore my neighborhood more, just to see how the old Florida was holding out against the new one. Modern houses were all painted mint, flamingo pink, and turquoise. New lawns grew tough, spiky grass—the only kind that could flourish in this intense climate. But there were no sidewalks to speak of, only bleached-white gravel pebbles of the old Florida that had been there long before. Around me, Miami stretched out in quadrants, cut by Flagler Street and Eighth Street (nicknamed Alligator Alley down past the Calle Ocho part), toward an infinite flatness. The flatness made every destination—the A&P, the tailor shop where my uncles worked, the post office—a horizon without end; as if God himself had ironed Alligator Alley and our wait for eternity began right here with it.

That night, my father called from Massachusetts.

I stood by and listened while Mami chatted on the phone. It seemed that the "short time" he and my uncle had expected to remain up north was about to be cut shorter. Their Puerto Rican roommate was facing eviction after little more than a month. Rent was expensive there, so Tío Paco was looking into replacement jobs for them in Hartford, Connecticut.

"Connecticut?" she asked fearfully. A few moments of silence passed before I heard her tell my father to come home.

I ran to my brothers' room at once with the distressing news.

"Why doesn't she let him go?" Manolo complained, tossing his *Flash* comic at Pablo, who reached out and caught it.

"Yeah," Pablo chimed in. "She could tell him we have to move out too."

"Pablo, she can't make up any old thing," I said. "Papi's not a fool."

He laughed out loud.

"He's not," I insisted. "He's just—odd."

Manolo stared at me. "He's totally crazy, Gabi! *Lo-co*." He eyed me like there was something wrong with me too.

"Yeah, well, you guys better get your heads together in case he does come home." I stood up to leave. "I hope Mami doesn't show him your teacher's letter, Pablo."

Pablo's face fell, and Manolo gave me a dirty look that instantly filled me with remorse. "I'm kidding, Pablo," I backtracked. "She's not gonna do that."

For the next few days, though, Mami got easily upset over

simple things that went awry. She obsessed over the silly letter
Pablo's teacher had sent home about his constant talking, and she
bemoaned our many broken wares, like the lazy Susan. All these
problems, she insisted, perhaps to convince herself, were due to the
absence of a man in the house.

"I'll fix that, Mami," Manolo promised as he inspected the broken cabinet. And to our surprise, he retrieved my father's toolbox
from the shed and bolted the lazy Susan so that it swung again.

"How'd you do that?" I asked, impressed.

"Papi used to show me things." His crooked tooth shone brightly
when he smiled.

But Mami only found new subjects to complain about, namely
me, my wardrobe, and my American influences.

"Are you wearing those faded pants to Rita's, Gabriela?" she
challenged, as she stared intently at me from the doorway before
our outing that Sunday.

"Most of my clothes are like this," I argued.

"Please change out of ese hipiado," she ordered, disparaging the
jeans she considered "hippie" attire. "Cámbiate."

Literally, her command meant "change *yourself*." All I could
really do, though, was force myself into a dress, the least close-
fitting one available that wouldn't mark me too obviously as a
female, attractive to nasty men like the sicko who'd chased me
around the Laundromat and the chorus of Calle Ocho lechers who
beeped when I walked down the street. My best choice was a faded
Nehru from the donations bin at St. Stephen's. I hated that dress. I
never knew when the original owner might show up and tell the
whole free world that I was wearing her hand-me-downs.

My mother appraised me silently in the mirror. "You have to *try*
to look like a lady, Gabriela," she reminded me. A big believer in
making the best of one's limited resources, Mami herself dressed
to the nines even for public hospital check-ups. Judging from her

expression as I halfheartedly brushed my tangle of hair, I wasn't trying hard enough. With her hand on one hip, she shook her head and frowned. "Ay, ay, ay, Gabriela," she muttered, then asked—rhetorically of course—why I had to part my hair in the middle, sin gracia, without any grace or style? "You look like una india," she complained, forgetting all about the Chibcha in the shadows of our family tree.

"Cut it!" I abdicated in frustration, throwing down the wooden brush. "Chop it all off, if that means so much to you!"

Cutting my hair wasn't going to bring my mother real happiness, though, I knew. Not if what she longed for was a soap opera daughter like the one with the fairy-tale outfits my mother so admired on *As the World Turns*. I wished I could tell Mami: *Be grateful I don't care about nice clothes or hairdos!* But it was all so tiring, being the object of someone's eternal disappointment, that I lost the will to explain what was okay about how I was turning out, that I didn't want to *change myself.*

Mami took my hairbrush, began pinning my hair behind my ears, and then shot me with her can of hair spray. "Ya," she said, "That's more civilized." I knew the bobby pins wouldn't outlast the afternoon, that the sorry mess would come tumbling down. My tough locks, like the slaves of the Caribbean, would free themselves. But for peace's sake, I let her keep her illusions. After all, hair was a small thing she could fix while my father's broken spirit haunted the air.

Late that night, after we'd returned from Tía Rita's, I heard the phone ring as I washed my face. I had an intuition that it might be my father so I finished quickly to go find out what was happening.

In the kitchen Mami sat grimacing through her pink reading

glasses at the bills splayed on the table: one big, bad hand of cards. With a tired glance at me, she removed her glasses and rubbed the bridge of her nose. "I don't know what to do. Should I put the seventy-five toward the mortgage or other bills?"

I slid into a chair across from her. "Is Papi coming home?"

She sighed. "I don't know."

"Mami." I hesitated. "Don't you think it might be good if he keeps working there a little longer? You know, so we can pay more things."

"But paying for two homes—" she started to explain.

"You said before he could go for a year."

"Are you complaining about your own father?" she snapped.

"No! But maybe a year would give Papi time to, um, recuperate." That was her word, I recalled, the one she'd used at Tía Rita's after the tailor shop fiasco.

My mother peered at me over her glasses. "Where do you get these americanismos, Gabriela? What kind of girl thinks that way?"

*Not a backward person like you*, I wished I could toss back. But I had no freedom to be mean. I could only dream of a golden ticket out of this place into some imaginary one, where conflicts wouldn't barrel down on me like the Greyhound bus heading home from Massachusetts.


Tío Victor delivered my father to us in his wrinkled ivory shirt and gray pants. My lone ranger uncle Paco had decided to move on to Connecticut.

A living soap opera, Mami embraced my father with tears in her eyes. "¡Por fín!" she proclaimed. At last he was home!

Smiling with embarrassment, my father accepted a quick peck on the cheek from each of my brothers, who then willingly went to bed.

"Hola, Papi," I said, trying to muster up enthusiasm as I kissed him too.

"You're taller, mi'jita," he observed proudly.

"Uh huh. Everyone tells me that lately," I said, carrying his bag into his room and then returning to mine. From there, I heard Mami begin to enumerate the outstanding chores, as if my father had never been away. A family should always stick together, she'd taught me fervently. Even if a couple didn't get along well, like Lydia's parents, my mother would object to divorce, whether or not it was legal in the Church. I didn't know how I felt about that part anymore. But as I lay in the dark and tried to ward off a vague disappointment, I divined what she couldn't from the paltry homecoming—that although our family was together again physically, forces bigger than us had already started to pull us apart.

My father slept peacefully through the entire next day.

Then he got up early the following morning and dressed. Donning his old visor cap, he marched purposefully to the shed. I was heating up café con leche when I happened to glance through the screen and I saw that he'd taken out his silver wrench. *Wow,* I thought, how tickled pink Mami would be if he actually tackled her number one complaint besides me these days—the bathroom sink. But instead of coming inside with his tools, he shouted loudly for Manolo and Pablo to join him out front. My brothers quickly threw on their shorts and rushed out, as Mami and I tagged along to investigate.

My father had wheeled our rusty, scraped blue two-wheeler bike around to the street in front of our house. The ancient bike, bent and haunted by the remains of its silver and white streamers, was a present he'd given us back in the day when he worked regularly. But it had been too small from the outset, and after an obligatory trial run he'd demanded of my brothers, they had declined to ride again.

Now, standing next to the hated bike, Manolo frowned at a mint green house up the street where his friend Johnny lived. The smarty-pants had made fun of my brother for riding it.

"This is a girl's bike," Manolo protested. Not that he'd won with that point before.

"It doesn't matter." Tersely, my father pushed the corroded blue handlebars at him.

Shaking his head, my brother grabbed the bike. He pedaled slowly, with his knees turned out, almost bow-legged, while the sun beat down. The rest of us watched, some neighbors joining in from across the street, as he circled the block and came to a halt.

"Hah!" exclaimed my father, grasping the handlebars joyfully.

"It wobbles," said Manolo as he dismounted. "It's no good, Papi."

"Qué va." A vein appeared on my father's red forehead and he cuffed Manolo really hard.

That rattled me, especially when I glimpsed that our neighbors, elderly Mr. Krantz and chatty Mr. Anderson, were observing the whole thing with their arms crossed. They took a few steps toward us, and my father made a show of straightening a bike spoke with his wrench. "Sin petroleo colombiano," he announced loudly, and I flushed in embarrassment.

Mr. Anderson and Mr. Krantz looked at each other. Neither of them had any clue what my father had said in Spanish, but the weird petroleum comment seemed to distract them from the whack he'd given Manolo. "Sorry?" Mr. Anderson called out, cupping his ear.

"Tell them your father is fixing the bicycle, mi'ja," my mother murmured quietly.

"Um, my brothers are practicing," I yelled over in the neighbors' direction as Manolo shoved the handlebars at Pablo.

Pablo saluted, mounting the bike. Luckily, he rode around without any antics. On his return, my father slapped his hands together. "Again," he ordered enthusiastically, sending my brother out for another tour instead of letting him dismount.

My father continued to order Pablo and Manolo to take turns in the hot sun, and it became apparent to me that he intended to keep them out riding, over and over, as if to force them to appreciate his gift. When the neighbors had finally retreated to their houses, I absconded into ours, glad, despite my guilt, that I wasn't required to participate. Mami had made it clear to my father that bicycle riding wasn't ladylike, particularly while trying to hold down one's dress to keep the underwear from showing. Since feminine morals of any sort were wildly popular with my father, he'd agreed. Manolo had scowled at me from across the table at the unfair result, but I'd merely batted my eyes in response.

Now, as Mami stood watching from the window for my father's bicycle whim to pass, I wondered if she was as disturbed as I'd been by my father's comportment. Even if hitting your own kid wasn't the same as Assault on a Minor, it had been a distressing reminder that my father was still in that probationary status and needed to keep his temper under control.

Later in the day, when things settled, Mami managed to sweet talk him into taking Manolo to the hardware store for sink washers. A nice, normal, fatherly activity.

"Bring back a newspaper," she added, before they took off.

Manolo smirked at me, as if to say, *payback time.*

When they returned, I was reading in my room and overheard Mami reprimand my father for having bought "those useless magazines" instead.

"No fue nada," he protested tersely. "They cost next to nothing. Less than five dollars."

"That's a few more we could apply to the chairs," she complained, despite the fact that we'd long ago stopped paying off the layaway for the remaining furniture. "¡Ay Roberto!" she lamented. "We can never invite people over."

How little my mother wanted, I realized suddenly. The meager wish for a few matching chairs consumed her. Into my mind slipped the saying she'd often recited when I wanted something I couldn't have: *Hay que aceptar lo que Dios ha puesto.* Accept what God has given.

"As long as the house is clean, Evangelina, you can invite people," my father pronounced pompously, his own Godly pride more important than hers.

"Humph," she muttered, growing silent. After a moment, though, she regained her momentum and added, "Maybe to ride that rusty bicycle. Nobody else wants to." She traipsed off, ordering Pablo to wheel himself right back to the Farm Stores for the newspaper my father should've gotten in the first place.

A half hour later, she appeared in my doorway with the hefty Sunday *Sentinel* in her arms. "Mark all the factory jobs, mi'ja," she said, dropping the bundle near my feet.

"But they don't always say if they're factory jobs," I explained, reaching for the newspaper. "How am I supposed to know?"

"Ay, mi'ja. Read and see."

"*All* of them?" I lifted up Section F to show her how thick it was.

She shrugged her shoulders. "If necessary."

"Why don't you ever make Manolo do this stuff?" I demanded.

She completely ignored the question and walked out.

I threw the paper back on the floor and propped myself, arms folded, against my pillow. From the floor, the head on the mast of the *Seminole Sentinel* stared sternly at me, as if to imply that I was being petty. It was supposed to be the head of a Seminole chief, although Mr. Lanham had informed us that the term "Seminole" was a bastardization—he'd paused to make sure no one giggled—of the Spanish *cimarrón*, a person who has escaped something like the slaves in Cuba or the Creeks into the Everglades.

In that case, we were all Seminoles, I'd concluded. Everyone who'd come to Florida. The elderly white people, referred to as "snowbirds," who escaped winter by claiming South Beach with their rocking chairs; the Cuban refugees who'd escaped Fidel for Calle Ocho; and my own family, fleeing the Queens Urban Renewal Plan that tore down our brick building to make room for a highway. Here we were, the lost tribe of Seminoles. United at last.

The next morning on the school bus, I passively listened to Lydia boast about things she'd gotten that dumb Rique boy near the gas station to do for her. When she'd drifted on to a glum monologue about her adulterer father, I was tempted to share my conflicted feelings regarding my own kooky father's return, but Mami had prohibited me from ever disclosing our domestic problems beyond the family. The only thing I was allowed to say was that he was experiencing temporary difficulties finding work; under no circumstances was I to "disrespect" him by divulging personal details.

I confined myself to carping to Lydia about the classified ad searches that would now be keeping me busy. When I complained in a similar vein to Alina during math class later, I accidentally lapsed into Spanish and got into trouble. Mrs. Goddard blinked at me in surprise and said she had no choice but to punish us both. I felt ashamed. But the punishment turned out to be nothing more than consignment to separate seats on the patio outside our classroom trailer with the sprinklers pleasantly spraying nearby. But the fresh afternoon air couldn't quell my growing disappointment over the return of my hot-tempered father and his oil fixations. Whatever the future held for my father, I sure wasn't going to be la-di-da'ing with Lydia and Alina anymore.

## SIX

Although my father zealously followed the classified ads, the jobless days continued. Thanksgiving recess arrived, and every day I faced the taunting black-and-white block ads: Clerk, Lab Technician, Physician's Assistant. The gray columns of entire categories: Professional, Services, Sales.

All the jobs my father couldn't have.

At night in bed, I struggled to conjure up from darkness an image of my father at work somewhere, perhaps piecing mechanical bits together, perhaps building them into equipment and machines, although the job I searched for by day—the disappearing GRINDER position—involved breaking things down.

The applicable *Sentinel* listings had definitely shrunk.

When Tío Victor dropped by one evening to see how things were going, he tried to reassure me. "It's just that those heavy industrial jobs are getting phased out," he said. "Look for different ones."

Other jobs, however, required special training, licenses, the fluent English my father didn't speak. More important, they required a person without my father's difficult *temperamento*. As he ranted to my dubious uncle about people at job sites who failed to comprehend anything at all about the refinery business,

I began to speculate that the story about the lost apartment in Massachusetts had been made up: No doubt my father and the shoe factory chief had had one of those harebrained oil drilling conversations—or worse.

When Mami came by my room after my uncle had gone that night with her usual "sleep with the little angels" refrain, I sat up straight in bed. "Mami, I don't know if any of those jobs will work out for Papi," I said.

"Keep trying mi'ja," she encouraged, coming to sit beside me. "We're all depending on you."

"Tío Victor thinks he might get into one of those...discussions with somebody," I warned vaguely.

She studied the butterflies trapped between my bedside lampshade's wax paper layers. "We have to find something," she said, sighing deeply. "In Colombia, we'd end up in some desolate jungle with only a pitiful chance of finding work. And even then, with miserable pay!" Bitterness cracked open more of her fears. "Dios mío, how could we leave como unos miserables, deported! What a disgrace! No, mi'ja, that can't happen to us!"

"Us?" I asked abruptly. "Would they deport us all? With handcuffs and everything like those people on TV?"

As the images took hold, Mami's eyes, still fixed on the lampshade, filled with melancholy. "You always expect to return to your tierra, but only to be buried, and with honor."

Silently I began to rue my own loss—the place I'd found for myself in the world was *here* now, not in Colombia—but then Mami shook herself and stood up. "Let's not be ridiculous, Gabriela. Nobody's going to be deported."

"But somebody has to make sure," I trailed faintly as she planted a good-night kiss on my forehead.

After she'd gone, I spun the lampshade with my finger. Were

the trapped butterflies real? I wondered sadly before finally turning out the light.

A couple of days after Tío Victor's visit I learned that Mami had borrowed money from him to pay our December mortgage, though my proud father didn't know it. She remained uneasy, brooding aloud to me, "How can we impose on your uncle again if things continue like this?"

I told her that some Cuban kids I knew in school received government help.

"Your father would never hear of it," she told me firmly.

One night, though, much to my surprise, the same U.S. Department of Agriculture surplus food provided to refugees mysteriously appeared in our kitchen: boxes of pale yellow powder to which you added water for scrambled eggs; cans of pre-mixed peanut butter and jelly; and a thick, pink meat spread.

It made for a very strange dinner.

"Yuck," said Pablo, pushing away the disgusting pink-and-white sandwich.

"Where'd we get this stuff?" Manolo asked.

"It doesn't matter." Mami tilted her head toward my father to signal an end to the conversation. "Eat, please."

Even my father responded with a puzzled smile. "No meat, Evangelina?"

"I thought you liked eggs," she replied, digging into hers.

My father picked up his fork and explored the dense clumps.

I tried the fake eggs too. "Very good," I mumbled encouragingly with my mouth full.

Manolo, who'd pushed his plate away as well, reluctantly pulled it back to eat.

My father devoured his pink ham spread sandwich. "One more, please," he said, holding up a finger and smiling at us. Suddenly and very oddly, his other hand began to jerk of its own accord against the table. Was he doing it on purpose? I wondered, glancing at my mother and then back at his spastic hand. Like a reflex test, the hairy knuckles jumped up and down. I couldn't keep my eyes off them.

"Gabriela!" Mami admonished.

Afterward, while cleaning up in the kitchen, I asked her about my father's unmistakable tic, but she brushed it off as a case of nervios.

"But he wasn't acting nervous," I pointed out.

"Ay mi'ja, don't contradict me so much. Please." She straightened up, rubbed her back, and leaned back down to finish scrubbing.

To expand the employment possibilities, Mami chatted over fences with neighbors about prospective jobs. "With all the building going on in South Miami," she began explaining to me the following day, "your father should find something." But when her gaze fell upon the unmarked *Sentinel* pages in my lap, her tone changed and she cried, "¡Dios santo! Is there nothing good in that newspaper?" Her desperate eyes darted around the yard like a pair of wild birds, alighting on the back wall where Pablo had indulged his latest pastime, knife throwing. Straight to the wall she suddenly marched. "See?" she said, jabbing the gouges. "This is what happens when parents are so distracted they can't provide their sons with guidance." Sadly, the gold glints faded from her eyes.

This was my mother's State of Worry. It provided some variety to her alternate State of Complaint, but not any relief. In the shadows of our backyard, I watched her work herself into a frenzy. How thankful I was when she finally went inside the house.

Not long after, though, she summoned me in too.

"Augh!" she began, starting another soliloquy on the endless chores to be done while tossing degreasers on the stove.

I picked up a scraper and braced myself.

"How am I going to get the house papers out of here without your father seeing on Monday?" she continued, moving on to some beef my father had with our mortgage company. According to him, they owed us, but Mami said it was the other way around.

"Do it when he's eating," I suggested.

"Don't be a boba. You think he won't notice? He checks those papers every day. I don't know where this strange interest comes from." She stopped to glare. "Gabriela, that's not the way to clean a stove! You have to pay attention. Why don't you do what I ask? What a soñadora!"

Some nerve she had calling me a dreamer. She hardly let me sleep! "I've done every single thing you asked me to, Mami. Who cleaned the bathroom? Who swept the living room?" I rose. "If my help isn't good enough, why don't you do it yourself!" I threw the scraper on the stove and stormed off to my room.

But she followed, unwilling to let me retreat. With her hand on the door frame, she pressed on. "Everything is sacrifice, Gabriela. I'm killing myself inventing ways to get through the month." Pausing to take a breath, she continued, "I have no water in my bathroom because of those pipes your father still hasn't repaired...." She forced me to listen to her headaches and heartaches until she finally ran out of steam and left.

Likely my mother would have returned for another round had Tío Lucho and my cousins not dropped in on their way back from the orthodontist. Mami offered my uncle Cuban guava pastries and coffee that she took out to the much cooler Florida room. My brothers and I were dispatched to attend to the three cousins in the yard.

I didn't care too much for my know-it-all older cousin Marisol, as much as I liked the fact that their family lived in a funky trailer park no one ever drove out of; the residents had planted colorful gardens and fenced themselves right in with cement bricks. Tía Elena was always complaining, but my mother swore, "Lucho will never leave that place."

In our yard, my cousin began to brush her long, black hair while the rest of us sat on the grass and watched. Marisol's modus operandi—a term I'd learned from reading a mystery once—was to choose the oldest kid in a group and make that person part of a team that looked down upon everyone else. On this occasion, the lucky person was me. Marisol informed me that she was mad because her bottom teeth were crooked but Tío Lucho wouldn't spring for braces. The dentist had said he would still have to straighten the top teeth in order to match the bite, so Tío Lucho had shaken his head and said, "In that case, no."

"She's so conceited," said her younger brother Luchito. "Her teeth are fine. Look at Cari's."

Little Cari, who was used to being picked on, gazed up at the trees and wondered aloud if we could knock down some mangoes. Manolo found a stick and began collecting fruit.

Eyeing him, Marisol commented, "I wonder which one of us has your father's sickness."

Manolo threw a hard green mango at her, but she caught it and hurled it back. "My mother says there's too much intermarriage between cousins in this family," she went on, "and that messes up the descendants' brains."

Everybody stared at her in stunned silence.

Finally, Pablo held up his right hand. "See this," he said to me, pointing to his index finger. "It shakes sometimes if I hold it out a long time. Just like Papi's hand."

"Mine does too," said Luchito.

We all held up our right hands and admitted they trembled too—except for Marisol.

"What about your eye?" Cari asked her sister. "Remember when your eye wouldn't stop twitching?"

"Man, I get that too!" Manolo said.

Marisol stood up. "You guys are all crazy." Into the house she waltzed, swinging her long black mane.

The rest of us stayed and kept discussing unusual things our bodies did—like Luchito's jaw slipping out of place when he ate an apple—and trying to predict who would inherit my father's nervios. Although it got to be a joke, I couldn't help but worry a little about whether there was any truth to what Marisol had said, that we passed these things down from generation to generation.

After my cousins and uncle had left, I fled to my room to work on a vexing autobiografía assignment for Señora Rubio's class. It was for the unit titled, "Turning Inward." Stories of our common patriot Simón Bolívar and the glory of independence that had paved the way for poetry, first by Cuba's José Martí, then by the chilena Gabriela Mistral, and soon by others. I'd gathered that our teacher was trying to be inclusive, since not all the students in class were Cuban, but it made little difference to me whether the sea that washed past Pilar in Martí's *Los zapaticos de rosa* was Cuban, Chilean, Venezuelan, or Colombian—the beautiful pink shoes in the crystal case were beyond the reach of all poor girls, wherever we might be from.

Unfortunately, though, whatever global truths I could glean from the literary panorama, my peculiar home life made me wish that rather than "turn inward," we could continue to write about other peoples' history. My home troubles were too global, with the deportation possibilities. And how could I openly memorialize the ad searching and typing that had become my calvario, as my aunts would say, my cross to bear? Or the sadness of being around my cuckoo father? No, our code of family silence did not permit such inward revelations.

I had to go back in time.

Through the gauzy curtains of a hospital window, my autobiography reeled out with my grandfather holding the infant me against his white guayabera, the one with the rows of embroidery tacking and shiny nácar buttons down the front. I didn't really remember that moment, though I had the leather frame photograph of him in that shirt. A little inventing was okay, anyway; Señora Rubio had explained that an autobiography fell somewhere between the stories of historical figures, with their many accomplishments meticulously chronicled, and the stories of poems and novels, which were truthful at heart.

One page devoted to each of my eight years in Cartagena, I wrote out my life; then I copied out the draft in elaborate penmanship that made the flowery sentences look beautiful.

On Monday, Señora Rubio asked us to read our autobiographies aloud in Spanish class, and I discovered that everyone's story, not just mine, had ended at the border. None of us could return to that time in our past when we'd left Cuba, Colombia, or Venezuela.... We'd all left tías and tíos or a grandfather behind in some patio scented by hibiscus and frangipani, where the mountains or the sea were never too far off. Away with everything had gone the smell of the fritos, the comfort of my own grandfather's arms, the silver saltwater spray in my face, and the soft susurro of waves that lulled my whole childhood to sleep.

I'd written my autobiography with pure sentimiento, an excess of feeling that would have raised the English teacher's eyebrows but earned me an A+ from Señora Rubio and a "Bellísimo" unfurling like a bright red flag of independence across my life.

Thankfully, Tío Lucho found my father work following the guava pastry visit.

My father's new agricultural job was on some unincorporated land near Homestead. As usual, I called the Dade County Metro number to find out the bus schedules. Mami woke my father before dawn and prepared his breakfast and two lunches. He had to ride all the way to the outskirts of Miami and transfer to another bus, since the routes ran parallel and perpendicular across the county without a diagonal line in between. In Homestead, a van gathered up the workers and drove them to the fields.

My father worked every day that week, in between riding those tiresome buses back and forth. He got home late, ate, washed up, and went straight to bed. Though his weariness saddened me, I was grateful that it depleted his energy for fighting. Tomato picking seemed a much better fit for him than most other jobs he'd held. With all the bending, he wouldn't be able to talk and get himself into trouble as he had at the tailor shop and the Hialeah job, and perhaps at the shoe factory. People weren't as likely to discover his peculiarities and get him fired up.

When he forgot his lunch the following Saturday, Mami made me call the Jamaican crew leader about arrangements to bring it over and I got to see for myself that Homestead was exactly the sort of hardy pioneer land its name suggested. On the bus, Mami and I passed fields of plants glistening from the morning's chemical sprays. Rows of tiny people knelt before the tall plants, as if in obedience. I thought about my father's pride and his great desire to be strong. Was he out there on his knees now too?

The fields yielded to a desolate region with numerous canals, flanked by razor-edged swamp grass that, as I'd learned in school, trickled down from the Kissimmee River to the Atlantic. So much water had been irrigated and diverted to deep, unfenced canals, in fact, that our state's scholastic essay topic that year was: "Why I Stay Away from Florida Waterways."

Where the canals ended, the bus stopped too. Before us

stretched a cloudless expanse without a house or anything remotely human in sight. After a while I began to wonder, where was the Tanaka Farms sign for us to meet the Jamaican crew leader's van? Mami pushed me toward the driver. "Ask him where we are," she instructed. "And find out how to get out."

From him, I learned that this was the genuine *Everglades: River of Grass*, untamed by thirty years of post-war development, where Indians lived whose name no one could spell.

"Seminoles?" I asked him with curiosity.

"They ain't Seminoles," said the driver, staring out over his steering wheel. "They're the alligator wrestlers. You know, the county fair? Mickosouuk—Miccosek." He tried to sound it out, but the consonants were like alligator teeth waiting to snap. "Anyway, they're the ones who own most of this land." He gazed across the swamps. "Florida's paradise."

I mulled that over while recalling Mr. Lanham's talk about the cimarrones and walked back to confer with Mami about whether to transfer buses or ride to downtown. Either way, we would be too late for any lunch break. She shook her head, infuriated with herself for failing my father. I tried to distract her with tidbits the driver had shared about the Everglades, but she glanced dismissively at the surroundings and said, "This is no paradise, Gabriela. This is a jungle."

Her view was one shared by other members of my family, as well as most Latinos I knew—the vast plain, a reminder of centuries of cane cutting and campesino misery. It made sense to me that the only people who stayed here were those clever Miccosukee, who seemed to have managed fine and dandy for nearly two hundred years. They remained invisible to everyone else, true to their cimarrón roots, except when invited to wrestle alligators at the Dade County Youth Fair.

As the bus neared downtown, Mami perked up. "¡Gracias a

Dios!" she proclaimed when the driver turned the corner toward the dilapidated McCrory's Department Store. We'd reached civilization!

Her anti-nature prejudice, though, was nothing compared to her distress over my father's presence in the ranks of the humilde—the humble people of the world. *Or maybe it was the humiliated people?* I wondered when she lamented tragically to me after we'd gotten home, "Your father shouldn't have to do this kind of work."

At the end of the week, along with his pay, my father brought home a huge bag of tomatoes that bloomed so red it was hard to believe they'd grown out of the sun-beaten Florida dirt.

But then the picking stopped.

## SEVEN

TWO DAYS AFTER his agricultural job ended, my father entered the kitchen, tossed the *Seminole Sentinel* into the garbage, and swore off that "¡condenado periódico!" for good.

One look at my mother's face, her mouth gaping open, squelched the sudden relief I felt over my liberation from *Sentinel* duty. As my father turned and reentered his dark chamber, Mami managed to choke out a "¿Cómo?" and followed him in. Moments later, I heard her low-voiced attempts to reason dispassionately about the importance of continuing ordinary job searches, but my father remained impassive. In my mind's eye, I pictured a mad medieval king with his arms crossed as his advisers counseled against war with the enemy.

I was only too glad to flee that gloomy castle for the silver steed of a van that arrived to transport me to a Junior Achievement meeting. A program teacher had paid us a visit earlier, during which my father smiled broadly and, upon hearing the student interpreter translate "the spirit of entrepreneurship" as "responsibility," decreed that I could participate.

At the peculiar meeting, poster boards were filled with lists of businesses' missions and the Ingredients of Success. It reeked of my father's fantastic moneymaking schemes and I glanced around at my fellow Achievers, Latino faces doubtful like mine. We were then divided into teams to create fictional companies and list their Key Marketing Strategies, with the program leaders promising that over time we would add to the Life of Our Company. Aside from feeling like a minor character in a chapter of a very boring book, I took one lesson home from that session: Moneymaking consisted of cold psychology, i.e., convincing people to buy whatever you had to sell whether or not they needed it. I had plenty of proof that such psychology didn't work in everyday life, since my father, who had only his labor to sell, had been hugely unsuccessful in finding buyers through the standard marketing methods or via his hopeless magazines. I tried to stifle a rebel voice whispering inside me that maybe my father had nothing worth selling to anyone anymore.

In response to my father's unorthodox new business plan, Mami began to secretly sell Avon products. She was gone for hours the next day while I pretended to listen to his pseudo-scientific lectures and anxiously contemplated how I would extricate myself to dress for the Cuban fund-raising party Mami had given me the okay to attend—Alina's mother had allowed Alina two invitees, Lydia and me.

I eventually managed to remove myself from my father's clutches to go shower and change into a party dress that still fit. Shortly afterward one of our neighbors, an elderly fisherman named Nicky who'd often brought over extra fish, stopped by unexpectedly. When Pablo complained to him of an earache, Nicky offered to cure him the way they used to do it in the Old Country, and I went with them to the yard to watch. While Nicky was in the process of lighting a newspaper funnel in Pablo's ear to smoke the pain out, Mami came home and greeted him appreciatively. But then my father, who'd evidently been observing from his window, came out shrieking like a lunatic. "*¡Imbécil!*" he cried at the old man and furiously whacked the funnel out of Nicky's hand. Stunned by my father's reaction, Nicky backed off, sputtering some explanation in hysterical Italian. My own hysterical heart began to beat *Oh God! Oh God!* as my mother feebly dropped her Avon packages and begged my father to restrain himself. But he merely kept yelling in vulgar Spanish and raised a threatening arm—and the poor, terrified neighbor fled.

The instant he took off, I leapt to my senses. "Papi?" I squeaked bravely between threats.

Jaw clenched, he looked at me.

"Wouldn't you like me to finish your work now? I'm all done studying." Nervously I held my hands out in humble supplication.

My father nodded in surprise. "Pues, sí," he agreed happily, straightening his shoulders and marching officiously toward the house, while Mami seized the opportunity to gather up her illicit Avon packages. I followed my father but hesitated at the back door. "I'll, um, be right in, Papi," I stammered. "I just have to tell Mami something." When I shut the door to turn around, my gaze fell on the tips of my patent leather shoes: black mirrors, empty as the hours ahead of me. With a sigh, I shook off disappointment and went to rouse Mami into action. "*Do* something!" I urged her. "Didn't you see Papi hit that man's hand? We have to keep him *away* from people!"

"No seas exagerada, Gabriela," she retorted, scowling. "Your father was trying to look out for your brother's welfare."

"What if Nicky reports Papi to the police like that lady?" I tossed back furiously. "Don't you think about that stuff?"

She glanced apprehensively toward the neighbor's house and back at me, her face registering surprise at the regalia I'd donned for my now defunct party. "All right," she said wearily, handing me the Avon bags. "I'll go over and apologize."

Back in the house, I changed into regular clothes, called Lydia and Alina, and fended off self-pity while feeling as wilted as a Saturday night wallflower. With my father's illogically constructed paragraphs before me, I worked stoically until dark arrived.

There was a method to this madness, I assured myself. Suborning my father's oddball writing was the only way, short of a real job, to keep him out of trouble until El Chino dismissed that criminal case and we could all be free.

The lone festive moment of my night came when Nicky's wife, Pia, brought over a plate of warm, powdered sugar cookies—like a sign that Someone had forgiven my father his trespasses.

Someone's tolerance waned by the following weekend, though. As my brothers and I stocked groceries Mami had left for us to put away, the high cabinet my father had once nailed into the wall for extra storage suddenly shifted slightly. Instinctively, I stepped back. Then, with a great shudder, the entire cabinet succumbed to the great weight inside and tumbled toward us. I let out a wild shriek and jumped sideways as the cabinet came crashing to the floor with all its contents.

"Holy cow!" cried Manolo, open-mouthed. Shattered oil and syrup jars, crushed spice packages, and rice were strewn everywhere.

My father raced in. When he saw the wreckage, his face went red-hot. "¿Están locos?" he screamed. But he was the one who looked crazy as he rushed toward Manolo and Pablo across the cans rolling in oil under his feet. My brothers tore out of there, and I ran too, uncertain where my father's furious arms would land. Into the bathroom I fled, trembling all the while, and shrewdly locked the door behind me. From there, I listened to him scream his head off and pound whoever he'd managed to seize. For the first time in my life, I feared that he could actually kill a person.

When things quieted, and my father seemed to have retreated, I slipped out, tiptoeing into the kitchen and surveying the disaster. Gingerly, I navigated a path toward the back door and looked around outside for my brothers.

There they were—in Johnny's front yard. I ran over.

Manolo's face had a throbbing pink welt. "Feel this," he said, gesturing to his skull.

I touched the bulging knuckle lump, shook my head in sympathy, and looked at Pablo.

"He didn't get me," Pablo offered.

"You guys better stay here until Mami comes home," I advised.

I returned to the house, then forced myself to carry out a rapid clean up operation as quietly as possible to avoid rousing my father's ire. A short while later, though, a hoarse voice behind me made me flinch. "¿Cómo puedo trabajar así?"

I froze up, immediately feeling on edge again, but when I ventured a quick peek, only the echo of his old pathetic self lingered as he stared at the floor.

How could he work indeed? Who was left out there to give someone like him a job?

I waited cautiously for a little longer, then bent down to extract a piece of glass from our long, sad river of oil.


My father's temperamento spread: Colombia, New York, Miami— everywhere and everyone became a bewildering jumble of refineries and people who had stolen his money. It was hard to decipher the subjects of his ranting as I transcribed increasingly illogical letters that had replaced classified ad searches. I was relieved when the holiday recess arrived, if only for the extra time. Never had life seemed more difficult than that period between my father's return from Massachusetts and our first Christmas in Miami. Enlisted to help with the expansion of Mami's secret Avon business when she began sewing Communion dresses to sell at St. Stephen's as well, I struggled valiantly to keep my father happy.

As people failed to answer his confusing letters, my father had become obsessed with the mail. Now either Mami or I had to make a mad rush to claim it before he did, so that he wouldn't angrily destroy something important, like a legitimate letter from the government. Only holiday cards were safe for him, along with one genuine letter he received from his sister, my Tía Consuelo, who'd helped raise him in Colombia. Hers was the only letter that actually made him smile and converse instead of fly into a rage or a frenzy of further composition.

We didn't have much of a Christmas that year. We attended the family party with not a single gift for Tía Rita, Tío Victor, or anyone else. The only noteworthy event was a worrisome conversation I overheard between Mami and Tía Rita about some mysterious debt my father owed to his former boss in Massachusetts.

At home later, I rifled forlornly through Gothic novels I'd long before finished reading and wondered vaguely if not returning a library book was a crime and whether you could be deported for it. Unhappily, I flipped through a familiar favorite, *Dark Victory*, and tried to suck a little more joy out of passages I'd read before, but the jumble of my father's block printing superimposed itself across the book pages like a dark and hopeless code.

Lydia called near the end of the break to suggest that we go buy materials for our Home Economics projects. Everyone at her house, she reported as we headed toward the fabric store, had been busy fighting. She unleashed details of the latest melodrama: Her mother had locked Lydia's two-timing father out of the house one night, and he'd had to break in through the back door. "You should've heard what a lío he caused! My mother was about to call the cops," Lydia exclaimed. "She told him he'd have more time to think about his family in jail!"

My eyes widened in dismay. "Lydia, that could get him deported."

"Says who? Cubans don't get deported."

"What do you mean?"

"Politics," she said authoritatively, entering the store.

"But what if—" I hesitated, "if the person assaulted someone?"

Lydia whipped her head around. "He doesn't *beat* us, Gabi. He's just a two-timer."

"Oh, I know," I mumbled embarrassedly, then rushed off to search for my dress pattern. I'd said more than I meant to, but it was hard to stay off home issues when chatting with Lydia.

After I'd located a recommended A-line pattern, I waited near the register for Lydia to join me with her selection—a sexy sundress pattern, plainly not on the recommended list, that she apparently intended to sew out of the bolt of canary eyelet she carried in her arms. Quite a contrast from the drab brown fabric my mother had procured for me from the uncles' shop for free. At least Lydia would have something in the right color for our spring concert. The concert was supposed to be a big deal, and guidance staff had already started notifying us that girls were supposed to wear yellow.

"Very cute," I commented succinctly to Lydia as I examined her wares, though I couldn't help but picture her as a well-endowed middle-aged Cuban lady trying to squeeze into old baby clothes.

Lydia stuck out her tongue. "Don't be jealous, chica."

I rolled my eyes and grinned, relieved that she didn't return to the subject of angry fathers.

When I showed Mami my Simplicity pattern package at home, she frowned. "What nonsense. What kind of sewing is that?"

"It's logical," I assured her. "See? There's directions. Step by step. I'll explain it to you as we go along."

"I don't think so. I was sewing long before you were born," she countered.

"So was the teacher," I pointed out.

But when school resumed a few days later, Mami's skepticism began to trump my faith in the logic. The process—from reading instructions, to pinning sections of pattern correctly along the fabric's grain, to drawing darts with a chalk wheel and finally cutting the dress sections out of cloth—proved unnecessarily complicated. Mami's old-fashioned methods were admittedly superior. Not only did she rely solely on remnants instead of the precise lengths and widths mandated by instruction sheets, she didn't use prefabricated patterns at all. Freehand sewing was second nature to her. She could easily have made the St. Stephen's frocks blindfolded. In record time, she pinned, cut, and sewed, then emerged from the closet where she kept her Singer machine with the pretty ready-to-wear item on a hanger. By contrast, at the rate we were going in class, I might be able to wear my Simplicity dress to graduation.

One night, while I was painstakingly basting over a bodice I'd done wrong, I listened to a radio program my parents had on, and Lydia's remarks about Cuban immigration rules came back to me. The radio interview was about people who wanted to immigrate here to be with relatives but weren't permitted to do so. I couldn't get to the bottom of who was responsible for the poor families' problems—the Cuban government for not letting the relatives out of their own country, or the U.S. government for keeping them out of this one? Whoever was to blame, it was all so mean!

Little did I know that an innocuous immigration rule would soon throw another monkey wrench into our family life. The following Friday, as Mami hounded my father for the third time in a row about some alien reporting forms we had to turn in, he got very testy with her.

I anticipated the worst, but she came out of their room looking merely exasperated, carrying our green cards and some blank white cards. She dumped it all on the table in front of me. "Fill those out, please," she said crossly.

"I'm typing for Papi."

"Do this first," she said. "Tomorrow's the deadline."

"All right," I said, glancing at the immigration forms, then lowering my voice to ask, "Is this because of Papi's problem?"

"No," she said, pushing aside his paperwork to give me room to write. "We just have to do it." She went on to explain that despite our green card status, in the eyes of the U.S. government we were considered "aliens" and had to report our whereabouts every year.

"We could get in trouble just for not turning these in?" I asked, holding up one of the plain white cards.

"Por supuesto," she agreed. "That's why I keep telling your father. Tomorrow's the last day to bring them to the post office."

"What kind of trouble, Mami?" I pressed, frowning at the card. "Is it one of those crimes El Chino talked about?"

"I don't know, Gabriela! Just write the information!"

"Okay, okay," I said, bending my head to the task. Neatly, I recorded our alien whereabouts on all five cards, along with our registration numbers, and gave everything back to her.

It wasn't until the next morning when I heard more quarreling that I appreciated the gravity of the little white card situation. My father was arguing vehemently that he'd already written to the government, and here was the proof of it, so the cards were unnecessary.

"No, they're not!" Mami insisted. "No, they're not!"

I glanced at the kitchen clock—almost noon. The post office closed at 1 P.M. on Saturdays. *Time for reinforcements*, I decided valiantly as I downed my glass of fortified fresh Florida orange juice.

In one corner of their bedroom was my mother, angrily waving her handful of white cards.

In the other corner, my bellicose father, fiercely gripping an envelope.

"Papi," I ventured, putting on my neutral Most Able Assistant voice, "Don't you think the government might pay more attention to your letter if you go ahead and give them their little cards?"

My father's brows pulled together in thought.

"You could try it," I suggested, gaining confidence. "You always say trying is good, right?"

"No," he rudely disposed. "I'll mail my own letter to those thieving burócratas!"

Mami dropped dejectedly onto her bed and issued me a final pleading look, while he ransacked the closet for his good shoes.

I studied the cards in her hand. "Papi," I said casually, "I'll go to the post office with you."

"Muy bien," he answered, pleased as punch. While he bent down to tie his shoes Mami surreptitiously handed me the cards.

Another deceit slipped into our family toolbox like the cards into my jeans pocket.

The walk down Calle Ocho toward the post office felt interminable. It was so extremely hot I worried that the ink might run off the sweat-sogged cards in my pocket. To compound the unpleasantness, men called out lecherous invitations from their clankety cars, despite the presence of my father beside me, and then slowed to a crawl as if I would actually accept their lewd proposals. Worse than the lechery, the heat, the distance, or even the anxiety over how I would dispose of the soggy cards in my pocket without my father noticing, was having to listen to him boast, his ticking hand drumming onto my shoulder, about the latest moneymaking schemes. "La invención más importante, mi'jita," he exclaimed, leaning closer to confide in me at one point. Now he was becoming an inventor too.

I crouched lower to relieve myself of the added weight on my shoulder.

"What we need," he continued, "is a system that doesn't require injection." At the traffic light, he paused and smiled at the stopped cars. "And I can make it!"

I squinted into the bright sunlight as he abruptly switched gears and added knowingly, "You need the right experience to manage that company, mi'jita."

"What company, Papi?" He jumped around so unpredictably that I couldn't tell if this tidbit was connected to the invention or to some job referenced in one of the letters he now carried in his batch of envelopes.

"The Louisiana company, mi'ja. I'll be the engineer," he explained, his free hand conducting the air with the envelopes.

My father had always worked as a laborer. Wasn't that a far cry from a professional job? I sighed deeply, tired of searching for the parts of what he told me that might amount to something in his junk yard of twisted logic.

We finally arrived at our promised land: the air-conditioned post office. My father went to stand in line while I wandered around anxiously, canvassing the place. Finally I spotted a box labeled "Alien Registration" under the poster of those Wanted for kidnapping children. Keeping a steady eye on him, I sauntered over there and pretended to study the kidnapped children, all American. When his turn at the counter arrived, I swiftly dumped our cards into the box and strode back nervously toward where he stood.

The clerk flipped through the envelopes my father had handed him and returned one with a question. My father looked back blankly. How I wished he would acknowledge people talking to him, even if he didn't get what they were saying. Instead, he held his envelope out with both hands, as if he needed glasses, and turned to me. I popped up to the rescue.

"It needs a more exact address," said the clerk, with his finger on my father's trademark block letters. The addressee was: "United States of America "

In Spanish, I asked my father who that letter was supposed to be for.

"El gobierno," he answered impatiently, though that much was obvious. He tilted his head toward me and smiled at the clerk as if apologizing for my slowness. The clerk shifted his gaze from my father to me and back.

As calmly and respectfully as I could, I told my father that it was necessary to include the name of the person in "The Government" as well as the street and city.

"Give me that letter!" He plucked it out of my hands. "Tú no sabes nada," he barked rudely, storming off.

*I* didn't know anything? Flabbergasted, I watched him leave. With an embarrassed shrug and without money for stamps, I turned to the clerk. "I'm sorry—could I please have our letters back?"

Outside, my father sped down Eighth Street and I raced to catch up. The envelope agitated in his hand like a handkerchief in Tía Rita's lumbering old washing machine. I certainly hadn't typed any letters to the U.S. government. What on earth, I puzzled silently, could he have written to them about? Perhaps I should have encouraged the clerk to mail it anyway, even if it didn't reach any destination; neither did letters to Santa Claus.

When we got home, my father, red-faced from the intense heat, marched straight into the house.

I sat on the back steps and listened to Mami criticize him for failing to mail the mortgage check. Listlessly, I lay back. The journey had worn me out. Clouds drifted behind the dark leaves of our mango tree.

My father yelled tersely at Mami about that scoundrel government owing him for work in the Colombian oil fields, eons ago. "We're not paying them a single centavo more," he warned her angrily. "Not until I receive my money."

"But it's not true, Roberto," she protested. "You were always paid by that company, very punctually. What are you talking about? You know we have to make our mortgage payment."

"I repeat, Evangelina, we're not giving them another penny. That money is ours!"

As I listened to him stampede away, the voices falling silent, I studied our crossed lime/grapefruit tree. The tree reminded me of my cousin Raquel's younger brothers, Ricardito and Robertico, whom everyone addressed indiscriminately as "Mello" or "Twin"—as if their identity lay solely in being related to each other. I remembered how when we'd first moved in, my father had caught me inspecting the tree curiously. "Which one grows?" I'd asked, and he'd pinched a lime and yanked it off to chew on the twig at the end. With a smile he'd offered me a try, but I declined, shaking my head. "The lime is good," he'd insisted, laughing. Despite the unusual form of his fruit testing, my father's words had proved true. The limes were always good.

My mother suddenly came outside and dangled a mortgage payment envelope over my face.

I sat up. "Mami! I already snuck those cards over there for you!"

She ran her fingers through her hair and looked skyward. "¡Ay Dios mío! ¡Ayúdame con esta casa!"

Should Heaven help her with the house, I speculated critically, or with the people in it? Silently, I amended her prayer, though she hadn't even thanked me for solving our alien registration crisis.

"Mi'jita," she begged.

I shook my head. "Make your little beaver Manolo go."

"He's not here. I'll keep your father occupied."

I glanced toward the closed blinds of my father's window, sighed, and surrendered my weary hand.

As I retraced my steps down Eighth Street, I couldn't help but worry about all that time my father was spending alone with his magazines. Even though it kept him away from people he could cause trouble with, it couldn't be good for his mind. In fact, the more he stayed in there, the more he seemed to be completely fading out. Granted, he'd never been totally present in our family, but the other absences had felt normal. Like back in Colombia when he'd worked long hours doing measurements around the refinery near our town. His longest absence, when I turned eight, was for the faraway United States. There, he had told us, a person could work for overtime pay, hold multiple jobs, and earn dollars instead of meager pesos. He'd sent for us as soon as he'd secured a steady factory job at night. After that, there was the daily absence of working, but we saw him on Sundays and holidays. Periodically, my mother would show him my report card and he would pat my back and praise my intelligence, and then remind me that A Good Education Is the Most Important Thing in the World. My mother finally revealed to me once that he'd never had the luxury of finishing high school himself.

That evening, with the post office debacle behind him, my father babbled on and on about how delicious the dinner was. "¡Arroz con pollo!" he exclaimed in delight, oblivious of my mother's stony silence.

No government treats for us that day.

In the kitchen afterward, as Mami passed me plates to wash while she proceeded to scrape the hardened cuquillo from the bottom of our rice pot, I thought more seriously about my father's actions. Because we hadn't socialized much with anyone but relatives, I'd gotten used to seeing him as the aunts and uncles did— taking for granted that in addition to his temperamental outbursts and moral extremisms he sometimes acted a little odd. But now it was obvious that his occasional mild eccentricity had turned into persistently illogical, disturbing behavior that was difficult to brush off. "Something's wrong, Mami," I blurted out.

My mother ignored me and kept on scrubbing.

"In the first place," I continued, "even if some Colombian oil company owes us money, what does that have to do with our mortgage? And in the second place, why should the U.S. government care if we get ripped off or pay our bills? Something's wrong with Papi."

She swung around with the pot. "Never repeat such a thing," she hissed.

"But what's happening?" I felt like a giant child beside her— grown tall on the outside but still small inside.

Shoving her pot into the cabinet, she faced me. "Listen now," she whispered. "There's no such thing as a perfect family. God gave you this life, now you concentrate on helping us resolve our problems. Not on complaining to anybody about our misfortunes. ¿Me entiendes?"

I nodded.

She grabbed the laundry basket and went out for the clothes. Her reaction frightened me. This went way beyond ordinary immigrant confusion over the everyday things done in this country, such as parents letting kids sleep over at each others' houses or girls leaving home before getting married. It felt scarier, even, than losing our green cards. As I watched through the window and waited for my mother's return, dusk filled the sky. Something spread through our house without my being able to see exactly what it was.

## EIGHT

THE LONGER MY FATHER STAYED in his room writ-
ing letters instead of looking for real work, the angrier he
became at the magazine people who refused to answer his inqui-
ries. "When are they sending my money?" he cried out to my
mother one morning at the start of our cleaning hour. But time
didn't mean anything to my father anymore. When he realized
that Mami was determined to ignore his endless interrogation, he
came to bug me. "You know how much they owe me?" He waved
his *Home Mechanics* magazine in front of my face. I stopped sweeping and shook my head.

"¡Son millones!"

I didn't bother to ask who owed him the millions. Now I knew
it was the big, bad American government.

Rarely did my father bother to go talk to my brothers about that
stuff; they'd also lucked out of the mandatory bike riding my father
had entirely forgotten about in his preoccupation with paperwork.

When my birthday came around in February, I tried to buoy
my spirits by helping to bake the family cake. It weighed a ton by
the time we removed it from our cast-iron rice pot, because the
recipe called for a pound of butter, flour, and sugar and a dozen

eggs. Mami fluffed it up with dulce de leche frosting and inserted candles around the edge. After dinner, she put the cake on the table and lit the candles. Then my father belted out an out-of-tune rendition of *Cumpleaños feliz* which my brothers sang in English under their breaths. Pablo had made me an origami butterfly, my only gift, and as I blew out the candles and cut my father a slice of cake, I wished we could celebrate without him. His presence left a hollow feeling like a hole in the middle of my birthday.

The next morning, the mailman delivered a pale blue envelope with the birthday letter my grandfather always sent me. It wasn't really a letter but a poem, handwritten on a thin sheet of paper. Bible paper. Other years, I'd given his poems back to my mother to save because the dense Spanish vocabulary words were too challenging. She would always get sentimental, reminiscing about the poems he used to write to her.

This time, I kept my grandfather's letter to myself. I went outside, stretched out on the grass under our acacia, and held the poem up to the sun. You could almost see through the paper. The poem was called *Norabuena*, basically Congratulations.

It was about a girl of Eden with blue gondolas in her soul and winds of love breathing her into a faraway port. I lifted the sheet with two fingers so that the feeble Miami breeze could turn the ends up a bit. I wondered how my old grandfather, who hadn't seen me in so many years, had guessed that my soul was full of boats searching, like the thin waters of the Everglades, for the place where they could be released. I went inside for a pen, thinking I might write back. But what came out instead was a waterfall of sadness—wingless angels, unrequited love, and waves of sea beating their helpless hands against the shore. I titled it *Las Magdalenas*, after the saying in Spanish "to cry a magdalena," which is what a person does when he or she is inconsolable.

• • •

My birthday sadness soon gave way to more manageable worry over the much touted eighth grade concert. Girls were supposed to wear a yellow dress, which I didn't possess, and I dreaded the humiliation of standing out like an odd duck. Who knew what antiquated thing my mother would come up with if I told her, and Lydia was too busty for me to fit into anything of hers. So when a few weeks past my birthday, another pesky notice was sent home about proper attire, I thought to phone my cousin Raquel to see if she had a dress I could borrow. Mami summoned me into the dining room before I could make the call, however. She seemed to be holding court at the mahogany table while my brothers were sweating it out before her on the padded burgundy chairs she'd protected with plastic covering. It crunched under their butts as they shifted position.

They'd run all the way home, she explained to me. A couple of sinvergüenzas had chased them.

"Why?" I asked Pablo.

"I don't know," he shrugged. "They don't like us." He reported that a kid had shoved him when he left cello practice and that the kid and three others had chased him and Manolo home with a pole. "They were sixth graders," Pablo added.

That was Manolo's grade, Pablo's was fifth. Both had repeated a year—one among the many reasons my parents treated me as the "smart" one. Though Manolo and I were technically closer in age than he and Pablo, my parents preferred to lump Manolo in with our younger brother.

As they finished their story, I tallied my resentments over the number of times something had gone awry with my brothers and I was put in charge. Once, long ago in Queens, Mami had anxiously anchored the three of us on her bed while she went for medicine for my sick brothers and my father slept. "Don't let the boys off this bed for an instant," she'd warned me, and it had seemed like forever that I sat upright, my shaky nine-year-old hands planted on my brothers' hot tummies until she returned. That was pretty much how the rest of our childhood had gone too.

In the middle of the mini-conference, my father shuffled in. "Hola, mi'jita," he greeted me, as if I were the only one present.

"Not now, Roberto," Mami said, frowning at the papers in his hand. "The muchachos are having a problem. It seems their school is a haven for delinquents."

"¿Sí?" My father tilted his head. "¿Qué pasó?"

Manolo shifted on the plastic. "Nothing, Papi. Some kids bothered us."

"Nothing? How can your mother be upset over nothing?" He yanked Manolo's hair.

"It wasn't Manolo," Pablo said guiltily.

My father swerved. "Then who was it?"

"Nobody, Papi," I said. "It's over. We're just discussing it."

"Over?" Mami threw in. "What about those sinvergüenzas?"

I wanted to smack her as my father suddenly began surveying all of us for the right person to clobber. "¿Qué pasó?" he demanded again.

"Shameless delinquents chased them home!" she answered. "With a weapon!"

I stood and said with false brio, "I'll call the school, Papi, okay?"

"¿Delincuentes?" my father responded in disbelief.

"Oh my God!" Mami exclaimed with an exasperated wave of her hand. "Let her call!"

My father blinked. He began to swallow repeatedly in a very awkward manner, as if he'd tasted something foul. Then, just as oddly, he went back to the repeated blinking. What was wrong with him? The four of us watched until the swallowing and blinking ran their course and he seemed to return to us.

"Sí." He nodded at me. "Go ahead."

Officiously, I went to the phone and dialed. Only the vice principal was at the school, and I explained the situation. Evidently not too worried about my brothers' safety, he said he would "chat" with them the following day.

I hung up and summarized for my parents.

"Is that all?" Mami asked.

"I'm sure they'll fix everything," I assured her.

"No," my father said abruptly. "I'll resolve it. ¡Vamos!"

"But—but school's closed, Papi," Manolo stuttered.

My father turned toward Mami for confirmation.

"That's true," she decreed from her royal throne.

Examining the papers in his hand, he thought it over. "No lo creo," he pronounced at last. "Manolo, Pablo. Get up. Let's go see."

My brothers stumbled to their feet, and I looked beseechingly at my mother. Aloud, I suggested nervously, "Maybe we should all go." The only school visit my father had ever executed was on the day of my Confirmation, and that had been in a church with nuns and other parents around.

"Yes, you go, Gabriela," Mami replied.

*Just me?* My eyes widened, but she looked away.

After my father had deposited his papers in his room and changed out of the ubiquitous slippers into his shoes, the four of us set out on our long, silent march of doom.

It was one of those odd Florida days when you actually needed a sweater, though we wore short sleeves. On the path in front of us, a brisk wind knocked a coconut down from one of the trees that had survived the pest eradication campaign. Maybe that's a bad omen, I surmised darkly. God hadn't dropped the coconut directly on my father's head.

The sprinklers were turned on when we reached Rickenbacker, which meant that somebody was there. Manolo bravely led us around toward the front.

The large blue metal doors were chained blessedly shut.

A joyful Pablo whispered, "Yes!"

Of course, my hardheaded father had to shake the chains and rap his knuckles insistently on the metal.

I timidly suggested, "Papi, the teachers must be gone."

"It can't be," he retorted indignantly, then began to shout "Who's there? Who's there?" in Spanish while pounding more vigorously.

An elderly woman in a housecoat and cardigan came out of her lime green house across the street to see what was happening.

"Maybe we should come back another time, Papi," I encouraged my father, who only continued to yell in Spanish and broken English while banging on the impenetrable door. To my horror, he started kicking it when his raw, reddened knuckles tired out.

"*Help,*" I mouthed to my brothers, who shook their heads in resounding defeat. As we passively watched our demented father kick and bang, I could only pray silently that he might exhaust himself before doing any physical damage to the door. In point of fact, the heavy metal looked too sturdy for anyone to harm. *Is assaulting a door even a crime?* I wondered wildly, biting on a fingernail. *What about making a spectacle of yourself?* I peeked at the lady in the lime-colored house. What was a "moral turpitude" crime anyway? It dawned on me then, with amazing clarity, that no one in my family had bothered to ask El Chino what *kind* of trouble could jeopardize our right to remain in this country.

"Can I help you folks out?" A craggy man's voice startled me, and I turned around.

He was a pudgy older black guy in a uniform-like shirt and pants.

"Um—" I stepped to the fore, but my father barked out a demand in Spanish that the door be opened.

"My father just wanted to talk to somebody," I stammered.

The groundskeeper or janitor or whatever he was hobbled forward unevenly as if he had a bad ankle. "Uh-huh," he said, nodding at my father, who looked completely disheveled from his door-kicking offensive.

My father's ticking hand started going a little nutty right then, and he began shaking his arm aggressively as if to rid himself of the tic.

"It's a problem with some bad kids and my brothers," I offered, though Pablo and Manolo were gesticulating madly for me to leave them out of it.

"Well, the school's closed," the groundskeeper stated matter-of-factly as he continued to regard my father, who was clearly stronger physically than the old hobbling groundskeeper.

My father swiped his brow in exasperation. "¡Qué carajo!" he erupted, turning toward me and demanding to know, "Is he going to open the damned door or not?"

"Oh sure, sure," the groundskeeper-janitor answered him calmly in English. "I can open that for you, sir." He fished a pair of metallic reading glasses out of his pocket and carefully put them on. Then, leaning on his good leg for balance, he slowly worked a key ring off the collection on his belt. "Okay now," he said, facing the door. "Let's get this chain off."

Four locks and keys later, he opened the door and invited us in.

I glanced at my father. *Now what?*

"Vamos," my father declared, walking in purposefully. He marched up a darkened central hallway and peered into one locked, empty classroom after another, while we stumbled along behind him like a band of escaped mental patients. The click of his shoes on the floor and the rattling of the groundskeeper's keys added a queer soundtrack. When we'd traveled up and down all three hallways, my father halted in his tracks, uttered a nondescript "Hah," and stared into the dark with a foolish smile, as if he were dreaming of something.

Then the groundskeeper did an unusual thing. Limping up to stand close to my father, he placed a friendly hand on my father's arm, looked up at him with a smile, and then just waited. After a moment, in an infinitely kind and gentle tone of voice, he murmured, "You see, my friend? They're all gone."

My father's expression began to relax into that of a shy kid instead of the foolhardy madman he'd become. To my surprise, he let the groundskeeper turn him around and lead him peacefully in the direction we'd come. My brothers and I trailed along, equally subdued.

Once outside the entrance, the groundskeeper shook my father's hand and told him his name. "Abi for short," the groundskeeper added with a grin, before addressing me. "Young lady, you tell my friend here that the building's always open by 7:30. Most folks stick around until about 2:30 or so." He gave my father a nod of encouragement. "You come back any of those times, and you should be okay, my friend." I obediently translated the schedule for my father, without mentioning anything about coming back, which prompted Pablo to poke Manolo conspiratorially in the side.

Abiasaph studied my brothers over his glasses as he commenced the elaborate door-locking process. "You kids watch out for your father," he said quietly.

Then we left. It was only after we were walking back that I felt the true meaning of his words rise up out of the "watching out" I'd heard him say into the watching *over* he must have intended.

At home, my father's perfunctory summary for Mami left

me unsettled about what to tell her privately about the peculiar visit, but I put it all behind me because the immediate crisis was resolved—or so I thought.

That evening my brothers came and told me they'd overheard my father planning another visit to Rickenbacker on Monday.

"Oh great," I groaned, wishing there were a chain like the groundskeeper's to lock up my father until the era of his criminal probation had ended.

"We won't be so lucky next time," Manolo warned.

"Lucky?" I felt like it was my turn to Assault a Minor, say the culprit behind this school fiasco, for instance. "What's the story with those kids you fought?" I demanded to know.

"I didn't do anything to that kid," Pablo swore, not very convincingly.

I looked at Manolo for an explanation.

"I wasn't there," he reported honestly, though I could tell he shared my doubts about Pablo's innocence. In the past, my brothers had tended to stick together in misdeeds, Pablo with big-eyed charm and Manolo with plain old silence, but maybe there was hope that Manolo would outgrow all his training in dumbness. "At least it's not tomorrow," Manolo noted. "Maybe Papi will change his mind over the weekend."

"What are we gonna do if he does come?" Pablo whined.

"I don't know!" I burst out. "Go to the park or something."

"I'll miss cello practice," Pablo protested.

"That practice isn't doing much for your playing," I said nastily, before I could stop myself.

"You got that right," Manolo added with a snicker that exposed his crooked front tooth.

Pablo pulled out his borrowed school cello just to spite us, although Manolo had hidden Pablo's sheet music somewhere. While Manolo and I debated the chances of our father actually getting a paint job call from the neighborhood contractor, horrible cello sounds screeched out of the bathroom, where Pablo practiced to avoid pissing off Papi. Pablo actually longed to play guitar, and even claimed not to mind the fruit bowl haircuts Mami gave him because he believed they made him look like a Beatle, but his school didn't offer guitar. Cello or violin, those had been his options. "Only girls take violin," Pablo had informed us the day he showed up at home with his large instrument of harmonic torture. Now, as he tried to practice from memory without the sheet music, he played that *Ode to Joy* so slowly and painfully that Manolo eventually felt bad and slipped him the music under the bathroom door.

I mentally prepared myself to convince my mother of the folly of letting my father loose on Rickenbacker. But when Manolo and Pablo returned home from school the following day, Friday, she only stirred herself up over the incident again. "Were those sinvergüenzas punished?"

"Nothing happened, Mami," Manolo assured her as he peeled a mango and bit into it.

Fists on her hips, she looked back and forth between Manolo and Pablo. "Why are you so late?"

"We stopped at the playground," Pablo explained.

"Playground?" she replied, aghast. "All these problems and you go to the playground instead of coming home?"

"I'm sorry, Mami," he said, with his black eyes rounded and seemingly contrite.

After she'd gone inside, they confessed that everyone involved was getting detentions.

"But why are you getting punished?" I asked Manolo, suddenly anxious that the friendly groundskeeper might have reported something after all about my father's rowdy encounter with the door.

"I don't know," he answered. "I don't care anymore."

To get Mami off their backs, I revised the facts, telling her that the principal had given detentions to the shameless good-for-nothings, as she'd called them, and that, as a safety measure, my brothers were supposed to come home on variant schedules. She believed every word. She wouldn't have wanted to hear the truth anyway, if it meant accepting that the problem had no solution.

My anxiety over my father's Rickenbacker activities had overtaken my own minor worries, such as the dreaded concert problem. Instead of turning to my family to bail me out, I'd resorted to more lies. In the morning, just before the concert, I'd taken the metro bus to the stop near school, waited there for a couple of hours until I was sure the performance had ended, and eventually shown up at the main office with the story that I'd been sick and my mother didn't think to write me a note. Lying was getting easier.

Unfortunately, my father remained determined to go to their school, despite my brothers' swearing up and down that there was no problem left to solve. My father even told Mami that he was looking forward to stopping in afterward on his "friend" Abiasaph the groundskeeper!

Mami paid scant attention to any of that, concentrating instead on keeping everyone off the phone throughout the weekend so we wouldn't miss a call from the contractor. With no sign of it by Sunday morning's Mass, I devoted all my prayers to that one miracle. To my faithless brothers, I merely suggested, "Cross your fingers."

Sunday night, we waited in our rooms, each of us silently willing the phone to ring. A little before eleven o'clock, Manolo came to talk to me. "What are we gonna do?" His pajamas were way too short for his legs and the fruit bowl haircut that looked so cute on Pablo made Manolo look like a mentally challenged adult instead of a normal teenager. Since he was funny-looking anyway thanks to his bad tooth, Mami wasn't doing him any favors cutting his hair that way.

I racked my brain for solutions. "I don't know." What could we do? With a vague sense of duty, I swung my legs off the bed. "I'll try talking to Mami again." Making my way to the kitchen, I began to putter around and prepare lunches before eventually calling out, "Mami! I can't find anything for sandwiches!"

She charged in with her head partially covered in rollers. "What are you talking about?"

"You can't let Papi go to their school tomorrow," I said in a low voice.

"Don't be ridiculous," she retorted.

"What if he yells at the principal? What if he does something worse?"

"Yeah," added Manolo, who'd snuck in behind me. "We might get in trouble."

"Your trouble is not paying attention to homework," she reprimanded my brother.

"Mami, that's not the point," I said.

"The point is your father has to protect your brothers from bad people."

"Oh yeah," Manolo muttered in English. "Protect us."

"Go to bed!" she ordered him.

"The bad kids already got detention, Mami," I argued. "What's the use?"

She raised her chin and refused to answer me.

She'd called the bad kids sinvergüenzas, but if she was such a big fan of shame, where was hers? "At least go with him, Mami. We were lucky the school didn't arrest him before!" I tried to control my voice as I pleaded with her, "Do you really want to take a chance?"

"You know everything, don't you?" she said tiredly, bending down to retrieve a roller that had fallen out of her hair. "Everybody just go to sleep," she said, waving us away.

Manolo and I found Pablo with his face buried into a pillow. "I hate my life," he mumbled. "I wish I could die."

"Oh, shut up," Manolo snapped.

Instead of fighting back, Pablo began to cry. I had an impulse to lean over and hug him, but I was too frustrated by the whole family to make anyone feel better. I went into my room, shut the door, and turned off the light. Then I closed my eyes, trying to dream myself into a blue gondola sailing away somewhere with my grandfather.

The sound of my mother's footsteps, followed by mumbling voices next door, jarred me awake. A few minutes after she'd left, I crept to my brothers' room.

Pablo sat up, his eyes gleaming in the dark. "Papi's not coming!"

"You musta convinced Mami," Manolo whispered. "Thanks."

"Yeah, thanks, Gabi," Pablo echoed.

"It's okay," I said. "Just stay away from sinvergüenzas."

They laughed as I tiptoed back to bed.

## NINE

THE FEAR THAT MY FATHER would jeopardize our family's precarious legal situation by causing a school fracas didn't end with the Rickenbacker crisis. A few days later, I got into some good-for-nothing trouble of my own when I took Alina's side in a foolish but heated fotonovela exchange with another girl at school. The teacher snapped and said she'd "had it with the Spanish violations" and sent all three of us, with the fotonovela, to the principal's office. Although I wasn't certain whether I was more in trouble for speaking in forbidden Spanish or for having a fotonovela, I intended to fervently apologize for both, whether or not I'd been at fault or agreed with the school's stupid language prohibition. Imagine my horror when the interrogation session concluded with the principal, operating on what he termed "the honor system," handing me a folded-over note to take home for my parents' signatures. Dumbly, I took it from him and stood like Superman holding a rock of Kryptonite. My weak hand trembled as I imagined my father scrutinizing the note, the word "foto-novela" emblazoned upon it.

Somehow, I managed to walk upright to my next class. During recess, I stood under the aluminum awning outside the cafeteria and tried to get guidance from Alina. "What are you going to tell your mother?" I asked.

She shrugged her shoulders. "My mother can't understand this stuff. To her, everything is persecution." Alina's father had been imprisoned in Cuba and her mother spent her spare time writing letters to the U.S. House of Representatives and raising money for the cause.

After we separated, I continued to brood over my angry, moralistic father and his ferocious scribbling. There was just no way I could let him see that principal's note. Mami might have managed to derail the crazy Rickenbacker site visit, but I had zero confidence that she could perform that trick this time.

I quietly unfolded the note during my next class. It was actually a form with checkmarks placed inside the box for "Violated Classroom Rules" and in front of the lines for parental signatures. The form didn't say a thing about fotonovelas or reveal what I'd actually done wrong. I recalled that Mami often turned Pablo's letters of reprimand over to me. "Sign it!" she would say, annoyed that the school officials didn't dish out their own punishments.

On the bus home, I mulled things over with Lydia. "Maybe I shouldn't give it to her," I considered aloud.

Lydia raised her eyebrows. "What about your favorite commandment?"

"It says *honor*, not obey." I paused. "What does that mean, anyway?"

Lydia shook her head. "God helps those who help themselves?"

I had to crack a smile. I knew what Lydia would do.

"How 'bout 'What they don't know won't hurt 'em?' " she volunteered.

"My Tía Rita has this other dicho," I told her. " 'Why throw water into the sea?' "

"¿Qué?"

"You know, it's like, 'adding fuel to the fire' or 'pissing in the wind.'"

"Yeah, like a stick in time will save your butt." Lydia held out her pen invitingly as I shook my head.

But as the bus got nearer to home, my feeling of imminent doom only began to grow. From the height of my window, I saw the empty bus benches gleaming in the Florida heat as if their orange paint were melting. People with overloaded bags trudged slowly down Flagler Street like prisoners on a chain gang. No wonder heat went hand in hand with evil. "I'm getting off here," I announced abruptly. Heaving my books on my hip, I disembarked and hightailed it toward St. Stephen's.

It was cool inside the vacant church. Up front at the roll-away table, I slid a dime into a slot and lit the only candle. Maybe that was a good sign: I had all the saints' attention. I knelt down, but an Act of Contrition seemed improper since I didn't feel sufficiently contrite. In despair, I closed my eyes and waited for the wisdom to know what to do with the note from the principal.

I tried to imagine Mami reading it. No doubt she would be confused, and maybe she would get angry with the school officials. How could they mistake her straight-A Catholic school daughter with some hooligan who'd "violated classroom rules"? And when I'd confessed that it *was* me—not a case of mistaken identity—she would fight to find the part of what I'd told her that she could throw back to me as wrong; she needed a place to put the blame.

Or—would there just be more disappointment?

I stared sadly at my small, burning candle. Above it, the pale blue stone of Mary's veil obscured her face, bent in perpetual sorrow. Our Lady of Sorrows—dolor. Singular or plural, in the end all sorrows became one.

That evening, after I helped Mami cook dinner and clean up,

I typed a very long, moderately confusing letter my father had written to a laboratory in Pasadena; at least it had some tenuous connection with employment. After these and all my other tasks were done, I sat restacking textbooks on top of each other in my room until Mami startled me by coming in and sliding two pages in front of me.

"One of those notices came about the house," she said with a grimace, rubbing her dry hands together. "Those people! They don't give you a break!"

Glancing nervously at the letter, I reached for the Ponds jar and offered it to her. "Want some?" I asked.

She massaged the cream into her hands. "No sé," she said. "I'm so tired. If they take the house, we lose everything, mi'ja. I don't have any more rabbits to pull." Her eyes began canvassing my room. There was plenty of disorder to pick on had she been game, but none of it seemed to inspire her right then. She simply shook her head wearily as a person might who has said "no" so many times she can't utter the sound again.

Silently, we wallowed in our respective miseries. When she couldn't take it anymore, she got up, declaring, "We have to find a way." Off she went, searching for something to clean, fix, or put away.

My gaze drifted toward the empty hall behind her. Was it true? Were we really in danger of getting evicted or was it more excessive worrying?

I picked up the bank letter and frowned at the highlighted parts. It sounded serious. But I thought the uncles were helping us? Maybe we should call El Chino for guidance?

A sudden commotion on my parents' side of the house got me up, and I made a beeline for the kitchen, where Manolo and Pablo were slurping bottles of malta. "What's going on?" I asked.

"He's mad about some magazine," Manolo explained.

I tiptoed over to peek into their bedroom. My father's angry face leaned toward Mami's. "¡No te lo permito!" he shouted as he reached for a magazine in her hand.

"¡Déjamelo!" she yelled back righteously.

Back and forth, they tugged at the magazine. I darted back to where my brothers were sitting. "Is she trying to take away his *Home Mechanics*?" I whispered.

"Nope," said Manolo. "Some Corín Tellado novela that Tía Rita gave her."

"That's not all. He called Mami dirty," Pablo added.

"What?" Panicking, I recalled a Corín Tellado Alina had loaned me. Could I have left that one in the bathroom by mistake? How many fotonovela crises did one person deserve?

I darted back to spy on my parents. Mami held a fotonovela that I didn't recognize out of my father's reach. "¡No me vas a quitar la mirruñita de diversión que me queda en esta vida!"

*Oh come on!* Although I did sympathize, she was being dramatic. Was he really robbing her of her only crumb of pleasure? What a fotonovela she was!

His response was to loudly and roughly straighten his chair, then sit with his back to her.

I stepped back into the kitchen.

"She won," Manolo observed without expression.

Both my brothers' bottles stood empty. "Hey," I asked, "does Mami know you guys are drinking those?"

As if she had a sixth sense my mother, eyes ablaze, burst into the kitchen. She clutched the fotonovela to her chest like a life preserver from the capsized ship of her family. "Why are you drinking those?" she challenged my brothers. "You know they're for company!"

"Sorry, Mami, we were thirsty," Pablo explained, tossing his bottle into the garbage can. He pecked her on the cheek before she had a chance to react, while Manolo shrugged apologetically. Then they both scurried out.

I tried to take quick stock of the cover of the fotonovela, just to confirm that it wasn't mine, but Mami tucked it closer to her person while grabbing a sponge and vigorously wiping water rings from the table. "He's not going to convince me with that nonsense," she muttered.

I didn't know who she was talking to, but I decided to leave her alone with her tiny victory.

The next day, I turned in my forged note. One thing had been illuminated by the eviction threat: School difficulties weren't worthy of such torment. I told the principal a white lie about the punishment I'd garnered—no television—just so he wouldn't worry about an "honor system" student like me going astray.

I also confessed to Lydia about the forgery. Then I returned all her fotonovelas. "I can't take this stuff anymore," I informed her. "From now on, don't even show them to me."

Lydia packed her magazines away and stayed quiet for a few minutes. Finally, she spit out what was on her mind. "Gabi, what does your father really have?"

"I don't know," I mumbled, rebuckling my bag in humiliation. Despite Mami's dire warnings against divulging family secrets, it had gotten harder and harder to avoid Lydia's direct questions.

"What do they *think* it is?"

"I have no idea, Lydia," I repeated. "Some kind of nerve disease. I'm not sure if there's a name for it."

"Oh." Shrewd Lydia said no more.


The crisis over our mortgage intensified. For three days, Mami was constantly on the phone with family, wringing her hands unhappily after each call and then escaping to her friend Camila's house. Months had passed since my father had worked, and Mami's secret Avon and dressmaking sales hadn't brought in the income to cover our payments. Manolo had taken a part-time hardware store job, but his wages were measly. At least he got free stuff like wood glue with which he repaired the holes Pablo had gouged into the back of the house. Tío Victor and Tío Lucho, along with Tío Paco—who'd finally returned and landed a job with a fancy builder in Opa-Locka—took up a collection to cover our April mortgage balance. They slipped the money to Mami that Thursday evening when they came by the house after work. The opportunity presented itself after my father excused himself to go retrieve one of his peculiar letters. The uncles exchanged troubled glances, apparently recognizing my father's increasingly flimsy connection to the material world.

"Evi, you have to find a job," Tío Victor said at last, putting down his coffee cup. "There's an ad up at the 7-Eleven."

"But Roberto should find something," she replied, with a light tremble in her voice. "It just takes time to find the right one."

"That's the problem," Tío Victor said gently. "You don't have any more time."

Tío Lucho stood up and jiggled the loose change in his baggy pants pockets. "Mira, Evi," he said. "You can't keep depending on us. We don't have much more to spare. You know that. What good will it do you to stay in the country if you lose the house?"

"But how can I work?" she despaired. "You know how he is."

Tío Victor sighed. It was true that my father had acceded to Manolo's job, but he was morally opposed to jobs for women.

"¡Jamás!" was precisely how he responded when Mami broached the topic at dinner that night. It was definitely a not-in-your-wildest-dreams answer.

"Yo soy el que mantiene a mi mujer," he huffed loudly, thumping his chest like a boxing champion. But we all knew he wasn't supporting anyone, let alone "his woman."

"As if anyone could tell I was a woman in these rags I have to wear," Mami retorted, storming out

Luckily, Tío Lucho soon solved our family's income shortage, at least temporarily, by arranging for Mami to do piecework at home for the factory where his wife, my Tía Elena, was employed. My father didn't object to that, since Mami was always sewing anyway.

Despite Mami's disdain for the paltry sewing skills I'd acquired in Home Economics, I was enlisted to help. The piecework would keep me occupied during the upcoming summer recess, she told me. Never mind that I already had plenty of chores to occupy me for a lifetime.

Mami and I took turns at the Singer, an old-fashioned pitch black sewing machine with faded gold letters. To make the machine go you leaned your knee against a side pedal; but unlike the quiet, beige, state-of-the-art models at school, this one zoomed loudly and threateningly across the fabric. I released my grip in panic the very first time I sewed my pieces together.

"But you control it, mi'ja," Mami explained, putting two firm hands over mine as she showed me how. Cautiously, I pressed my knee to the pedal, and as we guided the cloth together, I learned to trust the machine.

Piecework was hard. We'd sew identical fabric pairs together as fast as possible in a continuous chain that we clipped apart at the end. Collars, cuffs, sleeves—you name it, we made it. Speed was key, of course, otherwise we got ripped off. But sewing at that accelerated pace lost its novelty for me in the poorly lit closet after a couple hours of hunching over the Singer with the sleeves of my father's clothing swaying creepily across my neck.

For Memorial Day weekend, Tío Lucho suggested that Mami and I try a stint at the factory with Tía Elena. Sewing went faster on industrial machines, he pointed out, and we would make more money. Mami told my father that my aunt was overwhelmed with an unexpectedly large order and needed temporary help.

At the factory, a warehouse with lightbulbs dangling from the ceiling, middle-aged Cuban ladies with the same shade of Clairol Medium Auburn hair sat before large metal sewing machines listening to Latin music as their flying needles dissolved the fabric into a dust that thickened the air. The ladies complained frequently about how stuffy the place was, despite the air-conditioning, and everyone ordered me around. "Tráeme una colada, Gabrielita" or "Súbele el volumen al radio, mi amor," they would say, reducing my so-called workday to coffee errands, the switching around of radio dials, and other helper duties.

When the weekend stint was over, Mami and I returned to piecework at home. She admitted to me that she wished she could stay at the factory and earn more money. "But your father's awfully proud," she rationalized. "It would bring him shame, his wife working when he isn't."

"That's stupid," I blurted out, "when we obviously need the money."

She snapped at me. "Insolent girl! How can you sit there criticizing your father?"

I didn't reply. *She* was allowed to criticize. But *her* rules never applied to me. In silence, I kept clipping sets while she sewed. Only the whirring and clipping kept us together, my mother, huffy and righteous, and me, just plain mad.

## TEN

THE WEATHER BEGAN to suffocate me. By the second week of summer vacation, the air had practically stopped circulating over Miami, and I stood on our front terrace contemplating my Sunday pilgrimage to St. Stephen's. My mother had begged off with a handful of coins. "Light a candle for us, mi'jita."

Upon my return, I found my father in an especially cheerful mood. Apparently, he had new "plans" for me. Putting his arm around my shoulder, he escorted me to the makeshift desk he'd set up in his room. A solitary chair faced the *Seminole Sentinel* and two sharpened pencils lay atop the dresser.

"Siéntate, mi'jita," my father said, gesturing to the chair.

Hesitantly, I sat.

He stood behind me, placed a hand on my left shoulder, and pointed to the newspaper, curiously opened to a crossword puzzle. "Léelo," he instructed me.

I looked at him dubiously. Didn't he know that you didn't *read* a crossword puzzle?

"Papi," I asked at last with trepidation, "did you want me to translate these questions for you?" I indicated the clues.

"No, mi'jita," he answered, containing his excitement. "Es para ti." At my quizzical look, he added, "We have an opportunity! Read this." Even his good hand quivered as he showed me a paragraph that described a $5,000 prize.

Now it all made horrible sense. He wanted *me* to do the puzzle.

I gulped down my distress. It was bad enough that I'd become his personal typing robot, but I thoroughly detested puzzles! They only defeated the purpose of words, which was to form sentences, to communicate. They *wasted* meaning.

Eagerly, my father handed me a pencil. I studied the first clue and worked through the answer with growing uncertainty. Eventually I had to move on to the next equally difficult clue. This puzzle was so much harder than most. Some answers varied by a single letter or they depended on difficult distinctions, such as *contusion* and *confusion*, *refrain* and *reframe*. The dictionary helped somewhat, but looking up so many words slowed the process to an excruciating degree. My knees started to hurt from pressing the dresser handles. While I struggled to finish, my father paced back and forth like a great animal in his cage—periodically pausing to roar out the window at Pablo and his friends, then returning to paw my shoulder as I crouched lower into the uncomfortable dresser-desk.

"Muy bien," he approved mildly at one point, after my mother had entered the room with an armful of factory linens. She gave him an intense look before inquiring loudly whether anyone needed a break.

"No!" I retorted, wanting only to get the horrible puzzle over with.

I didn't finish until dinnertime. Though I wasn't feeling terribly sure of my answers, I turned the puzzle over to my father, who slid it into an envelope he'd addressed to the P.O. Box provided in the *Sentinel*.

My mother watched him with her lips pursed. "Good," she said to me. "Your father can take it to his office tomorrow."

"Office?" I asked, dumbstruck.

"The post office," she replied sarcastically.

My father ignored her.

While my father waited for his $5,000 ship of Good Hope to come in, Mami grew frantic that the factory tablecloths weren't bringing in enough income. But then her friend Camila informed her about a part-time job a few evenings a week at El Palacio de Venezia, the discount department store where Camila's husband had worked before his leukemia. Rightly apprehensive of my father's reaction, Mami told only the uncles and me about her new job. I had to help lie to my father and big-mouth brothers.

"Roberto, I'm going to stay with Camila a while," my mother announced that first evening, since my father never seemed to mind her going over to help her friend whenever Hernán took a bad turn. "Gabrielita will manage dinner," she assured my father. Then she gave me a bear hug.

"It'll be okay, Mami," I said, swallowing my doubts.

Around half past nine that night, he came to my room in his pajamas. "What time is your mother supposed to be home?"

"Um, I called a few minutes ago," I fibbed. "As soon as they finish turning over Hernán's bed, I think. You want me to do something, Papi?" I asked faintly, hoping he didn't. The prior days' typing requirements on top of my Sunday puzzle trial had already made porridge of my brain.

"No, no." He blinked repeatedly, the new visual tic making me nervous too. I lowered my face guiltily into my summer reading book, *Diary of Anne Frank,* to avoid inadvertently exposing some clue as to my mother's whereabouts. Eventually, he padded away.

She arrived at 10:15 p.m. "How did things go, mi'ja?" she asked nervously in a low voice.

"Okay. But Mami, Papi gets agitated after dark."

"Let's see how it goes on Wednesday. Maybe I can request an early shift."

"All right," I said, not that confidently.

Every day that week, my father checked the newspaper for the puzzle contest results. On Sunday, the *Sentinel* published an announcement: no winner. I rejoiced! I felt triumphant at seeing my father foiled for forcing me to do something I hated so fiercely.

Along with the announcement, though, they published a second puzzle. When my father told me I had to complete that too, I stared at his sharpened pencil and fantasized about stabbing myself in the heart. Would my mother save me?

I went looking for her.

"Humor him, mi'jita," she said, squelching my only hope. Why did she never help me when I asked for it? She didn't have the guts to stand up to him. All she did was hide things, like the Avon and the dresses and now her job, not to mention the mortgage payment we'd collected behind his back. No, she wasn't about to help me escape the second puzzle trial.

My fighting spirit dissolved, I dragged myself back to the dresser-desk and sat gazing into the newsprint until the letters blurred. The new puzzle turned out to be as difficult as the first. I got some answers right, but most words were too closely related, which made the coordinating Down and Across clues harder to figure out. My knees ached from the pressure of the dresser drawer handles digging into me. After struggling for an hour, I wanted to throw myself to the floor and weep. But it wouldn't have made any difference. I had to go on, like a slave in a Hercules movie.

After four impossible weeks my knowledge and patience, two of the qualities puzzles challenged, according to the dictionary, wore out completely. All I had left was the third—ingenuity—to *guess* my way to completion. My father couldn't tell. That afternoon, as I silently put his puzzle into his envelope and handed it over, he actually praised me for finishing so quickly!


Throughout that summer I deceived my father in numerous ways. On the weekdays Mami worked at the Palacio, I invented stories to keep him from catching on. I told him that Tía Elena was temporarily short of help at the factory; I whipped up spiritual retreats for parish mothers at St. Stephens. The rest of the family knew we needed the money and went along with our tall tales. But nobody knew exactly what Mami did at the Venice Palace until the Saturday morning that I found her uniform, all by its lonesome, in our washing machine.

The uniform was white polyester with Mrs. De Paz—the *la* omitted—embroidered on it in red lettering. I stared in shock. *My mother reduced to a cleaning lady?* Cleaning was one of those jobs she believed gente decente shouldn't do, probably because a cleaning lady in Latin America was like an indentured servant. Day and night, she cleaned, cooked, tended, and ran errands in her slipper sandals—even for visitors—before retreating to the crude cement room built for her in the interior patio of each middle-class home.

Suddenly I heard Mami's footsteps outside the shed and quickly shoved the uniform back into the washer.

"Didn't you hear me, Gabriela?" she asked as she approached, a dirty plastic shower curtain hung over one arm.

"I'm sorry, Mami, you want me to wash that?"

"No, I'll do it. Get the other one, please."

I went inside to the bathroom, unhooked the moldy curtain, and shook it out. Holding it out at a distance in front of me so as not to soil myself, I carried the curtain outside.

"Gracias, mi'ja," Mami said, scooping the slimy plastic to her chest without hesitation. As she turned toward the washing machine, her silhouette widened on the ground behind her like the shadow of a much bigger person. I thought of the beliefs she was forced to defy for the sake of her family, and my complaints about the brain-wasting puzzles and the aches and pains of typing and sewing suddenly felt selfish. Like Mami, I should swallow my pride and become a bigger person. We had to each do our part for our family, connecting our individual pieces to make it whole.

Pablo began to do his part too, delivering *Seminole Sentinels* on the rusty bike my father used to force him to ride. Normally, Pablo did the route alone, but one quiet and eerily humid afternoon when I wasn't puzzle-bound and my mother wasn't working, she stood in the Florida room with the front door open, stared at the moving clouds, and suggested we start bagging before the *tempestad* came. Pablo had gone to fill a flat tire, and Manolo was on duty at the hardware store again—my brothers' former twosomeness had begun to crack.

As Mami and I bagged *Sentinels*, the room became unusually dark. A breeze picked up, banging our door and shaking its old bent screen. When Pablo biked up on the rusty two-wheeler, he was surprised to see the bagged newspaper stack. "Hey thanks," he said, with a grateful smile, and sat down with us to finish.

Thunder rolled in and the wind got stronger, sweeping away garbage can lids and madly spinning the wheels of the bike. You could see how Frank Baum had imagined a house blowing off its foundations and sailing through the sky over to Oz. Though our glass-paned Florida door was shaky, I had faith in the house's thick walls and the furious energy of the three of us working together to get the job done.

The rain came in long, elegant strides that paused and yielded to a greater wind. Mami instructed Pablo to put on his slicker, though he complained that it would blow around, delaying his progress. Finally, he packed the *Sentinels* into his canvas shoulder bag. With his thick black hair falling into his eyes and the enormous bag on his back, he looked like an orphan about to peddle his wares in the Olde London of English novels. Pablo was the only one of us who'd gotten happy eyes; Manolo and I inherited the sad, deep-set family eyes. As little kids, when jealousy got the best of us, we'd teased Pablo that he was adopted, but he only grinned. Everyone loved him best and he knew it.

I offered to help distribute newspapers on foot in the immediate vicinity, la vuelta a la manzana, as we called it. It was hard to know why we used that phrase, once around the apple, when neighborhoods—at least in Miami—were strictly square, as if a giant had drafted the blueprints with an enormous slide rule. Maybe in the ancient villages of Latin America, houses had been round like the huts of the Miccosukee and streets unpeeled around the huts, giving the poor hungry people the apple idea.

As I set off with my bundle of *Sentinels*, I was handicapped by Mami's long raincoat that the wind kept lifting up over my head. I slapped determinedly at the coat's tails with one of the bagged newspapers, but it fell and scuttled up the street. Quickly I ran to catch it while clutching my bigger bundle to my chest. By then, Pablo had zipped through his first round and spotted me chasing the *Sentinel*. He started laughing, and I had to laugh too. Warm rain came down then and washed us both. I felt the weight of my T-shirt and shorts as the wind whipped them close, but the water itself was light, dissolving as it touched me.

The rain stopped by the time our deliveries were done. Pablo and I turned around and skipped backward with the wind, our scarecrow arms dangling the leftover bags of *Sentinels*. Pablo took a sheet of newsprint out of one bag and threw the other papers into a dumpster. We ran forward into the wind, the sheet held high between us like a kite gliding home.

I spent the rest of the summer bent over the weekly puzzles while my father buzzed around, constantly sharpening pencils before releasing me to the piecework I helped Mami complete so that she could sneak off to the Palacio. The *Sentinel* finally suspended the crossword puzzle contest after seven weeks without a single winner. Despite my intention to rise above selfish feelings, the Sunday puzzles came to infuriate me more than anything else in the exhausting crusade against our family's threatened exile into poverty and disgrace. Unable to express my fury directly—afraid to—I began to fantasize about my father dying in any number of gory ways, thus liberating me from his oppression: a heart attack, a burglar's blow to the head, a bus careening into him on Eighth Street as he walked to the post office clasping his precious puzzle envelope.

Little by little, I began to hate everything about him. Not just his Assault on a Minor; not just the assaults of his wild temper all put together; but also his laugh, his idiosyncrasies, his tics, his inadequate English. Most of all, I hated his inability to recognize that he would *never* win the money—that the stupid puzzle victory was, like so many things we had and would encounter wherever we lived, totally beyond reach.

## ELEVEN

THE SUMMER ENDED and I gratefully returned to school. Hoping to evade my father upon my return home that first day, I gathered money saved from helping with Avon, piecework, and Pablo's paper route to go buy supplies at Osco's for the big-deal Dade County Youth Fair project.

My father stopped me before I got out the door. He wanted to acompañarme.

I hustled into the kitchen. "Mami, he's so difficult," I whispered. "Can't you please keep him home?"

She rolled her eyes at me but called out, "Roberto, Gabriela doesn't have time for errands. She has school things to do."

"¡Claro que sí!" he said, joining us. "She's a good student." Then he added. "Como yo."

Like him? I raised an eyebrow for my mother's benefit, but she dismissed the remark with a tight-lipped shrug, abandoning her halfhearted effort to deter him.

"Vamos," my father urged.

Sweating my way there with my father's hand jerking against my shoulder, I tried to ignore his unintelligible babbling so that I could conceive a topic for my exhibit. But an evil voice inside me whispered, "Oil drilling."

Jealously I recalled that Lydia and Alina were collaborating on some Santería project.

"What does that have to do with science?" I'd challenged.

"Chickens," Lydia replied matter-of-factly. "People sacrifice them to Changó, like if somebody is dying."

"They won't let you bring dead chickens," I'd said knowingly.

"Tch! It's gonna have pictures, chica," she'd replied.

Now, while my father drifted off in search of pens, I carried around my hurt that Lydia and Alina had excluded me to plan an exhibit about their own culture. Nothing about my own Chibcha ancestors seemed comparable, but as I stood before the poster boards, it occurred to me that maybe I could turn to the indigenous people who had survived right here in Miami—the Miccosukee. History was science, no? With a surge of enthusiasm, I gathered rainbow markers, laminate, and posters for an exhibit that might show why the lost Everglades mattered.

I went to find my father examining pens despite the many writing implements we had at home. It seemed he would be a while so I took off, paid for my supplies, and waited for him. Finally, balancing boxes of pens and envelopes, he emerged triumphantly and headed toward the cashier. She rang up his items and waited for him to pay, but my father smiled inanely, and she caught my eye. "Doesn't your dad speak English, honey?"

I shook my head, leaning close to him to whisper in Spanish, "Papi, did Mami give you money?"

"Ha!" he answered, looking at the cashier as if I'd done something cute.

*Oh God, how humiliating.* Furiously, I pulled out a crumpled ten-dollar bill.

"Here you go, hon," she said, handing me the change.

I stomped out and rushed up the street, pausing only for my father to appear, moving along at a turtle's pace with his two bags a-dangle, so that he could see me before I finished my mad hare's race home.

"He doesn't need that stuff!" I cried to my mother. "It's a big waste of *my* money!"

My mother poked diffidently through my wares. "Those Osco prices are ridiculous," she concluded.

That night, my mother came into my room and fiddled around gathering empty glasses off my dresser. The dillydallying bugged me, and I frowned in mock concentration at a book on my lap. As she was about to make her exit, she hesitated in my doorway. "You know," she started to say, "Your quince will be here before we know it. Maybe we should go to that new jewelry store on the corner and put something on layaway."

I looked up. "My birthday is *months* away, Mami," I advised, returning to my book. "Anyway, you don't have to get me a present." The quince reference had briefly reminded me that wealthier girls at school would soon be planning lavish quinceañeras, each celebrant choosing her corte of fifteen girls in matching ball gowns and choice male escorts. Quinceañeras were not for the likes of me, though.

"Why not?" my mother challenged, lifting her chin high as she turned to leave. "I'm not going to let your quince go by without at least getting you a gift."

But my real gift was the happy news that Tía Consuelo, my father's eldest sister, was coming from Colombia in October: her first visit since we'd come to Miami.

The day she was due, Mami and I cleaned prodigiously. I liked the smell of Pine-Sol cleaner, but that morning's scrambled eggs in my belly combined with my menstrual cramps to make me feel ill. I sat down on the toilet to wait for the floor around me to dry.

When my mother's exasperated yells reached me from across the house, I threw open the bathroom door and did some shouting of my own. "I have cramps!"

"Go lay down," she called back. "And pick up your feet!"

I got up and mopped my way backwards toward my room, kicked off my flip-flops, and jumped into bed. Mami had this crazy notion that when you were sick, your feet shouldn't touch a cold floor. I didn't know if there was any scientific basis to this line of thinking or whether the cold floor theory was a superstition, like sprinkling holy water over our doorstep. As Catholic as my mother might be, I knew her heart belonged to voodoo.

It was quiet in the house. My eager father had gone with my uncles to the airport. Outside my window, a breeze scattered blossom bits through the sky, like rice from someone's wedding. The smell of jasmine and Pine-Sol blended with whiffs of the celebratory sancocho my mother was stewing. Sleepily, I rubbed the pain from my belly and daydreamed about Tía Consuelo and her presents. On prior visits, she'd brought dresses, fine ones sewn by hand like my white Confirmation dress with the voile skirt and shiny pearl buttons down the back, and others I remembered backward from my pink tulle party dress with its satin sash, to my very first tiny pinafore, yellow taffeta peeking through white eyelet....

When I woke up, Tía Consuelo was sitting at my bedside. A gold filigree medallion beamed like her heart from the center of her torso. She hugged me, put a cool hand in mine, and, with a confidential smile, asked "Así que ya eres señorita, ¿ah?"

Although I'd become a young lady some time back, I nodded affirmatively. "I'm almost fifteen now, Tía."

"So I'm told," she said with a twinkle in her eye. "Qué bueno, ¿no?"

She had a way of slowing down her enunciation, like kindergarten teachers do, and then letting an "¿ah?" or "¿no?" linger at the end of a sentence, so that you had to give a reply. I willingly became her kindergartner when she spoke to me. Her face, with its small crooked nose and wide-set eyes, was so kind. She was the first person in my family to tell me that my own face, my carita, was pretty. I loved her, deeply.

Leaning over now, she whispered. "I have something special for you, ¿ah?"

I grinned with joy as if I'd just remembered how.


After phone calls from the rest of our family, we convened in the living room. My father was still wearing the ironed shirt, dark pants, and buffed shoes he'd worn to the airport. Without his slippers or scribbled sheets, he looked like a normal person.

My brothers and I plopped ourselves at Tía Consuelo's feet as my parents and aunt discussed who had married, who had died, who had lost his job; the country's economic crisis that had gotten so serious; whether the Hotel Caribe was renovated; and the economic problems all over again. Gradually, my father's hand jerking slowed down. His legs, lightly crossed at the ankles, seemed to relax too. Every so often as he chatted with Tía Consuelo, he chuckled, shook his head, or shared a smile with her, and she patted his knee affectionately. For the first time in eons, he was actually participating in a conversation. My own exchanges with him had been reduced to monologues he conducted while I listened for the part where I was supposed to chime in with the obedient servant's "Sí, señor." In a burst of conscience, I recalled Abiasaph the groundskeeper's lesson of kindness and wondered, could my father's being with his sister return him to himself? Maybe Tía Consuelo had the kindergartner effect on him too. A wisp of longing passed through me.

Eventually Tía Consuelo pulled her chair closer to her enormous brown suitcase, its leather worn down as if our family had been using it for centuries. Laughing, she eyed Pablo, whom she'd promised to let unbuckle the belts. "Bueno," she said. "Open it."

Pablo unbuckled and unzipped and then lifted the top. Mixed scents of lavender, rosewater, and department store ambience rose from within. My brothers and I leaned forward, inhaling the possibilities amidst my aunt's pressed nightgowns. There were packages meant for us, as well as others that had been wrapped with brown paper, tied with string, and addressed in cursive handwriting. Those were encomiendas—packages sent in my aunt's care by people who had paid her to deliver them to relatives in this country. Jewelry, birth certificates, and other valuable possessions people feared the postal service wouldn't deliver safely. Even cash was entrusted—encomendado—in her care.

My aunt squinted at the writing on one package. "Ay, Lita, bring me my glasses, ¿ah?"

Pablo and I traded smiles over my childhood nickname. As a toddler, he couldn't pronounce my name in the diminutive form, so everyone had started calling me Lita instead of Gabrielita.

I brought my aunt her reading glasses, and Tía Consuelo passed out packages: a doe-brown leather handbag and a letter to my mother from her parents; thin wood boxes packed with guava bocadillos from Abuela Matilde for my father; and sweets and dress up clothes for my brothers.

"Bueno," Tía Consuelo said, her eyes playing with me, "¿y para ti?" As she teased me, she smiled and began untying a package in her lap before finally holding out a dark green satin box.

I took it with a shy smile. "Gracias, Tía." Inside was a pretty velvet case the same color. And inside the case was a ring so beautiful that my mother and I gasped at the same time. A sleek gold band bore a tiny pyramid of golden steps leading to a sparkling emerald. "¡Qué lindo, Tía!" I exclaimed, so overwhelmed by wonder and joy that I could only stand and throw my arms around her.

Tía Consuelo slipped the ring jubilantly onto my virgin finger.

"Look at that!" said my mother.

It fit perfectly, though it was almost too beautiful for that rough hand. The gold gleamed luminously beneath the emerald crown, and I felt like a great queen.

Tía Consuelo took my hand with tenderness. "Do you remember where emeralds come from, Lita?"

I shook my head "no" in kindergartner fashion.

"Ah bueno," she said, "let me tell you then." Tía Consuelo began telling us all about the Andean foothills where indigenous people had first scraped crystal from the rock. "They polished the cloudy green stone until it had extraordinary clarity," she gushed. "That's why the Colombian emerald is the most beautiful in the world!" She clasped her hands. "And do you know, buried in those very mountains, many centuries later of course, the archaeologists found gold and emerald masks? The indígenas hammered them thousands of years ago, Lita. Imagine. Gold masks with the same emerald eyes as your ring! Chibcha eyes."

My father asked to see the ring, and I passed it to him. Holding it up to the light, he squinted, scrutinizing the gem closely. "Muy lindo, mi'jita," he agreed, handing it back.

I hugged my aunt in gratitude. For the ring, the story, and her scents of rose and lavender, and for making each of us feel so cared for. How much we trusted Tía Consuelo, as did the many people whose encomiendas she safely delivered. If there was one thing to be when I grew up, I vowed then, that was it. *Trustworthy.* The kind of person everyone could depend on.

I gathered up the wrappings and said good night, then carried my treasure back to my room. After I'd changed, I climbed into bed and took out my ring to marvel at all over again. I held it up, just as my father had done, for the moonlight that shone in through my window. Back and forth, I tilted the crystal to catch the light traveling through it into the dark beyond. Long, beautiful rays bounced back, as if someone out there had finally said, "I'm sorry, Lita, I'm sorry."

My aunt's visit passed too quickly, though the special scent of her presence lingered through our house after she'd gone. My father remained agreeable for a while, but eventually he regressed into his Mr. Hyde character, scribbling with vengeance in his room only to emerge with rambling letters for me to distill sense out of on the typewriter. At least he didn't blow up or provoke a crisis. I sent many prayers of thanks to Heaven that we still had our green cards, given Tía Consuelo's alarming descriptions of the economic problems in Colombia and my mother's heightened terror of being sent back.

Mami valiantly cobbled together that month's mortgage payment from her part-time wages and our spottier income sources. Flitting restlessly through the house, she recited litanies of economic woe and did no decorating at all as Christmas approached, though my brothers and I cut up and hung paper ornaments. In one of those moments where distress overcomes caution, she spilled the beans on the mysterious debt I'd caught her discussing uneasily with Tía Rita several times. We apparently owed the shoe factory for some expensive machine my father had damaged in Massachusetts. When Mami registered the *aha!* on my face, as my suspicion was confirmed that his sojourn hadn't ended so benignly, she rushed to undercut what she'd revealed. "It wasn't any kind of police thing," she assured me defensively. "We just have to pay a lot."

A different and sadder revelation unfolded for me at Tía Rita's holiday party. My aunt had completely covered the yard with white nylon filament to imitate snow, but it lifted up each time someone slammed the door and exposed our tropical reality. As was always the case, we split up by gender and age. When I passed Tía Rita's room on my way to my cousin Raquel's, I overheard Mami telling Tía Rita and Tía Elena about the difficulties of her job. The description of the store's detailed accounting needs perplexed me, so I slowed down and stopped to listen—and what I heard was quite a surprise. Without directly lying, Mami made it sound as if her job were *counting* the inventory, not cleaning it. This deception, for some reason, disheartened me more than all our outright lies. I had to chide myself: even my mother was entitled to her pride.

Still, the bad feeling stuck with me for a while, despite Raquel giving me an unexpected gift, a scented candle, and other gifts that followed. My cousin Marisol passed on her old transistor radio, and I got a box of cute hair clips from Fernandita, Mami's niece de crianza—a term she'd long before explained simply meant that Fernandita was raised alongside her father's true children. Marisol snidely reminded Raquel and me that it really implied Fernandita was illegitimate. I told Marisol that I didn't care one whit how Fernandita had been born.

Marisol scoffed at my response. Maybe she didn't know what a "whit" was, or maybe she was just taken aback at my standing up to her. Sweet and trustworthy Raquel gave me a sympathetic look. She knew that I was really standing up for my mother.


As if my father's way of thinking were spreading, my brothers started inventing their own imaginary moneymaking schemes to supplement the portion of their earnings my mother let them retain. Pablo suggested entering a TV musical competition. He was kind of musical and cute but, as I pointed out, no prodigy. It would take a lot of bathroom cello practice before anyone would pay to listen to him. In the middle of that dumb discussion, Tío Lucho showed up with a huge bag of factory pieces.

"Don't worry," Tío Lucho laughed as I groaned. "They're remnants," he said, dumping the bag on the couch to light his cigarette. "Maybe your mother can use them."

My brothers scavenged through the bag and unloaded cutout sleeves, bodices, collars—skeletons of clothing waiting to be whirred alive. When Manolo pulled out a whole bolt of fake tan fur, Pablo proposed making rabbit's foot key chains like the one a girl had given him the year before on Sadie Hawkins Day. Manolo got excited too, and I saw dollar signs in his eyes. Here was something to be made and sold out of a worthless nothing we didn't have to pay for.

"They won't look real," I noted, holding up the synthetic fabric.

"It *feels* real," Manolo replied, rubbing the cloth.

"We could call ourselves The Fuzz Shop," Pablo added, pretending to smoke a joint as I rolled my eyes.

Rabbit foot key chains, granted, were a big deal. But from the little I'd gotten out of that Junior Achievement meeting I attended, I doubted my brothers could make any money. They didn't even know how to sew. Still, a couple of hours later, I found them madly cutting up fur rectangles by the hundreds.

I took pity on them and volunteered to sew their rectangles together on the rickety Singer in my mother's closet. The thick fur kept getting stuck under the needle, which aggravated me. Mami must have heard me cursing, because she suddenly came over and put a human foot down on the project. "You think I have money to buy another machine when you break this one?"

"I'm sorry, Mami," I said before going to report the disappointing news to my brothers.

Scissors in hand and surrounded by mounds of rabbit fur, they stared at me in disbelief.

"That means sewing by hand," I pointed out.

"But my hands are tired from cutting," Pablo complained.

"Yeah," Manolo agreed, "It's not worth it." He tossed the shears into Mami's basket and got up to raise the TV volume on some game show.

All moneymaking enthusiasm dissolved in a matter of seconds.

Gabriela the Helper, of course, gathered the cut-up scraps into the bag, then hoisted the bag up to carry away. Defeat weighed me down too. All I'd hoped for was a little extra money to buy a Christmas present for each person who'd given us one, so that we wouldn't feel like moochers. The problem with Junior Achievement business plans, I concluded depressingly as I lugged the bag toward my room, was that they assumed everyone had more control in the world than was actually possessed. Like the power my father lacked to find and keep a job, despite succeeding in Colombia and New York. At least he was still trying with his pathetic, disjointed letters. As I passed the kitchen, I overheard him speaking loudly in his room about the La Cira Infantes oil field. He paused briefly, as if someone might ask him a question, but there was no one in there with him. It was so weird.

Back in my room, I tried to shove the unwieldy bag into the closet, but it burst, spilling the lifeless animal tails. Morosely, I threw myself onto my bed and stared at them. How stupid to have thought the scheme would work. At least my brothers and I had recognized that the project was doomed without necessary tools. Not so with my father; he repeated things that failed and failed. It was his great mental tic.

Yet I preferred to blame him for his nervios, or whatever malady he had, and for everything that followed from it—the criminal case, the immigration problems, the lack of money, my mother's awful negativity, and both my parents' total ignorance of the bad things sickos like the Laundromat jerk did to children. Because to consider my father a hapless victim of some flawed Junior Achievement business plan only filled me with doubts. What was the use of trying to help everyone around you stay calm, do the right thing, obey the law, or generally make life better if your own efforts could never be certain to produce good results? And how were we supposed to know if any of our betterment efforts were crazy without trying them out?

Some things you just knew ahead of time. For instance, no one in their right mind would dive into the ocean if they didn't know how to swim, because other people had already drowned that way.

But what of things no one had tried yet?

You would have to trust your instincts, your own thoughts.

But what if your thoughts turned out to be defective?

I started to cry. What else did I have but my own thoughts?


Melancholy stayed with me until Mami dragged me along with her to the bank on some mysterious errand.

The bank was in another strip mall that had replaced The Palms, a pale pink motel whose two neon palm trees used to illuminate the intersection before the traffic light was installed. The elderly year-round residents must have moved on, I eulogized silently, nearer to the quiet palms of God's Gulf Coast.

Between the bank and the jewelry store was a sandwich shop with another lean-in window for people to sip coladas, cortaditos, and other Cuban coffee variations. Mami suggested we share a café con leche there. After we downed the coffee, she smiled conspiratorially and said, "All right, let's go into the jewelry store."

*Oh, so the bank excuse had been subterfuge.* "I don't need a birthday present, Mami," I reiterated hollowly. "I already have Tía Consue-lo's ring." I held up and wiggled my finger, the pyramid emerald glittering. "Don't waste money on me."

"You're too generosa, mi'jita." A small furrow appeared between Mami's brows. "Sometimes I worry about you," she said quietly.

"Me?" I asked in surprise.

"Of course." Her eyes softened as she gazed into mine. "A mother never stops worrying," she said with a smile. "Ya verás, when you grow up." Then she turned and led us toward the Joyería Marbella, and it struck me that predictable as Mami was, I didn't completely understand her.

When we paused in front of the display window, I couldn't help but admire the pretty gold bangles and rings. Delicate clusters of seven tiny medals twinkled on each ring. The bangles glowed in sets of seven too. Cuban girls, even Lydia, who disdained copycats, wore semanarios, as they were called—one bangle for each day of the week. The only bracelets nearly as ubiquitous were the metal POW-MIA cuffs engraved with a soldier's name and the date he went missing in Vietnam that some American girls wore. The gold bangle sets didn't bear that kind of weight, but they shone as brightly as my memories of the jewels the ancients would throw into their sacred lagoon for the First Mother, Bachué. Mami used to read me those stories from her own treasured schoolbook.

"So pretty," she murmured now.

In a moment of weakness, I admitted how much I liked the bangles myself.

She grabbed me by the wrist and ushered me inside, where she asked the Cuban saleslady about the price. Mami's eyes widened when she heard the quote. "Oh. Do you have a layaway plan?" Of course, that was how my family had purchased everything nice we

owned, like our dining room chairs that had come two by two—
like candidates for Noah's Ark—only to be encased like mummies
in the plastic of eternal life.

"Sí, of course," the lady answered, her glasses bouncing on their
chain against her bosom as she bent down for the forms. "¿Son para
la niña?" she inquired.

"Sí," Mami nodded, turning in my direction. "Tell the lady which
ones you like, mi'jita."

Without hesitation, I chose the plain rims that had no engravings
to dim the glow of their gold. The saleslady took one bangle out,
lifted its miniature price tag up to her nose to read and held it out
for my mother.

Mami bit her lower lip, then looked up. "May we have three?"

*Three?* I tried hard not to show dismay  but *three?*

Nodding politely, the lady gave us one of the cards to fill out and
placed her chubby arms on top of the counter to watch my mother
write. When Mami handed it back with our cash down payment,
the lady recorded the amount due on our card and slipped the
money, card, and my three bangles into a plastic Baggie. She locked
everything behind the glass counter with the gleaming, golden
bangles I couldn't have.

On the way home, I didn't say much. As soon as we arrived,
though, I went to retrieve my personal savings stash and counted out
fourteen dollars that I brought into the kitchen. "Here, Mami."

She stared at the bills in dismay. "But it's your birthday present."

"It doesn't matter," I replied, leaving the money there.

It did matter. Contributing to my present didn't bother me.
What did was that I had to get it in such a peculiar way. I mean,
if we were buying the bangles on layaway anyway, why didn't we
buy a *normal* set? Who ever heard of half a semanario set? Bitterly,
I tried to imagine a store letting you put one shoe on layaway. I

wished I could feel grateful to be getting any bangles at all, but like our chairs in their hard plastic, I was trapped in my negativity without a way out.

I resolved to buy my own semanario instead of depending on my mother for her fractured gift. Later that day, I called Tío Lucho and asked him to bring over more dreaded piecework, and he laughed at my sudden "reformation."

All the money I earned after that I applied toward the full bangle set. My mother, ashamed that I was paying for my own gift, didn't try to talk me out of it. But she looked at me sadly every time I returned from the Joyería Marbella as if every one of my payments took a little more life out of hers.

Finally the day arrived for me to give the saleslady the final payment. She removed my semanario from the bag and crossed out the balance due on our layaway card forever. My golden bangles lay on the glass, the morning sun shining upon them. How they gleamed, prettier than the first time I'd seen them. *Dear*, I thought to myself, a two-sided word from English novels. The dear of costliness, the dear of loved.

## TWELVE

M Y BIRTHDAY REALLY BEGAN when I received my grandfather's poem, "Tempestad," a day early. Although I took my time reading it, the bleak stanzas, the last one particularly, utterly confused me:

> Don't say no to me, Light—constant,
> panoramic, faithful in distance;
> illuminate this solitary shore.

I put the page down. What had happened to Abuelo's sentimental odes? My rueful gaze drifted out the window toward the three stumps the city's eradication crew had painted with white lime. Once, our cheery coconuts had stood there. Could my grandfather's poem be about death?

Mami only wrinkled her brow when I showed it to her. "I don't know, mi'ja," she said, returning it in frustration. "We'll study it some other time."

The next day, my actual birthday, Lydia gave me a wallet, along with my own pack of cigarettes. I distributed that cheerfully after school, while saving a few singles for myself, before I terminated the festivities to walk home.

The sun poured down, soaking my sleeves in the simple effort of moving my arms and legs. When I arrived at the house, I shut my eyes for a moment to absorb the cooler kitchen air.

Mami came up and kissed my forehead. "Habla con tu papá," she whispered.

My heart sank. Seeing my father was code for another assignment. "But my shirt is wet."

"You can change afterward."

My father heard us and came into the kitchen. As if planning to attend his court hearing totally ahead of schedule, he was strangely dressed up in a baggy suit and tie that made him look frail. Clenching and unclenching his hands excitedly, he confided that he had "algo importante" to discuss. Of course, with him there was always "something important."

I glanced morosely at my mother, who merely nudged me toward their room with her chin.

There, my father had already set up the typewriter next to a pile of encyclopedias.

Some birthday this was turning out to be.

"Mi'jita," my father began.

The endearment made me wary.

"You know how hard we have to work," he continued.

*Work?* I tried to keep a straight face. Only my mother believed in that miracle.

I said nothing, though, since what I wanted never really mattered.

What *he* wanted was to take advantage of this "oportunidad."

I hardened when I heard the same word he'd used to justify my consignment to the horrible summer of puzzles. "Opportunity for what?" I dared to ask.

"Dinero, mi'jita." My father waved his arm like a wand across

the typewriter. "Aquí," he said, displaying his perpetual solution to all our woes. "And here." He opened one of his expired
magazines. The trembling of his knuckles as he held it open to an
article about a Baton Rouge petrochemical plant distracted me,
but I read enough to learn that the company had brought wealth
to a poor town.

Next, he pulled out another faded article, "Fractional Distilla-
tion of Crude Oil." That seemed to mean boiling, since a chart
illustrated the boiling points of different components of oil. "Todo
es refinería, mi'jita," he concluded, pleased with himself.

This sounded like another of his oddball letters. I still didn't see
where the new money aspect came in, except that now he picked
up a *World Book Encyclopedia* volume. We'd purchased the set a long
time back from a persuasive visiting salesman with a pay-over-time
offer. The S-U volume my father was holding up had slips of paper
sticking out of it, but they fell out as he flipped pages. He started
praising articles he'd "read" in his fragmented English, while I
finally figured out the essentials:

1. The people in the magazines owed us millions of dollars.
2. We were going to get it all back.
3. I was going to help him.
4. By doing even *more* typing.

Suddenly I got why he'd put on the suit. He'd decided that this
was his job. Here was his office. And I was his secretaria.

"But I have to go to school," I protested.

"Claro que sí, mi'jita," he reassured me. I would report for
work *after* school. Handing me the encyclopedia volume in his
hands, he thumbed to "The Solar System" entry and pointed to it.
"Necesito tu colaboración con esto."

Taking a deep breath, I ogled the entry and ventured a wild guess about how it related to our new million-dollar opportunity: Maybe my father thought he'd found a mistake, something to report to the *World Book Encyclopedia* so that he could collect a handsome reward? But my eyes widened when he informed me that he expected me to retype the entire article—nine single-spaced pages, charts and all. He was going to send it to the magazine as proof.

"Proof of what?" I inquired with dread.

He answered with one word. "Refinación."

Refining! It was all I could do not to throw the book at him. Even if there were some remote connection between refining and the Solar System, my father could never put that into words other people would understand.

"Why don't we make a photocopy, Papi?" I asked faintly, hoping against hope I could cajole him with the Xerox machine they'd installed at the post office.

"No," my father said point-blank as he shook his stubborn head. *He* was going to write the article. "Yo," he repeated, patting his chest.

In stunned silence, I tried to absorb his intention to write an article someone had already authored. Kids in school weren't allowed to copy. That was plagiarism. The more distressing thought crossed my mind that my father was too far gone to believe in anything anymore but what he invented. Helplessly I stared at the halves of his white shirt split by his ugly tie. Where oh where was the father who used to work, chat with my mother, give us quarters, sign report cards, and take my picture on my birthday? The father before me now was like one of those figures in a Picasso painting from my art class slide show. You knew they were there—the title told you so—but the human features were broken up by objects you had to struggle to see beneath.

By now, my mother had come into the room. "Let Gabriela change her clothes, Roberto," she urged my father.

"Claro," he agreed, sitting down to wait.

In my room, I sank glumly onto my bed and fixed my gaze on the black specks that marbled our terrazzo floors. I tried counting dots on my dotted Swiss curtains. With unhappy fingers, I traced the embroidery lines that curled back and forth across my bedspread—a labyrinth with no beginning or end. Fleetingly, I considered putting my foot down once and for all. Sure, I'd typed his convoluted, illogical job letters—they kept him happy, quiet, out of trouble. And there had always been that sliver of a chance that the letters might help. But this stuff?

I didn't have the courage to defy my father, though. I was afraid. I'd been good at staying on his good side, but now he was prone to lash out at anything that angered him, no matter how innocent. Grimly, I tabulated the victims: the tailor shop customer, her daughter, the old Italian fisherman who'd only tried to cure Pablo's earache, and all the inanimate objects of my father's wrath like the Rickenbacker doors, the faraway shoe factory machine, and our poor TV.

My mother was observing me from my doorway. "Aren't you going to change?"

I looked up bitterly. "Why don't *you* help him?"

She walked toward my dresser and opened a drawer.

"Ay mi'jita." She handed me a clean blouse. "I can't see well. Anyway, your father wants you. You're the smart one. Think of it as a chance to practice."

"Practice what?" I blurted out. "Being crazy?"

Her slap shocked me. I stared back with utter contempt, willing myself not to touch my face, though it stung.

She rubbed her hand without looking at me. "Help your father," she said, turning away.

Silently, I stood and went to retrieve the Royal, then carried it into the kitchen. At the table I sat with the typewriter in front of me and the *World Book Encyclopedia* propped between two cans of black beans.

Humidity made the keys sticky, so I gently wiped the letters with a napkin first. The typewriter was innocent. Its solidity and its order—the square box it came in, the rectangular opening where the legs of each key kicked up toward paper, and the square black keys, each with a proud white letter in the middle—braced me against the hopelessness in which I felt myself whirling as I began to type.

To calm down, I tried to make believe that I was *watching* instead of *being* the person at the table. Mutely, I watched the typing hands peck out the letters and pick up correction paper strips to fix mistakes, then furiously roll out a sheet to start over when there were too many to correct one by one.

*Someone help me,* cried a tiny voice inside me.

I had to stop, seized by fear that I too could be splitting apart like my father, some of me stuck inside and the rest gone who knows where?

The *World Book Encyclopedia* was a vast universe. What if, after I finished this, my father required me to type whole books—or the entire encyclopedia? Weeks would become months in the clutches of madness. What good would it do to save myself from deportation if I couldn't keep my own mind from disintegrating?

As hours that felt like eternity passed, I managed to type over all the dense pages of text. But there were still charts and diagrams left—one of the planets, a rainbow of spheres moving toward the large flaming sun. Dejectedly, I inserted a final sheet into the Royal. All I could to do was type the captions, which I did in order like a list. But they read so oddly—disconnected from their pictures like my father from human reality. I stared at the diagram's flaming sun and the tiny gray Earth near it while my father paced behind me, as if he couldn't stop himself from dragging me into his doomed orbit.

In the wake of that depressing fifteenth birthday, my father whipped up many fresh batches of encyclopedia-related concoctions for me. Exhausted, I complained to Mami that my back ached from so much typing. She became silent for a moment, wiping her hands with a towel and thinking. Then she went to get Pablo, who seemed to have a lot of free time on his hands, and enlisted him in reading my father's assignments aloud so that I could sit up straight. The typing did go faster, plus with Pablo cracking jokes I began to feel a little less alone in the world.

I plunged back into despair, though, when one of my textbooks went missing. "It has to be Papi," I told Mami darkly, after I'd searched just about everywhere except his chambers. I went in there and carefully scanned his cluttered pseudo-desk, but it was hard to tell what was under the large plastic lime planter in which he kept his treasure trove of sharpened pencils and cartridge pens and the slide rule he'd confiscated for his diseños—as if he were the one taking Manolo's drafting class. Sure enough, the corner of my science book peeked out from where he'd buried it under the planter.

I turned on my heel.

"Mami, he has my book!" I hissed. "He's taking over my life! First he takes my money, then my supplies, and now *all* my stuff. When is this going to end?"

She sniffed disdainfully. "Don't exaggerate, Gabriela. He borrowed a book. It's not going to kill you to be without it for a few minutes." Then she went into the lion's den as I listened from a safe distance.

"That book, Roberto," she asked innocently, "isn't that Gabriela's?"

"This? Sí, but I have to examine it."

"Roberto, your daughter needs it. Give it to me, please."

"It's important for my research."

"I'll get you another one."

"You don't know, Evangelina. We need 1.9 million barrels."

"What I know is that your daughter needs that book to study," she replied. "Gabriela!" she yelled. "Bring me the book Pablo didn't return last year! From his closet!"

I ran into my brothers' room, which Pablo had decorated with posters of rock bands whose names had "Black" or "Dark" in them. On the closet shelf I found a social studies book, *The World We Live In*, with a Rickenbacker sticker inside. I ran back, extending the book to my father in both hands like a peace pipe. "Here, Papi."

As he took it, Mami nabbed the science text and passed it to me.

My father began blinking at the wall in front of him, as if he were thinking very hard. Blink. Blink. Blink.

I frowned at Mami in puzzlement and left.


Things got worse as my father recognized, despite the looseness of his thinking, that Pablo's reading aloud enabled me to type faster. He assigned more of the *World Book Encyclopedia*, *The World We Live In*, and his dog-eared magazines, and combined it all with his illogical handwritten notes. Having to retype entire encyclopedia entries from scratch was bad enough, but connecting my father's incomprehensible sentences to those disparate sources just about taxed my remaining mental capabilities. When Pablo suggested skipping parts to see if my father noticed, I refused—only because I didn't want to use up the brain cells that survived figuring out what to omit. Clinging desperately to reason, I resorted to adding a concluding sentence here and there so that his documents wouldn't end so abruptly—vague summaries like "Thus, Seismic Stratigraphy is very important."

When at last my father assigned us an article about global seismic activity that appeared to have some miraculous connection to oil drilling, Pablo and I got our hopes up. Maybe, just maybe, our father understood more than we appreciated. It might all come together in some mysterious way, like our purpose here on Earth when God was through with us.

The letter to Miami-Dade Junior College wiped out my illusions once and for all.

Happy and energized, my father emerged from his room one bright April morning, his special letter drafted and ready. Pablo had gone to some thirteen-year-old's pool party, leaving the unfortunate task to me.

I followed my father into his room. Sunny as it was that day, he'd turned on the lamp to show me his letter in all its glory. His own private solar system.

On top of a pile of the usual volumes and periodicals was the introduction in his unmistakable block print:

DEAR SIR:

PLEASE YOU BE SURE THAT I AM WRITING WITH RESPECT AND HOPES OF SPEAK AS SOON AS POSSIBLE. WITH THE PROPOSICIÓN OF DISCUSS MY TÉSIS.

My father had failed to translate "proposal" and "thesis" of course. As usual, he'd also forgotten that English didn't have tildes, accent marks.


HERE YOU WILL HAVE MY EXPERIENCE IN REFINERY. SECONDARY RECOVERY TECHNIQUES IN THE OLDER FIELDS, SOME OF WHICH DATE BACK TO 1918, EXTEND THE PRODUCTIVE LIFE OF THE FIELDS. OFTEN, THEY INCREASE ULTIMATE RECOVERY TO MORE THAN 20 PERCENT. THESE TECHNIQUES GENERALLY INVOLVE INJECTION OF WATER TO DISPLACE OIL, DRIVING IT INTO THE WELLBORE (NATURAL GAS IS OFTEN PRODUCED SIMULTANEOUSLY WITH THE OIL FROM A RESERVOIR).

This whole paragraph I recognized from an article I'd typed before.

I WORK TOO MANY YEARS IN COLOMBIA REFINERY.

This was clear enough, but underneath he'd clipped a letter that the *Sentinel* rejected when he'd looked for work in a more or less normal manner. The work experience paragraphs of the old letter were circled for me to insert, but they included jobs that had *not* been with Colombian refineries—like picking tomatoes, sweeping the shop, and making shoes.

The page ended there. I looked at my father. He put a hand on his pile of *Home Mechanics* magazines and *World Book Encyclopedia* volumes. They contained excerpts for his letter, he explained, petting the pile like a pet.

Wordlessly, I counted twenty-six lengthy entries he'd clipped, including the beloved Solar System article that I'd already retyped once. He handed me another handwritten page that he'd signed, despite its draft status, which read:

AND I WANT TO BRING TO YOU THESE PAPERS OF PETROLEUM INDUSTRY AND STUDY MORE WITH YOUR UNIVERSITY THE PROBLEM, WITH YOUR ASSISTANCE. AND RECEIVE THE PAYMENTS.

SINCERELY YOURS,

This was followed by my father's signature and beneath that, a title,

"EXPERTO EN REFINERÍA."

*Expert in refining?* I wearily asked myself. *To be paid for his petroleum studies?*

All my father's obsessions and delusions were now coalesced in a single document.

*Okay,* I quietly but sternly told myself. *No more fixing.* No more trying to make this garbage rational. Pablo was right—trying to fix things was hopeless. My father was nuts. My mother was nuts for going along with him instead of me. There was only one sane response to life in this insane asylum: escape. Whenever and however I could manage it. With that conviction, I picked up my father's materials and marched into the kitchen. I inserted the first clean sheet into the typewriter.

The letter to the first of the thirty Miami-Dade addressees was a pain to cobble together out of my father's multiple inserts. But I drew some satisfaction in leaving the bottle of Wite-Out untouched. As I moved on to the second letter, my mother prepared a café con leche for me with lots of sugar. The coffee jolt gave me the sense to go buy carbon paper, after which I typed three letters at once, adding the individual addressees later. The addresses corresponded to phone book listings in the community course catalog that had arrived a few days earlier—for *me* of course, although my father had appropriated that like Manolo's slide rule, my money, and whatever he could squeeze out of my mind.

For the envelopes, I resourcefully converted Mami's leftover return address stickers from St. Stephen's with the red and green Christmas crosses on them by scratching off her name and substituting my father's. He insisted that I go drop off the letters, though at least he didn't tag along.

Pablo found me dumping envelopes into the post office mailbox. He had a towel around his neck and offered me his goody bag. "Want some candy?"

"Thanks," I said, grabbing a pack of Red Hots. "Was the party fun?"

"Yeah, it was really fun. Hey, Gabi, let's detour over to Tuttle and see who's there. I don't wanna go home with the crazies yet," he said with a grin.

"I don't know," I replied tepidly, but I wasn't too eager to return home either so I let him talk me into it.

Tuttle was the typical clean neighborhood park, complete with swings, sandbox, and a slide. In the back, however, the chain-link fence had been pushed down, yielding an overgrown swath of land adjacent to rusty railroad tracks. The park was named for Julia Tuttle, the one woman studied in our Florida history unit because she'd given money for the railroad that "civilized" south Florida. Now, the abandoned tracks were littered with beer bottles, Coke cans, tampons, and empty Frito bags. Pablo and I walked past the litter and situated ourselves on the grassy part between the jasmines and a lone orange tree that sometimes dropped dried-up fruit. No one Pablo knew was around. Tossing me his goody stash, he pulled a small paper bag from his pocket and removed a tube that he uncapped and squirted into the bag. Then he lifted the bag to his face and sniffed.

"What's that?" I asked, getting serious.

"Glue," he said as he inhaled deeply. "Want some?"

"What are you doing that for?"

"It's good." He flashed me his baby smile. "Wanna try?"

"No. I have enough mental problems." I watched with concern as Pablo tossed his head back, seemingly dizzy, and laughed.

"I have pot too," he admitted, reaching into his pocket for a joint and matches. He started lighting the joint.

"That's illegal!" I said angrily as I reached forward to snatch it away.

But Pablo was quick, pulling the joint back with a sly grin. "Who's gonna find out?" he asked, gesturing toward the desolate grounds.

"If they did, Pablo," I explained patiently, "you could get arrested. Or deported. Or *both*." Black versions of our future were the only kind I could foresee.

"They have good pot in Colombia," he joked, not taking any of it seriously while smoking.

"The only good thing," I replied dourly, "would be seeing Abuelo."

"I hardly remember him," Pablo said, then offered me the joint. "Take a turn."

I shook my head. "Drugs are bad for you, Pablo."

"Not this," he urged, holding it out with an impish grin. "Just try it."

I frowned at the marijuana, but Pablo kept shoving it at me teasingly.

"Okay, okay," I said finally. "Let me see." I took the joint and briefly inhaled. "Hmm, no menthol," I remarked blandly.

Pablo laughed. "Hold it in more, Gabi."

"All right." I tried another puff, then gave it back. "That's enough."

As Pablo stretched out on the grass and smoked, I resumed my somber discourse on life after deportation. "We'd have to go to school in Spanish," I pointed out. "That is, if we even got to go. Maybe in Colombia they'd make us live in a home like Tía Julia or maybe in a mental institution with Papi." Depressing only myself, since Pablo was in the dark about the family's legal dilemma, I decided to drop the whole business. I was feeling lightheaded anyway, maybe from the pot.

"What did Papi make you do today?" Pablo asked.

"College applications!"

"What?"

I giggled. "Not really." I told him about the wacky letter and suddenly I was laughing so hard I felt like crying.

Pablo watched me quizzically out of one eye until I finally tumbled backward onto the grass beside him. "Oh my God," I said, catching my breath. "And get a load of this—he wants to study your old social studies book. To *study*!" I wiped a tear from my eye.

For a minute, we both remained silent.

"Yeah, pretty fucked up," Pablo said at last, getting up to look for his glue tube. When he found it, he pocketed it again and added, "You know, Papi could still invent something. Like that drill thing. You can invent things even if you're loco."

I sat up. "No, Pablo. I don't think so. I think there's something seriously not right with his brain. It's not the fake nervios Mami blames it on either. All those motor tics, that blinking, and the hand thing."

"Yeah, and don't forget the swallowing," Pablo reminded me.

"I have to focus on not listening to him," I said grimly. "Like, block the words from coming into my head."

Pablo nodded. "Yeah. Keep it together. Or you could split all the time, like Manolo."

"I guess."

We stopped at Manolo's store on the way home and told him the pathetic letter story. Before we left, he promised to borrow the store's heavy-duty stapler for my exhibit construction.

That night after dinner, Manolo came into my room to help me create the frame. Afterward, I worked diligently on my display while he sat drinking a Coke and watching. After a while he spoke up and said he'd figured out what was going on with Mami's frequent absences to Camila's house.

I shot up straight. "She'll kill you if you tell Pablo."

"Hey, I'm the one who helps the old lady," he retorted, meaning repairs I guessed. Manolo was good at those. The store owner had even given him a hammer that he forbade any one of us to touch. Manolo hammered back kitchen drawer fronts that fell off, put on washers to stop leaks, changed lightbulbs. But while he'd raised his stature in my mother's eyes, I didn't have the heart to tell him that his accomplishments would never amount to much. My mother would wait forever for my father to resume his manly duties again.


Pablo and I began tricking my father after the Miami-Dade disillusionment by leaving out small sections of paperwork. Once, a couple of weeks into that, Pablo even managed to temporarily avert typing duty altogether. My father had gone to gather his papers and Pablo dashed into the bathroom. Papers in hand, my

father followed in that direction. "Pablito?" he inquired outside
the closed door. There was no answer.

"Where did your brother go?" he asked me.

"I don't know, Papi," I said, retreating nervously back into the
kitchen. As my mother gave me a suspicious glance, I gazed back
with all the innocence I could muster. Then I returned to check
on my father, still standing with his hand on the doorknob. When
he saw me, he emitted a goofy "Ha!" and pushed the door open,
then looked around in confusion. There was no one inside. If he'd
thought to move the bath curtain aside, he'd have found the window obviously utilized for Pablo's escape. Instead, my father only
shuffled to his room and didn't even ask me to type.

How guilty I felt for conspiring to make him sicker in the head
than he already was. But it was only a small way of trying to pass
the craziness back, to keep it off me. I *had* to resort to trickery, or
he would take over my mind.

Before I'd realized it, though, my mind tricked me right back.

It was the moment they passed out the red, blue, and yellow
ribbons for the winning Youth Fair exhibits. The colors of the
Colombian flag, I'd pointed out to Lydia when I'd proudly turned
in my own elegant and well-constructed—not to mention thoroughly researched and documented—Miccosukee land exhibit.
Adorned with sketches of native people in their natural habitat
before the conquerors arrived and excerpts of *Sentinel* articles
blasting the excesses of south Florida development, *The Misuse of
Science* illustrated how badly artificial drainage had damaged the
Everglades and literally siphoned off the Miccosukee land from
right under them. In contrast to my father's incomprehensible
manuscripts, my exhibit exposed the truth beneath *The World We
Live In*. It deserved a ribbon, at least a yellow one.

I could only blink like my crazy father when the names of the boys who'd won were announced. I couldn't believe it—my own country, taken from me.

"They only have three to give, Gabi," Lydia rationalized afterward.

"It's not fair, Lydia," I blurted.

"Óyeme, chica, don't get bummed about every little thing."

"It's not little," I insisted, slamming my locker shut. How could I explain to her why I felt so betrayed?

"Want to ride downtown?" she urged, trying to be nice.

I shook my head. "I don't think so, but thanks." That was Lydia's hobby to avoid returning to her own empty home. Since the divorce, her mother was always out trying new boyfriends, and Lydia's brother Emilio was hardly home either since he owned a car now. It was a lonely life for Lydia. Sometimes I rode the bus to keep her company. But not that day.

"Well," she said, offering me her cigarettes, "take a couple."

"Okay." I tucked one into my case. "Thanks."

I waited until the downtown bus arrived and waved her and Alina off. The area where they were headed was a depressing land of discount department stores and urinated alleyways. That ride would not have cheered me at all.

As I crossed the street and waited for my own bus, I stared forlornly at another new strip mall with a batido stand in front. Actually, it was a wrinkled Cuban guy who had attached an awning to an ice cream wagon and started selling mango and banana shakes from a blender he rigged up with an extension cord connected to the beauty salon behind him. Ladies in rollers and painted toes came out, ruining their lipstick on his shakes. Bits of the Old World—or the Third World, as Mr. Lanham would say—poked through the fancier development my exhibit had railed against.

I rode my bus to my stop, got off, and trudged the long blocks home. New houses and driveways being built were unhappy reminders of the time elapsed since my father had had a real job. The construction workers I passed were dark from laboring in the sun, and you couldn't tell who was Cuban and who wasn't until the familiar chirp of the "Oye, niña" began.

At home, I found Mami cutting mangoes. I swiped a piece, kissed her cheek, and sauntered off quietly to my room, hoping my father wouldn't notice I was home.

No such luck. No doubt he'd waited all afternoon with his ears perked up like a dog hoping to be let out. "Mi'jita." There he was, scratching at my door.

I shuffled some books around. "I have homework, Papi."

"Bueno," he said. "After."

It was a tricky dance, trying to keep him at bay with worksheets, English papers, and, until today, my exhibit.

Morosely, I considered that the winning exhibits had touted *Ultrasonography: The Future of Swine Breeding*; *Phosphorus in Crop Fertilization*; and that old standby, *Pasteurization*. Maybe those county farmers had been upset by my exhibit's anti-agriculture slant.

But was the problem losing? Or was it thinking I would win at all? Why had I let my thoughts take over—like my father, convincing himself he was writing a thesis instead of gibberish?

I lay in my bed. If only I could share my worries with someone....

When my father shuffled in later, I pretended to sleep. In the distance I heard Mami say, "Déjala que descanse." Let her rest.


When I woke, the sun had set.

For some reason, I took out my grandfather's poem. It wasn't the comforting kind, but at least it reminded me of him, and that was comforting. My mother's indifference to the poem had reassured me that my grandfather wasn't obliquely telling me he was dying or anything horrible like that.

*Don't say no to me, Light, constant. Illuminate this solitary shore.*

Was he telling me to ask God for help?

## THIRTEEN

T HE SHADOW OF MY GRANDFATHER'S POEM grew ominous when I found my mother holding his photograph in my bedroom after I returned from school a few days later.

In a small voice, I said, "Hi Mami," and sat down fearfully beside her.

My grandfather smiled back at us from the photograph, his hands tucked inside the pockets of his guayabera. He looked amused that someone thought his picture worth taking.

"Your Tía Julia resembled him," Mami told me mournfully. Then she spilled out the sad news of her sister's death.

A surge of momentary relief filled me that my grandfather hadn't passed away, but I quickly tried to summon up heartfelt grief over Tía Julia, whom I couldn't remember well as she'd lived in some institution since before I was born. When Tío Paco joked once that it was a place where old ladies recovered from being unmarried, Mami had slapped his arm while he cackled at his own wit.

There would be no joking now.

"I'll have to go," Mami told me ruefully.

"To Colombia?" I asked, startled.

She nodded and put an arm around my shoulders. "I need to see my parents."

"Papi too?" I probed nervously.

"No. That would cost too much."

"But who'll stay with us?" I asked, trying to quell the mounting anxiety.

My mother shook her head. "Nobody." Her gaze drifted, not really seeing the room. "It's only for a few days, mi'ja. You'll look out for your father as always. I'll talk to Pablo about behaving himself. And you know Manolo's responsible." She rose and put my grandfather's picture back.

They were to go for ten days—Mami and Tío Paco. Another sister sent my mother her ticket, after which Mami began calling around to ask relatives to keep an eye on us. "Fernandita promises she'll look in on you," she comforted me vaguely.

With school about to end, I worried about how I'd manage my father full-time. What if, while she was gone, he came up with some crazy impromptu visit to the bank to demand his millions? What if he got into a fight with someone? But every time I opened my mouth to beg Mami not to go, her sadness over Tía Julia's empty life and death silenced me.

That Saturday, my brothers and I sat outside and watched Tío Lucho drive away with our mother. My father couldn't go to the airport because Tío Lucho was due at work directly afterward.

As the hours passed, my feelings of unease coalesced into a more specific fear that something might happen to Mami's plane or that the immigration officials—God forbid—might never let her back because of what my father had done. All day, I tried to reassure myself, but my worries began to spread into each other: If Mami never came home, I could be chained to my father forever. I would be locked away in our house like Tía Julia in the institution. Tío

Paco's black joke echoed in my head. How would I ever attain freedom, if the only route my parents accepted for a young woman to leave her home was marriage?

The next morning I left the pot of café con leche prepared on the stove before heading to St. Stephen's. At Mass, I lit a candle and prayed for my mother's safe return.

When I got home, I found Fernandita with her boyfriend, El Loco, in our living room. They'd brought pastries that my father and brothers were demolishing.

"Such a good girl, going to church when your Mami's not home," Fernandita said with her pretty smile, then hugged me to show that she meant it.

El Loco started to have fun with my father. Enunciating loudly, he asked my father about his "work."

"Bueno," my father began, launching into refinery talk.

Eyes big and round, El Loco examined my father as if genuinely listening for a few minutes, then suddenly burst out laughing. "That's great, Roberto!" he said, slapping my father on the back.

My father laughed too, though none of it was funny.

I saw Fernandita giving El Loco the eye, but he ignored her.

Fernandita said they wanted to take me out to a Colombian restaurant in Hialeah. From the corner of my eye, I checked my father's reaction, but he didn't seem to object.

Fernandita added, "Just you, nena. Let's let the boys play and keep your Papi company."

I turned to my father. "I can leave some sandwiches made," I offered.

"Muy bien," he said, smiling.

Fernandita followed me into the kitchen to help.

On the way to Hialeah, she tried to give El Loco the what-for about teasing my father, but El Loco only tried to make out with her, while I pretended to study the most interesting highway in the world. Though I was glad to get a break from home, these two embarrassed me and provided further confirmation that male-female entanglements should be avoided entirely. I was grateful when we finally parked in front of the restaurant.

El Cerro Maravilloso was not as marvelous as the name suggested. The tables were set with stained tangerine tablecloths and plastic flowers, and a fan hung from the ceiling. El Loco ordered a beer and with the same mock laugh he'd used with my father told me to order anything—beer or even aguardiente, that colorless liquor only men drank.

"No seas idiota," Fernandita reprimanded, giving him The Look.

El Loco laughed and blew her a kiss.

I ordered a Pepsi, forlornly wishing they'd taken me to McDonald's, which was air-conditioned and offered French fries we never got at home. As Fernandita handed me the menu and said everything was good, El Loco ordered sancocho and leaned his chair back on its hind legs, his beer glass askew. Although I didn't want to align myself with him, I ordered sancocho too, since Mami hardly cooked that anymore.

El Loco gave me a chummy smile. Tall and slim, with curly hair, he had eyes that laughed even when he wasn't joking. I was wary of him, above all, because of his nickname. Why would anyone be called The Crazy One if he were all right in the head? Of course, Latinos threw the word "loco" around loosely. This made it possible to think that some people who weren't crazy, in the medical sense, might actually be so, which made it harder to distinguish the people who probably were crazy. Like my father. Maybe calling more people "loco" than actually were was a way to hide the true craziness floating around and our shame over them.

Afterward, El Loco ordered an overly candied and slightly revolting dessert for me. On the way home, I regretted it bigtime. The unforgiving heat cooked the sugary guava into the meat already inside my stomach, making me nauseous.

As we arrived at my house, Fernandita encouraged me to call if I needed anything while my mother was away. "Don't be afraid," she reiterated.

A suspicious part of me wondered why she had put it that way. But I just said, "Okay," and thanked them for lunch.

The house was hot. My father was at his desk safely surrounded by pages of accent marks and exclamation points.

Too stuffed to do anything else, I went to rest on my bed and wait for the churning in my stomach to stop.

A short while later, Manolo burst in. "Pablo fell. He can't stand up. His leg hurts."

We ran to the yard, where Pablo was leaning back on his hands, his legs splayed in front of him. Johnny from across the street, a mangy dog, and an ugly older kid who owned the dog surrounded him.

Pablo shielded his eyes from the sun while smiling affably at me.

"What happened?" I interrogated him roughly.

"I think his leg is broken," the ugly kid said.

"It was their fault," Pablo added, pointing at Manolo and Johnny. "They didn't hold the dumb dog."

"He was jumping from the tree," Johnny volunteered. "Trying to land on Petey's dog."

Pablo started laughing.

"It's not funny," I let him know. "We're gonna be in big trouble." I turned to Manolo for ideas. "What are we supposed to do now?"

"You shouldn't move a broken leg," the big-shot ugly kid interjected.

Pablo grinned. "I can't, stupid."

I checked the bedroom window nervously for my father. "Are you sure it's broken, Pablo?" I dropped to my knees to check, but my brother slapped my hand away. "Ouch! Don't touch it. It hurts," he said.

While the four of them waited, I leaned back on my haunches and anxiously assessed the situation. I remembered Fernandita's offer to help. Maybe she could take Pablo to the doctor? But how would I keep my father in the dark about the incident, especially since he was bound to hear El Loco's car and big mouth? Calling an uncle would require telling my father, who would get mad at us for causing trouble, and then—? *Oh God!* Why had Mami gone to that funeral? I *knew* something bad would happen.

I stood up and gave my brothers a look of grim defeat, "I better get Papi."

Pablo put a protective hand over his leg.

"Don't move anything," I warned. "I'll be right back."

As I approached my father's bedroom, his compulsive scribbling stopped and he looked up at me bug-eyed, like a person who hasn't slept enough. "¡Mi'jita!"

"Pablo fell, Papi," I announced bravely.

My father gulped hard, then did it again and again. He was so bony-looking now that his Adam's apple made the tic especially conspicuous.

"Pablo hurt his leg," I repeated, waiting for a response.

He didn't answer. Perhaps he hadn't understood? "Pablito hurt his leg," I reiterated.

"¿Sí?" At last, my father slid the chair away from the dresser and followed me out.

Petey and his dog were gone. Johnny started to explain the obvious, but I cut him off. "My father doesn't understand English."

With his bug eyes, my father examined Pablo slowly, as if he didn't recognize his son. Pablo squinted up without the customary charming grin.

Suddenly, my father turned on Manolo and started viciously whacking my brother's head with the knuckles of his right hand.

"Whoa," said Johnny, backing away as the knuckling intensified.

"Get out of here," I told him in a low voice.

Johnny took off right away. He looked a little shaky, glancing back over his shoulder to watch my father pound Manolo harder and harder. My father was muttering weird, angry gibberish while Manolo struggled to cover his head and cry, "No, Papi, no." The fierce knuckling alternated with manic shaking of my brother by his hair. I feared Manolo's brains would be scrambled forever, but when I opened my mouth to scream "¡Papi!" the sound refused to come out. It was like screaming in a dream.

My father's high-pitched threat, "¿Quieres que te *mate?*" shocked me into reaction.

*Kill?* With two hands I grabbed Manolo with all my strength and he stumbled out of my father's grip and fell. My father swerved furiously toward Pablo and me. "¡Mierda!" he cursed, eyes wild. He lifted a foot to terrified Pablo on the grass.

"¡Papi!" I screamed at last. Something had gone terribly, terribly wrong. "¡Papi!" My father looked so strange, as if he were in some mad killer's trance. "Papi, listen. *Listen.*" I tried to control my voice, to slow it down and sound normal and gentle like the old groundskeeper's. "It was that other kid who pushed Pablo and made him fall," I pleaded softly. "The *other* kid," I breathed, desperately holding my father's eyes in mine. "It wasn't us, Papi. It wasn't us!"

My father stared at me with such a wild expression that my body trembled a little.

All of a sudden, blinking hard, he seemed to recognize me. He looked down at Pablo with surprise. "¿Qué fue?" he asked.

"Pablo's leg, Papi," I said quietly.

"What's wrong, Pablito?" my father inquired solicitously.

"I think it's broken," Pablo practically whispered.

"¿Sí?" My father stared at me. "We need a doctor, mi'ja."

"Yes, Papi," I replied, giving Pablo a look of relief. "Why don't you call Tío Victor, Papi?"

He nodded calmly. "Sí, está bien."

We watched him go, the door swinging shut behind him.

Manolo got up, wiping his face with his T-shirt. "I hate this fucking family," he spit out in bitterness and then ran across the street. Pablo and I traded guilty looks. Why did Manolo always get the brunt of my father's anger? It wasn't fair. "I'm sorry!" I yelled out after him, because no one else ever would, I guessed. "Come back before it gets dark!"

I turned reluctantly back to Pablo. "I better go check on Papi."

My father had finished making arrangements and was just hanging up with Tío Victor.

I suddenly realized how badly I needed to go to the bathroom. As I raced in there and dropped onto the toilet, my legs and arms began to shake. I couldn't get up for a while, not even when I heard the ambulance, quickly followed by my uncle's Chevrolet and his voice as he disembarked. Finally, once my trembling subsided, I rose and went outside. Tío Victor was talking with the paramedic.

"Do you want to come?" my uncle asked me.

I shook my head, still feeling ill. "I better wait in case Manolo wonders where everybody went." I hesitated for a moment over what to tell my uncle. "Tío, I don't think you should leave Pablo with Papi," I suggested. "Just in case he might form a problem."

"What do you mean?" Tío Victor probed.

"He was acting sort of badly, Tío." I glanced at my father, who was waiting peacefully in the Chevrolet with his arm propped on the window. "Papi had some kind of attack."

"But Pablito said he fell from a tree."

I nodded. "It happened after—" I took a breath. "After Pablo fell, Papi started hitting Manolo really hard, talking crazy, about killing. It didn't make any sense."

My uncle pursed his lips and pulled his pants up higher by the belt loops while studying my father. "We'll resolve this later, Gabrielita. I'll call you from the hospital."

They took off then, and I went into the house, but the sudden switch to its cooler environment brought on a cold sweat. After another mad dash to the bathroom, I barfed all over my arms as I reached the sink. Never again, I swore to myself while heaving up the rest of the marvelous lunch, would I eat ñame, carne de res, yuca, maíz, plátano verde, or plátano amarillo.

When there was nothing left to throw up, I felt profoundly empty. How could my mother have abandoned us like that? How *could* she?

A while later Manolo crept into the house carrying a small package. "Where's the old man?" he asked.

"They're at the hospital. Tío Victor's taking Pablo to his house after."

Manolo grabbed a screwdriver from the drawer, along with his personal hammer that Mr. Byatt had given him and the package he'd brought. Purposefully, he carried the stuff toward his room.

"What are you doing?" I asked, following.

"I'm putting a fucking lock on my door."

"I think Papi's staying at Tío Victor's until Mami comes home," I said.

"I still need a lock." He twisted in a brass screw.

"I guess we should have locks on all the doors, huh?"

"I can get you one, if you want," Manolo offered.

"Oh no, I just meant, you know...."

Obviously, the door against my father was a door against Mami as well. I couldn't help but chew on my lip and worry as I imagined the expression on her face when she found the lock Manolo had installed to protect himself from his own father.

Moments later, that became the least of my worries. A vigorous rapping called me to the door, and I opened it to find a cop, who greeted me pleasantly.

"Hello there."

## FOURTEEN

T HE SMILING OFFICER ASKED to speak to my
parents.

"They're not home," I answered politely, my hand fixed
tightly on the doorknob. It occurred to me that in the universe of
immigrant-only rules perhaps my mother wasn't even supposed to
leave the country. Fretting over that, I switched tracks. "My father
had to go to the hospital, on account of my brother. He hurt his
leg. I'm not sure which hospital."

"That's all right," she answered mildly, tilting her head to examine
me better. "What's your name?" The officer's high blond ponytail was
pulled up so tightly that her blue eyes beamed bright as searchlights.

"Gabriela de la Paz," I responded, then for some reason felt
compelled to add, "I go to Flagler Junior High."

"Uh-huh." Cracking a smile, she glanced behind me and asked,
"You live here, Gabrielle?"

"Yes—" I nodded, pausing. *Should I call her M'me?* "Yes, Officer," I resolved, "with my family."

"I see," she replied. "So—was there some kind of incident here
today?"

"You mean, my brother's leg?"

"Sure, tell me about that." She aimed her blue lights at me.

"They were in the yard," I began cautiously.

"Who was?"

"My brothers. And their friends."

"What about your folks?"

"Well—" I parsed my words. "My mother had to go to a funeral. But my father was home."

"Outside with the boys?"

"No, in the house. Working. That's why he didn't hear it when my brother fell. I didn't either," I clarified. That sounded suspicious, so I added, "I mean, I was inside too. So then Pablo—my little brother—jumped out of the tree and broke his leg and my other brother came to get me. Us, I mean. My father and me."

"And then?"

"Oh, then—" I twirled my hand around the aluminum knob. "I guess my dad was kind of mad at them for fooling around, but he just said we had to see a doctor so he went inside to call my uncle—we don't have a car," I added, by way of explanation. "Then my uncle came, and the ambulance and everything like that."

She turned her head slightly right when a sound drifted out of my brothers' room, then gave me her friendly officer smile again. "We got a phone call earlier from one of your neighbors. She seemed concerned."

Neighborly concern only disconcerted me. *Remain silent*, I advised myself.

"Everything looks pretty quiet now," she noted.

"Mmm, fine," I murmured.

She gave her ponytail another swing and shot me one last smile. "Let your folks know we stopped by, okay? Maybe we'll come around again. Toodle-doo," she added, wiggling her fingers good-bye as she left.

"Bye," I answered faintly.

I forced myself to wait a few seconds before going inside to give Manolo the blow-by-blow. Afterward, the two of us watched the squad car idle out front for a while before it drove away.

When I called Tío Victor later about the house call, he wanted to pick Manolo and me up right away, but I was more worried about no one being at our house if the lady officer returned. There was also the difficulty of getting Manolo to work, so my uncle relented.

"It's only a week until Mami returns," I reassured him. "We'll be fine."

That night, though, as we slept alone in our house for the first time—Manolo locked in his room, courtesy of his new lock, and me hyper-alert in mine—fears stole in and grew large.

In the morning when I awoke, I ransacked my parents' room for a business card I remembered El Chino providing. I left three phone messages with Arthur, who finally suggested it might be simpler to book an appointment for my parents to see Mr. Korematsu in person. "He has a hard time keeping up with calls," Arthur explained.

"But I just have one question," I repeated for the millionth time.

El Chino finally called the next night way past normal office hours. "What's up?" he asked. "Arthur says you've got a question." Though his tone sounded mocking, I was grateful he'd called back.

"It's about my father, Mr. Korematsu," I explained. "This police officer—"

"He got arrested again?"

"Oh no, he's okay. They just came over. But the thing is, I don't know what might happen with my mom. She's in Colombia and she's supposed to come home, like, this week. But I'm worried because of all the stuff with my father. So what I wanted to know is, well, do you think they could not let her back in?" The teensiest decibel of panic trilled out.

"What happened?" he asked sharply. "Why did the police go to your house?"

In a flash, I unleashed the story, including my father bashing Manolo right in front of that Johnny kid. Since El Chino knew about my father's temper, I thought it was safe to be honest. El Chino asked me questions and with surprising patience began sorting through each of my fears one at a time. For one thing, he said, it didn't seem like my father was being charged with anything, at least as of yet. The police visit was probably a routine domestic violence unit check, and I shouldn't worry too much about it.

"As far as the surveillance," he went on, "it wouldn't hurt to keep a low profile—you know, cut it out with the loud noises, family arguments and all that—just so Protective Services doesn't come calling while your mom's gone and happen to find two juveniles living there unattended."

"I'm fifteen."

"You're a minor."

"Oh yeah...but there's a kid at my school who's sixteen and... lives unattended."

"Maybe he's emancipated. The law's kind of slanted. Though I'm sure you're very emancipation-worthy," he wisecracked quickly. "But we don't have to get into that. What else?"

"About my mother, about her coming back."

"Right, the immigration issue. But she doesn't have an immigration issue. Or am I missing something?"

"I thought we could lose our green cards. If my father got the two crimes, like you said."

"*He* could. Not your mother. We don't have collective punishments here."

"But what if he gets arrested for another one of those crimes? Wouldn't she have a problem getting back then?"

"No. Not unless she's gun-running or smuggling drugs or something herself. Orphans. Parrots. Something."

"She doesn't do any of those things, Mr. Korematsu," I declared earnestly. "But I was worried. I thought they could kick us all out, on account of my father—"

"They're not going to kick you all out just because your dad got busted," he said kindly.

"Oh. I guess I didn't get how it worked."

"No problem. So, any more questions?"

"No, I guess that was it. Thanks."

The questions I had left weren't legal.

Had my mother deceived me—or had she been confused?


In the days that followed, I watched the windows uneasily. A police car sometimes passed on the street, but none stopped.

Manolo reported that it was Johnny's mother who'd called the cops.

"Why did you have to go and blab?" I chastised my brother. "You want to get Papi arrested?"

"Johnny told her! Anyway, that didn't happen!"

"It could," I replied angrily. "What if Mami came home and found out Papi got kicked out of the country because of *you*?"

Manolo gave me a puzzled look. "What are you talking about? You know we would just go too if something did happen."

I folded my arms and stared at him dubiously. What if I told him about my talk with El Chino—and that maybe our family could just split up if my father got deported. *Fat chance!* I could hear Manolo retort, and he would be right. Mami was more likely to fight tooth and nail to drag us along with my father into the Colombian village mud she so dreaded.

Tío Victor finally brought her safely home from the airport without any of the immigration problems I'd feared, just as El Chino had assured me. Home, too, came my prodigal father and a grinning Pablo, proud of his cast. My father headed directly to the trunk and pulled out Mami's heavy suitcase. As he lugged it toward the house, he tried to muss Manolo's hair with his free arm, but my brother pulled away. A lump in my throat kept me from answering the "Hola, mi'jita" that my father threw in my direction.

Tío Victor waited for my father and brothers to go inside before addressing me. "We told your mother about what happened Sunday," he reported. Then, looking Mami in the eye, he said, "You can't let this situation go on, Evi. We have to sit down with Roberto."

Lines deepened in her forehead, as if every worry she'd left in Miami returned all at once. "Ay, Victor," she sighed, "what good would it do?"

"Maybe there's some kind of treatment, Evi. You can't avoid it forever. He might get worse." Tío Victor nodded in my direction. "Ask your daughter."

Instead of facing me, she looked away.

Tío Victor suggested a heart to heart talk with my father.

"All right," she capitulated.

I hustled inside so I could question Pablo. "What did you and Tío tell Mami?"

"That Papi beat up Manolo," he answered matter-of-factly.

"What about that stuff Papi said?" I pressed on.

"Like how he was gonna kill everybody? She wouldn't let me talk about it."

"Did Tío Victor tell her?"

"He just said Papi's temper is outta control, he's a peligro to his family."

"He said Papi was dangerous?" I asked.

"Yeah."

Hearing it from Tío Victor sounded much more frightening.

I went to the kitchen, where Mami was busy but uncharacteristically silent. After watching her for a minute, I decided to broach a less loaded subject—summer work for me. But she sent me off with an "ahora no" as her eyes clouded with a worry she hadn't yet found a name for.

To my great relief, Tío Victor called the next morning to say he'd gotten my father a medical appointment, and that he and Tío Lucho would come over soon to confront my father. Later that day, Mami's friend Camila visited, singing the praises of the disability checks she'd received for her husband who didn't work anymore because of his cancer. Mami pondered hopefully to me afterward, "Maybe your father could get a check too." As she washed out the coffee cups, I tried to ride her wave of optimism.

"Mami," I began, "could we ask Tío Lucho to let me work in the Hialeah factory? They're letting Marisol do it."

My mother frowned. "I don't know. How would I explain to your father?"

"We could pretend I'm keeping Marisol company."

"Lucho can't be driving you back and forth from Hialeah."

"I could go on the bus!" I offered desperately.

"All the way to Hialeah alone? No, mi'ja. I don't think so. I have to resolve this situation with your father. Then we'll see."

I bit back disappointment and tried to steel myself to be patient. But pessimism's little cloud hung around. "Mami, did you tell Camila about Papi's attack?"

"¡Cómo va a ser posible!" she exclaimed in shock. "And don't refer to it that way either." She eyed me suspiciously. "Have you been talking to anyone?"

"No!" Guiltily I thought of El Chino. He didn't really count, did he? Aloud, I only argued, "What difference would it make? Why should we hide it?"

"Hide it? It's respect for your family. You say you want to go and work like a grown woman," Mami shimmied her shoulders to make her point, "but you talk like a child who needs bringing up."

"You're the one who left us!" I blurted out.

As her jaw dropped, I turned on my heel before she could get the last word in. Then I took off on the pretext of delivering new Avon literature to her customers.

Camila saw me in the neighborhood and invited me over to meet her niece.

The niece, Olguita, was vacationing from Colombia to help out with Hernán. She had shiny, blue-black hair gathered into a large peinado high on her head. Her eyes, honey brown as her skin, were blackened with eyeliner that curled up at the edges like elegant script. She looked like a beautiful alien in a sci-fi movie.

I was shocked to hear she was seventeen, only two years older than me.

"We have to teach Olguita English," Camila said, smiling as she served us glasses of tart tamarindo juice.

"I don't understand a word, mujer," said Olguita, using "woman" the way Cuban girls used "chica" or "girl," and waving her beautifully manicured hand in a casual dismissal of the entire English language.

She invited me to come over one day for makeovers—undoubtedly intended for me, given my "natural look."

"That sounds nice," I replied with tepid enthusiasm.

But I did return, two days later, since I didn't have much going on besides trying to keep an arms' length away from my father, who fortunately hadn't shown signs of the explosive anger with which he'd pummeled Manolo—except for one brief outburst over a movie Mami was watching.

At the makeover, Olguita chatted about her fleet of older brothers and pushed my hair into a headband while I sat pinned to a chair she'd set up in the bathroom. As she dolled me up, she said so many nice things about my cheekbones that she managed to mesmerize me. "Models have operations, you know," she observed, "but you have them muy *au naturel.*"

I grinned at her unconventional but chic blend of French and Spanish. This mujer was growing on me. In between sharing beauty tips, she put on cumbia records and danced around drinking saccharin-laced iced tea. Now and then she'd pop into her uncle Hernán's room to get a smile out of him too.

When she was done with me, heavy shades of taupe eye shadow were gilded by Olguita's trusty eyeliner and signature curl at the end. It was the makeup style modeled on Colombian album covers by women whose breasts bulged out of bikini tops. I didn't think I would ever choose to let my womanliness bulge out like that, but Olguita's ministrations pleasantly distracted me from thoughts of home. Plus, I had to admit, I did look glamorous.

Even my mother offered cautious approval of Olguita's work. "Very nice," she remarked, studying me.

For the rest of that afternoon, however, she was in "No Mode," as Pablo called it. Stuck with his cast, he asked for permission to eat in front of the TV, but she refused. "And why did your brother have to put in that yellow brass lock instead of aluminum?" she complained again. She went on and on, pretending it was the color that bothered her rather than the fact that Manolo had installed a lock at all. I figured she was feeling anxious about the looming face-off with my father; we were all counting on it to resolve our familial difficulties.

When Olguita called later to say she was hosting a cocktail party on Saturday, my mother expressed relief at my getting an opportunity for more feminine socialization. She'd long before tried to teach me the lessons of her adolescent girlhood, a Dark Age of formal dancing and queer manners; but then the problems with my father had started and she had no time for frivolity or even for fighting off my Americanization. All she could do, really, was rue the fact that I'd abandoned el castellano as I conversed with my brothers almost exclusively in English.

When Saturday came, Mami cooked my father Aunt Jemima pancakes and slathered them with syrup. He was in excellent spirits by the time his brothers arrived.

Pablo was shooed away from the TV.

"Please, Mami!" he protested, "I can't do anything with this cast."

"Read a book," I encouraged, feeling a little sorry for him as he hopped away on his crutches.

My father greeted Tío Victor and Tío Lucho. "Siéntense, siéntense." Gaily, he gestured toward the couch and pulled over a couple of dining room chairs for extra seating.

"Gabriela, make some tinto," Mami instructed.

"Okay." The kitchen post let me hear everything in the living room, so I took my time washing out the espresso pot and matching the coffee posillos to their tiny saucers until things got under way.

"Roberto," Tío Victor began. "How do you feel?"

My father laughed. "Good, good," he answered. "A little full this morning."

"I'm referring to your mental state," my uncle said sternly.

I heard timid Tío Lucho offer cigarettes to everyone.

"Not now, Lucho, thank you," said Tío Victor.

"My mental state is good too," my father announced.

"I don't think so," said Tío Victor. "These illusions you have of getting rich."

"You're mistaken, Victor, they're not illusions."

"Roberto," Tío Victor continued, with customary gentleness. "Something has taken over your mind. These conditions have a solution."

"We want to help you," Tío Lucho added.

"Gabriela's helping me," my father declared.

"I'm talking about a doctor," said Tío Victor.

"But nothing's wrong with me," my father answered. "Sometimes I feel tired, but with my vitamins, I bounce right back." The obsession with vitamins was one of the relatively milder eccentricities my father had developed after seeing some of their strength-promoting qualities touted on *The Jack LaLane Show*.

From the kitchen, I could only imagine Tío Victor's uncomfortable glance in my mother's direction when my father mentioned his "vitamins."

"A doctor can prescribe better ones," I heard Tío Lucho say, as if coaxing a toddler to eat.

Mami intervened then. "Roberto, it's not that. Your brothers are talking about your nervios. Your hand, mi'jo, the shaking." She hesitated for a bit before pressing on. "You're spending so much time thinking about those papers."

"¿Cómo?" my father barked, his voice rising. "I keep explaining it to you, Evangelina. You don't understand a thing." His chair scraped the floor loudly as he stood up. "Let me get the letters," he begged my uncles, then called out, "Gabrielita!"

"Hombre, I don't want to see more papers!" Tío Victor declared. "You have children, Roberto. This can't continue. You have to get a hold of yourself."

"But my check is coming, Victor," my father insisted. "Gabriela! Bring me the papers from my office!"

I walked halfway into the living room.

"Roberto!" Tío Victor was losing his patience. "The only checks that come here are the ones your wife brings home and the ones from Lucho and me! Take responsibility, hombre!"

Mami gasped in horror.

"Evangelina?" My father's voice rose as he turned toward her. "What's he talking about?"

"Nothing," my mother said. "Nothing, mi'jo. Victor is referring to the time I went to the factory with Lucho." Her eyes flashed in anger at my uncle, then turned patiently back to my father. "Please, Roberto, sit down." She patted his chair. "If you go to the doctor, you *will* get a check. Like Camila's husband, I told you about that. People get checks until they can work again. It's like a pension. You get a pension."

My father kept looking from my mother to his brothers and back.

"Roberto," Tío Lucho ventured, "we're all getting older. It's a good idea to go to the doctor sometimes to make sure everything works, eh?" He gave an unconvincing chuckle.

"I *do* work, that's what I'm trying to show you," my father objected, falling heavily into his chair. "Neither of you knows about refineries, Lucho. I can explain it."

Tío Victor sighed. "Roberto, we scheduled you a doctor's appointment. All we're asking—"

"I don't need a doctor!" My father popped up.

"Everybody needs a doctor sometimes," Tío Lucho corrected.

My mother nodded. "Yes, mi'jo, like Lucho says, we're all getting older."

"*He's* getting older!" my father retorted, the vein in his forehead in full throb.

I ducked into the kitchen.

"Roberto, por favor," Mami implored.

"¡Basta!" My father came marching into the kitchen where I'd hastily retreated. There I stood at the ready with the coffee pot lifted. "You want some, Papi?" I offered meekly.

"No gracias, mi'jita."

I waited for him to go into his room before pouring the tintos and carrying the tray of cups into the living room. My mother and uncles stared up at me. Finally, Tío Victor took a cup.

"Didn't I tell you?" my mother said.

"You have to convince him, Evi."

"Nobody can convince him." She shook her head. "He's too stubborn."

"He always was," Tío Lucho added.

"How are you going to avoid another episode?" Tío Victor nodded in my direction to indicate what he meant.

Mami's eyes smarted but wisened up. "Victor, that was because I was gone."

"Well, Evi," he said, handing me the empty cup. "You know the situation. You drive. We're the passengers."

*Yeah, right,* I thought, thinking of that show *Lost in Space* and of my mother at the helm of some wildly orbiting space ship.

Even the cups on my tray shook as I carried it to the kitchen.

Later, after the uncles had gone, I anxiously sought her out. She was gathering sheets off the line in the yard. "Mami, how are you going to get Papi to that appointment?"

"Appointment?" She grimaced, handing me two corners of a sheet to help fold. "He won't go. Your uncle doesn't understand your father like I do. He's a proud man."

She didn't understand my father like *I* did: He was a knock-somebody's-brains-out man. Deportation was hardly our gravest problem anymore. "I think you'd better make him go, Mami," I advised soberly, joining my ends of the sheet to hers.

Her eyes narrowed. "No te vengas a igualar."

*Don't make myself her equal?* I jerked a pillowcase off the line. How was I supposed to respond to that?

Mami dumped a clothespin into the bucket and sighed. "He'll come around in his own time."

"You're just going to wait?" I exclaimed in disbelief.

She put a fist on her hip and stuck out her chin. "And what choice do I have, smarty-pants?"

"Trick him! Try something!"

"Nobody can make your father change, Gabriela," she said wearily. "I make do with what God gave me." She swung the hamper onto her hip and turned toward the house.

With my mouth wide open, I watched her go. I couldn't believe it. She was totally giving up! What about what Tío Victor had said about my father being a peligro?

I stormed inside, dumping my hamper on the table. Then I furiously gathered my party clothes. Boy did I need to get out of that place!

Things were happy at Camila's. Dance music played and Olguita had placed chairs against the wall with portable TV tables in-between. Plates lined with paper doilies were stacked with sandwiches that Olguita had cut into tiny triangles filled with chopped olives and Velveeta cheese. She and Camila were drinking whiskey and laughed when I admitted I'd never had liquor. Camila added water and lots of ice to a drink before handing it to me. The whiskey had a smoky taste.

Olguita ushered me into the bathroom. She said she had a surprise for me, the *pieza de resistencia*. From my one French class, I knew it wasn't proper to translate *pièce de résistance* that way—she made the *pièce* sound like an apartment for revolutionaries. But Olguita would have waved her hand in the classy way she always did whenever I tried to correct her, so I just shook my head and smiled.

The surprise was a pair of false eyelashes like hers. She was giving them to me, she gushed, because with my eyes—"esos ojos divinos"—it would be a crime to ignore the lashes. Then I donned the silky orange V-neck top she'd lent me, although I didn't like how the material curved so closely around my breasts.

By the time her invitees arrived, I was no longer the scruffy girl I'd gotten used to.

Olguita's cousin, Antonia, hugged me and introduced her tall boyfriend, Mauricio, and two cousins, Jairo and Tomás, visiting from Colombia. Olguita offered each guy an aguardiente to "remind them of home," she said charmingly, then poured me a second whiskey drink with less water than Camila's rendition.

I started adapting to the taste.

Everyone took their drinks to the chairs. I was the youngest, and Olguita explained that I'd come to the United States years before, like her aunt. The handsome cousin, Tomás, asked if I liked aguardiente, and I grimaced. He laughed and all the guys started talking about what they missed most when away—the women or the food. Olguita held up her glass, offering a toast "to Colombian women," and gave me a quick smile. Then everyone got into a conversation comparing American and Colombian schools, which interested me now—just in case we did live to survive my father's peligro and end up in one of those mudslide-prone villages that tormented my mother.

"We come out more educated than the gringos," Jairo concluded boastfully.

"Maybe it's our Catholic discipline," Antonia suggested.

Eventually, they mentioned plans to visit the Miccosukee village, and I warned them about the noisy airboat rides. "Everything else in the Everglades is so quiet," I said, "even the alligators."

The guys compared American alligators to caimanes and birds of the Colombian interior to birds of the coast. This led to a debate about where the better Spanish speakers lived, whether salsa had originated in our port city of Cali, rather than Cuba or Puerto Rico, and back to the women. "Who won the last beauty pageant, ah?" challenged Mauricio. "A girl from the interior!"

"You're drunk, hermanito," Tomás replied. "The Cartageneras consistently have the best legs," he said with a wink in my direction.

As Olguita changed the album, I lost track of the whiskeys I drank. Quite honestly, I didn't know when to stop. Tomás invited me to sit beside him on the couch and I did, fighting off a few unpleasant heart-flutters of the TV-kissing type. Together, we began to read titles off the album cover as the songs changed, and eventually I drifted into the pleasant scent of his cologne until the rise and fall of the music, like the sounds and scents of my own life, were somewhere far, far away.

At some point close to midnight I wobbled up for a bathroom break. I managed to keep my footing, pee, and wash my hands, but when I sized up my lovely lashes in the mirror, the right one seemed a little precarious. I thought I ought to remove it and wondered, *Does Olguita have a case?* It took a while to find paper cups. Then, carefully, I removed the lashes and plopped them into a cup. I stood staring at myself for a long time with an uneasy feeling. My de-lashed eyes looked slower and sadder than before.

Olguita knocked on the door. "Is everything okay?"

I had trouble speaking. "No sé," I admitted, opening the door. Something overwhelmed me, and I started crying.

With a worried look, Olguita hugged me and encouraged me to go sit in her bedroom. As she went to get her aunt, I heard the voices in the living room go low.

When Camila came and saw me crying, she turned to Olguita. "She's drunk. Evi will have a heart attack."

I began sobbing in earnest, telling them I couldn't go home, I just couldn't.

"Of course you can." Olguita patted my arm and laid me back on the bed, shoes and all. "As soon as the alcohol wears off a little."

I shook off her hand. "I can't!" I cried. "My father has a knife under his pillow and he'll kill me!"

They stared at each other. The living room grew completely silent behind us.

"I'm going to make her some tilo and tell Antonia it's time to go," Camila said. "Why don't you get a warm washcloth and wipe her face."

Olguita left, and I heard her saying good-bye to the guests. After the door slammed shut, I cried harder. What a spectacle I'd made, ruining Olguita's party. And no one had even come to say goodbye! I cried and cried until I wore myself out.

When Olguita returned, she placed a warm, wet towel over my face. I started to drift off as she and Camila talked, their shapes passing by me like the Guardian Angels the nuns had taught me about in elementary school. Afterward I didn't know what time it was, but Camila coaxed me into sitting up to drink the tilo. Then she said she would drive me home.

"Okay," I said, lifting my legs off the bed one at a time.

Olguita patted my hand. "It was a fun party, no?"

I nodded gratefully. "Your cousins are nice," I told her with sincerity. "I'm so sorry I ruined your party. So, so sorry."

"Oh no. Don't worry," she said, hugging me. "I had a good time."

I was ashamed of what I'd said about my father, but I didn't know how to take it back. Being with him *was* killing me, though not in the way I'd described. The knife my father actually owned was only a blunt, rusty instrument for cutting cane or high grasses—one that he probably kept for protection in that beat-up sheath under his bed. I didn't know why I'd brought that up out of the blue. Maybe it was just the weariness of trying to cover up so much. Every once in a while things squeezed out.

I concentrated on getting myself to Camila's car, but as we headed toward my house, I began to worry about what she would tell my mother. When we got there, I stumbled out toward the house and headed to my room without listening to whatever they were saying to each other. I let the voices slip away, my house becoming a separate thing, hard and fixed, to which I didn't belong. I was a whiff of cologne that floated, motherless and fatherless, through the dark air....

When I woke, Mami was plopping down a large cup of café con leche on my dresser. She sat on my bed and wagged a finger at me. "That vast quantity of alcohol is not to be repeated. ¿Sabes qué señorita?"

I nodded with my eyes closed as everything from the night before collided in my brain.

"Only a miracle prevented that drunken aroma from reaching your father," she added with the usual exaggeration. "I can't imagine what Camila was thinking. She said you didn't eat anything! Why didn't you, Gabriela? Un traguito, a social drink, is one thing—but multiple whiskey glasses! Since when did we bring you up to borrachear in public? Why didn't you follow Olguita's example? What's wrong with you? What if your father..."

Suddenly I remembered what I'd blurted out about the knife and my eyes popped open. But Mami merely appeared to be inspecting with the typical jaundiced eye my evening's apparel, scattered on the floor. I closed my eyes. *No, Camila must not have told her.*

Willing myself to sit up at last, I reached for the cup on the dresser. "Don't worry about it, Mami," I said, taking a sip of my café. "I don't even like the taste of liquor."

She glared at me. "Taste?" She shook her head in disappointment.

"And you think you have the maturity to work like your cousin Marisol?"

There went my hope of a summer escape from my angry father. "But the money would help us," I offered weakly.

"You can help with Avon," she retorted, standing to leave.

At least her positive comment about Olguita had reassured me that I could go on visiting.

Negativity returned, however, when Tío Victor called and I heard Mami advise him to cancel the doctor's appointment. "I'll resolve things somehow," she claimed.

I almost hoped then that my father *would* kill me with his sugar-cane cutter. Wouldn't Mami be sorry.

[ FIFTEEN ]

In the wake of my drunken episode, I occupied myself with collecting Avon orders to appease Mami while staying out of my father's way as much as possible. I lied to him that Camila had asked me to teach Olguita English. Camila's only reference to my embarrassing episode, fortunately, was a teasing remark that I should go for the aguardiente next time. Olguita just shook her head.

In the days before her departure, Olguita hauled out Hernán's old guitar to teach me some Colombian songs. Singing along to "El pescador barquero" helped put the sorry knife business out of my mind, though I knew the songs wouldn't sound so great with just me singing. Lydia, my only other friend, seemed pretty busy with some boyfriend and was hardly home. My summer days would soon fill with the papers my father had been amassing since the doctor talk failed so miserably. On the good news front, there was no-news from our friendly community police officer, so I finally stopped worrying about her.

The day before Olguita's trip home, I went over to help her pack and found an unusually tall woman, who'd apparently moved onto that street, visiting Camila. "Mi amor," Camila greeted me, apologizing that Olguita hadn't returned from her expedition and then inviting me to sit and wait.

"Bien," I said, taking the empty rocker beside the neighbor.

Camila introduced Lara, who smiled up at me out of curious gray eyes. She had a lanky build and thin shoulder bones that protruded. Her hair was a mass of evenly gray and black curls—surprisingly, she didn't dye her hair.

Lara was German, Camila explained, and had lived in Spain and Latin America.

In native Spanish Lara added that her husband Walter was from Argentina.

Her daughters, little wispy blondes, were running around with a boy from the neighboring yard. The girls spoke to their mother in a mix of Spanish and German that Camila said was enchanting. Lara laughed as if Camila had said something witty, and then Camila went inside to make us coffee.

"What grade are you in?" Lara inquired with a warm smile.

"I just finished ninth," I replied. "I switch to high school in September."

"I see. And what subjects does one study in that grade?"

I ran through my report card classifications, leaving out the questionable Physical Education curriculum.

Lara nodded, as if she were actually taking in what I'd said. "And do you enjoy these subjects equally?"

"I guess," I said, considering her question. Most people—namely, my relatives—wanted to hear that I was a good student but weren't too interested in the specifics. As long as their kids stayed out of trouble, parenting was on a need-to-know basis. "Mostly I like classes where we read."

Camila pushed through the screen door with a tray of demitasse cups and Lara switched back to Spanish. "Let me help you," she offered, opening the wooden folding table.

Camila's cups had colorful miniature paintings of ladies who stood in 1800s-style bustle dresses and parasols under great leafy trees. Lara smiled when she caught me admiring the cups. "I think they're pretty too," she said.

"At your service," said Camila with a proud tilt of her head.

Lara gulped her coffee. "Delicious," she pronounced, then turned to me. "Do you care for children, Gabriela?"

"You mean babysit?" I glanced at Camila, who was absentmindedly watching the older little blonde jump rope. "I think so."

"Wonderful. Would you like to take care of mine?"

"Yes," I replied. "I mean, if my mother says it's okay."

"Vale. Ask your mother if you can come Saturday, around nine in the morning. I have to go to the university for a few hours." She rose from the wicker chair, beckoned her daughters over, and asked me to phone her. "Camila can give you my number, yes?"

"Claro," Camila agreed.

Lara shook our hands, thanked Camila for the coffee, and left.

Camila mused aloud over the peculiarity of the handshake. "Muy raro," she commented.

I agreed that it was odd for women to shake hands. Out of the blue, like Lara herself with her wild salt-and-pepper hair. She seemed so foreign to tropical Miami.

When Olguita returned later, I helped her pack. As a parting gift, she bequeathed me a taupe eyeliner pencil. "Don't forget the twist," she added, curling her wrist and smiling. Regretfully we hugged farewell, and I felt as if I'd known her for longer than the few weeks she'd been in Miami.

The next day, with Olguita gone, I sat dejectedly in front of the typewriter and tried not to engage in direct conversations with my father. Things were resuming their uneasy, unreal state, though I remained on edge around him after the Manolo attack.

When Saturday came, I was only too happy to flee to my new

babysitting venture. Mami had assented to my helping out Camila's neighbor with the children but had asked me not to tell anyone in the family, including my father of course, but also the aunts and cousins, that I was to be paid.

I showed up at Lara's right at nine o'clock sharp.

Her house turned out to be as unusual as she was. It had little furniture and absolutely no trace of the Pine-Sol scent so popular in my household. Lara apologized about the sparse furnishings and ran around gathering books while pushing a wayward curl behind her ear. "We've only been here a few weeks," she explained. "Walter is teaching. He has to put in long hours at the university. I'm trying to do a little research too, for a book." She giggled nervously. "It's a bit difficult when one's children are young,"

The girls, Luna and Sol, were four and two. I found them playing with huge squashy red blocks in their room. The younger one cried when her mother left, but Luna and I distracted her by holding the blocks against our chests and throwing ourselves on the mattress that served as their bed. When I'd settled them with the game, I went to prepare their breakfasts.

I had to open the living room shades for more light. In that room, between two armchairs, a coffee table was scattered with magazines, newspapers, and index cards with neatly printed quotations. Books were stacked in piles that came up to my knees, and the stacks extended from that room into what was supposed to be a dining room. There was no dining table, though. Lara had downed her morning yogurt while standing in the kitchen. I guessed they ate dinner at the plastic table in the backyard.

While the girls' oatmeal cooked, I counted twenty-five stacks. The books were written in English, German, Spanish, and French. I moved carefully among the piles, in case they'd been arranged in a particular order, and proceeded to open books and scan contents, comparing the French with my Spanish here and there. Most of the books were hardcovers with heavy-duty titles like *Symbolic Logic*, *La poétique de l'espace*, *Modernism and Rubén Darío*, and *The Origins of Consciousness*. Lara's books distinguished her home from any other I'd seen before. My parents and relatives owned some books, mainly paperbacks that reminded me of fotonovelas, but I rarely saw anyone read anything except for my father. Of course, it was hard to say how much of what he did could be called reading. To me it seemed that when he lifted paragraphs into letters, he *wanted* to understand, but the understanding was another fantasy.

By the time Lara returned, breathless and loaded with more books, I'd decided that either she or Walter was a history buff. She smiled, thanked me for putting the girls down for naps on time, and gave me five dollars for the four hours she'd been gone. "Next week?" she asked.

"Sure."

I waltzed home and found Mami popping overgrown eyes out of old potatoes.

"Lara wants me again next week," I informed her.

Mami nodded without looking up. "But don't forget what I told you," she said.

"I won't," I agreed.

"No sé cómo vamos a hacer," Mami continued, moving on to the daily mantra. "How am I going to put together the total?" Aloud, she subtracted phone and gas balances from what was left of last month's income, then deducted water, electricity, etc. It was such a wearisome arithmetic.

"Here." I put the bill Lara gave me on the counter.

"No, mi'ja," Mami said with embarrassment. "You keep it for your things." She dried her hand on a towel, shoved the money into my pocket, and picked up her peeler.

I grabbed a knife to help with the potatoes.

Confident about my new employment, I decided to broach a

matter I'd been brooding over. I'd finally pinpointed the root of my father's evil anger at the world: those people who'd ripped off his money. Why had that one incident meant so much?

Mami raised her eyebrows. "Those are your father's cuentos, mi'ja. Don't pay attention to them."

Cuentos? So she believed the things Papi said were just stories?

Lowering her voice, she explained that he'd always been paid for his work. The trouble was that it didn't pay enough. "But nobody owes us, mi'ja. On the contrary, *we* owe. The bank, Southern Bell, that Massachusetts factory...."

Off she went, trying to fix the pieces instead of what was broken. I put my knife down in frustration and turned to leave.

"Wait," she said, motioning toward the cabinet where she stashed important mail for me to read. "A letter came."

I retrieved an opened envelope from behind the jar of naranja agria. The letter, written in Spanish, was from Miss Lucy Prado, Family Unit Officer at the Dade County Office of Protective Services. "You can read this," I said, puzzled but becoming alarmed as I skimmed the letter.

"I need you to make the appointment," she explained, peeling away.

"It doesn't say you and Papi *have* to go."

"Of course we do. Why would they send a letter?"

"This is the government, Mami," I said, shaking the letter in front of her. "It's like...going to the police. You know Papi can't do that. He's still in his probation. You want them to find out he has...dementia or something and can't take care of his own kids?" Unattended minors, I remembered El Chino calling it. "*You* might get in trouble, Mami," I warned anxiously. "Isn't there enough trouble with *him*?"

My mother stared. "First of all, your father is forty years old!

No one who is forty gets dementia." She aimed the potato peeler at me. "Además, you kids are lucky you have a house and don't live in some miserable place where people are killing each other back and forth through eternity!"

"Who's that shouting?" my father called from his room. "I'm working!"

"Nobody! Calm yourself!" Mami answered, before resuming her furious potato attack. "Help, please, Gabriela, instead of giving me things to worry about."

"I always help," I said, staring into the pile of peels in front of us until they became the muddy fields of the Andes. Quietly I shoved her letter into its envelope and put the envelope back in the cabinet. My mother wasn't going to save anyone, not even herself. "Fine," I said. "I'll call those people for you."

Bitterly, I tramped into my room and tossed my babysitting money on top of the nightstand. Money wasn't my problem. What undid me was the living balance sheet my mother shoved my way: plus this, plus that, always more of her demanding mathematics.

The only math I believed in was the kind that distanced me from our problems. Like skewed lines in space or the infinitesimal points between any two others, no matter how close. *That* kind of math, the geometry of imagination, was the only kind that had ever helped me.

As I'd been instructed, I scheduled her Protective Services interview for a date in late July when she didn't work. Later, I called Tío Victor, who very rationally agreed that my father had no business paying visits to inquisitive public officials. It eased my mind to turn my mother over to my uncle, who indicated he would contact El Chino, or maybe Tío Paco's old divorce lawyer, about the peculiar interview business.

•  •  •

Saturday, I eagerly tapped at Lara's door again.

"Come in!" she called out. From the living room, I could hear her bickering with Walter about some private school where she wanted to send their daughters. He declared the school too expensive. Apparently they had math problems as well.

When Walter came out, I saw that he was taller than Lara. He had a young face, like a kid whose body had grown up before he did, and he wore wire-rimmed glasses. Nodding briefly, he downed his coffee and went out to the car to wait for her.

Lara emerged with her bedraggled hairdo and gave me an apologetic laugh. "Walter doesn't think ahead about the children's needs," she offered. "It's the woman's job, no?"

I returned a half-smile, wondering if Lara had any friends. "Is your family in Germany?" I thought to ask.

"My father is there. My mother died long ago." She gulped some coffee. "You know, when I was a girl, he was a diplomat and took me all over the world. That's how we ended up in your beautiful birthplace." As she talked, Lara quickly made herself and Walter lunches while taking her unstocked groceries out of bags. We heard Walter beep his horn.

"I can put those away," I offered politely.

"Oh thank you!" Lara swallowed the rest of her coffee. "Let the girls sleep as long as possible, please. They're not feeling well."

"Okay."

After I'd stocked the groceries, I heated milk in a saucepan and prepared instant Nescafe. As I waited for the girls to wake, I looked through the book piles for something interesting to read. No novel was in sight, and I was reluctant to upset the piles by digging down too far. The closest reader-friendly material I found was the *Modernism and Rubén Darío* book, which at least concerned literature, so I sat down to read that.

Three chapters were devoted to one of Darío's poems, "Divagación," through which I wandered, in homage to the title, until compelled to read the whole thing. Unicorns, horns of gold, incense burners, roses! What a strangely beautiful world *that* was! It was like my grandfather's. The book's text, however, was harder to understand with its maze of undefined references I'd never heard of: *dithyramb, aboulia, gauchesque.* I skimmed the Prologue to determine what "modernism" meant, which turned out to be a literary movement in Latin America and not modernism as in "now." According to the book, people had had difficulty seeing themselves as Latin American instead of Spanish—with breaking away from their past.

*Lara is modern*, I concluded, *as in "now" and as in breaking away from the past too.* I'd gathered from her comments that she was in favor of Women's Liberation, a popular discussion topic at my school. Was my family liberated, I wondered, since the females—my mother and I—planned and organized around the males? On the other hand, we had to do everything around my father's temper, so maybe *he* had the power. Still, didn't we kind of control him with our lies? I put the book down, confused. My parents were nothing like Lara and Walter, with their equal jobs and the independent bank accounts I'd heard about from the morning quarrel. But Lara had to care for the girls and deal with groceries on top of her equal research. Modernity apparently required more than the old-fashioned ways.

By the time she and Walter returned hours later, I'd bathed, dressed, and fed Solita and Luna. I'd even helped them draw pictures they were allowed to tape right onto their walls. Walter greeted me with a brief nod as Lara pulled the girls into her arms and checked their foreheads for fever. "Are you better, my little stars?"

When Walter saw the Modernism book on the coffee table, he glanced at me. "Were you reading this?"

"Oh, I'm sorry, I'll put it back," I answered apologetically.

"No, leave it. Please."

"I didn't really understand it," I admitted.

Lara stood with Solita in her arms to see the book. "Oh, maybe the words," she said dismissively. "The ideas are simple."

Walter looked askance at her.

"You know what I find so interesting?" Lara put Solita down with a kiss. Her gray eyes twinkled as she looked from Walter to me. "Darío was from Central America. And Modernism, of course, united the continent just as European colonialism had broken it into parts. He was a bridge, like his country." She touched her fingertips together to make the bridge.

"That's too much," Walter argued. "Bolivarian nonsense."

Even though I knew who Simón Bolívar was, I wasn't quite sure what Walter meant. But Lara hadn't finished her point. She held up a hand. "What happens," she continued, looking toward me but aiming her remarks at him, "is that Walter is not a true modernist. Isn't that interesting? Given my being the European and all."

Walter studied her without any expression, then turned to me. "Would you like me to drive you home, Gabriela?"

"That's okay," I replied. "I can walk."

The girls protested my leaving, but I gave them double cheek kisses as their mother had done. I slipped the money Lara had given me for babysitting into my pocket.

"We'll see you again, yes?" Lara asked.

"Sure," I replied. "Bye, Walter."

He lifted his hand in reply.

With disappointment, I declined Lara's next babysitting request, as I had a stored up jumble of petroleum letters to complete before our family outing. With Pablo's aid, I finished the typing quickly, avoiding deviations I no longer dared attempt.

Afterward, we headed to Tío Victor's for the twins' Confirmation party.

Once there, I couldn't help but notice how the fathers, including my own, got to decide so much about family life. Even small things, such as which room the fathers would play cards in, were determined in the same unquestioned way as the big ones, like which country we lived in and who was allowed to work outside the home. In my cousin's bedroom, I asked Raquel if she thought Latino families were more sexist than others.

"Well, definitely that stuff about girls not being allowed to leave home for live-away colleges," she said. "I had to talk my parents into that one."

Such talk would never fly at my house, I knew. "But Raquel, do you think your mother and father are equal?" I probed.

"Mami says she can get Papi to do anything she wants," Raquel replied, smiling at her mother's puffing.

"Your father's nice," I acknowledged, then persisted, "How about Tío Lucho and Tía Elena?"

Raquel laughed so hard that her headband slipped across her eyes. "I vote for Tía Elena!"

I laughed too. True, our aunt bossed Tío Lucho around. But then again, he got to call the shots on other things such as their trailer park residence and Marisol's braces. From the bed, I untucked one foot from under me and swung it out to compare its shiny patent leather toe with the worn one of the other shoe. Shiny or worn, the two shoes were equally ugly.

Raquel watched me through the mirror as she readjusted her headband. "You can't really compare your mother and father to other parents, Gabi. You have to wait for your father to get better."

I examined my ugly shoes. "Yeah, but how?"

Her brow furrowed. "I don't know. Maybe my parents will come up with something." She came over and put an arm across my shoulder. "Don't worry, Gabi."

The following day I realized Raquel must have known something was up because I stumbled upon my mother oddly grinding a pill with the majadero we used for garlic and spices. "What's that, Mami?" I asked.

"It's for your father," she replied nonchalantly, pressing the pestle downward. "A sleeping pill. Don't say anything to your brothers," she cautioned.

*Aha!* Now I knew why there hadn't been any blow-ups. "Where did they come from?" I asked, lifting the small brown envelope.

"Dr. Sanabria. Your Tía Rita gets them. I'm just giving your father half a pill to relax."

On the envelope, "Dalmane" was scribbled above the signature of that Cuban doctor who'd gotten me out of Phys. Ed.—if in fact he *was* a doctor. "Is that okay, Mami, for Papi to take Tía Rita's pills?"

"Oh, they're not hers. She just bought them for us." Mami stirred the ground pill into an orange juice and raw egg tonic that my father had taken to drinking—it was yet another fantasy of making himself stronger that he'd heard about on *The Jack LaLane Show.*

"Will the pills do anything besides make Papi sleepy?" I asked with concern, wondering about the legality.

"It's only a calmante. Your aunt swears by them. She takes them now and then."

As I took my father his glass of calm I felt a bit uneasy. For one thing, I'd read *Valley of the Dolls*, which introduced me to downers and uppers and the fact that people overdosed on such drugs. But if Tía Rita, Tío Victor, and that could-be-a-doctor in Little

Havana all believed it would prevent another vicious attack like
the Manolo-bashing, then who was I to doubt that Dalmane
was a force of good in the world? Besides, as Pablo had shrewdly
observed about pot: Who would ever find out? And even if the
pills *were* illegal, maybe such law-breaking was morally justified
because it kept my father from hurting people.

Later that week, after phone calls were traded among my
mother, my uncle, Miss Lucy Prado, and our ever popular family
lawyer El Chino, it was decided that Mami would attend her interview alone. Though relieved to hear that my father was out of the
picture, as calmed as he was by the calmante, I was bothered that
all the capable men had left my mother alone with this responsibility. "Why isn't Tío or somebody going with you?" I probed as I
watched her repair a run on her nylons with pink nail polish.

"The lawyer doesn't recommend it," she said tersely.

"Why not?"

She blew on the polish to dry and avoided answering.

Finally, I suggested, "I better come, Mami."

"No, they speak Spanish," she said, adjusting her stocking to be
sure it didn't run.

"But somebody should be with you."

"Well *you* aren't permitted!" she blurted angrily. Then, adjusting her tone of voice to an ordinary level, she added, "No children."

I opened my mouth to demand further explanation, but I
noticed—like the bright fuchsia threads that flashed above her
knee when her skirt moved—the trace of vergüenza in her face. I
knew that my father's behavior had often shamed Mami, despite
her denials, but couldn't she dissemble as much as she needed
to without him present? This particular shame, though, seemed
oddly and sadly all her own.

She wasn't terribly forthcoming after her interview either.

"Nada, nada," she said, dismissing it. "That Cuban woman, who as a matter of fact isn't old enough to be a mother, wanted to lecture me about how *differently* things are done here and how everyone can improve. Hmph! As if Americans didn't punish their children!"

"What punishment was she talking about?" I inquired uneasily.

"None!" my mother shot back.

Well, I decided, whatever had happened, there was no point in fighting her over it. My uncle and El Chino had left me out, so they were in charge of this one.

My own charges—Lara's peppy girls and my tenuously calmed peligro of a father—were more than enough to keep me busy.


By the end of July, the already humid temperatures had risen high into the 90s. Walter installed an air-conditioner in Luna and Solita's bedroom, and I gratefully took to napping with the girls there. Solita liked falling asleep in my arms.

"You're spoiling her," Lara told me a few appointments later when she found us like that. She helped me loosen the child's grip on my neck, and we slid Solita onto her pillow.

"Her skin is so soft," I whispered.

"Mmm," Lara whispered back. "Our world hasn't toughened her up yet." She touched my cheek lightly, as if it were soft too. Then, as was our new custom whenever Lara returned home from her own research without Walter, who spent increasingly longer stretches at the university, she and I took our coffees outside. We sat at the plastic table underneath a large umbrella, and Lara inquired about what I was reading. She'd read practically every novel I checked out of the library, but this time she wanted to know what I read in Spanish.

"Nothing, really," I responded. "I got tired of those fotonovelas."

Lara stared at me in amazement. "But Gabi, there is an *abundance* of good literature published in the Spanish language. You don't have to read comic books."

"They only have English books at the Chekika branch," I informed her.

"Oh, that's absurd. We have so many books here!" And with that, she went rummaging for novels by Spanish and Latin American women writers. "Here," she said, returning with a pile, "a community of heroines."

Almost immediately I became absorbed in the Spanish-language novels she plied me with. My father's calmante had slowed down the production of illogical documents, so, in the timelessness of summer, I stayed up reading until three or four in the morning.

Lydia rarely called. The hollow created by her absence and Olguita's made me grateful for the friendship I was developing with Lara, if you could call it that, what with her being an adult. But I admired the way Lara lived so confidently inside her thoughts, unlike me, always doubting my own.

On my last babysitting Saturday before high school began, we sat outside again with our coffees, and Lara asked casually, "Tell me how your family is, Gabi. Is Evi still working hard?"

I nodded. "She'll be starting full-time when we go back to school."

"Wonderful. I'm sure she'll be glad for the extra income. And your father?"

"He's fine." I sipped my coffee slowly so that I wouldn't get too sweaty. I got the impression Lara understood more than whatever Mami had shared—or that Camila had, if even she knew the whole of it. I wished I could be more open, since Lara was kind and didn't seem like a blabbermouth. But if she let out anything I'd revealed, how ashamed my mother would feel!

"Poor man." Lara put her feet up on another chair. She was wearing socks and brown loafers with her skirt. She wasn't exactly what people in Miami would call a snappy dresser, but she seemed comfortable in whatever she wore. "And you, Gabi?" she asked, "Did you finish *Nada*?"

"Oh, it was great! I left it on your coffee table. What a family that girl had," I exclaimed enthusiastically.

"Mmm. I thought you'd like Andrea." Lara's gray eyes drifted over me. "So fatalistic as young women can be."

I asked Lara if she thought love had to be fatal.

"Oh, I don't know about that," she replied. "Maybe some kinds of love." Then she told me about the Greek classification system. There were four kinds, she explained. First, there was *eros*, passionate love. Next came *philos*, friendship, and then *storge*, the familial form. Last, but not least, there was *agape*, divine or selfless love.

"But great love," she concluded, with a look so soulful that I didn't know who it was meant for, "contains all four."

## SIXTEEN

THE DALMANE TAMED MY FATHER'S MOODS, but his writing seemed more incoherent than ever. At least when he used to compose job letters, the structure anchored his free floating associations, probably because having to address someone forced him to try to communicate. But since the advent of his "thesis," nothing structured his writing. I couldn't tell why one page followed another, though he became distraught if he dropped a page and disturbed the mysterious sequencing. He'd started using index cards too—mine, of course—which unfortunately reminded me of my exhibit failure. But at least that inspired me to vow fervently never to fantasize beyond what I had the power to control.

High school became my only antidote to evenings at home with a drugged, deluded father. Unfortunately, because of the desegregation lawsuit, my Alina gang from the other side of Flagler had been redistricted to Tamiami High, which left just Lydia and me at Royal Palm High. Here, students were divided almost evenly between Latino and Jewish, and the school was so big that Lydia too quickly disappeared into the masses flooding stairwells. At the end of orientation week, I eagerly signed myself up for a part-time work program, the AfterCorps, that ran three days a week. Since it was at school, Mami agreed that we could sneak it over on my father.

In ACs I was pleased to find quiet Claudio Sotomayor, whom I remembered from eighth grade Spanish class. He still had that tiny black stain in his eye, as if the pupil had smeared, but other than that, he'd actually gotten cute. He was taller, his black hair curlier, and he had a lazy smile like Pablo's. When the rest of us bickered over plum assignments—like wrapping dittos around the spirit duplicator and cranking its lever until whiffs of fresh purple ink filled our lungs—Claudio politely accepted whatever tasks were left.

In that uncomplicated environment, I could almost trust in a world beyond the fears and pressures I was used to at home. Gladly, I accepted extra jobs offered on off days, while willingly signing my weekly AC paycheck over to my grateful mother.

Sadness, however, soon came calling.

One morning, sobs woke me from sleep, and I sat upright—only to realize that the crying was coming from outside. I peered out my window and saw Mami comforting her friend Camila. The sun was shining on them and the dewy grass under their chancletas shone too, but the two women in their faded housecoats and bare faces looked like rag-tag survivors from some tragic fire. I dove tiredly back under the covers until the clanging of the café con leche pot and coffee aroma lured me into the kitchen. The back door was open. I poured myself a cup and went outside, where Mami sat drinking her own coffee in a chair under the mango tree.

Grabbing the other lawn chair, I wiped dew off with one hand. "Did something happen to Hernán?" I asked, sitting and squinting at Mami in the sunlight.

She lifted a hand wearily. "He's back in the clinic. It's terrible."

"Poor Camila," I said with sympathy. "What's she going to do?"

"Do?" Mami frowned, shaking her head. "A todo se hace uno."

I reflected for a moment on the import of that proverb. "Just because you can't do anything about leukemia," I offered finally, "that doesn't mean you have no power at all."

With a melancholic look in her eyes, Mami replied, "Ay Gabriela, someday you'll have to learn what it means to be a woman. Don't give yourself illusions just because we're in this country."

I leaned forward in my chair. "But things *are* different here, Mami. Look at you. You're the head of the household."

"That's a disgrace, Gabriela, not something to be proud of."

"But why? What's so horrible about women working and becoming independent?"

She gave me a long, hard look. "When the proper time comes," she said, "you can get married and leave this family to form one of your own. Así, like I did," she added, "not without sacrifices."

"That's the problem!" I burst out in exasperation. "Why should you make the sacrifices and be stuck with them forever just because he—"

"It's *not* forever," Mami said firmly. "Those pills are relaxing your father. You don't realize, Gabriela, how hard he had to work all these years. He needed a rest. Later on, you'll see, he'll start to find his happiness. Then he'll look for the right job." Before I could rebut any of that with a point-by-point summary of the manuscript-without-end that my "relaxed" father had been creating since he psychotically attacked his own son, she'd stood up. "I have to get dressed. Are you coming in?"

I shook my head with disappointment. If only I could have opened her eyes, illuminated the truth for her as Lara often did for me with her repertoire of knowledge. But all that came to my mind was a simple dicho I'd heard Tía Rita say many times: Quien espera, desespera.

Too much hope deceives.

●    ●    ●

That afternoon, Mr. Lanham, whom I'd been surprised to find teaching my World Geography class at Royal Palm, unexpectedly borrowed me from the AC office for a project in his classroom. Its walls were covered with great posters of colorfully costumed people, mountains with snow, and the pyramids at Tucume, Perú. He handed me the staple remover. "Okay, Gabi. Take the old ones down." He patted his shirt pocket for cigarettes, but there were none in there.

I pushed a chair against the wall, climbed up, and started unstapling. While I worked, he unzipped a flat, wide case and emptied the contents onto his desk. "We're going to Giza next," he explained, studying the fresh batch of posters. He looked up. "Do you know where Giza is, Gabriela?"

"No, Mr. Lanham."

"Egypt. Some of the greatest achievements of all time happened in Egypt. A Wonder of the World, as you will soon learn." He held up a crisp poster printed with huge pyramids, stark and perfect. "Bigger than Huallamarca," he pointed out. Then he confided to me that he'd worked in the Nile Valley as a graduate student, doing his thesis on the Great Nubian Civilization.

*Maybe Mr. Lanham is lonely here too,* I thought as I carried a Peru poster to his desk.

"Trade you," he offered, handing me a new one. "What colleges are you thinking of, Gabi?"

*Colleges?* Recalling my morning's foray with Mami into the unchartered waters of women's independence, I could only mumble, "Um, Miami-Dade?"

"Oh, you can do better," he replied authoritatively. "What are you interested in?"

"History, I guess. Maybe geography." I positioned the poster to see if it was even.

Mr. Lanham looked pleased. "Oh?"

"Well, not so much the dates and stuff," I said apologetically. "More like how people and places got to be what they are."

"Cultural anthropology," he pronounced with conviction. "That's a great field." He handed me the pushpins. "You know, there are such good financial aid packages, your parents shouldn't worry about cost."

I smiled agreeably, though sparkling colleges felt light-years away from life on my planet. Even if I got to attend college, it would be next to impossible to obtain an exemption from living at home. *Blessed Virgin, will I really have to marry someone?* I despaired silently. *Who? How?* I didn't want to get married! The search for a passageway out confounded me even more than the unsolvable puzzle of my father's mind.

I resolved not to think about those intractable problems, though, as I quietly finished installing Mr. Lanham's posters. The straightforward task brought me a simple pleasure. Being a girl in high school was going to have to be enough for the moment.


Mr. Lanham led us into Egypt by way of a local museum that housed a sarcophagus; then he launched us on research expeditions of our own. My adventures with the spirit duplicator and my anti-adventures transcribing my father's hieroglyphics inspired me to ask if I could investigate the invention of paper rather than the popular topic of pyramids.

"That would be great, Gabi." Mr. Lanham wrote down the Latin name of the plant, *Cyperus Papyrus,* for my research list.

At home later, the assignment released me from my father's grip to visit the library. His moods had become more agreeable with the sleeping pills, and sometimes he even took naps; I could almost swallow Mami's diagnosis that all he needed to become well was a good rest.

Quickly, however, I was disappointed to learn that the Egyptian invention was less like paper than a cardboard mat, and I complained about my pitiful findings to Lara and Walter when I babysat that weekend. Surprisingly, Walter returned later that day with a papermaking book he'd borrowed for me from the University of Miami library. He watched tolerantly as Lara and I pored over the beautiful illustrations of the ancient process.

In ACs a few days later, even the normally reserved Claudio asked where I'd gotten that nice art book.

"It's for my geography project," I replied.

As he gently opened the book, I wondered if the black teardrop in his eye affected his vision.

"You can still make this paper," he told me in Spanish, admiring the illustrations. "But nobody uses it for routine writing anymore. It's more of an art."

"How do you know?" I asked.

"In Venezuela, I have an uncle who does this. The ancient indígenas made paper in a similar way."

"Really?" I glanced at the oversized black pad he always carried. "Do you know how to?"

He extended a slow, sweet smile to me. "No, I have other traditions."

Without understanding what he truly meant, I grinned back. Claudio had such an oblique, professorial way of speaking. Maybe his formality came from spending so much time with his abuelo. Claudio had told me that he helped care for his sick grandfather, sometimes missing ACs on account of medical appointments. I couldn't help but envy the fact that his grandfather was afflicted with a physical illness one could discuss in the open. The secrecy over my father's condition, though, wasn't the part that most distressed me. My main fear was that he would really hurt someone—and who knew what horrible crisis would follow?

But months had passed without an eruption, and my fear began to fade—and with it, the whole saga of crimes and punishments and lost green cards. It was hard to believe that the end of my father's probation was actually approaching.

What never diminished were his delusions. One Saturday only a couple of weeks after I'd started on my school project, Mami waylaid me from a library trip to help clean the paper mausoleum that had become her bedroom. My father wouldn't throw any of his stuff away—it was like his family, now that no one really conversed with him. "¡Estoy harta!" Mami muttered, swooshing across the buildup with her broom. How sick and tired indeed she must be, I sympathized silently while heading into her bathroom with a bucket of cleaning supplies.

My father chuckled.

"I don't find anything funny," she said indignantly. "I live here too."

"Everything will be improved," he replied, "when we receive the new house."

From the bathroom, I had to shake my head as I scrubbed.

"Don't start with those cuentos," she warned him, while walking toward me with a sheet of newsprint that I took, dampened under the faucet, and tamped to the floor like a dust pan for the debris.

My father leaned over his pencil and wrote so hard that his point broke. "You'll see," he pledged, sharpening the pencil point anew.

"I'll go blind first," she answered with biting sarcasm.

*They're both crazy,* I thought, and eventually left them—my father, writing himself through a frenzy of imagined education into imagined riches, and my mother, sticking to her tried and true forms of ignorance.

Afterward, I went to the library all the more determined to ground everything in my own life on objective, irrefutable fact. That became more complicated with my report, though, the more facts I read. In the book Walter had borrowed, I discovered that the true inventors of paper weren't even Egyptian, but Chinese. One Chinese: Ts'ai Lun. He mashed up plant fibers in a vat, then filtered them through a screen. When the intertwined fiber dried up, presto!—a smooth sheet like the paper we used nowadays. They named his invention Distinguished Ts'ai's Paper, and he became known as "The Saint of Paper." But as those facts took me very far from Egypt, I made an appointment to see Mr. Lanham.

He nodded thoughtfully over my draft as he read the story of the Islamic warriors who'd captured a caravan of Chinese papermakers and brought papermaking to the Muslim world—and eventually to Europe when the Moors invaded Spain. "Interesting material, Gabi," he said approvingly. He said he wanted to enter my report in the state Ambassadors competition, but I would have to revise it into an essay. "You don't need any more research," he cautioned. "All you need to do is think about what it means to you."

Fátima, a smart girl I sat beside in class, suggested I write about what a society would be without paper. "They'll like that. Trust me." Fátima had very strong opinions and was the kind of person who would clearly go places—whipping out lists before each class; tucking away elaborated outlines afterward.

"But I think it should cover the things *I* care about."

She shrugged as if she knew better.

I decided to seek Lara's advice.

On Saturday, as we sipped our coffees, she admitted that she was struggling with the same questions I had about the implications of research. Her research was for a book she was trying to write on how women had evolved physically. "You see, Gabi, there is not so much neutrality. Histories depend on your point of view. You have to consider the prism through which you have decided that this particular history is important."

"You mean like me as a student?"

"Or it could be as a Latina."

I nodded gratefully.

Talking to Lara always gratified me. She led me to believe my thoughts mattered. Because of my father, I'd become fearful that the germs of craziness could spread through my brain from too much thinking, like a fatal tropical disease. But with Lara, thinking—even a lot of it—seemed normal.

What was my prism?


People had invented great things from their limited and humble environments, I wrote finally. The story of paper was imagination in its purest form. In places as different from each other as the Egyptian river's reedy banks were from the sacred forests of the Otomi people in Mexico, papermaking possibilities evolved and were passed along by each culture until the world knew them all and had more choices. My prism was Freedom.

I finished and turned in my essay after the Columbus Day holiday.

"Fantástico," Mr. Lanham said, mispronouncing the *a* and *o* with his American accent. "Geography is the material everything derives from," he quoted, putting my essay in his folder. "Once you understand the relationship of a people to their environment, you have real history. Not the history that can be cooked up. That's Wolé Soyinka." He gave me a ditto sheet with the quote on it, and I hurried to the AC office to mimeograph his copies. With disappointment, I learned that the school was going to be purchasing a much-desired Xerox machine. I had to admit, as I cranked out Mr. Lanham's copies that afternoon, that the pages did all turn out slightly different on the duplicator because of the way the ink spread. But I *liked* that the copies the spirit duplicator made were unique, that each spirit was an original.

Soon, I began to feel similarly about Fátima, who chose me to partner with on an Antilles map project. Fátima had, in addition to her elaborate outlines, a grand unified theory of how everything led to a bright future. There was no room for fatalism with that girl—she'd broken free. As I headed eagerly toward her house for the first time, I hoped we could become good friends, especially now that Lydia had dumped me big-time for her boyfriend.

When I arrived, a huge German shepherd barked at the gate, and a muscular man with a mustache, the strict father Fátima had warned me about, came out and restrained the dog by the collar.

"I'm Gabriela," I said meekly in Spanish.

"Sí, I know. Pasa." He gestured toward the house.

Fátima, wearing her trademark ponytail with the tortoise-shell barrette that matched her glasses, led me to a room she shared with two sisters. "My oldest sister, Mirén, works at the mall with my mom," Fátima explained. "At the Imperio Femenino Boutique." As she tucked notebooks into her satchel, she pointed with her chin at the middle sister, who was talking on the phone. "That's Rosalía. She basically communicates in orders."

Sure enough, as we left the room, Rosalía interrupted her call to tell Fátima, "Hey, use your own card. I don't want fines on mine."

Fátima put out a what-did-I-tell-you hand.

"It's the opposite in my family," I said, walking behind her. "I order my brothers around. But honestly, they need to be ordered." As much as I hated to admit it to myself, though, Pablo hadn't been heeding too many orders lately. He'd quit helping me with typing too, because he preferred to go off with friends to have fun.

At Chekika Library, Fátima and I headed toward the wide table in the back. For a moment I missed the good old days of Gothic novels with Lydia. When Fátima unpacked a light blue test booklet from her bag, I gave her a quizzical look and she explained, "My Truth Notebook." She flipped through it to show me a repository of handwritten quotations.

"What's it for?" I asked.

"English papers. You stick Truths into your paper to illustrate your point. There's all these books full of proverbs," she said, motioning toward the library walls. "You want to start one?" She offered me a blank booklet.

"Sure," I replied agreeably.

After we'd completed our archipelago maps, I went gamely truth-searching until I'd perused enough proverbs to last me a lifetime. Then I began to roam around in the Dewey Decimal System until I found a poetry book I liked and carried it back to our table. Reading through the book, I was delighted to find lines an English teacher had once written in my yearbook: *Through the field wonderful, with eyes a little sorry, another comes, also picking flowers.* Immediately, I copied the e.e. cummings lines into my booklet.

"Huh," said Fátima, tapping the desk with her pencil. "I hadn't thought of putting in poems."

I was pleased that I'd managed to impress her.

The next afternoon, as if I'd conjured her ghost while at the library, Lydia herself appeared at my house unexpectedly. "Want to go to Osco's?" she asked brightly.

"Okay," I replied. Glad to see her, I put away my father's latest typing gibberish.

All the way to the store Lydia complained about her guy troubles. The tricks she'd tried to keep him from straying and the stupid ways he was always lying. "Like I call him when he's not supposed to be home, right, and I catch him, but he just makes up more lies."

I said nothing while attempting to stare down the Calle Ocho oglers.

Abruptly, Lydia turned and said, "Chica, you're so serious lately. How come you hardly talk anymore?"

"What's wrong with being serious?" I countered.

"I didn't say anything was wrong with it. I was just asking." She tossed her hair back awkwardly, reminding me that her old pixie cut had been way cuter.

I shrugged as if I didn't care about what she'd said. Maybe I didn't. As much as I'd admired Lydia for her toughness, in reality she was the one who'd changed. She let that nasty boyfriend boss her around and then acted like it was no problem that he didn't bother to honor his promises. She was doomed to live her mother's life. That truth seemed written in the stars.

A few afternoons after we'd embarked on our truth-collecting quest together, Fátima confided in me about her parents and their strong views of Cuba as a terrible place to live. "My dad's finally working in an accounting office again," she shared, "like he did before Fidel."

"Before Fidel" was the line, I knew, that forever divided Cuban time in the world.

I told Fátima about a newsreel we'd been shown in junior high of the "Freedom Flights"—how the TV people pointed out that although thousands of refugees came here after the Revolution, they were only a small fraction of Cuba's population. "How horrible could it really be, Fátima?"

She got up and closed her bedroom door. "Well, my family lost a lot of stuff, Gabi," she said soberly, sitting back next to me. "The Castro government took our house and my grandfather's jewelry store. We pretended to be going on vacation and put on tons of jewelry. That's all we had to live on when we got here. My father thought the Americans would kick Fidel out, but then that didn't happen so we had to stay. Thank God the Church helped us." She gave me a grave look. "Whatever you do," she warned, "never say the word 'Revolution' in front of my parents. Say 'Dictatorship.'"

"Okay," I promised, then admitted, "It wouldn't be too much fun for me to go back to Colombia either." As the old dark cloud passed over me, I realized that in different ways, Fátima and I were both stranded.

"My father says we can't believe what relatives write in letters," she added. "About how great everything is, how all the black people live in nice houses in Velado and Miramar, and how everyone gets free medicine." She shrugged her shoulders. "It's hard to know for sure."

Whatever the truth was about her country, I could only imagine tiny Cuba afloat on the vast Caribbean, with survivors hanging on to their beloved island, whatever its faults.

When I got home, my mother complained about how long I'd tarried at Fátima's.

"Mami, we study," I said, rummaging through the cabinet for a Coke can I'd hidden from Pablo but not finding it.

A minute later the phone rang. Fátima again.

"You saw her less than twenty minutes ago," Mami said with annoyance. "How much more is there to say to each other?"

"¡Ay Mami, por favor!" I replied, hanging up. "She just wants to invite me to church tomorrow with her family."

"Hmm," my mother answered, stymied about how to object to that.

I headed outside for a replacement Coke from the 7-Eleven. The afternoon was so bright, the light looked artificial. As I walked, I mused over the notebook truths I'd been collecting with Fátima and the truths my own family collected. Crazy things my father said and wrote were often composed of truthful information, like

facts from the The *World Book Encyclopedia,* but they were twisted
into an incoherent and shapeless form that was the opposite of
truth. No, facts alone would not net my father the millions he
dreamed of; they hadn't even gotten him a job.

I caught up with Manolo en route from his home-away-from-
home job. "Hey," I called out. "Did you remember Mami's lightbulbs?"

Manolo stopped and frowned at the traffic signal. "Somebody
should light a bulb in her head."

"What?" I responded, taken aback.

He glanced up as the signal changed to Walk. "You know she's
giving the old man pills?"

"She told you?"

"I saw her. She doesn't tell me shit."

I reached out a sympathetic hand, but something like guilt
pulled it back. I wished I could explain that Mami telling me
"shit" didn't count for much, that she didn't like me any better.
But Manolo was another island broken off from the mainland to
which we'd both belonged. He'd drifted from Pablo too since the
broken leg episode.

"How does she know that stuff doesn't make the old man
worse?" Manolo blurted out to me. "He keeps making up new
shit, like the house thing."

"Tía Rita takes those pills. She says they're okay."

"Yeah, but she's not crazy."

"That's true. It makes him quieter, though."

"I guess," Manolo concurred.

That time when the light turned green, we went our separate
ways.

As I continued toward the store, I pictured the disturbing image
of my father, blindfolded and tied to his chair while our family
surrounded him. The ground-up sleeping pills were an antitruth

serum. Instead of confessing the truth, my father was forced to sleepwalk in our land of make-believe.

Make-believe number one: the "vitamins."

Make-believe number two: the lies we fabricated around things that might upset him, like Mami's job.

Make-believe number three: the incessant typing and retyping of illusory words that lulled him into faith that his delusions were real.

We were poisoning him with antitruths. *Why?*

Because it was easier than dealing with his temper, with its consequences.

And, maybe, because we felt sorry for him. Because the truth might break his heart.

Mami disappeared for most of the next day with Camila, whose husband had been steadily declining since his hospitalization. When the phone rang, I didn't realize that the Palacio had called until Pablo came to stand in my doorway.

"Guess what?" he said, throwing me a *Sentinel* left over from his delivery. "Mami's a cleaning lady."

I pictured her polyester uniform in the washing machine and sadly recalled her meticulous fibbing to Tía Rita about the fictional inventory she supposedly tracked at her job. The land of make-believe was overgrown with untruths. "Pablo, you keep your big mouth shut," I warned, staring him fiercely in the eye. "You're too old to be a blabbermouth. Mami would die of shame."

Pablo held both hands up. "Hey, I don't care. Why are you always blaming me?"

I let the frown linger on my face for a moment. Sometimes you had to hammer the message in with a bit of meanness to get it through Pablo's thick skull. But that was how Mami acted toward me, I realized with a twinge of regret. Maybe her meanness wasn't the truth either.

"Sorry," I said, getting up. "Let's go water Mami's tree."

We went to the yard, and Pablo uncoiled the long rubber hose. I pulled it around to the front and waited for him to turn on the faucet before starting to water the níspero tree. The sun dipped behind the back of our house, then slowly rolled across the shoulders of the other houses and escaped. As my gaze trailed the diminishing evening light, I wished for a more certain truth. Did one even exist, like God you couldn't see or prove but still might be there? Through all the twisted layers of falsehood, I thought I sensed it, a truth that I alone believed in, though I didn't know what it was, or where to look for it.

Later, with Mami gone, my father came out of his cave and surprised my brothers and me by plopping down at the table where we were doing schoolwork. He had the old textbook we'd given him. Casually opening it, he nodded over a page before looking up to ask what "conspiracy" meant.

Manolo and Pablo traded smirks.

"Let me see, Papi," I said, frowning at them. I leaned over, reading the passage about laws against labor unions to myself and then explaining it to him.

"Ya," he said, bending over the text again.

I could tell from the way he nodded and blinked at the page that he wasn't actually reading. But when Pablo hunched over his own book and blinked rapidly in imitation of My Father the Student, I kicked my brother hard under the table. Still, just letting my father pretend he was one of us deepened my feelings of foreboding about the layers of untruth that thickened through our house, as if they might someday suffocate us all.

## SEVENTEEN

W E FINALLY GOT A CALL from El Chino's secretary
informing us of the date of my father's near-mythical court
hearing. Almost incapable of believing in it still, I plied Arthur for
details about where and when we should meet Mr. Korematsu.

"Oh, honey, your whole family doesn't have to go," he said.
"It's a dismissal, they just sign and file papers. Stop-and-go."

"Really?" Could my father's absolution come that easily?

"Sure, like five minutes," Arthur declared. "Your dad probably
won't have to talk."

"Wow. That's great. Thanks," I added, before he hung up.

I relayed the astonishing news to my mother and then by phone
to Tío Victor, who decided he didn't need to miss work in that
case. Mami roped Tío Lucho into giving us a ride.

For his court date, my father shook out his moth-scented suit
jacket. As I watched him put it on, the pessimism I'd struggled to
fend off since he'd last donned the baggy suit to induct me into typing his encyclopedia memoirs reared its ugly head: *Nothing was really
going to change.* Sure, his criminal assault case would end and its atten-
dant deportation threat. But as long as my father remained himself,
even a calmer replica, what would free me from his chains?

Our courtroom experience was every bit the drive-by event

Arthur had predicted. I barely saw anything because everyone up near the judge remained standing; no chairs were provided for lawyers or defendants or even in the witness box. From where I sat in the back, everything contrasted markedly with the sober impressions I'd formed while reading *To Kill a Mockingbird*. The main goal here was the finish line. Even the judge's recital of each defendant's rights was delivered in such rapid-fire fashion that a couple of lawyers near me took bets on how many minutes each advisal would take.

El Chino joined the courthouse speed race. In the lobby afterward, he handed over copies of my father's dismissal orders, shook hands, and was preparing to scram when a startled Tío Lucho detained him. "But—is that it? Is my brother free now?"

The lawyer returned a droll smile. "Yes sir, your brother's case is finito. Don't worry, I went over everything with Mr. De la Paz. You guys are all set." He fished out business cards and started handing them out.

"Could I ask just one thing?" I inquired anxiously in English.

"Shoot," he answered with an amused wink. As an afterthought, he gave me a card too.

"What else could someone be deported for?" I probed. "Besides these things?" I indicated the court orders.

"Oh, there's a long list of grounds," he said, then translated that for the adults.

"But—what *are* they?" I persisted. "Like, not turning in those white forms in January? Not paying library fines? What?"

He shook his head as if the matter were way beyond me and turned to my parents. "I think your folks know it's a good idea to avoid convictions. Period. But as for the rest," he shrugged, "I'm not an immigration lawyer. You guys call Arthur." He tapped the card I held. "He'll get you a referral."

On our way back, thrifty Tío Lucho promptly discounted that
idea as a big waste of money.

When we got home, Mami came into my room to stash the dismissal orders in the Important Papers box in my closet. I watched
her as I changed out of my dress-up clothes.

"It's not over."

Startled, she looked up. "What?"

"The problem with Papi."

"You know very well that what happened to him wasn't fair,"
she scolded, before turning and leaving the room.


The next day at school I learned that while I'd been absent, an
enthusiastic Madame Imbert had entered me and another French
grammar wizard, Octavio, into an interscholastic competition. I
suspected familial authorization would be difficult to procure for
the drive with Octavio, an unknown male, especially to the hotel
hosting the cultural component of the *concours*; but I decided I
would wait and see how well he and I fared on the qualifier exam
before broaching the topic at home.

Octavio was a friendly junior who owned a car and smoked
long, skinny cigarettes. After French class that day, he unexpectedly joined me, Fátima, and her friend Amy Kaplan at lunch,
and I discovered that he had a wicked side. A new student from
Jamaica—where of course English is spoken—had joined us too,
and some dumb girl questioned him about what they ate in his
country, only she used that artificially loud, slow tone of voice
people do for the hard of hearing. Observing her, Octavio pointed
to his temple and said to the Jamaican kid in the same affected
tone: "SHE'S NOT VERY BRIGHT." I instantly wanted to put
Octavio in my tiny constellation of friends, the Gemini twins of

Fátima and Claudio—who wasn't a friend exactly, though we had meaningful talks during ACs.

Octavio and I took the qualifiers just before Thanksgiving recess and scored well enough to perform at the cultural event. Since neither of us knew much about French culture, though he did subscribe to *Life* magazine's French edition, Madame Imbert—or La Plump, as he began calling her privately—offered to help make *les costumes* and bake a French *tarte*. She went above and beyond the call of duty, though, when she bought me fabric for my mother and me to sew up my costume.

Mami greeted that request with the usual scowl over the latest nonsense from the public school system. "Why don't they stick to books?" she protested.

"Mami, I had to *earn* the right to participate. It's not like a stupid fruitcake fundraiser." I decided to defer mention of the ride with Octavio to the Miami Beach hotel until after my costume was already sewn.

Mami peered over her reading glasses at Madame's sketch. "Hmm. I guess they're trying to teach you about being a lady in past times."

*Yeah, a Lady of Pastry*, I chided myself with a smirk, recalling that Lara had also been puzzled over "the pedagogy" of the dress-up competition.

The long blue-and-white striped dress Mami and I sewed looked oddly suitable for an Amish candy striper, if such a thing existed. Lucky Octavio got to wear a blue shirt and white slacks under an apron Madame had adorned with blue and white fringe to match mine. Both of us had tall hats she'd constructed from white paper doilies.

At the *concours*, Octavio and I stood like royal guards beside our pastry, which the contest judges weren't allowed to eat until the end of the program. The whole time I worried that my hat would topple out of the bobby pin contraption Madame had *composéd* in my hair. Both the hazelnut *tarte* and our costumes turned out to be a big hit, and when our Second Prize victory was announced, I threw my arms elatedly around Octavio: I was so happy to win! My fatalistic fear of lifelong failure had finally evaporated.

We headed home in Octavio's Beetle with a blue and red ribboned *Certificat* for the school and our two gift certificates. By then, we'd loosened up enough to poke fun at the *concours*. "They should make teachers participate," Octavio commented, as he drove onto the expressway. "Wouldn't you love to see La Plump squeeze into your skirt? That would be worth a *tarte* or two."

Chuckling at her zeal, we began to gossip about other people we knew in common. "That guy you always talk in Spanish to is kind of interesting," Octavio said out of the blue.

I scrunched up my face.

"You know, that AC kid, the one with the funny eye? Some skinny girl's always tagging along waiting for him?"

"Oh. You mean Claudio." I hadn't realized that Claudio was the one person outside my family with whom I spoke only Spanish.

Eventually, Octavio pulled up in front of my house, where Mami was already waiting for me in a chair on the terrace. Octavio got out of the Beetle to go greet her and introduced himself with a smile.

"Would you like to sit for a moment?" Mami asked, patting her hair.

Octavio and I plopped awkwardly down on the stoop in front of her.

"We won Second Prize, Mami," I announced, handing her the *Certificat.*

Though it was printed in French, she studied it closely. "Very good," she said, smiling at Octavio. "Did you win too?"

Octavio flashed me an amused look, then returned her smile. "Same thing, señora."

With the ice broken, interrogation began. Mami asked where Octavio lived, how long ago his family had left Cuba, what his parents did for work, and basically circled the wagons to determine whether he came from gente decente.

My father must have heard our voices, because he shuttled out in his slippers and mad scientist hair.

Feeling rattled, I stood up and dusted my bottom.

Octavio stood too. Politely, he extended his hand to introduce himself again, but before he could get any words out, my father loudly inquired, "¿Quién es este hombre?"

Octavio glanced at me and promptly announced, "Octavio Rodríguez Pereira, señor," like a soldier reporting for duty.

"What are you doing here?" my father demanded to know in an even louder tone.

I threw a fearful look at my mother: What had happened with the Dalmane pills?

"I gave Gabriela a ride home," Octavio explained innocently.

"Mi'jo," Mami interrupted, as she rose to her feet. "This young man brought Gabriela back from a school program."

"Who gave him permission?" my father shouted, like a one-man holy war.

He made me ashamed, as if I'd come home compromised or something. But when Octavio threw me a what's-going-on look, I only widened my eyes in warning.

"She had to travel there somehow, mi'jo," Mami explained, as if reason could go it mano a mano with my father. "There's no bus." Lightly, she pressed my father's arm and tried to encourage him toward the front door.

"¿Este carajito?" he shouted, his vein popping as he gesticulated at Octavio.

*Oh my God,* I moaned silently, *now he's calling Octavio a shit!* Why wasn't the sleeping pill working?

Mami pressed firmly on my father's arm. "Vamos p'adentro, mi'jo," she urged intently. "Por favor."

Snapping into action, I murmured, "Time to go," and pushed Octavio in the opposite direction. While my father continued to curse and threaten in Spanish, Mami navigated him indoors.

When Octavio and I were safely at his car, I apologized profusely. "I'm so sorry. Really, really sorry."

With a thoughtful expression, Octavio fiddled in his pocket for his keys. "Um, that's okay, Gab, but—" He glanced at the door my parents had left ajar, then looked me in the eye. "What's with your father?"

"It's a long story," I answered, evading his eyes. "I can't really talk now. Thanks so much for the ride, though." As I turned and ran toward the house, my humiliation spread. What on earth would I do now? Save that one drunken outburst in front of Olguita and Camila, and some sanitized complaints I'd made to Lydia, I'd never told people outside my family about Papi's condition. I'd observed Mami's golden rule: silence. Only now, I realized, I believed in the rule too. I didn't want people to know what kind of family I had!

In my room, after quickly packing away the French victory remnants and then changing my outfit, I sat completely distraught before a homework assignment. Could it be that everything we'd been doing to control my father—isolating him from strangers, molly-coddling his delusions, and even the sleeping pills—still wasn't enough?

Mami walked in, interrupting my private panic attack, to tell me that she was going over to Camila's.

I couldn't help but blurt out, "I told you it wasn't over! Those pills aren't a cure. He's going to get in trouble all over again!"

"He will certainly not!" she retorted, though she glanced quickly away as if I'd caught her in something.

I considered my words and then said in a very measured tone, "El Chino told me that if Papi did get into more trouble, we wouldn't all have to go."

She stared at me. "What?"

"Just because *he* got deported," I elaborated carefully, "doesn't mean we would *all* have to leave."

Mami went pin-drop still.

Dropping my eyes to the notebook in front of me, I nonchalantly turned to a blank page and initialed a Jesus–Mary–Joseph logo at the top, then began drawing a circle around it like we used to do in Catholic school.

I sensed my mother slowly walk toward me and stop, standing over me until I looked up.

"I would never leave your father alone," she declared proudly, drawing herself to full height. "Or you either. That's one thing those people who do things 'differently' here would never appreciate." With that, she trounced out of the room.

I kept on tracing over the JMJ logo until it became a blue-black oval that threatened to rip through the paper. Other letters began to spell themselves out of my pen into a word El Chino had once tossed out casually. E-M-A-N-C-I-P-A-T-I-O-N, the legal form of F-R-E-E-D-O-M.

L-I-B-E-R-T-É.


On Sunday after Mass, I typed edgily for my father, who'd conveniently forgotten his fundamentalist ravings at Octavio and had returned to more relaxed displays of lunacy. In between agitating over what had gone wrong with his sleeping pill, I obsessed over what I would say to Octavio when Monday came around.

The only thing I could think to do, though, was avoid him. Too humiliated for a direct encounter in French class, I went to the nurse's office in the morning with fake cramps. At lunch I sat with hippie girls he didn't know. Then that night, I gratefully welcomed a diversion from all my dilemmas when Fátima and her friend Amy invited me to my first football game.

On the tallest bleachers where Fátima and I sat, my illuminated patch of reality seemed to diverge from the dark beyond, as if I were alone on a special raft in space. The light scattered the air around my raft like lovely particles whose names I'd paid scant attention to in Biology. It was so much better not to know how things worked, I felt suddenly, with a pang of sympathy for those poor scientists we'd read about who'd had to give up their Spontaneous Regeneration theory when they found out that life couldn't appear just like that, out of rot. I sighed, and when Fátima's parents arrived to pick us up, I left the illuminated city of football behind for good.

The following day I tried to slide casually into my seat in French class. Madame Imbert had brought a bottle of fake champagne, and she began passing out paper cups of it along with *pain de chocolat* to celebrate our *victoire mervellieuse*. Octavio kept shooting me pointed looks I tried to ignore.

After class, he caught up with me at my locker. "Why aren't you talking to me, Gabi?" he demanded to know. "And why did your father throw me out of your house?"

I shut the locker tight. "Look," I said. "He has these nervios—"

"Come on, Gabriela. Tell me the truth."

*The truth.* I opened my mouth, closed it, then slid to the floor and buried my face in my hands.

Octavio joined me, his legs crossed, on the floor. "What's the deal, Gabi?"

A part of me wanted to cry and another to laugh in helpless embarrassment. How could I tell a coherent story about my father? "Ay Octavio, I'm so humiliated at the way he treated you!" I burst

out. Then, taking a deep breath, I started letting everything spill
out. The temper tantrums at the lady in the tailor shop and at any
sexy embraces on TV. Our legal problems and the whole green card
saga. The puzzles and encyclopedia articles and my endless typing.
    The strange, sad mess that had become my familia.
    Except for recoiling slightly when I got to the part about my
father's attack on Manolo, Octavio simply listened. He didn't laugh
at my descriptions of my father's bizarre typing projects and rants
against the U.S. government, and I ended my jumbled confession
with the fear that people at Royal Palm High would find out about
my family and look down upon me.
    "Gab," he said. "I would never tell a soul. Honestly. But—" He
hesitated. "You guys should probably tell someone before anything
bad happens. I mean, I know Latinos don't like to admit this kind
of stuff, but maybe your father could get cured."
    "He won't go to the doctor. My uncles tried once."
    "Can't they, like, commit him or something?" Octavio asked.
    "What do you mean?"
    "You know, someone signs him over to the State. Like your
mom."
    "You mean to an insane asylum?"
    "I don't think they're like that anymore. Are they?"
    I was horrified at the thought of having my father institutional-
ized. As bad as he was, how could we send him off to one of those
dungeons? "Octavio, we could never do that. My mother would
kill me for even suggesting it."
    After going at it for a while, I convinced Octavio that there was
nothing for me to do but wait out my time until I could figure out
a legitimate reason, besides getting married, to leave home.
    "But that might be a long way off," he said.
    "I don't know. If I got desperate, my father's lawyer told me
about this thing once, emancipation."

Octavio raised his eyebrows. "Come on, Gabi. How would you support yourself?"

"You're right," I admitted, sighing.

Lockers began to rattle around us, and Octavio and I stood up.

We parted ways, but as I walked down the hall an unusual, almost euphoric calm seemed to carry me along. Telling Octavio had placed my family in some oddly suspended state of being; as if, for a moment, I might just be free.

Octavio kept his word too. He didn't tell anyone about his expulsion from the Garden of the de la Paz, as he began to call it when we were alone. Nor did he tire of hearing cuentos about my father's obsessions, such as the mortgage records Mami hid to keep him from sending the bank inappropriate letters. Ironically, my father had provided me with someone to confide in about him— and I was especially grateful now that I was unsure whether the sleeping pills could be trusted.

Octavio encouraged me to confide in Fátima too. "She's your best friend, isn't she?" he asked.

"Yeah, kind of. But I can't." It was hard to explain exactly what made me so reluctant, but Fátima's family seemed sort of perfect, helping one another out in ways you could be proud of. And I'd already lost so many people—like Lydia, the junior high gang, and Olguita...I didn't have the strength to tell Fátima my truth yet.

## EIGHTEEN

THE OCTAVIO BLOW-UP left me anxious that my father might, without warning, throw everything out of equilibrium. With Mami overwhelmed by her secret job, I easily persuaded her to give him whole sleeping pills, which I suspected might be more potent than diluting the ground half-pill in a drink. Mami fooled him that the new "vitamins" were from my aunt. The only problem was, my father refused his "vitamin" once, saying that his egg and orange juice tonic made him healthy enough. Mami had no choice but to let it go, sighing. "As long as he takes them most of the time," she said to me in private.

I began to reflect, as the holidays approached, that if worse came to worst, I could always go to that cozy-looking Dominican convent in the Gables. The convent wasn't such a bad prospect, I thought nostalgically, recalling my childhood aspirations. The legal emancipation alternative, as Octavio had exposed, was pretty ill-formed, even if I overcame my Latina training that girls didn't leave home that way.

I was attending church with Fátima's family often nowadays, undoubtedly the reason I overheard Mami telling Tía Rita that Fátima was a good influence on me. What Mami didn't know was that Pablo was the one in need of good influences. In junior high, he'd expanded his extracurricular hobbies to include not only glue and pot but also, queerly enough, the Wite-Out in ample supply at our house. Mami poked around, almost instinctively, for evidence of wrongdoing in his room but had no clue what to look for. Once, after she'd left, he imitated her peering through an imaginary spy glass into his laundry hamper. I had to giggle, and he joined in.

"Crack yourselves right up, huh," said Manolo, placing a pillow over his face.

"The old lady's getting as crazy as the old man," Pablo quipped back.

"Yeah, but you better clean out the pockets before throwing anything in your hamper," I advised.

Manolo reached for a pair of jeans on the floor and checked them.

My eyes widened. "You have stuff too?"

"Relax. I don't do Wite-Out or that glue shit." He tossed his pants back.

Pablo laughed.

"You're fucking yourself up," Manolo warned.

"I don't feel fucked up," Pablo said, laughing again.

"Well, you'll be going to a nice village school in La Güajira when you get yourself deported," I informed him sardonically. "All by yourself."

Manolo looked up to see if I was serious. "Nobody's gonna bust us, Gab."

Sighing with resignation, I left. Maybe he was right. Look at those hippie kids who smoked dope in the Royal Palm parking lot. No one seemed to get caught. Maybe you just had to be smart about it. Anyway, "illegal" drugs—at least pot—weren't as bad as they were made out to be; nothing extraordinary had happened to me when I'd tried the joint with Pablo, who seemed to smoke without consequence. The only drug that really altered him—turning him hyper and sometimes hysterical—was the glue, which wasn't even illegal.

By contrast, the pills Tía Rita obtained from Dr. Sanabria *were* illegal, according to a "diverted pharmaceuticals" lecture in my Health Education class. Yet all they did was calm my father down. It was hard to know what to think about drugs anymore, or about legality. Besides, the double standard applied to us immigrants in this country had left me with more than a few doubts about The Law.

My father was fully Dalmaned at Tío Victor's on the 31st, and that brought everyone else the peace of the New Year. I eavesdropped on Mami's conversation with Tía Rita about my father's grosería toward Octavio, a story that led Tía Rita to toss out the foolhardy doctor notion again. Mami responded by trying to justify my father's aggressive fundamentalism as no more than concern for his daughter's morals. Tía Rita rose to get another drink.

The following morning, I accompanied Fátima's temperate family to New Year's Day Mass. The priest's sermon on the Holy Family's plight to save the baby from persecution explored the meaning of refuge. His hopeful words filled me with gratitude that at least the Holy Family had made it safely into Egypt.

That night, my own family enjoyed a relatively quiet meal together. When Mami brought out a bottle of cidra, Pablo released a bizarre whoop, as if the cider were a gift from the gods. Manolo grinned stupidly and I realized that he was stoned too. Then my father gave us his beatific calmante smile and I was dumbstruck: Was everyone in my family on drugs?

"Toma, mi'ja," Mami said, carefully pouring my serving.

No, my mother certainly wasn't high.

When the holiday break ended and I returned to school, Amy invited me to her brother's bar mitzvah. "Something to do with the Old Testament," Fátima explained to me afterward. The Adam and Eve story was the one that stuck out in my mind the most, probably because of Octavio's wisecracks about his "expulsion from the garden," but reminders of a naked Eve disobeying God were clearly not likely to go over well with Mami. Fortunately, she so admired the ivory invitation I showed her that she decided Amy's family must be gente decente and that I should attend.

I went to the gringo mall that weekend with Fátima, who bought herself a red print dress before we picked up Amy and headed back to Fátima's house. I asked Amy about her own bar mitzvah, and she explained that girls had a *bat* mitzvah, though she hadn't had one and they weren't common. "I guess it could be sexist," she added, shrugging as if it didn't matter.

"We don't have quinceañeras for boys either," Fátima pointed out.

"So Latin girls become women," I threw in, "and Jewish boys become men." I suspected Lara would have something interesting to say about this particular gender difference.

Amy scrunched up her face. "It's different. Boys come into the faith, not just their manhood. But Jewish women carry the faith. Like, if I married a non-Jew, my kids would be Jewish. But if my brother did it, his wife would have to convert. Maybe it's reverse sexism."

"In traditional quinceañeras, you're supposed to go to church first," I observed neutrally, before Amy went on. But suddenly it seemed to me that she and I had more in common, despite her wealth, than I did with those other American girls at school who seemed like me in not having much money but who weren't Latin or Jewish. Amy was connected to her gente—her people. Did those hippie girls even *have* a people?

Fátima's sister Rosalía insisted on giving me a practically new dress that she said didn't fit her anymore. It was ivory, a crushed-velvet with tiny gold flecks and a white lace collar. At everyone's insistence, I tried it on.

"You look sooo adorable," Amy cooed.

The dark-eyed girl in the mirror reminded me of my mother in some old-fashioned, painted photograph from Colombia days.

"It shows off your figure better than mine," Rosalía admitted, studying me. "Why do you wear baggy clothes so much, Gabi?"

"To cover my hips," I replied reasonably.

"You don't have to worry in that department," she retorted, eyeing Amy more critically.

"Welcome to Bimbolandia," Fátima quipped airily, grinning.

I laughed.

"What are you gonna do with that hair?" Mirén asked.

"What do you think?" I responded democratically, as everyone inspected the thick brown locks that only gravity's weak force kept hanging down my back.

"Tie it down. Use a ribbon," advised Mirén. "But gel it so you'll look dressed up."

*Gabriela Cinderella*, I mocked myself. *What I could do with a real fairy godmother!*

At the bar mitzvah, Fátima, Octavio, and I sat together watching Amy's little brother, who was spruced up like a good do-bee in a suit. Something about his bearing reminded me of Manolo, forever trying to compensate for his smallness by acting manly.

Octavio drove Fátima and me to the party afterward, and Amy introduced us to her cousin David. Blond streaks shone in the shaggy hair that fell over his hazel eyes. He was good-looking, despite a twine he wore in lieu of a tie around his neck. Amy explained that he'd interrupted his first year of college and was working at a Coral Gables daycare center.

When the Temptations came on, I danced with Octavio and Fátima until it became uncomfortable in the three-inch "little heels" she'd loaned me. I strolled over to a glass-domed enclosure where Kaplan relatives were admiring flowers.

David came up with a beer in hand. "What's happening?" he asked.

"These plants grow all over," I replied. "It's like putting a giant jar over your yard and calling it a grass collection."

He laughed, showing his dimples. "Yeah, some people don't figure things out very well."

"Where do you go to college?" I asked.

"I'm taking time off. To clear my head," he added, then glanced at the glass doors. "Wanna check out the outside gardens?"

It was 90 degrees out, but I said okay.

David led us to a hammock situated where the path split. The shady island was thick with hardwoods, and we sat on a bench to inspect the signs. Sable Palm. Mahogany. Strangler Fig.

"This is like the Everglades," he observed. "You hang out there?"

"Not really. When we first moved here, we went to the airboat rides. You know those?"

He nodded.

"That's more like an amusement park. Everything around the village is pretty much Everglades though. Grass. Big birds." *Should I tell him about the birds?* I considered self-consciously.

"How long have you lived here?" he asked.

"Since I was thirteen."

"A long time, huh?"

"I'm seventeen," I stated defiantly, studying the Strangler Fig.

"Oh yeah?" He squinted out of one eye and cracked his dimpled smile. "I'm getting another beer. Want one?"

"No thanks. But maybe we should go back to the air-conditioning," I suggested.

"What if I bring you a cold drink?"

"Okay."

When he returned, he was balancing a plastic drink cup between two beer cans. "Saved myself a trip," he said sheepishly. As I took the cup, he immediately downed one beer while standing and threw that can in the trash.

I sipped my soda and watched with keen curiosity.

"Okay," he said, back on the bench. "Time to party." He pushed his wild hair behind one ear, popped the new can open, and turned toward me. "So what's the deal? You go to school with Amy?"

"Yeah." I couldn't think of anything intelligent to add. "Where did you used to go?"

"NYU. I'm thinking of living on a *kibbutz* now."

"What's that?"

"It's like a community, kind of a socialist thing. In Israel. It's pretty cool. You never heard of it?"

When I shook my head, David explained about the *kibbutzim* movement. How people owned land in common and raised their children collectively. You could live on one that farmed or one that made or fixed things.

"You know about farming and stuff?" I asked, surprised.

He laughed and finished the beer. "No way. I'm a *tabula rasa*. I don't know anything."

"So can anybody go live there? Like—me?"

"You probably have to be Jewish. Are you Cuban?"

I shook my head. "Colombian."

"Oh yeah! García Márquez, right?" He nodded at me with interest. "Great book! My Spanish professor made us read that." He reached into his pocket. "You get stoned?"

I was taken aback. Why did he think I did? Maybe it was my Medusa hair that gave him the impression. I hadn't followed Mirén's gelling and tying advice.

"There's nobody around," he added.

Despite the disconcerting drug offer, I was flattered that this college guy wanted to hang out with me, but I'd started to feel uneasy about spending all that time with him. "Fátima and those guys will be looking for me," I said and stood up to leave. "I'd better go in."

David looked up, suddenly less confident.

"I'm sorry," I added.

*"No problema,"* he answered, giving me a peace sign.

I left him staring into the trees with one hand in his pocket. *Eyes a little sorry,* I thought, inexplicably.

Inside the dome, I found Fátima. She raised a neatly plucked eyebrow, then dragged me to one side. "What were you doing with that guy? Amy says he almost got kicked out of college."

"Really? We discussed history," I said. "He's very informative."


A few evenings later, Fátima's family dropped us off at the Gables Cinema to meet Octavio and Amy, who showed up, lo and behold, with her cousin David. He was wearing a baby blue T-shirt and his arms were really tan. He looked cuter than in that dark suit he'd worn to the bar mitzvah, and I felt tacky in a snug Cartagena de Indias T-shirt my relatives had sent me.

"Aren't you coming?" I asked him casually, after Amy got out of his van.

"Nah, not my thing."

The comedy turned out to be about a bunch of guys who wanted to have sex. Even without my mad moral custodian around, I didn't find it too funny.

At the pizza place where Fátima and I waited afterward for her parents, David reappeared to pick up Amy. When Octavio started mimicking characters in the movie, David smiled playfully and sat down. Something about the way his eyes grazed over me made me feel very self-conscious, and I grew quiet. After a while, I excused myself and went to the bathroom.

When I came out, David, who was taller than I'd realized, was leaning against the wall facing me. "Hey," he called softly.

"Hi." I nervously pushed my hair behind my ears.

"So I have to drop Amy off," he said. "How 'bout a little party afterward?" He gave me a dimpled, irresistible half-smile.

*Party with me?* My heart skipped, but in a good way for once. "The thing is," I said hesitantly, "I'm not really allowed to go out. Except sort of like this." I waved toward where the others were sitting.

"What about during daylight?" he asked, looking amused. "Like, could you skip out Saturday?"

What I wanted to skip out with was a cool, sophisticated answer— but all I could say was, "Sure, I guess so."

"We could check out a park or something," he added.

I flashed immediately on Tuttle, where Pablo hung out with his little girlfriends. "There's this place in my neighborhood," I offered. "It's got jasmine trees and stuff."

"Cool." He grinned. "How do we get there?"

Since I couldn't very well tell him where I lived, I had to give roundabout directions from the library and suggested we meet by the swings. I pretended my phone was disconnected, and he retrieved a crumpled daycare form from his pocket and scribbled down the phone number for his aunt's house in the Gables, where he was staying.

Then we walked back to the table. Flustered, I nibbled on my pizza crust. What had happened to my resolve about avoiding the opposite sex? But I felt dizzy with the consciousness of David's body across from me, as if I'd been knocked off kilter on a sudden elevator ascent.

•  •  •

Lara seemed especially flustered when I arrived on Saturday morning before my secret liaison with David. Apparently, Solita had contracted an earache, and Luna was fussy too. Running her hands through her hair, Lara complained about Walter in an unusually frank manner while she struggled to open a tight kitchen drawer. "I've had to take her to the pediatrician *three* times this week!" she exclaimed, shaking the drawer open at last. "And to the pharmacy every time they changed the antibiotic because, after all, where is Walter in all of this?" She threw up one hand in frustration while the other located the pharmacy card she'd been hunting. "Very busy preparing his research for Argentina," she answered herself mockingly as she shut the drawer.

"You're going to Argentina?" I asked, alarmed.

"Oh no." She smiled apologetically. "Just Walter. His team is going to do field studies in the pampas. 'Objects of permanence in the lives of migratory peoples,'" she explained, drawing imaginary quotation marks in the air. Her good humor returned as she talked and rummaged for cereal that she poured into a plastic Baggie. "In other words, what is 'home'?" she posited. "You could say it's practically a mimetic fallacy for Walter," she added with a wry grin, "since he's gone so much."

"Lara," I said, watching her dump the cereal lunch into her bag, "could I fix you a sandwich?"

"Oh, no thank you, Gabrielita, this is fine." She smiled away my concern. "I'll pick up Soli's medication first and drop it off before I leave, ah?"

I nodded, only slightly worried that Lara's delayed start might make me late for my secret rendezvous. But she returned as planned in the afternoon, and I regretted that she had to find both girls crying. Still, I had to make my excuses to leave instead of staying to help, since I was anxious to get to the park to meet David.

He was already there when I arrived. He'd brought along a cooler of Budweisers and chocolate Yoo-hoos, a rolled up sheet, and a large order of McDonald's fries.

Toward the back of the park, we found a shady place under the jasmines and away from teenagers. I helped David shake sand out of the sheet before we placed it on the ground. After we sat down, he fished through the cooler with his tanned arm, extracting a Yoo-hoo that he handed to me and a beer he kept for himself. He arched his eyebrows provocatively. "My uncle has a vast supply." He popped the beer open, took a long drawn-out swig, and propped himself up on both elbows beside me. "So what's your last name? Are you really seventeen?"

"No." I smiled timidly. "Almost sixteen. My birthday's this month."

"Great!" His dimples deepened. "Something to celebrate." Sitting up, he took a joint out of his pocket.

Why did illegality seem to follow me everywhere? I wondered forlornly.

David lit the joint, smoked, and passed it to me. I hesitated for a second but then took it and just puffed, all my reason abandoned.

Then, with genuine interest, he asked me about my family. How long we'd been in this country, what kind of customs my parents had.

In between trying to smoke correctly, I awkwardly answered his questions and started to feel warm and fuzzy. Maybe it was the buzz Pablo had described. I found myself talking about my family's unconventional chaperone code. How the chaperones could be stupider than the chaperoned. "Like when my idiot younger brother got assigned to watch me at the Laundromat," I said, taking another toke.

David grinned. "What did he watch you for?"

I sidetracked into an explanation of my parents' perplexing "decent" family exception. "Like, I can go out with Fátima and her sisters but not on rides alone with Octavio, who's older than her and me but I guess not as 'decent.' As a girl, I mean." I paused. David seemed to be enjoying these lessons, but suddenly I began to feel guilty about ratting on my family. Maybe the Octavio confession had started to let my cat out of its bag. "What's your family like?" I inquired abruptly.

"My dad's a TV producer. My mom teaches dance at a private school in Manhattan. Isadora Duncan style."

"Oh." His parents sounded rich.

David added that he'd graduated early. "Big mistake," he said, shaking his head. "Now I have to figure out whether to go back to college or do the Israel thing."

*All those choices must be nice*, I thought.

"It's either that or Vietnam," he added on a somber note.

"Vietnam?" I asked with dismay.

He gave me a bemused look. "Don't look so freaked. I got a 203."

"What's that?"

"My lottery number. You know how it works?"

I shook my head no.

"It's a roll of the dice. They use these Ping-Pong balls, according to birthdays. None of the numbers they picked were in the hundreds, so I should be okay. But if they did call my number, I wouldn't go. I'm no My Lai murderer."

The mental picture of him gunning down Vietnamese kids, like that horrible Lieutenant Calley in the newspaper, made me shudder. "Maybe you could do something good instead, like medical work," I suggested.

"They don't exempt you for being into Peace," he replied soberly.

"But if you run away from the Draft, don't they hunt you down—like a criminal?"

"I'm already a criminal," he said with a sly smile as he put out his joint. "I'm conspiring with a minor."

He could joke, I thought with chagrin, because he wasn't an immigrant. But the way he was looking at me was making my heart start to flutter again. "Why are you in Miami?" I asked nervously, to buy some control.

"My parents went to Europe. They didn't want me hanging around their apartment, so my aunt and uncle let me stay here while I get my shit together." He grinned affably. "Miami's as good a place as any."

"What do you mean, get your shit together?"

"Oh, the usual. My future." He gave me a wry smile. "Girls."

Suddenly feeling self-conscious again, I tore the aluminum ring off his beer can and slipped it onto my pinkie. He reached across and lightly spun the ring, then looked at me as he spun it again and again. Each time his finger touched mine, it gave me a thrill. He turned my arm over, ran his hand slowly up my pinkie and along the lines of my palm to the soft skin at my wrist. I wanted him to keep going up my arm. I was so paralyzed with wanting it that I had to close my eyes to keep him from seeing. I felt him pull me onto the sheet and start to kiss me, deep, with his tongue. Suddenly, the sky was darker and his fingers were grazing the skin below my ribs and climbing. "Me vuelvo loca," from one of Olguita's records, played wildly in my head, or maybe it was my body. But then a freakish echo, like an aural memory of my screaming father, shook me out of the kissing spell and forced me to stop. Gravely, I stared into David's eyes. I feared that if I opened my mouth, strange sounds might come out. Forked tongue language. Voodoo.

He gave me a crooked smile. "Hmm, let's see. I'm guessing you're a fifteen-year-old Latina virgin?"

I shook my head hard.

"No?"

"Yes," I gulped out. How could he think otherwise? "I—couldn't talk for a minute."

"What?" He laughed and rolled over on his side to check me out. "So I guess sex isn't in the cards right this minute, huh?"

I sat right up. "No." The very thought of sex stirred up every kind of fear, confusion, and shame I'd stored up through all my father's fits of violent moralism.

David only laughed, leaning across me for the fries. "*Quieres* french fries?" he asked engagingly.

"Sí, quiero." I smiled gratefully and took a couple from him. They were cold and salty.

Then I lay back, and we watched the jasmine blossoms fall on our sneakers. "I love fries," I said and reached my hand out for more.

Later, as I walked home, I couldn't help but smile stupidly to myself while reliving the unusual afternoon. His eyes roaming over me as he twirled the beer can tab around my finger. The cheeky way he'd brought up sex—disconcerting but still sort of seductive.

Some nun I'd make, I mocked myself.

When he'd said we should get together again, I'd felt ecstatic, though I cautioned him that it had to be on the sly. Saucily, he quipped back, "Sounds like fun."

He would make it fun, I knew.

It was near dark when I reached my house, and Pablo came out to report on the lies he'd told Mami about my being at some high school thing while she was out.

"On Saturday?" I asked, frowning at his idiocy. "You were supposed to say I was at the library."

"She doesn't know, Gab."

Luckily, Mami seemed tired, already yawning and rubbing her eyes as I greeted her in the kitchen. "Gabriela," she said sharply, "I can't have you in the streets in the middle of the night." She took foil off a plate of fried fish she put in front of me.

"I told you," I said, retrieving a fork from the drawer. "I needed to go to the library for a school project. It's not my fault." I prayed she wouldn't pick at the discrepancies between my story and Pablo's.

"Well, tell your teachers to assign less." She plopped down a glass of water. "Do they think we have a chauffeur to escort you around at all hours?"

I was tempted to poke her hand with my fork. "It's only 7:47 p.m. What are you talking about?"

"I'm talking about young girls wandering around in a dangerous city. Don't you know what happens out there? What terrible people there are?" She folded her arms over her chest as if she were cold and perched herself on the edge of a chair. Almost immediately she pulled herself to her feet again, unwilling to let fatigue come between her and the struggle against evil.

"Nothing's gonna happen, Mami. I take care of myself."

When the phone rang, she went to answer. Carefully I picked out the baby bones from my fish. A long-ago memory of my grandfather, tenderly removing a fish bone from his panicked terrier's throat, came flooding back. Poor Mami, I sighed. If only she would give the world a chance to be good.

## NINETEEN

THE WHOLE-PILL REGIMEN SEEMED to be working well, because the production of missives slowed and my father became more "mellow," to quote David. Sometimes Papi would even bumble around like a dreamy old person, letting me float away from everything I'd obsessed over—his volatile temper, The Law, who would be exiled, who would remain, and where to find the hidden door out of my family prison.

Big chunks of my free time suddenly and fortuitously became available for secret larks with David. In his blue van, he would pick me up at a park with a lonesome eucalyptus tree. Then, slouching in his seat, he'd grin through dark granny glasses and ask things like, "Anybody spot me?" before getting out to let me in the van from the outside, since the passenger door was dented. He took me to banyan-filled parks he loved in Coral Gables and Coconut Grove; to the funky Grove shopping area with its beautiful but dilapidated Playhouse that evoked the Grand Old South; and sometimes just for a drive around quaint historical Grove neighborhoods that my one black teacher had told us were built by his Bahamian ancestors out of nothing but trees and breeze. The houses were called "shotgun houses," he'd explained, "not because you could shoot through them, but for the Yoruba word, *shogun*—God's house." David

turned me on to a record shop hangout, where the employees
burned incense and let him play me albums, like one by an unusually deep-voiced Canadian named Leonard Cohen, who must have
been Jewish but seemed obsessed with Christian imagery—and
women. Even the *Sisters of Mercy*—nuns!—had slept with him.

A couple of times, David just parked and left the van running,
slipped in a sitar music tape, and coaxed me into the back to smoke
with him. I'd decided to quit worrying about that, despite my
initial qualms, since David, like hippies at school, only got high
in places police didn't frequent. I followed his lead, climbing onto
the colorful Indian pillows, sewn with tiny mirrors, that covered
the van floor. Pretty soon, we'd be into the mirrored pillows, the
original Gabriela de la Paz dissipating into the ether with all the
brain cells lost by smoking illegal drugs. I could drift along pleasantly enough until the sobering reminder of my Jehovah father,
furious and apocalyptic, always brought my kissing to a halt.

Whenever I returned from these airy adventures, it was hard to
focus on whatever I was supposed to be doing. If I read English
assignments, Odysseus would morph into David and I'd have
to shut my eyes, conjuring up images of him rescuing me from
mythical storms, wandering sea rocks, and a mad Scylla who
looked suspiciously like my father. Movies I'd seen or read about
in *TV Guide* would play out behind my closed eyes with David in
the lead role, brandishing a sword, musket, bow and arrow. Fighting movies inevitably changed into romantic ones, and suddenly
I'd want to fly around the room and sing with my arms out, like
Lesley Ann Warren in *Cinderella* or Audrey Hepburn after her ball
with the professor.

On my birthday, I woke to such daydreams, but my reverie was
interrupted by a long forgotten snippet of the "Las mañanitas"

song—Mami's pretty voice was singing it as she entered, carrying a gift wrapped in rainbow tissue paper. My brothers poked their heads in behind her. "Happy Birthday, Gab," they chimed.

"Thanks." I smiled, sitting up to reach for the gift. Inside I found a lavender and white skirt and top. "So cute, Mami!" Grateful for something at last that we both liked, I hugged her hard.

Fátima called later to congratulate me, and she invited me on a beach outing to escape the latest heat wave. I accepted gladly, relieved not to have to invent another lie in order to sneak off with David, who'd gone to a family wedding. Embarrassed about my liaisons with him for some reason, I'd been unable to confide in Fátima at all.

Lara was driving Walter to the airport that morning, so I already knew the girls wouldn't need watching. I felt badly for Lara, since I'd learned from our last conversation about his research trip that she wasn't too happy he was going off to the Argentine pampas while leaving her alone with the girls.

After I'd finished dressing and stuffed a beach bag, Mami called out that Lara had dropped by on her return from the airport. Surprised, I went out to the Florida room, where the two of them sat, a bakery box between them. The front door was open as Luna and Solita played outside.

"Lara brought you a cake, mi'jita," Mami announced, handing me the box. "She saved us the trouble of baking on this atrocious day! Muy atenta," she added appreciatively.

"Wow," I said, peering in at the meringue roses. "It looks like a wedding cake!"

"But dark chocolate inside," Lara pointed out, smiling.

"Mmm. Thanks so much, Lara!" I ran up and hugged her. "Should I call the girls in?"

"No, Gabi. You save that to enjoy with your family."

"Mi'ja, why don't you make us both a tintico before you

leave?" Mami pleaded, then told Lara, "Gabriela has an excursion. But the girls seem happy out there. Stay a while."

"Vale," Lara agreed.

As I prepared coffee, I heard Lara begin to explain the modern day mysteries of Walter's trip.

"Argentina..." Slowly, Mami sounded out the syllables, as if she were measuring the distance. "So far... ," she murmured. I was sure she wouldn't understand why Walter couldn't do his research here instead of abandoning his family.

"Yes," Lara admitted with a forced laugh. "I imagine we'll get a little lonely."

"You'll get accustomed," Mami said kindly. "Roberto had to leave us for a short time too. And those boys were difficult! But you have girls," she added reassuringly. "Girls are much better. Se portan bien. And your two are sweet."

"Thank you, Evi."

On that note, I waltzed in with the coffees.

It felt odd to leave them together afterward with their distinct forms of loneliness. But my mother, I realized, was more practiced at hers—and Lara seemed to want to stay.

When I arrived at Fátima's, she welcomed me with the gift of a blue leather diary with gold-edged pages. "It's from all of us," she declared warmly, hugging me.

Mirén and Rosalía hugged me too.

As we drove to Crandon Park afterward, it seemed that all Miami was on vacation, but we managed to find a shaded grill at the beach, and Mirén and Rosalía parked themselves in chairs while Fátima and I lay on our towels on the sand nearby. When Fátima's parents arrived separately, I turned over on my stomach to wave, then rolled back over. After a couple of hours, though, my skin started to sting. I threw on my big yellow T-shirt to cool off under a palm tree and drink a Coke. The light had changed and the water deepened its blue hues. In the distance, I recognized Claudio from my AC crew. He'd recently been conscripted to the school arts magazine, after the adviser saw his drawings on display. Waving, Claudio walked over.

"Hola," I said, saluting him with my Coke. In Spanish, I introduced Rosalía and Mirén.

"That was a good sketch you did of Gabi," Fátima commented, leaning up on her arms to squint without her glasses on.

Claudio returned a small smile. "Thank you for your kindness." I almost expected him to give her a bow.

I'd blocked the sketch from my mind out of embarrassment. Along with his bodega drawings, Claudio had exhibited a crayon drawing of me with a sad expression on my face and my hair draped around me like some Florentine Madonna. I couldn't imagine what had made him draw me instead of the slouchy older girl who sometimes hung around waiting for him.

"Would you like to take a walk?" he asked now.

No one responded until I realized it was me he was inviting. "Oh!" I glanced toward Fátima's parents.

"You don't have to ask them, Gabi," she said, smiling.

"Okay, I'll come," I told Claudio, wrapping a towel around my hips.

We walked with the sun behind us. Claudio didn't have a shirt on and was burnt to a crisp like me. His hair was wet and curly at the neck, and he walked with sudden stops to study the landscape. He said his family came here often and that he liked this time best. "Where is your family?" he asked in Spanish.

"Home. My father isn't feeling well. Besides, we don't have a car."

"It's hard when your family has difficulties," Claudio said sympathetically. He used the word "dificultades" as we did in my family— vaguely, so that problems serious or small could be included.

As he pondered the sky, the water, and a patch of pines we were passing, he stopped and pointed. "Look. Where the sunlight pulls away, it gives the world back its color."

I looked and saw that he was right: The blues and pinks were more distinct without the afternoon glare.

"Did you like the sketch?" he asked suddenly.

"Well—" I studied the tranquil water. I didn't want to hurt his feelings. "It was *good*. I just don't like standing out so much, or people looking at me."

"But your face is good, not imperfect like mine."

I examined his face without knowing whether to contradict him or ask about the tiny black teardrop that ran down his iris.

"Es una pupila derramada," a spilled pupil, Claudio explained with a gentle smile. He'd been born with it.

"Oh," I said, nodding. "It's not that noticeable."

That wasn't true, but he looked handsome anyway. The pupila derramada suited his quirky yet dignified personality.

"It doesn't make any difference," he said, with a wave of his hand. "We are what we are. Do you remember *La negrita cucurumbé*?"

"Sure. My mother used to play those albums when we were kids. Isn't that the one about the little black girl who goes to the sea?"

"Wishing she were white," he added, then quoted, "como la espuma que tiene el mar."

*White like the foam of the sea.* "Pretty," I murmured, as we watched the blues deepen in the water.

Claudio recited a verse about the fish telling the negrita how pretty her face was. His voice was low and textured, making the words sound mournful instead of corny.

"She didn't see her beauty; it appeared in another's eye," he concluded after he'd finished.

I had a feeling that he was complimenting me, but how conceited of me to think so. "That song always made me cry," I said humbly.

"Me too," he admitted.

The bands of blue water near the shore were nearly the same color now as the distant horizon, all the blues becoming one. I asked Claudio about other songs I distantly remembered from *El rey de chocolate*, and he resuscitated words I'd forgotten. Our childhoods in Colombia and Venezuela had followed the same coastline. As we walked back, it seemed that we'd traveled a long way together, our common history more solid than the bits and pieces of childish memory. The neon sun dipped slowly into the water, like the great criollo dream of a Gran Colombia.


Over breakfast the next morning, I tried to piece together in my memory Claudio's sketch of me. With belated pleasure, I recalled the soft silver shadings he'd used, how they'd illuminated the portrait—as if some secret might be revealed if only you waited long enough.

Did I like Claudio? I wondered in a burst of surprise. There was a kind of gentility with which he always listened to others that suddenly made me hope he wouldn't feel out of place with those cynical gringos I knew he would be joining at the *Persona* magazine. Claudio was so noble that thinking of him moved me to feel guilty about how much I'd ignored my poor father lately with fake library trip excuses while I gallivanted with David.

Contrite, I went to find my father, and he was so pleased at my unexpected offer to type that I felt a new kind of tenderness toward him. As we sat in the kitchen together, he pressed creases out of a letter so that I could read it better. How quiet he was then, the exact opposite of the Jehovah God looming over me whenever I kissed David or watched the fictional kisses on TV.

Around me, the kitchen had aged. Wallpaper was splattered with fried oil residue, and the dusty overhead light no longer shone brightly. I got the impression that I'd typed these pages of my father's before, but I'd lost track of his latest petroleum theories. I didn't begrudge him the work this time, though. *Let him be*, I told myself gently. He isn't hurting anybody with his strange hieroglyphs.

And as he sat so childlike beside me, I remembered being a little girl myself, riding the bus back once from our first public library visit. He'd taken me there, to the nice part of Queens, one sunny morning. The library was bright and spacious, and he'd admitted with embarrassment that he'd never been inside a library before. At first, shyly, he'd waited in the doorway and watched mothers read to their children. Eventually, he took a seat while I walked among the shelves. There were so many books to choose from, and no one had told me that I could borrow more than one. The one I chose had a cover full of shining leaves in every green hue from emerald to sea. The leaves reminded me of the Río Magdalena, especially the part where the thickest trees had once enclosed my grandfather and me on a canoe trip. Through the leaf images, the feeling of the little girl in the canoe—that the green world ahead would stay good and beautiful forever—returned to me. Joyfully, I took my book to the librarian, but she informed me that she had to talk to my father about it.

"He doesn't speak English," I'd explained anxiously after I called him over.

"Tell your father I need to see his driver's license, dear."

My father had looked at me quizzically. Finally, he said—and I translated—that he didn't have one.

"Does he have mail—a bill or something?"

My father emptied the scuffed brown wallet and his jacket pockets and waited for the librarian to poke around with her finger and tell him if anything in there was good enough. Finally, she found something that allowed us to borrow the book.

On the bus ride home, my father looked out the window and didn't speak.

With a sorrow I hadn't known before, I held my hopeful green book on my lap without opening it, my fingers folded tightly around the edge of something that I sensed I couldn't hold.

That night, I said good-bye to such nostalgia.

Tía Rita had invited us over. "Put on something nice, please," Mami urged, and I donned my lavender birthday outfit.

When we arrived, Manolo and Pablo—who'd decided they were too old to associate with the twelve-year-old twins—threw themselves, legs spread out, on a couch in front of the TV in my aunt's new recreation room. Tía Rita cajoled Raquel into distracting the twins outside, and I helped her until I got fed up and went to see what my own brothers were doing.

In the recently paneled room, Tío Victor and Tío Lucho were standing on either side of my father, who frowned ominously at the dark television. *Oh no,* I thought, shooting a nervous look at my brothers sitting silently in the shadows.

"Heh heh," Tío Lucho forced a laugh and patted my father's shoulder. "We'll have to get the government to hire you as their TV censor."

*Good, the blow-up happened already,* I thought, sighing inwardly with relief.

"¡No seas estúpido!" my father exploded.

*Or maybe not,* I decided fearfully, turning to leave. What a shock it was to hear him call his older brother stupid. As I glanced back, I saw that trusty Tío Victor had a hand on my father's arm, whose fists remained tightly clenched. My own hands felt shaky, like my current confidence in Dr. Sanabria's sleeping pills.

"Man," said Manolo, who'd clambered after me. "I told you those pills weren't too good."

"What pills?" Pablo asked as the three of us headed outside.

I frowned at Manolo. "Some medicine Mami gave Papi for his nervios," I improvised quickly.

"What kind?" Pablo persisted.

"Go ask the old lady yourself," Manolo blurted out.

"Don't you dare," I warned Pablo. "It was just something she was trying to see if he would feel better. But it might not be legal, so just keep it to yourself, okay?"

"Maybe we should score some," Pablo laughed.

Rolling my eyes in exasperation, I left to find Raquel.


I went to speak to Mami alone when we got home. Tiredly, she shared Tío Victor's latest proposal for dealing with my father. Tío had suggested we choose a good day to double-dose my father with the Dalmane and then telephone my uncle to come over on some driving pretext, only he would take my father to a doctor instead.

Mami admitted that she was worried about what would happen after my father returned home if the doctor didn't do anything.

She had a point. What if my father reacted badly to her betrayal? If the sleeping pill really wasn't strong enough, who would survive that volcano? Still, we had to do something.

"Why don't you get Camila's advice?" I urged anxiously. "She's got so much experience with doctors, especially now with Hernán in the hospital."

No, she concluded, she would sort things out and decide.

I opened my mouth to plead with her, but the expression in her eyes revealed that maybe she hadn't fully confided everything to Camila either.

"Rita's checking the dosage," Mami added reassuringly.

I tried to reassure myself, too, that my father's blow up hadn't been that unusual, except for his turning on my uncle a little harshly. But when I heard Mami officially decline my uncle's proposal, on the phone with Tía Rita later that night, I felt deflated. "Roberto will have to go to a doctor eventually," Mami rationalized over the phone. "He's got that gall bladder problem."

For a few days, I couldn't shake a feeling of doom that we were living in purgatory, waiting for my father to commit the act that would start the cycle of criminal and deportation threats all over again. I was so weary of worrying about what could happen. Wistfully, I wished I belonged with the nuns who cared for one another in the convents of the world. Or the socialist *kibbutzim* David praised, in which everyone seemed to be cared for too. Wasn't there some place out there for me?

I was more than ready to be cheered up by the time David pulled up to our meeting spot that week. *"Al parque, niña?"* he greeted me.

I smiled back and hopped in. "Yes, please, the park. Me encantaría."

*"Encantar.* I remember that—enchant! I gotta ask you something, though. Why are guys in Spanish textbooks always named Esteban? I had three different books with that guy's name in them."

I giggled as he drove off toward our day's adventure, a rendezvous at the house on Alameda Avenue where he'd been staying. His aunt and uncle had apparently gone AWOL for the week. We stopped at a park to get high beforehand so that their cleaning lady wouldn't detect any mischief. As we sat on a log together, David lit up and talked music, and I shared Pablo's dream of turning primitive cello sounds into groovy rock 'n' roll. That got a laugh. "Yeah, maybe I'll learn to play Israeli folk instruments," David ruminated, "maybe accordion."

"We have those," I said, explaining cumbia and vallenato music.

"I'd love to check out South America," he said, smoking.

"Machu Picchu, Patagonia. And after that, maybe the Seven Wonders. I wonder which are left?" While he thought it over, possibilities flew around tempting him.

"The Pyramids," I replied authoritatively, taking a small toke when he offered the joint. His ruminating made me wish I could jump up and seize one of the winged possibilities for me. "What about sailing the Nile on a barge?" I proposed enthusiastically, as if we might go together.

He laughed. "Yeah, guess I better make more dough before the *kibbutz*."

The wings of possibility flew away, dropping me precipitously into the cage of my life.

Abruptly, I asked him what he was really going to do with his life.

"It's too much work, figuring that out," he said, smiling and offering me the joint again.

I shook my head, refusing. "Maybe you could start by ruling out what you don't want to do," I encouraged.

"Well, I don't want to work all the time like my father. I don't want—"

"David, that's not what I meant," I interrupted.

"Tell me what you want to be. Maybe that'll inspire me." He put the roach away and, folding his hands like an altar boy, scuttled close to me on the log. "Shoot."

"Okay. I guess I wouldn't mind being a history professor, or maybe do what the lady I babysit for does. Write books. But I'm not sure how you get a job with that, I mean that you can live on. I know the things I *don't* want to be."

"Let me guess." He fiddled with my blouse. "A doctor?"

"How'd you guess?"

"You hate science."

"That's true." I closed my eyes and let him slide his hand up my belly. "What I would *really* hate to be is a petrochemical plant worker." Firmly I took David's still climbing hand out of my blouse and gave him a Fernandita-to-El-Loco look. "How about you now?" I demanded.

He leaned forward and whispered in my ear. "Do you want to be a nun?"

I whispered in his, "Do you want to be Leonard Cohen?"

He laughed out loud.

"You shouldn't take your luck for granted, David. You have so many choices. Nothing's stopping you from choosing."

"Sure it is. I want to be here now. In the moment. My parents say I have to be productive."

All his freedom was pretty invisible to him, and I felt the tiniest bit mad. But something compelled me to him anyway, very physically.

Afterward, we drove to the house, which was large and shaded by ficus and palm trees. Inside, the temperature was cool, but David jacked up the air-conditioning to the max, then poured us beers in two refrigerated glasses and showed me his room. He put on a Moody Blues record I liked and, as we drank the beers, I began to relax out of my own moody blues. Eventually, we climbed into the twin bed and had fun rubbing each others' bodies for warmth under the blankets until I nervously pushed him off.

"What's the matter?" he asked, scrunching one eye open to appraise me.

"I'm not that used to this," I admitted.

He slid back over me with a smile. "You get more used to it with practice."

I had to grin back, though I couldn't help hearing that stupid song, "Me vuelvo loca," in my head. Did people actually go crazy with love? Was that what love was supposed to be? Crazy? Shutting my eyes tightly against all that, I let myself float back into the warm bay waters of kissing, and then David removed his T-shirt and pulled me close. "Come on, Lita," he whispered, partially unzipping my jeans, "just a little." I cracked up trying to zip them back up, because my pants were too tight and I couldn't do it with one hand. Laughing too, he unzipped his own pants and took them off, then started roaming around in his underwear and slid a hand down mine. That instantly shot the crazy-in-love feeling straight into my blood. But I didn't want to be crazy—not even for love. Panicking, I rolled myself into a blanket and dropped to the floor. "Cut that out," I said furiously.

"Come on," he coaxed, his nearly naked body outstretched. "It's not even fucking."

My heart pounded madly at the sound of the word, and I scrambled to my feet, but David grabbed my leg and tripped me back down beside him. "What's the deal with you?"

I started to cry.

"Oh man, oh shit, Lita. Don't cry." He pulled me into a hug. "It's okay," he said. "I just don't get you." With a sigh, he clambered out of the bed. "Let's just get outta here. Help me find my sneakers, okay?"

It ended so weirdly, and I felt so guilty, but I had no choice.

The really bad feelings didn't start until he'd dropped me off and I was alone again, walking home. Suddenly, I was scared that David would dump me, but I grew even more afraid of my own body betraying me in some vague way, as I always feared my thoughts would. What was craziness anyway? That darkness took hold as I opened the door of my house and went inside.

"Mami's been calling you all afternoon," Pablo alerted me. "She's at Camila's. You better go over there. Hernán died."

## TWENTY

A DEFEATED-LOOKING CAMILA WAS RESTING in an armchair while relatives scattered around coddling her and assuming responsibility for things like checking with Pan Am about her son's flight. As I stepped up to tell her how sorry I was about Hernán, she smiled kindly and took my hand, then said what a good girl I was and how they'd always wanted a daughter like me.

I blinked back tears as Mami smiled in gratitude and led me away toward the master bedroom, where Lara was chatting with the nail lady from a hair salon where I'd delivered many an Avon package. Both of them were charitably gathering Hernán's old clothing for the St. Stephen's donation bin, but one glimpse at the neatly folded male apparel on the bed made me teary again. Lara stopped what she was doing to come hug me, and Mami patted my arm comfortingly as she handed me a plastic bag to start loading clothes.

"Many hands make light work, ah?" said Lara, simulating cheer. She was the only one of the three who looked herself in her black outfit, maybe because it went better with her salt-and-pepper hair. Zoila, the nail lady, and Mami seemed a little washed-out, especially Mami, who must have been crying with Camila and had to wipe off her mascara.

I shook my plastic bag open. "How come Camila and Hernán *didn't* have another kid, Mami?" I asked thoughtfully.

"Oh, they tried, mi'ja," she said ruefully, grabbing another shirt from the closet. "Believe me, they tried."

Zoila clucked. "Por lo menos, the marriage lasted. Sometimes all that trying squeezes the zumo right out of a relationship." She lifted her eyebrows knowingly at Lara.

Lara returned an amused smile and joked back, "Sometimes the zumo is just fine, but the orange is a problem."

Though Zoila laughed heartily, Mami derailed the joking. "A real marriage," she said quietly, her chin held high, "should be more than that."

Surprised, I tried to size up the exact meaning of her remark while discreetly studying her. Was Mami actually acknowledging the existence of *sex*? Or, more precisely, its nonexistence, in her case? Cryptic comments she'd made in the past about no one recognizing her as a woman anymore started to make sense to me.

"No relationship gives you everything," Lara offered matter-of-factly, as she briskly folded up clothing, not bothering with any creases. "We all make compromises."

Mami glanced at her with curiosity.

"Without a doubt," Zoila admitted.

But Lara *has* her man, I thought uneasily, unlike Mami. For a moment I wished I could throw my own zumo-squeezing difficulties into the mix and get somebody's advice, at least Lara's.

Aloud, I only dared ask, "Like what, Lara?" while pretending not to see Mami frown at me for breaching the silence expected of me when crossing the borders of adult territory.

"Oh," Lara smiled vaguely as she tied up a finished bag. "Sometimes, in periods of difficulty, love presents us with challenges. ¿No Evi?" she inquired, trading understanding glances with my mother.

Beside me, Zoila shook her own bag to test the knot and parked the bag back down. "Parece que we've finished, señoras," she concluded, fists to her hips as she looked around. "No one would even guess that a man had lived here."

I surveyed the pink and gray room with its ruffled bedspread and shams and Camila's matching robe that hung over a door. My gaze landed on her wedding photo. "Oh no," I said, clapping a hand over my mouth. "That's going to remind her."

"Ay Gabriela," Mami said ruefully, shaking her head. "She's not about to forget that he was her husband. Only that he's gone, mi'ja."

Whatever that meant.


Saturday, Mami went to the funeral with Lara. At first I was angry when Mami forbid me from going. "Funerals are no place for the young," she proclaimed righteously. "Too much sadness."

As if I weren't already familiar with sadness.

But as the hour of the service approached, I felt relieved to escape my thoughts of Camila and her loss.

I went to meet Fátima at the library until it was time for David to pick me up for our planned fishing expedition. I had finally gotten up the nerve to call him, and when he sounded completely normal and glad to hear from me I'd gratefully agreed to his suggestion.

I still hadn't found the courage to tell Fátima about him though, and the guilt was eating away at me. "Fátima," I said hesitantly, opening my copy of *Siddhartha*, "do you think any guys in our grade are cute?"

She twirled her ponytail with a pencil. "I guess if I were going to date anybody, I would pick Mark Pierce." At my scrunched-up brow, she added, "He's in Chemistry with me. Really smart."

"Oh yeah." A high achieving male to meet Fátima's standards.

No doubt David would qualify in the loser category on *that* subject list. I nodded and observed neutrally, "He's American."

She smiled. "I'm not about to get married, Gabi."

"Yeah, I guess your parents would let you leave home anyway," I said with envy. "Mine are more old-fashioned."

"They'll adapt," she predicted confidently, bending to highlight something in her book.

Unlikely, I decided, then promptly gave up the love talk to jot down sketchy thoughts about the *Siddhartha* cycles. A few minutes later, I glanced at my watch and abruptly told Fátima that I had to leave. "I forgot something I have to do for Lara," I invented. "I'll call you later and you can read me your paper, okay?"

She gave me a funny look.

"I'm sorry, Fátima," I said as I stood up. "It was stupid that I forgot." What a bad person I was, I felt then. Fátima was a friend of the soul—wasn't that *philos* love? But did all the forms of love in Lara's classification scheme count equally? I sighed to myself as I waited for the van.

Soon, David was driving us toward the Miccosukee Village while chatting blithely about all he'd learned at the tackle shop. When we reached the spot near the canal where a guy was already fishing, David parked and set up our rods. Then we waited a long time until he got a bite and happily managed to reel in a fat black fish.

"Mudfish," stated the Miccosukee guy, laughing when we asked if you could eat it. "Oh, sure. If you like mud," he quipped, before he cleared out and left us alone there.

We didn't get any more bites after that.

With disappointment, David folded up the rods. While he was packing them in the van, I mustered up the courage to tell him that I wasn't really ready for a sexual relationship.

He looked at me as if I'd said something funny. "What's 'a sexual relationship'?"

"Don't joke around. You know what I mean."

"No, tell me." He shut the van door and leaned back, arms crossed.

I studied the saw grass waving in the breeze on the opposite side of the canal. From this distance, you couldn't see that it had many tiny razor teeth. "I mean, I can't have sex with you, with anybody." I looked up at him and my lip trembled. "I'm afraid," I confessed.

"Oh, Lita." Reaching an arm out, he pulled me to him. "You're making it into such a big deal. Can't you trust me a little?"

I tightened my arms around his waist, my face to his chest. We stayed that way, close and quiet, as the low-key sounds of Miccosukee life whispered across the Everglades. I didn't want to let go. But the breeze was picking up, the sky threatening rain.

On our way home, a quieter David put on a Cat Stevens tape while I gazed out the window and brooded, absentmindedly breaking apart split ends in my hair. Eventually, he lit up and smoked, but when he passed me the joint, I could only hold it out in front of me like some foul medicine I was supposed to swallow. "What's your favorite drug, David?" I asked, before he finally took it back.

He considered. "This guy I knew used to cook his own speed. That was good. Mushrooms are fun. I don't know, probably pot. It's easy to share."

Like Pablo, David craved the solidarity of fellow druggies.

This time, when he passed me his joint I took it and inhaled for as long as I could. "David," I asked, releasing all my breath at last, "do you still want me to try something else with you?"

He looked curiously in my direction. "For real?"

I nodded with fake confidence. I wanted to make things up to him, but I didn't have anything else to give. "It won't be bad for me, though, right?"

He reached for my hand. "No," he said, grinning happily. *"No problema."*

And all I could think was, *we all make compromises.*


Twinges of anxiety stole over me during the weeks that followed, but I shook off my fears. Pot hadn't proved to be dangerous, so how much worse could David's other drugs be? If nothing else, trying to figure out prospects for sneaking away with him distracted me from my worries about my father.

I quizzed Lara about her future plans, but with Walter in Argentina and Solita's many pediatric visits, Lara hadn't needed me much of late. "It's so difficult to get things done," she'd apologized the last time she returned early from the university, and I sensed it wasn't me she was letting down but herself.

When Tío Lucho rang with a family barbecue invitation, I sang a private hallelujah! Tío Lucho's was so far that David and I could have the whole day to ourselves. Immediately, I fibbed up a babysitting excuse for Mami, which she acceded to since Manolo had begged off to work too. He'd practically disappeared into his hardware store job, the wages diligently stashed in the sleek, new Florida Savings & Loan: Manolo the banker, amassing the millions my father would never have.


I was jolted out of my rendezvous plotting during a school assembly when a voice suddenly boomed out my name from the stage.

Startled, I looked up: Why was the principal calling for me?

With a nervous glance at Fátima, who laughingly pushed me up, I climbed out of the row and hurried to the stage. There, I squinted into the high beams in confusion as the principal began shaking my hand and handing me an enormous plaque. I tried to read it quickly and almost couldn't believe what I saw. I'd won the essay contest! Someone else pressed a thick envelope into my arms. It was Mr. Lanham, smiling at me as the principal began addressing the audience and explaining the award. In a daze, I smiled back while struggling to hold everything. The lights were so disorienting that I couldn't quite catch what the principal said about some trip to New York.

When the assembly ended, Mr. Lanham and the guidance counselor came up to me. "I'm sorry we sprung this on you, Gabi," he said. "We thought it would be a great surprise."

Miss McWhorter smiled warmly, took both my hands, and asked, "Shall we back up a little, Gabi?"

I nodded gratefully.

"As Mr. Lanham must have told you," she began, "this program promotes intercultural understanding, dialogue. That's why the kids who win are called Ambassadors. They get to travel abroad and learn about other people."

"This year's country is Egypt," Mr. Lanham interjected eagerly.

"I won a trip to Egypt?" I asked in disbelief. A strange warmth began to fill me. *I had won my freedom!*

Mr. Lanham smiled. "Yeah. But it's not all shopping and bistros. You'll be there for a whole semester."

"A whole semester?" I echoed faintly as the winds of the Levante and the Khamsin swept me across the sand dunes of some other wondrous world.

"Sure. You'll go with all the reps from participating schools around the country," he explained.

"It's all in there," Miss McWhorter added, tapping the envelope in my arms. "You'll go to New York first, to the United Nations, and you'll get to attend their sessions. That should be fun." She threw an inquiring glance at Mr. Lanham.

"It will all be fun," he stated confidently.

"Oh, great," I said. But the lightness that had carried me along was dissipating. Who was I kidding? There could be no bistros, trips, or understanding dialogue for me. There was only the prison of home. "Mr. Lanham," I said bravely, trying to squelch the feeling of letdown, "I know this is an honor and all, but I don't think that the trip part will go over with my family. Couldn't I get the prize money without it?"

He looked disappointed. "There isn't any money, Gabriela. The purpose of the award is to give you an opportunity that you might not have otherwise."

"It's okay, Gabi," Miss McWhorter said, her brow furrowed. "This isn't something you have to decide now. You talk it over at home. The trip isn't for a year. You have to be a junior. Tell your folks to call me about it or to come see me, okay?"

"Okay," I said, though I knew only too well that parental visits to school weren't on the De la Paz itinerary either.

Slowly I walked back to my locker, placed my plaque and the envelope inside, and headed depressingly toward my next class. As I took my seat next to Claudio at the crowded communal table, our bare arms touched. Both of us immediately retracted them, and an intense shyness came between us, causing us to sit perfectly still. Thankfully, the teacher, Mr. Rubenstein, broke the silence to explain our next writing assignment. When class finally ended, Claudio stood by hesitantly as everyone else filed out. Then, offering me a generous smile, he congratulated me. "It will be a journey of greatness, Gabriela," he added, looking at me so profoundly that I wanted to give him something back too.

"I wish *you* could go," I blurted.

For a second, we stared at each other without speaking, and my heart began to flutter like a baby parakeet begging to fly.

"Would you like a ride home?" he asked me quietly.

"I'm supposed to meet Fátima."

"Ah." He picked up my bag and handed it over.

"Thanks," I said, falling silent while feeling like an idiot as we walked out. I finally found my tongue. "Is your grandfather any better?"

Claudio shook his head. "The cancer is making him even smaller." With both hands, he measured vertically, as if his abuelo were an infant.

"¡Ay Claudio! How sad!"

"The story is sadder," he said ruefully, admitting that his family had convinced the grandfather that he had osteoporosis, not bone cancer, so that he wouldn't know he was dying. "To save him the tragedy," Claudio explained as we headed downstairs.

But that meant more tragedy for Claudio, I realized sorrowfully. How could you share a room with your grandfather and watch him die while pretending not to know or feel anything? A great city of lies was crumbling into dust around us.

We reached the cafeteria where Fátima was waiting, and I paused at the door. A part of me wanted to go with Claudio, wherever that might be, but I said good-bye and went to meet her. Then I put Claudio's tragedy out of my thoughts as I returned to brooding aloud to Fátima about what to tell Mami about my award. I could only imagine her appalled reaction to the notion of a trip across the world.

"Give her a chance," Fátima urged as we rode the bus together homeward.

"Your father went to college," I said glumly, staring out the window. "He knows leaving home is part of modern life. My mother doesn't agree with that stuff. I'd have to get married, or else I'd turn into a persona non grata."

"Come on, Gabi," Fátima said, with a smile. "Think about it. You show up with a scholarship to Harvard, and she's going to say no?"

"You don't know the half of it," I said, frowning.

"Well, at least talk to her about what it means to you," Fátima encouraged, as the bus neared her stop.

As I rode on toward my house after she got off, the difficulties of negotiating the Egypt trip grew nearly insurmountable in my mind. And if leaving for one semester was difficult, I thought morosely, how would I ever leave my family prison for good? To be sure, the Holy Family wouldn't look favorably on my entering any convent under false pretenses. And false they would be, since I'd obviously exhibited physical impulses toward the opposite sex. That left me with only one legitimate escape route: marriage. And who was there for me to marry?

Claudio?

Whatever was going on between us, he had plenty of his own problems and wasn't going anywhere either, not for a while.

Octavio knew about my crazy father, I mused. I pictured marrying him—he was a good person. Would he do it as a favor?

Oh, this was ridiculous. No liberated woman would hang her life on a husband. That wasn't the kind of compromise Lara had in mind, I was sure. Sighing, I let myself off the bus and plodded home. Maybe I would wait and seek her advice, when she had some more free time, before saying anything to Mami about the Egypt trip.

That night I tried not dwell on the loneliness of not being able to tell my own parents about my contest win. Instead, I searched distractedly through my diary for something I could deliver in the guise of a writing assignment. The only possibility that seemed to fit the theme—personal portraits—was the unpleasant episode in which my father, screaming and cursing in furious Spanish, had whacked a burning newspaper funnel out of our elderly fisherman neighbor's hand while the poor guy mumbled back in confused Italian. Call it a story of men speaking in tongues under our lime/ grapefruit tree. Call it: The Tree of the Split Persona.

No, that wouldn't do. Even if I changed the names to make my father American, the whole school would speculate about me. With frustration, I continued to flip through pages until I came to a diatribe about how Mami never let me express my true feelings. I stopped, then grabbed a sheet of paper and started listing her favorite admonishments—from the innocuous "eso nunca se dice" ("that must never be said") to the more direct "ya" ("enough")— into a kind of poem, a mean one. I squeezed my eyes shut for a moment and tried to divine which clichés would follow an announcement from me that I was going off to Egypt. "¡Ni siquiera!" ("In your dreams!")

Adages from past fights quickly landed on my page, along with the timeless questions: "Who Do You Think You Are?"; "How Could You Ever Suggest Such a Thing?"; and the ever-popular "Who Gave You Your Life?" As I wrote, I alternated between English and Spanish—indenting the translated lines separately on the page, as though the two languages were yelling their Ten Commandments at each other. I suspected my darkly poetic teacher would love it. It was so *harsh*.

Fátima called, and I put aside the commandments poem to briefly report on my lack of gumption to bring up the contest win at home just yet. When I returned to my bedroom, I found Mami staring at my writing. My heart leapt.

"¿Qué es esto?" she asked.

"Homework." With my eyes, I willed the pages intact, afraid she might rip them.

"What kind of homework is that, criticizing your family?" she asked, frowning.

"It's an assignment," I told her quickly, reaching for the papers and tucking them safely inside a book. "It's supposed to be ironic."

"To be what?"

"Ironic. Mami, didn't you see Pablo messing around with the typewriter in his room? Papi will have a fit."

The anger dissolved in her face, leaving deeper crevices of anxiety. When she left, I felt relieved that she hadn't cried, though I resented bitterly her complete indifference to any of *my* feelings. The only persona she seemed to love was one who would march resolutely into martyrdom to save everyone else.

My piece, Mr. Rubenstein opined when I turned it in the next day, was "a cultural map of subtle dimensions."

David just laughed when I read it aloud for him on Saturday at the start of our special outing, which began with our ever-romantic McDonald's stop. I shared my contest victory news as well as my travel difficulty—that great big hole at the center of my cultural map.

"Well, if you figure out how to sneak off from your mother," he joked over his burger, "I'll meet you. Israel's not far from there."

"Yeah, right." I threw a whole salt packet over my fries.

"Parents are a drag," he admitted, folding his arms on the table. "You know, there's something I didn't tell you too." He hesitated. "I got busted last year after a concert. I didn't have that much, so they gave me a fine. But my parents said I'd better clean up my act."

"Oh, I guess that's lucky," I said, digesting the unexpected disclosure. But along with sympathy, I started to feel some bitterness. David only had to "clean up his act" and pay a fine, while my father could be dragged off in disgrace and exiled permanently for doing the exact same thing, just because he was an immigrant.

It *wasn't* fair: Mami had been right on the money about that. As I sat stewing on the injustice, David added that he'd only started working to become independent of his parents. "I guess I should get serious about this *kibbutz* thing," he concluded, studying the people eating at other tables.

"Yeah, maybe that's a good idea," I said faintly, my righteous anger suddenly abandoning me.

"It's not even my idea," he admitted. "A girlfriend of mine went to one."

*Girlfriend?* My fantasy of being his one and only quickly disintegrated, and I started grabbing our trays to clear until he stopped me with a grin. "Hey, no big deal," he said, playing with my hand. "Maybe I'll stay here and transfer to U of M. I could take the Lita bus and ride in back so your girlfriends don't discover your secret." His eyes twinkled. "I could write a mystery, like 'Bus Number 43 Romance' or something."

"Ha ha." I faked a smile.

But what would be left of my story with David missing? My mother and her Commandments? Pablo and his sniffing hobbies, Manolo the Banker? My sewing uncles and Tía Rita, the Saint of Diverted Pharmaceuticals?

And my father, the greatest character of them all.


As David drove toward the Everglades afterward, he gave me his dimpled smile, inserted a Taj Mahal tape, and said, "Let's get in the groove." The gold streaks in his hair lit up his face, and I suddenly wanted to move to the pillows in the back. *Eros* love, defying any human fear.

Beyond the populated areas, he pulled off to the side of the road. Rummaging through his drug satchel, he removed two tiny squares of paper and handed me one. "Lick it."

"Huh?"

"It's glued on there. The Blue Heaven."

I licked a few times, but I didn't taste much. Puzzled, I looked up.

"It's not a trick," he said, grinning and licking his square. "You'll see."

Then we got back on the highway to the National Park. Parking in the lot, David took out a visitors' guide to show me the board-walk trail he had in mind. He tucked the brochure in his pocket and we ambled over to the slough where the trail began.

Three alligators reposed in placid water. Our eyes riveted on their tails, we stopped and watched, waiting for one to move. Everything was utterly quiet, as if something ought to happen. But time here was indifferent: no fragmented hours, only a present that stretched out into perfect silence. As we kept watching, the biggest alligator finally glided across the slough into a clump of red man-groves until all we could see through the roots in the water was a dark, still mound of alligator head.

Eventually, we started down the boardwalk trail. Holding hands, we pointed out birds for each other. Anhingas. Blue herons, Little and Great. A beautiful pink bird the visitors' guide said was a Rose-ate Spoonbill. Where the boardwalk ended, we continued on a path sculpted with limestone sinkholes. I peered into one of the holes, and a rainbow unfolded in the water. "It's so beautiful, David."

"Maybe it's the acid," he mumbled back.

Beyond the limestone holes, our path led through a tangled can-opy of hardwood trees. Peacefully, we followed it along until both of us realized at once that our limbs and faces were stinging.

"Shit," David complained as he swatted. "I should've brought bug juice."

The stings multiplied and I began to scratch myself furiously. "Ugh! Let's go back."

Turning, we sprinted toward the trailhead. As the mosquitoes became completely unbearable, we tore maniacally down the path. I shook my arms in the air to simulate a breeze that might send the vicious insects away, but they were undeterred. It was one hot race to the van door. David panted as he fished for his keys and found them. Jumping in, we locked the doors behind us. "Fucking monsters," he said, catching his breath. "Bloodsuckers. Pigs."

I burst out laughing. I'd never seen David so mad before. I climbed on top of him and kissed his bitten face with all four forms of love. Then I straddled the seat into the back and dropped myself into the mirrored pillows. With my hands resting quietly on my chest, I lay there and perused David's posters as he drove us out of Paradise.

The posters were in 3D. In a blue concert hall, the Moody Blues were playing, but the sound traveled in rays of light that shone through the instruments. *Synaesthesia*—I remembered distantly, as snow fell across the Himalayas and each flake quivered like the long-held note of an electric guitar. The white doors of a church in Switzerland fluttered open. There was a swish of red leaves in the trees, a symphony of rain sticks. Everywhere I aimed my eyes the world came beautifully to life. I was so happy, so blessed. And for the first time in my life, I felt truly free.

I must have fallen into a trance, because David startled me when he opened the van door and the sun beamed in. "Wow," I said, rubbing my eyes. "That was great."

"Yeah. Except for the bugs." He looked chagrined. "It's kinda late. You hungry?"

"Full of joy."

He tumbled into the back with me and we fooled around briefly until someone beeped who'd been waiting for gas behind us and forced David to move the van.

On the road, we stopped at an IHOP and I checked in with a

call to Tío Lucho's. My father was playing dominos with my uncle.
That was a good sign.

"Everything cool?" asked David at the table.

"Yeah. We have time."

He ordered pancakes with everything on them: strawber-
ries, whipped cream, pecan bits, and golden syrup that I poured
gloriously over the buttermilk medallions. David reached for the
pancakes and cut into them. "Mmm, good," he said through a
mouthful as he slid the plate back over.

"David, I have to ask you something."

"Uh-oh." He wolfed down another big bite.

"Seriously. Say you could have only one kind of love. Like God's
love versus a person's. For example, mine. What would you pick?"

He chewed on the pancake. "Sounds like a rabbi question."

I waited.

"Okay, since I don't believe God exists," he said, licking his fork
adorably, "I'd rather have yours."

"Really?"

"Mmm."

"You don't believe in God?"

"Oh, I don't know about that shit, Lita. Eat the pancakes already.
I don't want to get you in trouble with the authorities."

"I'm sorry." I chewed a little, glanced up, and smiled. "I'd rather
have yours too."

"Yeah, yeah." But then he gave me the biggest smile of all.
"Love is all there is."


As I'd come to expect, the freedom and joy I'd felt that day didn't
last long. David began to zero in on his Israel trip, and as he did,
a sad-eyed fatalism returned to claim me. I couldn't laugh when
David twirled my hair in his fingers and sang a croaky rendition

of "So Long, Marianne," which made Leonard Cohen sound even more depressing, if that was possible.

When his departure date neared, we made one more rendez-vous to the park in the Grove, where I paid silent tribute to the banyan and mangrove trees that had always sheltered us. The low-hanging branches created a Hansel-and-Gretel darkness in the woods around me. Would I ever return?

David took off his silver pinky ring with the black and white yin yang stone. Flashing the dimpled smile he'd worn when he first asked me to party with him, he handed me the ring. *"Un regalo."*

I stared at the stone. "Thanks," I said joylessly, taking the divided ring. What had I given him besides a few dull rules of Castilian grammar?

We drove to my drop-off spot, but this time he parked before coming around to let me out. I stood facing the battered blue door with my hand gripping the broken handle until David turned me toward him. "Hey, Lita."

How solemnly I stared back.

He laughed and kissed me, then gave me a big hug. "Hey, it was really great to hang out with you. Even though you're saving yourself for somebody better."

I didn't laugh.

My broken "'bye" got buried in his chest. Whatever kind of love it had been was lost in the woods of sorrow, along with every other kind I'd known.

At home afterward, I tied the yin yang ring on a ribbon around the cover of my diary and stuffed the diary back into the cigar box I kept under my bed. Then I lay down. When Mami called for me, I pretended I had cramps.

## TWENTY-ONE

AN INTERNATIONAL CALL CAME the morning after I'd said good-bye to David. I could tell from my parents' shouting on the phone. In bed with "cramps," I put the transistor radio to my ear. Everybody had a broken heart. I tried to sing along on one of the peppier melodies, but I couldn't bear to push my voice out to meet the notes. I couldn't defy my nature, which was to be silent. Silent. Silent.

Getting up seemed pointless, like that part of *The Bell Jar* where the heroine wonders why we brush our teeth and hair day after day, over and over. Sameness was horrible. Why had God made us this way?

As the hours ticked, Mami became impatient and came to collect me. "Gabriela, please get out of that bed and help with dinner. Take some aspirin."

I stumbled up. If only I did have cramps instead of this terrible ache in my stomach, chest, head, eyes.

In the kitchen, she was subdued, refraining from the usual complaints. I added capers and raisins to her picadillo and replaced our plastic tablecloth with the washed-out but merrier one with the orange flamboyán flowers. As the food simmered on the stove, Mami sat and stared out the window.

"¿Qué fue?" I asked, suddenly conscious that something was wrong.

In a soft voice, she answered, "Hubo una muerte."

A death? My heart froze. "My grandfather?"

Mami looked startled, then shook her head. "No, mi'ja. Abuelita Matilde."

My father's mother. The one who, every year without fail, sent us—via Tía Consuelo or other visitors—treasured boxes of bocadillos veleños. Inside each wood box came the treats, wrapped in a pale green wrap that Tía Consuelo had taught us wasn't paper but plátano leaf enclosing each three-layer bocadillo. The thickest layer of rich guava paste was topped with a layer of dulce de leche, glazed with caramelized sugar. Nothing you ate in this world would be sweeter.

"What happened, Mami?"

"Ay, mi'jita," she sighed. "Old age. A respiratory infection."

I remembered how Abuelita Matilde's tiny crystals had jiggled from her earrings when she laughed. I remembered her face with its slightly bent nose, a miniature version of my Tía Consuelo's. I remembered, though more vaguely, my mother's spinster sister, Tía Julia, and other relatives we'd lost. It was as if our family had started to die away from us after we left Colombia.

Mami was crying. It made me want to cry too, but I held the cry in my throat. I put my hand on her shoulder and let my gaze follow hers toward our intertwined lime/grapefruit trees, each bearing its own fruit.

When my father came out of his room for dinner, everybody quieted. He wore the determined look with which he assigned me projects, but when he sat down, he didn't give Mami the usual goofy smile of anticipation or say everything smelled delicious. He simply looked at the plate in front of him, forgetting to eat. Even his ticking hand remained still on the faded flower tablecloth. I almost wished he would start raving about refineries again.

Across the table, Mami waited like a prisoner for a turn at the guillotine.

After exchanging uneasy glances, my brothers and I began our obligatory meal.

Tía Consuelo's call lifted our penalty of silence. With relief, I listened to my father start the familiar shouting process on the hallway phone. Suddenly, he broke into sobs—great, ugly sounds that stumbled across the room and engulfed us. My brothers and I had never heard my father cry. Pablo trembled on the verge of tears himself, while my mother pushed her chair back as if to rise but then thought better of it and pulled herself grimly forward. Next to each other, Manolo and I hunched over our plates to shield ourselves from the avalanche of my father's grief.

I felt terrible for Tía Consuelo, who had to listen to the sobs while trying to talk with my father. I felt the ache and sadness of each of the De la Paz brothers and sisters, of the family cloth that would not last. I felt saddest of all for my father and my tiny, lost abuelita. And me.


Abuela Matilde's death left my father a different person, a broken one who frequently cried in his room. No one thought it a good idea to send him to Colombia in that state, even with his brothers, and Tío Victor was convinced El Chino would advise against it anyway because of the immigration complications. Luckily, my father didn't bring it up himself.

I worried aloud to Mami about his constant crying, and she explained that he'd loved my abuelita very much, of course, and that a person always regrets not having done more to show his love.

But to me it seemed that my father cried out of loneliness, a kind of loneliness that maybe no one but his mother could ever take away.

My father's sadness made my own feel small and futile. With David gone, and now school ended, I sank into gloom and doom. Fátima had secured a job at her mother's store, but mine at the mall bookstore wouldn't start for a couple more weeks. While I waited for that and Pablo for his summer school course to start, we stayed home together and listened to my father cry. After a week of that, Mami quit giving him sleeping pills for fear they might be depressing him further—despite Tía Rita's admonition to wean him off gradually, so that he wouldn't panic. As his crying ceased, my father promptly resumed his manic scribbling.

That wasn't a big deal, but a couple of evenings later when we were sitting over dinner, something alarmed me about his overly excited predictions regarding the millions of dollars the government would return as soon as we stopped writing checks.

Pablo chirped up. "You said the government's gonna give us a house, Papi."

"No!" My father shook his head angrily, declaring that we would get the millions outright after he wrote to the bank. He raised his dinner knife and warned, "No more mortgage checks."

Mami stood and began loudly clearing the plates.

Though she'd already hidden the family's important documents in my closet, she took the checkbook to work with her on Monday. It was a lucky thing, too, since that day my father went hunting. Off the sleeping pills, he had surprising energy. Pablo and I hung around in our beds while anxiously listening to my father fight with the drawers. Pablo kept verbal track of progress. "He's in the silverware drawer again, Gab." Then, a while later, "Hall closet."

As much as Pablo poked fun at my father initially, all humor disappeared when his searches became frenetic. The house rattled with doors and drawers banging over the angry pitch of my father's muttering. A couple of nights later, when Mami got home from work, I alerted her that his bizarre behavior had intensified.

Her immediate response was to disregard all that and pick on me instead for hanging around all day without doing anything productive. "What's wrong with you, Gabriela?" she demanded, shaking her head.

Too deflated to mount any comeback, I only shrugged. Something *was* wrong with me, I knew. Fate had been stalking my fledgling future like my father on his relentless quest for the checkbook— and I was losing ground. I still hadn't told Mami about my contest victory, despite Miss McWhorter's cajoling for me to do so before classes let out. The counselor had taken pains to emphasize how great the field trip would look on my college applications, and she'd even plied me with pamphlets about college choices. But I already knew my college choices, if any: Miami-Dade or the University of Miami. Home with the family was my husbandless destino.

I tried to redeem myself by preparing dinner. When Mami saw the chicken stewing later, she planted a kiss on my forehead. "Gracias, mi'ja. You're a good girl." She took the wooden spoon. "I'll finish."

I sat at the table, momentarily at a loss. To make myself useful, I grabbed a napkin and began wiping the hard-to-clean crevices on our salt and pepper shakers. They were ceramic flamingos, the tiny salt bird's wings extended in flight and the pepper bird with both feet planted. A terrible longing seized me as the fragrance of spices filled the air and the evening light fell across my mother's shoulders like a shawl—the two flamingos stood mute, separated between the earth and sky.


In the morning, I walked to the library instead of vegging out with Pablo. Carrying a few college catalog trays over to a table, I read about the University of Chicago, Notre Dame, McGill in Canada, and even the University of Barcelona, where Claudio hoped to study some day.

Cold, damp places, thousands of miles away, where my family and its problems could never reach me.

If only I could get there myself.

I put the catalogs back in their trays.

The next day, Friday, was every bit as steamy and depressing as the day before. No hint of air broke through, and I lugged myself through the hours like a slug across the eternity of a tree trunk. I couldn't wait for my job at the book store to begin.

Gratitude struck in the form of an unexpected babysitting date the next morning, which provided an air-conditioned reprieve from the general meaninglessness of my life. That day, when Lara returned from her research and errands, she ran her fingers through her hair with an apologetic smile. "I haven't had a free moment for a cut." Carrying our coffees into the living room, she kicked off her shoes and said, "Oof, what weather! How is everything at home, Gabi? Your Papi?"

"I guess he's better."

"You must miss your abuelita too."

"I don't remember her that well." The kindly way Lara spoke made my words catch in my throat. "I wasn't—close with her, like I am to my grandfather Gabriel."

"Your mami's father?"

"Uh-huh. He and my Abuelita Julia took care of me when my mother was having my brothers. He writes poems."

"How beautiful, Gabi. To have a grandfather poet."

I almost started to cry, gripping my cup fiercely to stop.

As Lara sipped her coffee, she asked in a casual tone, "How are your studies of love going, Gabi?"

My head popped up. Had she seen me and David? "Oh, I was just..." I bumbled around for what to say. "Curious."

"It's a good subject for a young woman to be curious about," Lara said with a bemused expression.

"Um, when is Walter coming back?" I responded nervously.

Lara sighed. "A few months, perhaps. There's been so much difficulty with the research," she paused. "Sometimes—how can I say this? He doesn't calculate everything into his planning."

I was unsure how to answer, so I simply asked, "Do you miss him, Lara?"

"Oh yes." She gave me a wry smile, then patted my hand as if I shouldn't worry.

But it did worry me. *We all make compromises*, I kept remembering her say.

"You know," she went on pensively, "you can try to change other people or change yourself. Either path is wretched! Walter struggles with it, too, even though he's a man."

"Maybe it's better to be alone," I ventured.

"Oh no, Gabrielita," Lara protested laughingly. "You mustn't lose your faith in love."

The girls woke, and I hung around to help everyone gaily prepare lunch instead of heading back to my house right away. Lara praised her daughters' "cooking," and I suddenly found myself blurting out that I'd won the Ambassador essay contest.

Lara grabbed my face and kissed me. "That's wonderful, Gabi! You're a marvel!"

I blinked furiously as the little girls clapped happily, and I tried to explain my prize.

"What an opportunity," Lara exclaimed, scooting the girls outside.

"I don't know about the trip, Lara," I said dolefully. "I don't think my mother will let me go."

"Oh, you'll convince her."

I shook my head.

"May I help?"

Though I suspected Mami would simply discount the unconventional Lara's advice, it was possible that she might trust Lara's opinion as a professional. A seedling of hope took root. "Okay, maybe you could try talking to her."

"We'll do it together. You tell me when."

"All right. I don't have to turn in permission forms for a while."

When I got home, I found the back door open. A loud racket was coming from my parents' room, and I rushed inside. They were both shouting, though I couldn't see what was happening because Pablo stood in the doorway in front of me.

"Give it to me!" my father screamed.

"No!" Mami yelled, sobbing. "We're not losing this house because of your cuentos!"

"Leave her alone!" Pablo shouted, darting into the room with a fork that he clutched in his hand and brandished like a weapon while approaching my father.

"Oh my God," I heard myself utter desolately.

I could see Mami bent over, grasping a small prayer book to her chest with both hands. My father tried to wrestle it away, his face becoming enflamed. As she secured the thing in her hands between her dress folds and locked her thighs tightly, forming an awkward vise, he began roughly shaking her to dislodge whatever she held. "It's *my* money!" he screamed, his face sweating. "Give it to me!" Just as it hit me that what she held was the checkbook, he put his big hands around her neck.

"No, Papi!" I cried out.

Pablo lunged forward and decked my father hard in the face. The punch knocked him off-balance, and he stepped backward, wavering. Pablo rapidly retrieved the fork he'd dropped and held it up in the air again, but my father retreated, regarding Pablo in complete bewilderment. He glanced at my crying mother and seemed to notice me by the door, but suddenly it was like he was looking through us, or past us, as if we'd become his ghosts.

Pablo lowered the fork, pointed it at my father, and said softly, "Just stay there." With the other hand, my brother motioned for Mami to leave. She brushed by without looking at anyone. "I'll be at Camila's," she barely croaked.

I eyed my father anxiously, but he only stood staring at us in his disheveled and bewildered state, his cheek pink where Pablo had hit him.

Pablo turned toward me. "I'm cutting out of here too."

"Okay," I replied timidly, following him to the kitchen and watching him take off.

Then, unsure of what to do next, I went to my room and sat on the bed. With Mami and Pablo gone, I felt as lost and bewildered as my father.

A sudden burst of fear propelled me into my brothers' room, and I locked the door. I stood facing it—and the treacherous possibility that perhaps we *should* let my father get arrested. Hadn't he just tried to strangle Mami?

But he *loved* her. Even if he was crazy, he loved her, right?

An image of the cane-cutting knife I'd once told Camila and Olguita about flashed into my mind. What if my father, overcome with remorse over how he'd attacked Mami, turned the knife on himself?

The house was so hot and horribly quiet.

But quiet was good. No doubt it meant my father was all right...

Or was he?

Weak-kneed before the locked door, I felt physically incapable of going out there to check on him. Why didn't someone else come home? Why didn't someone else do something?

After a while, I undid the lock, opened the door, and quietly exited. I crept slowly into the kitchen and paused there for a moment before inching my way toward my parents' room. Some nerve-wracking minutes passed in which I strained to listen and eventually detected the sound of an eraser softly rubbing against the blessed, blessed paper.

With enormous relief, I retraced my footsteps.

Then I took a very, very long shower.

When I got out, Pablo had returned, and I found him sitting on his bed, sweat streaking his back.

"Hi," I said from his doorway.

He was staring at a mound of dirty jeans on his floor. "Hi," he said, turning toward me, his eyes swollen from crying.

"Where did you go?" I asked, walking in.

"Johnny's."

"Oh." Rivulets of warm water wended their way into the towel I'd wrapped around me. Tightening it better, I sat beside him. "Pablo," I asked quietly, "how come Papi blew up like that?"

"The old man caught her writing a check." Pablo shook his head. "Instead of making something up she just told him what she was doing, and he started with that crazy million dollar shit and exploded. His money! Man, he hasn't worked in so long he doesn't know what money looks like."

"Mami shouldn't have stopped the pills," I said with conviction. "I don't know, maybe Papi's getting worse?" Confused, I realized I'd always assumed my father would stay the way he was—that the only change would come in each of us taking our turn to leave. But if he hurt Mami...

"I just wanna get outta this place," Pablo blurted. "I hate him.

I hate her. I hate everybody." As his voice broke, I hugged him stickily, though he'd grown so big that he was hard to comfort.

"It was crazy, man," Pablo mumbled. "Hitting my own father."

"He could've hurt her, Pablo "

"Yeah, but my own fucking father."

The sweat, mixing with wetness from my shower, left me feeling like I would never get clean again, but I went and reshowered anyway. When I got out this time, Mami was slapping fish patties together in the kitchen. I watched for a second while leaning into the counter. "What are you gonna do, Mami?" I asked softly.

"It's over, mi'ja. Ya pasó." Her lip shook. "I gave your father the pill again. With his juice." I located our vegetable oil bottle and placed it in front of her. Mami poured oil into the frying pan and let it get hot. As she threw in the first patty, she pushed me aside with the other hand, so that the sizzling oil drops wouldn't burn me. *Storge* love. The kind you couldn't help. I wished that my father had tried to choke Pablo or me instead of her.


Tío Victor's double-dosing scheme began to haunt me, but each time I planned to raise it with Mami, I couldn't bear to remind her about my father's attack. And so a few days later, with blackness in my heart, I rifled through the purse where she kept the sleeping pills and lifted one out. It would be easy enough to grind and dilute the calmante into my father's juice as Mami used to do, I knew, and no one would be the wiser. My uncle, I comforted myself while guiltily pocketing the little pill, would surely absolve me later. But when I came across an envelope addressed to Tía Consuelo in Mami's handwriting, I realized that she must have written for help. Mami was looking for a way out.

A sense of right and wrong returned and flooded me with shame. What could I have been thinking? What if I overdosed

my father instead of fixing anything? Mortified, I put the pill back
and hoped against hope that Tía Consuelo would come quickly. If
anyone could help us right him, or at least get him to a real doctor, it was her.

That week, summer classes started for Pablo, and he all but stopped
coming home. When not in school, he hung out with druggie
girlfriends at Tuttle Park. The little time he was home, he just slid
Manolo's lock across their door and stopped popping into my room
to get laughs out of me. I began to believe that he really did hate
my father.

Whatever hate I had was impossibly entangled in *storge*. The
episode with Mami had really scared me. I wanted to believe that
my father hadn't understood what he was doing, that he'd only
choked her because he became overwrought over the missing
checkbook and confused her with the people who'd stolen his
money. The people he *thought* had stolen his money, I corrected
myself for the umpteenth time.

It was a welcome relief when my job began. My father in his
timeless universe assumed that I was still going to school. That day
before I left, I gave him the obligatory good-bye kiss and noticed
how the hair on his scalp had thinned. Despite everything, I felt
sorry for him, like when he'd cried continuously after Abuela
Matilde died. But with Mami plying him with daily "vitamins"
again, there would be no crying. Only our house's silence, as each
of us left him for work, school, or other peoples' lives. And for a
while things appeared to go back to normal—or at least as normal
as they could be in that house.

[ TWENTY-TWO ]

WEEKS PASSED DURING which I felt that time was changing for all of us—time in the Latin sense of *tiempo*, meaning temperature or weather as well as the time of stories. You could sense it like the thickened air before a storm or the way you smell rain before it falls.

In real time, fortunately, there were no further eruptions from my father. Mami didn't mention Tía Consuelo, though I closely monitored the mail. In the relative peace, my mother decided that it was okay to leave my three cousins home with us for a day while Tío Lucho drove her to Jackson Memorial's free eye clinic, since the glaucoma drops made her eyes blur.

"Cuidado con tu papá," she cautioned before she left, though I was always careful with my father.

"Don't worry, Mami," I reassured her. "We'll take everybody to the park." Manolo and Pablo were on orders to help me entertain our cousins.

Mami had predictably decked herself out in a nice outfit and the dangling emerald earrings from her wedding. The quantity of hair spray and perfume forced me to hold my breath as I kissed her good-bye.

"We'll be back in a few hours," Tío Lucho told my cousin

Luchito. "No funny business. Marisol and Gabrielita will report to me."

My thirteen-year-old cousin grinned.

After my uncle drove away, I announced, "Okay, guys. Just stay in the yard or go to Tuttle. Don't anybody come in the house unless you have to use the bathroom."

"I have to go," Luchito piped up.

"Well, hurry up, stupid," Marisol said, shoving him.

"Just kidding."

"You're hilarious," she said.

"Come on, Manolo," I urged. "You guys take Luchito to the park."

Manolo scowled, but the three of them headed off after Marisol gave her brother a dollar.

When they'd gone, I opened lawn chairs outside and volunteered to braid Cari's hair. As Marisol lay back in the chaise longue with her eyes closed, I went into the house for a comb and rubber bands.

My father, wearing Mami's pink reading glasses, intercepted me. "I need envelopes, mi'jita," he said.

"I don't have any, Papi."

"It's necessary to buy them."

"Papi, my cousins are here."

"What cousins?"

"Marisol and Cari. Don't you remember? Tío Lucho took Mami to the clinic." I regarded him warily. I trusted that Mami had given him his pill before leaving, what with everything that had happened, but you could never be too sure of anything around here.

"O sí." My father nodded docilely as he remembered. "But I have to send these letters, mi'jita."

Keeping quiet, I opened a drawer and rummaged for rubber bands. Maybe he would drop it.

"It's urgent," he said a little louder.

"I have to stay here, Papi," I explained. "Tío Lucho wouldn't like my leaving my cousins. That's not nice."

"They can accompany you."

I jerked the drawer shut. "Okay. I'll ask Marisol."

Outside, she was still reclining in her glamorous position. "Look," I told her, "I have to go to the store. You want to wait with Cari?"

"I'm not staying with your crazy father," she said, promptly putting on her sandals.

"What about my braids?" Cari protested.

"We'll do them after," I promised. "Maybe Mari will buy you some pretty bands."

"I'll buy her a lice comb," Marisol said.

"Marisol, you're mean," Cari said.

"She's grouchy from her period," I told Cari.

"No. My love life," Marisol argued glumly, as the three of us walked down the street. "He won't tell me if he'll be my escort for his sister's quinceañera."

"Bummer." I tried to remember—was she talking about that guy with the 1920s mustache? "Can't you go with somebody else?"

"Tch! Don't you know anything? No one's gonna ask me if they think I'm Guillermo's novia!"

We arrived at the light. "Maybe you should ask someone then," I suggested.

"Oh my God. You're so American. You think I would ask a boy *out?*" Marisol stressed the "out" as if it were a horrible disease.

I looked down at Cari, who returned a sympathetic smile. Though she was only nine, she was wise to her sister's superiority complex. "I don't know," I answered neutrally.

When we finally reached Osco's, Cari and I gave Marisol the slip and went to find my father's envelopes. The store was out of white ones, so I had to buy the thin, blue-tinted kind with "Air Mail" printed on a red and blue border. They were envelopes for international mail, but my father wouldn't mind; his oil empire spanned the globe.

After we got home, I tossed the box on my father's bed and scurried back outside before he could demand any more of me. Then I stationed myself behind Cari in a lawn chair and busied myself with her dense black hair. Sure enough, my father popped into the yard and stood watching us. I combed Cari's hair as slowly and laboriously as possible until he finally withdrew.

When the afternoon got hotter, I moved my chair under the mango tree next to Marisol to nap and closed my eyes as she began to complain about virtually everyone she knew.

Eventually my father reappeared at the kitchen door, tinted envelopes in hand. He'd handwritten the addresses, I figured, if he'd addressed them at all. As he came closer, I tried squint-reading the writing. *Of course.* They were letters to banks.

"I'm going to the post office," he announced.

No one answered, but I nervously gave the pale blue envelopes another peek. Already stamped. Good.

"Your father must be looking for a job, huh?" Marisol asked with her eyes closed after he'd started down the street.

I knew she was probably being sarcastic but I merely said, "I don't know what he's looking for," and sighed. I watched my father's shadow slide along the ground behind him as if his spirit were folding into the sidewalk.

"Poor Tío," said Cari.

I asked Cari to help me knock some limes off the tree. A little later, as we squeezed lime juice into a jar, I heard a commotion.

Manolo burst in, Pablo in pursuit.

"Hey!" I yelled, as Pablo banged into me. "Stop fighting! You guys are too old for this stuff."

Manolo pushed forward, arms outstretched to escape Pablo's grasp, but Pablo caught him by the hair and punched his face. Manolo couldn't see to punch back, but he kept swinging blindly behind himself to hit Pablo's chest.

"Cut it out!" I yelled as I tried to pull Pablo off Manolo. "Now!" But my brothers were too big for me to handle alone.

Luchito came into the kitchen with Marisol. "Help me!" I ordered them.

Instead, Marisol grabbed Cari and backed away while Luchito and I grabbed Pablo's arms. That gave Manolo the upper hand, which he used to hit Pablo in the eye. Infuriated, Pablo freed himself and dove for Manolo's neck. I wedged myself between them while pushing Pablo away with my butt, but Manolo picked up a knife and backed up like he was going to charge us with it. I stumbled back, scared, and Pablo snuck around me and lunged. At that point, Manolo dropped the knife and ran for his room. Pablo followed but Manolo slammed the door in his face and locked it.

"You asshole!" Pablo shouted, kicking the door. "I'm gonna kick your face in!"

"Yeah, you try it!" the other asshole yelled back.

"Pablo, it's over!" I interjected.

"No, it's not!" He shoved me away, gave the door another kick, and muttered, "I know what I'm gonna do." Pushing past the cousins, he ran out to the yard.

"Hey Manolo," I called through the door. "Stay in there until he cools off."

Pablo started a very noisy banging in the yard.

"Wait here, guys," I said to Luchito and Cari, who looked nervous. "I have to see what Pablo's doing. Marisol, don't let Manolo come out." For once, my older cousin seemed willing to follow my lead.

Before I got outside, the front door slammed. *Oh no.* Dalmaned or not, my father would surely have an attack and kill us all. Panicking, I raced to the front with my cousins trailing me.

"Mami!" I was so relieved to see my mother walk in, blurry-eyed but intact.

"What's this racket?" she asked. "What's going on?"

"Pablo and Manolo are fighting each other!" Cari burst out tearfully.

"Manolo's locked in his room," Luchito volunteered.

"Where's my father?" Marisol searched past my mother.

"What?" Mami gazed through her blur while putting down her pocketbook and patting Cari's head at the same time. "Oh, your father had to do some errands," she replied distantly as she tried to get her bearings. "Where's Roberto?"

"Mailing letters," I said quickly. "Don't worry. It's not Papi. It's the boys. Pablo's going crazy and won't stop trying to hit Manolo."

"How can that be? Where are they? What's that sound?"

The pounding racket had intensified. Pablo was screaming, "I'm gonna kill you, asshole!"

My mother rushed to the hallway outside the boys' bedroom as the rest of us followed her. "Pablo!" she reprimanded him. "Put that hammer down this instant!"

He was pounding the door with the claw side of Manolo's cherished hammer, the one Manolo proudly used to repair all the things my father had abandoned.

"Pablo! Stop that!" Mami ordered. "Don't you see you're going to break the door?"

But he continued to hammer, becoming as enraged as my father when he'd attacked my mother over the checkbook. It was terrible; as if Pablo didn't hear us; as if nothing existed for him but that door. His face was so contorted by hate that I hardly recognized him.

"Luchito," I whispered. "What were they fighting about?"

"The glue."

"What about it?"

"Pablo sniffed some, but then he couldn't find the tube and said Manolo musta took it."

"Did he?"

"How would I know?"

We watched as my mother chaotically commanded or cajoled Pablo to stop, though nothing seemed to work.

I tried too. "Pablo," I pleaded. "Papi's gonna get home soon. It'll be so bad! Cut it out, will you? Please?"

But he only hammered harder. Suddenly, the white paint cracked and a deep split rent the wood. My mother cried out, "The door!" She glommed herself onto Pablo's arm and hung there to keep him from raising the hammer anymore.

Pablo growled, "Get off me!" and shook her violently.

Weeping, my mother began calling his baby name. "¡Pablito! ¡Ay Pablito!" Then, with a low moan, she crumpled like a baby herself onto the floor.

"Mami!" I shook her. "Get up!"

But my mother kept lying there feeling sorry for herself. She was crying.

"Oh my God." I looked at Marisol, who was transfixed by the expanding fissure in the door. Luchito was a mirror image of her, the two of them totally useless. I could hear poor Cari whimpering into a cushion somewhere. If someone didn't stop Pablo, I realized, he was going to break open that door and hammer Manolo to death.

I ran to the phone, but my finger trembled in the O slot. How could I possibly call the police? That was like spitting in the face of all our efforts to save my father.

But this wasn't my father's fault—no one would punish him, right?

He would be back soon, though.

But I couldn't call the police against my own family. I just couldn't.

Why oh why hadn't Tío Lucho returned yet? Where was everybody?

Then I heard another *crack*! Succumbing to terror, I just dialed. "It's an emergency!" I cried, after the operator switched me to the police. "My brother's trying to kill my other brother!"

Only after I hung up did the sense of doom strike. Weakly, I dropped to my knees until comfort arrived in the form of a memory: my kindly fourth-grade nun, whispering, "It's in God's hands, child."

I got up and went to ask Marisol and Luchito to help drag my mother into the living room, where she fell into a weeping trance, listlessly reciting the Hail Mary while Marisol held her hand and Luchito and Cari timidly watched.

Then I went back to work on my brother. "Pablo," I pleaded softly. "Don't you know you're acting like Papi? Remember the checkbook? Won't you please cut this out before the police come?"

"Shut up! Get away from me!"

Afraid of getting whacked with the hammer, I stood back as wood pieces splintered and flew off. The hole in the door was now big enough for his arm but still too small for me to see where in the room Manolo was hiding. With relief, I finally heard the police. Two large men with sticks—an older black man and a young white guy with dark hair and blue eyes—clodded into the house and overwhelmed our tiny hallway. How grateful I felt for their size.

"Why don't you back up, hon?" the older one said. He waited

for me to move before sidling up behind Pablo, who'd now carved
a hole almost big enough to climb through.

"You're gonna be sorry, asshole!" he yelled. In his own crazy
world, he didn't seem to notice or care that the cops had come.

"Okay, buddy," said the older officer, who grabbed Pablo's right
arm while the young guy grabbed the left. "Gimme the hammer."

Pablo tried to shake them off to lift his leg across the hole, but
the cops twisted both his arms until he cried out. They forced
the hammer out of his hand, and the younger cop snapped cuffs
around his wrists. Swiftly, they walked my brother out of the
house toward the police car in front.

A minute later, the older officer came back. "Okay," he said
calmly as he took out his pad. "What's all this about?"

My mother shook her head tearfully.

"Why don't we start with your son's name?"

She mumbled something unintelligible.

"Pablo Roberto de la Paz," I added quickly.

"How old is he?" The officer looked back and forth between
Mami and me.

"Fourteen," I said.

He asked a few more questions, but most of her responses consisted of helpless whimpers, so I ended up answering. When the
officer had finished, he wrote something on a piece of paper that
he handed to her.

I heard someone at the back door.

Grabbing Luchito, I ordered, "Come on," and ran frantically to
the back door. I blocked the threshold while shoving my frightened cousin toward my father. "Luchito has to show you something, Papi," I said nervously, shutting the door after them. Then
I raced back to see if the officer was done, breathlessly asking if he
could take my brother with them until he calmed down.

"That's what we're doing, young lady." With his pen, he

pointed to the address on the paper he'd given Mami. "That's the Juvy Unit where you can bail him out."

I shook my head, not understanding but feeling extremely anxious for the cop to leave.

"Let him sit there a while," said the officer. "He doesn't have to be released for six hours. That'll cool him off."

"Okay," I said. "Thanks." I moved toward the door to urge him out.

My father and Luchito entered the living room just as the cop was leaving. He half-turned, held up a hand in greeting, and exited, while I held my breath in fearful anticipation.

"What are those men doing here?" my father interrogated my mother suspiciously.

She stared back, her hairdo undone and her eye makeup smudged. At least she'd stopped crying. "Ay Roberto," she said wearily.

My father's jaw tightened. "¿Qué hacían esos hombres aquí?" he repeated.

My heart began to flutter all over again.

"I'll explain it to you," Mami said quietly, picking up her pocketbook and lifting herself from the couch. Then, to my great relief, she managed to lead him away toward their bedroom.

I remembered to go tell Manolo it was safe to come out.

He was shaking in his bed. "Where's Pablo?" he asked.

"The police took him."

"He's under arrest?"

"I don't know," I admitted, bending to pick up a piece of door from the floor. "Why were you guys fighting?"

"It was—" Manolo shook his head. "Pablo just got too high, Gab."

"Oh no! Do you think he had pot on him?" *Why hadn't I thought of that?*

Manolo shrugged. "Hope not."

I stared at the shards of wood in my hand. Frowning, I threw
them into a wastebasket and tried propping a chair in front of the
door to cover the hole. But the slats of the chair were wide, and
the deformity was too big to hide.


My cousins were never so glad to see their father.

"You kids really missed me, eh?" Tío Lucho smiled as Cari
clung to his side, but my mother insisted on taking him out front
to talk out of my father's earshot and ours.

"Pshh! We saw more than she did," Marisol observed.

"Yeah, but you know how it is," I answered wearily.

"I feel sorry for you. You're the only one in your family with
any sense."

Ordinarily, a compliment from the ever-critical Marisol would
have been an honor. But now, I felt too tormented over having
turned in my own family to appreciate it. "It's not anyone's fault,
Mari," I muttered, confused about who needed more defending,
my family or me.

"Huh," she said, arms crossed.

We heard my mother crying again.

"Your mom has a lot to cry about," Marisol said with a sympathetic sigh, surprising me. "If you want to sleep over at our house,
you can," she added.

"We have to get Pablo," I said, with increasing nervousness
about what the consequences would be for having gone outside
the family.

"Oh, I forgot."

An hour later, Tío Victor and Tío Paco arrived. They came and
greeted my father and Tío Lucho in the dining room. "Siéntense,
por favor," my father said, pointing a fork at the chairs.

Mami had told my father that neighbors called the police when the boys got rowdy. Though upset by that, my father had no clue that Pablo was at a police station. Luckily, the uncles' arrival took his mind off the incident. As usual, my uncles had acceded to Mami's strategy of not telling the truth.

"No, no, Roberto," Tío Victor answered my father now. "That's not necessary. We've eaten. We're going to have a smoke outside. Relax, we'll talk."

"Buen provecho," Tío Lucho said, patting my father's shoulder.

My father finished his dinner while the uncles had their pow-wow in the front. Mami sent me out with a tray of tintos.

"Tell them I'll be right out," my father called after me.

I walked carefully so the hot coffee wouldn't spill. The evening breeze had picked up and was blowing acacia blossoms through the air. I put one hand over the three small cups to keep any red petals from falling into them.

"Gabriela," Tío Paco said, taking one of the cups without thanking me. His interpersonal skills seemed to have gotten worse since he'd bought that big Opa-Locka house so far away—the family couldn't visit frequently enough to help him keep up his manners. "Why did you call the police?" he challenged me now.

I stared in surprise. "You know why, Tío. Pablo was going crazy. Trying to kill Manolo."

"First of all," my uncle said, downing his coffee and fitting the cup back into its saucer, "never let those words come out of your mouth again." He handed the cup-and-saucer set back.

"Second of all," he said as he lit a cigarette, "don't ever call the police without permission."

"But Mami fell apart, Tío," I explained.

"Why didn't you call me, mi'ja?" Tío Victor asked. His tired brown eyes sloped forever downward.

"I didn't think there was time. I mean, before Pablo broke down the door or something really bad happened...and I thought Papi might come home and start attacking somebody like when—" I gulped. *Had my mother told them about the checkbook?* "Like when Pablo broke his leg," I finished desperately. "I thought Papi could get arrested or something and all that deportation stuff would start all over again!"

"Did you think about getting your brother deported?" Tío Paco inquired caustically.

Appalled, I answered, "They don't deport kids, Tío."

"They do so," he countered.

"But I—"

"Gabrielita," Tío Victor interrupted gently, "the problem is, the police are often more trouble than help."

Even agreeable Tío Lucho nodded and sighed. "No matter how long we live in this country, mi'ja."

"Now we have to go to the station to get your brother," Tío Paco added. "Your mother doesn't need this."

Stumped for words, I couldn't begin to exonerate myself. But all I'd wanted to do was get help. "I didn't know what else to do," I offered finally.

"Now you know," Tío Paco ruled. "Come on. You better come with me. No point in upsetting your mother more by seeing Pablo in that place."

Tío Lucho and Tío Victor headed inside to say their good-byes. Afterward, they climbed into Tío Lucho's car, with Manolo, who was to spend the night with the cousins. "Bye, Gabi," he said.

"Bye." I waved longingly at everyone in the beat-up Buick and went over to Tío Paco's shiny Chevrolet.

"Where's the address?" he demanded rudely.

How fiercely I wanted to slap him right then. Instead, I gritted my teeth, turned, and went inside to retrieve the slip of paper the cop had left. "Here," I said, handing Tío Paco the paper and getting into his car.

As we drove away, I made one last effort to redeem myself. "I didn't tell anyone to take Pablo to jail, Tío," I said quietly. "I asked them to take him somewhere to calm down."

My uncle turned on his radio and didn't reply.

I rubbed my hands together and listened to the sentimental boleros of his generation: slow songs, full of flowers and longing. Out the window, the passing city scenery became seedier. As dusk became dark, all you could see were the shells of down-trodden buildings with their broken-eyed windows and the occasional coconut tree survivor from the city's pest eradication campaign. The only light in this land of faint hope was the blue and white neon sign of the police station.

At the station, they directed us to the Juvenile Detention Unit. My uncle signed release forms and gave the Spanish-speaking officer twenty-five dollars. He handed my uncle a pink hearing notice and a bail receipt. When I started to explain the tiny English print to my uncle, Tío Paco grabbed the forms from me in annoyance. For the first time that day, I felt like I might break down and cry. The things I did well—reading and explaining—he wouldn't let me do.

My uncle took a bunch of quarters from his pocket and nodded tiredly at the vending machines. "Go get yourself a soda."

We sat for twenty minutes until Pablo came through the heavy door. His face was streaked, his hair mussed, and the top buttons of his shirt were torn off from the fight.

"Pablo," I said.

My uncle stood and patted my brother's back. "Let's go home, mi'jo."

On the ride home, Pablo sat in the front seat but barely answered my uncle's questions.

"Did they hurt you?"

"No."

"What did they tell you?"

"Nothing." He pulled a pink wad out of his pocket. "Here's the court stuff."

My uncle said, "Give those to your sister."

Pablo passed the crumpled papers back without looking at me.

"Your father doesn't know any of this," my uncle warned Pablo, as if he wouldn't have figured that out. "Keep it that way."

Pablo nodded and stared out the window.

We rode in silence, my uncle not even turning on his radio. Maybe he was contemplating the long drive back to his empty house in Opa-Locka.

"Pablo, you want some of this Coke?" I asked.

Pablo didn't answer. He didn't speak to me at all during the ride home.

When we got to the house, my mother hugged him like there was no tomorrow while my father watched with a perplexed smile.

"¿Qué pasa aquí?" he asked, finally sensing that something had happened.

"Nada, nada," my mother said. "Some good-for-nothing boys tried to fight him. He's all right now." She patted Pablo's shirt closed over the missing buttons.

"A fight!" My father's voice cracked.

For the first time, I understood what made my father's voice rise and crack like a girl's sometimes: fear. But what did *he* have to be afraid of?

"¡Ay Roberto!" she said impatiently. "¿No ves que el niño está cansado?"

But if my father didn't see that the "child" was tired, Pablo made it clear by removing her hands and stating in English, "I'm going to bed."

"Manolo's sleeping at Luchito's," I volunteered.

"Do I give a shit?"

His first words to me. I bit my lip.

Mami told me to heat up his dinner while she and my father escorted Tío Paco to the car.

It was quiet in the kitchen. When I opened the refrigerator, I saw the lime halves I'd cut up earlier. Tears smarted in my eyes, but I fought them back. It wasn't my fault that the fight had started, I told myself with a deep breath. It wasn't my fault that Papi was a maniac—and that Pablo was now one too. That Mami had given up, leaving everything to me.

*Why didn't you call me?*

I was too scared of Pablo bashing Manolo's head in, Tío. Too scared of my father coming home and bashing us all.

*The police are more trouble than help.*

But they saved Manolo, didn't they, Tío? Didn't they take the hammer away?

They took Pablo away.

I hadn't saved anyone.

Worn out by defeat, I left Pablo's plate out on the counter and went to my parents' bathroom. My father's lamp illuminated the black-inked pages he'd left strewn across his bed. I locked the bathroom door behind me, put the toilet seat down, dropped my head on my arms, and sobbed. Why did everyone expect me to get it all right? Why wasn't anyone ever there to help *me*?

## TWENTY-THREE

PABLO WOULDN'T TALK TO ME. He acted as if we'd never been allies against our strange, sad family. My only comfort came from El Chino setting Tío Paco straight about juvenile delinquencies not causing deportation. The juvy court gave Pablo a probationary dismissal and assigned him to Tuttle Park cleanup with other juvy kids.

Mami picked up a few peoples' vacation schedules at the Palacio, to keep from getting too depressed over the start of Pablo's juvy career, I guessed, as well as her own humiliating follow-up appointment with Miss Lucy Prado in Protective Services. Despite Mami's entreaties, Manolo refused to replace the deformed door. The splintered hole gaped grotesquely every time I walked by it.

As for my father, he was quietly composing another exegesis to a bank. I saw the letter one morning before work on his make-believe desk: pages of block print generically addressed to Chase Manhattan Bank, New York. He'd been mum on his old check theory since the day Pablo hit him, so I was no longer certain how we would get our millions—his letter would tell me soon enough.


August brought windy, tropical rain.

Fátima and her family had gone camping in it, somewhere in the Keys. Lara and the girls had rented a bungalow in rainy Naples. Even the cashier from my bookstore was sailing through the rain on a Norwegian cruise ship out of Biscayne Bay.

Inside the bookstore, you hardly knew weather existed. The mall had its whirring noise that shut the world out completely. I put price-stickers on books, shelved them, and filed invoices. The only words I absolutely had to speak were "yes" and "no" to the temporary cashier and "left" or "next aisle" to customers.

Some nights, the rain woke me when it tapped my window in bumpy syncopation, its natural rhythm thrown off by an unpredictable Caribbean wind.

Other nights, the rain purred softly, like the voice of the English lady who led the reading hour at our store.

Sometimes, the rain went by without a sound, like a dream I didn't have a chance to remember or a form of love that no one told me existed and that slipped away.

One night, I stayed up to listen. The rain dripped from the awnings and I began composing my own letter, one with no salutation, no addressee, no "Sincerely yours" at the end. No end, really. It was just an anonymous stream-of-consciousness running over with feelings that didn't amount to much or mean anything. Meaning itself was so wide and vague a thing that I would never reach it.

The next day at work, I treated myself to a book so I could cheer up. The one I bought was called *Solitude,* and when I got home that afternoon I lay on my belly to read it and found a poem that made me feel as if there might be some meaning left in the world:

*Young Girl: Annam* by Padraic Colum

*I am a young girl;*
*I live here alone:*

*I write long letters*
*But there is no one*

*For me to send them to. My heart*
*Teaches me loving words to use,*
*But I can repeat them only*
*In the garden, to the tall bamboos.*

*Expectantly, I stand beside the door. I raise*
*The hanging mat. I,*
*The letter folded, gaze out*
*And see the shadows of the passers-by.*

*In the garden, the fire-flies*
*Quench and kindle their soft glow:*
*I am one separated,*
*But from whom I do not know.*

How separated I was too—from everyone except her. I shut my eyes to picture her, and drops of the August rain trickled out. Around me, air whistled through the culms of the three bamboos: the girl, my father, and me, each gripping our letters that we couldn't send.

Labor Day neared, and my spirits lifted at last. Mami's announcement that Tía Consuelo was coming to visit us cheered me the most.

When my job ended, I spent the Friday before school's reopening cleaning the house to surprise my mother. "¡Ay mi'jita!" she exclaimed after seeing it all and coming into my room. "Everything looks so nice!" Her hair in a towel, she sat down beside me and asked how things had gone. As she undid the towel and started drying her hair, the gray roots showed that it was time to call Tía Rita to repaint.

I reported that there had been no trouble with my father and handed over my last paycheck.

"Thank you, mi'jita." Mami sighed as she slipped it into her pocket. "I'll be glad when Gladys comes back, though I'm grateful for the extra cash. I wished we'd fixed the roof when your father was working with that contractor. I'm afraid after all the rain, it might cave in."

"Maybe I'll get a better job this year," I offered.

With a smile, she patted my feet. A little breeze sauntered in through my window.

"Mami," I broached hesitantly, pulling my knees up to my chest. "There was something I was going to tell you—about school."

"Already?"

"No. It happened before. Last year, in Geography, I had to write this essay. The thing is, it was a contest. That I won."

"How nice, mi'jita. Did they just write you about it?"

"Not exactly. But, well, instead of a regular prize, the winners get something special."

"What?"

I pulled my legs closer. "The kids who won second place, they only got a plaque. But the kids who won first place, our prize was...is...a trip. A really expensive trip that they pay for, with teachers and chaperones—"

"A trip?" Mami stopped drying her hair. "Where?"

"Well, everyone goes to the United Nations first, in New York. You know, they get to meet officials and everything."

My mother was silent, so I forged ahead. "And then they take you on a special trip to a very important historical site in," I took a quick breath, "Egypt."

"¿Egipto?"

"Yes, Mami." I sat up very straight. "It's to teach us to get along with people from different backgrounds. You can't learn that if you don't have a chance to meet them first."

"There are plenty of people right here in Miami," she said, frowning.

"Yeah, but you know what? There are kids going from all over. Hundreds. It's a big honor. The principal wants me to represent our school."

"Let him send his own daughter!"

"She didn't win the prize, Mami! *I* did." My voice quivered.

"Why don't they give your family a prize? Like an air conditioner, so you can study without suffocating?"

"Mami! I thought you wanted me to do well! But then when I do, you don't even care!"

"I do care. Who brought you into this world? Why did your father and I make so many sacrifices?"

"*I'm* the sacrifice! I'm the one who's supposed to roll over and die!"

My mother stood. Haughtily, she went to the door and turned, pointing a finger at me. "That's what public schools teach. To prance around thinking you're better than everyone and can fly off without your family. Well, take those ideas out of your head, señorita, there's no room for them here."

As I watched her go, I felt completely demoralized. Would there be any point in Lara even trying to talk sense into her? How could Lara dislodge my mother's rock-hard views?

All I'd really wanted was for things to go back to how they used to be before I'd called the police—when my family still believed in me sometimes.

When Pablo heard me crying, he came and stood in my doorway. "You shouldn't argue, Gabi," he said. "It makes her more stubborn."

"I can't help it," I admitted, gratified that he was speaking to me at last. "It's hard to just listen."

"I know what you mean." He smiled. "Hey, I didn't know you won a prize. That's cool."

"Thanks, Pablo."

After that, things weren't exactly the same between us, but at least he continued to talk to me. Afraid of jinxing it, I refused to have anything to do with the forms Probation required from my mother. "Do them yourself," I told her, leaving the papers on the table.

That Sunday morning, Mami woke me with the surprise announcement that she was coming to church. No one but me had gone to St. Stephen's in a long while, and my own attendance had been spotty since the adventures with David.

The weather was sticky when she and I headed down the street. The only other person out and about was Jorge Cabrera, who'd bought the Andersons' house and was repainting everything a bright papaya.

On the bus, Mami informed me of the reason for her spiritual renewal. "We're going to ask the priest for help."

"With what?" I asked.

"Everything. Our situation. Your brother. You."

"Me?"

She nodded grimly, and we rode the rest of the way in silence.

When we arrived at St. Stephen's, the church was still refilling. Eventually, the Spanish Mass began. Unlike English services I attended, there were no lay people participating in this one, no guitars or youth groups singing folk songs. A single altar boy helped the bald-headed Cuban priest with black glasses who recited, in a stern voice, more Latin liturgy than I thought was required anymore. He seemed to be leading a one-man rebellion against every positive change brought about by Vatican II.

After Mass, we got into a line of families waiting to greet Padre

Felipe. When our turn came, he smiled blankly, taking my mother's hands as she introduced herself. Quietly, she asked to discuss a pequeño problemita—a little problem—in private. He gave me a sharp look and motioned us toward the rectory. I hoped he didn't think I'd disgraced myself in some way.

The rectory office was small and windowless. Dark, grim-faced paintings of male saints covered the wall behind Padre Felipe's desk. He offered us worn chairs and sat facing us. A dim lamp emphasized the contrast between this dark office and the intense brightness of the church. Even priests needed a place to retreat from God, I guessed.

"Bueno," he said, folding his hands.

My mother edged forward. "Father, I'm not sure where to begin. Ever since we came to Miami, we've had so many problems. First, my husband lost his work...."

I waited for her to enlighten him about my father's nervios and the legal woes he'd created, but she went straight to the bills, the roof, the end of her overtime pay, and—before the priest had a chance to open his mouth—The Difficulties of Raising Children. "And my younger son, Father, has brought me such anguish lately! He needs discipline, but without a father's guidance—"

Padre Felipe held up a hand. "Does your husband drink?"

"Oh no!" my mother protested. "Es un hombre recto." A correct man. "No, Father. He has—a sickness."

"Is that why he isn't with you?"

My mother looked down. "Yes, Father."

"His sickness is in his head," I blurted.

"Is that true?" the priest asked Mami.

"Sí, Padre," she said, quietly. It was the closest she'd ever come to an admission that my father was a mental case. I felt victorious but pitied her all the same.

The priest considered a moment. "And how can we help you?" he asked, more kindly.

My mother took out a package of papers fastened with rubber bands. She unloaded the contents onto Padre Felipe's desk— check stubs, phone and gas receipts, bank statements, and a recent estimate from the roofer—while orally subtracting bill balances from the amounts on her stubs. It was a litany I'd heard virtually every day of my adolescence, but in front of another person—how embarrassing! Why did she have to go into those details? I stared at the paintings on his wall while searching in vain for the symbols that told you who each saint was until I realized at last that they weren't saints at all, just popes!

"If we could place my son here with the Sisters," Mami continued, "for a short time, until he learns better discipline, but the program here costs so much, Father, and you see I earn so little."

"How old is your son?"

"Fourteen, Father."

"And the other children?"

"Only two, Father. My son who's fifteen, I haven't any problems with him, gracias a Dios." She nodded toward me. "And my daughter is sixteen."

The priest examined me, his thick lenses magnifying his eyes. I didn't like the way he stared at me while interrogating Mami as if she were a witness testifying against me in this courtroom. "Does your daughter help?" he asked, as if he'd already entered judgment.

"Oh yes, Father," Mami answered. "All summer she worked. And faithfully brought home her paycheck."

"Does she help with your husband?"

Help, help, help. I was sick of being the Auxiliadora!

"Oh yes," my mother said. "And she studies."

"Of course," he answered, enlarged eyes sentencing me anew. "But in two more years, she'll be finished with her studies. Then she can dedicate herself to these matters."

I opened my mouth to object, but thought better of it. This priest couldn't care less if my life became una miseria.

"Yes, Father," Mami repeated. "But in the meantime—"

"In the meantime, the Church will assist. But we cannot solve everything. You must find the way—with your family's help and God's guidance, of course—to arrive at a solution."

My mother nodded.

The priest rifled through a box and found our parishioner's card from when we'd joined. After writing a note on it, he explained to my mother that the Church would provide a tuition waiver for Pablo to attend St. Stephen's for one year.

*Pablo?* Whose favorite class at Flagler Junior was detention hall? Boy, were the Little Sisters of St. Stephen's in for a treat.

Padre Felipe removed a gray card from his top drawer. "This voucher you can give to Sister Teresa on Tuesday," he told Mami. Then he wrote out a check. "For your roof," he said, handing her both items. The deformed eyes absorbed me again. "You must help your mother," he decreed. "Her burdens are too much for her."

*Her* burdens? I tried to look neutral.

"Of course she will, Father," Mami replied, tucking the check and voucher securely into her purse.

The priest stood.

Quickly, my mother gathered up her bills. "Thank you, Father," she said, then hesitated. "It's not the same in public schools. I wish it were possible to place all my children here, especially my daughter." She nodded reproachingly in my direction. "The ideas they put into their heads, you can't imagine! Leaving home...even leaving the country! And without one's family! I don't know how those teachers come up with such things."

I glared at her. Why was she bringing that up?

"A daughter's place is with her family," the priest quoted, holding out his hand.

"With her family," Mami echoed before thanking him again for the tuition waiver, the check, and his wise guidance.

As he ushered us out to await the next devotees, I didn't say a word.

On the way home, while my mother obsessed about how to purchase Pablo's new uniform by Tuesday and find someone to cover her shift, I tried to quell my fury. That reptile priest had invoked the power of the Church to banish me to permanent servitude! And Mami had simply used me to win more sympathy!

By the time the bus dropped us off, I was seething. As we began the final walking stretch of our journey home, the sweltering humidity had me by the legs like a ball-and-chain while the sun lashed me from above. I felt like I might suffocate in all my synthetic fiber. When I couldn't take it anymore, I turned on her. "Why didn't you tell the priest to find us a doctor so Papi won't strangle you to death someday? Why didn't you ask him to get you a better job than cleaning disgusting bathrooms?"

Mami was taken aback. "Who told you I did that?" she sputtered, the turquoise umbrella swinging awkwardly on her wrist. "You have no right to talk that way!"

I marched ahead, my legs freed by defiance, until we arrived home. Then I slammed my door shut and threw myself on the bed, the linens crumpling under my sweat and tears.

That horrible priest was prepared to let me waste away. Everyone had decided everything was my responsibility. And if, God forbid, I should make a mistake while trying to solve a problem, like with my brothers' fight, I would be blamed for whatever had gone wrong in the first place! Why had I even been born?

*Who made me?* The words of my first catechism text lit up like a tiny neon billboard in my brain.

The textbook answer, *God made me*, was a complete sentence but incomplete in meaning. As my entire Catholic education had been, right from the time Mami left me to walk alone up a never-ending stairway to that alien classroom on the fourth floor of the United States.

As I cried now with my hot face in the pillow, I struggled to unravel the God the Father mystery all over again. While my human father had worked to take care of us, God the Father had only waited around, ever-present, for horrible crises and bad deeds to occur. My human father had punished us, but his belt had been more threat than weapon back then, and he'd given us chances: one, two, two-and-a-half, two-and-three-quarters, the fractions getting smaller as he neared ten because he believed in our ability to be good. Not like God the Father, the All-Powerful One who'd saved mankind only by sacrificing his own Son.

Tuesday I arrived gratefully at Royal Palm—an oasis in the desert of the past few months. I was overjoyed to see Octavio and Amy, even though Fátima was out sick.

Sweetness greeted me on my return home too; when I opened the back door, wafts of sugary burnt oil floated out. Mami was frying plantains.

"How did it go?" she asked, as I planted a perfunctory kiss on her cheek.

"Good."

"Your aunt Rita's here," she said. "We're doing our hair. Finish these when she comes out of the bathroom, will you?"

"Okay." I slumped into a chair, my book bag at my feet. "Where are the boys?" I inquired, eager to hear about Pablo's adventures with the nuns.

My father entered, wearing an undershirt with visible underarm stains.

"Hola, Papi," I said, glancing at my mother to see if she would criticize him for dressing that way in front of Tía Rita.

Suddenly my father shouted. "¡¿Por qué?!"

I gave Mami a quizzical look. She turned, greasy spatula in hand, and frowned. "What's the problem, Roberto?"

"¡¿Por qué?! ¡¿Por qué?!" he yelled.

The "why" wasn't really a question, punctuated as it was by the rising decibels. What was he so mad about? I eased toward the edge of my chair, preparing for flight, but I was wedged between my mother and the table and couldn't exit.

My aunt appeared, her wet hair tied up in plastic. "Vamos, Roberto, what's all this about?"

"¡¿Por qué?!" my father screamed, the vein in his forehead practically exploding now. As if he were about to exact the final revenge from mortal enemies, he screamed louder: "¡¿Por qué?! ¡¿Por qué?!" He was blinking rapidly and raised his arm.

Suddenly something sharp landed on me. "¡¿Por qué?!" Sharpness pounded my head again. "¡¿Por qué?! ¡Por qué?!" Down came his knuckles, driving the crazy "¡¿por qué?!" furiously into my brain again and again.

"¡Papi!" I cried, face in my arms. "I didn't do anything!"

"¡No, Roberto!" my mother shouted in panic as the knuckles ambushed me.

"¡¿Por qué?! ¡¿Por qué?!"

My scalp was on fire, a fire coursing through me down to my legs so that I feared I'd peed. "Please, Papi," I whimpered.

"Roberto, ¡por favor!" My aunt threw herself over me and pushed me roughly out of the chair and onto the floor.

As I rushed to crawl out of there on my knees, I heard the por qués start up again behind me. My mother was crying, "Mi'jo, please, return to your senses!" I reached my bedroom, got to my feet, closed the door, and leaned my forehead into it like a best friend. But the pounding seemed to continue, only it was coming from my heart. *Make it stop*, I prayed dizzily, as my mother's sobs and my aunt's stern rebukes rose with my own heartbeat above the mad, fading chant of my father's por qués.

Then: wordlessness, signals, space.

Later, someone knocked.

"What?" my thick voice answered.

"Let us in," my mother said.

"¿Por—" The syllable garbled in my throat. Why? Why?

"Open the door, please," she insisted.

I opened it, stepped backward, and sank into my bed.

"Mi'ja." My mother entered with a bag of ice.

"Let me feel it first," said Tía Rita, coming in to sit beside me, her hair still wet and spiky from the Clairol.

I recoiled. "No, it hurts."

"Sí, Gabi, you have to let me check." My aunt explored my head lightly with her fingertips, and I winced as she touched the goose egg on my scalp. "Well, it's not bleeding," she said to my mother with a grimace.

"Merciful God," Mami said. "Here, put the ice on."

"I'll do it myself." I wrested the bag away from her, but the sudden movement brought on a wave of nausea. I took a deep breath, then carefully lowered the bag onto my scalp. The ice cubes were a sharp reminder of my father's knuckles, and I let out a moan.

"Mi'ja, let me slide you onto the pillow," she offered.

"No!"

"At least she doesn't seem to need a doctor," Tía Rita concluded wryly.

"Doctor?" Mami dropped to the bed too.

My aunt touched my hand. "Look, Gabrielita. Victor's here. He gave your father a pill a little while ago."

"Why didn't the other one work?" However much I adjusted the ice, my head throbbed.

Tía Rita raised an eyebrow at my mother, whose ojeras darkened with fear and regret.

"¡Ay, mi'ja! He didn't take it!"

I looked out the window. "I wish I were dead," I declared firmly into the dark.

My mother drew a breath. "Eso nunca se dice."

Never Must It Be Said: always the passive voice with her.

But I didn't *want* to be passive or to help anyone.

Tía Rita stood. "I'm going to tell Victor that Gabrielita's all right."

My mother waited—for what I didn't know—as the ice pressed my head like a freezing marble slab. Outside, the street lights weren't yet illuminated. So dark. Even the ghosts of our three coconut trees, now amputated white stumps, had vanished like the Holy Family in flight from their persecutors. Who would I pray to now?

Mami finally stood. "I'll call you in a while to eat," she offered quietly.


I sat at the table between my brothers and began to swallow one forkful of rice, meat, and plantains at a time with great gulps of water. Nobody said a word. When I finished, I went and dumped my plate in the kitchen sink. Manolo followed, placing a hand on my shoulder. "I'll wash the dishes, Gab."

"Thanks." I returned to my room with my head still pounding and the rest of me completely bloated. Why had I swallowed all that rice? How disgusting. Resting on my bed, I closed my eyes. If only I could run away somewhere, emancipated from the entire world. I could glide magically in the clouds with a Coke in one hand and a book in the other. Maybe there was a place for me like the imaginary lands we'd read about in French. *Le pays où l'on n'arrive jamais*—a country never reached except through special kinds of remembering.

Out of the blue, I remembered our long-ago family picnic in Queens, the rose brocade tablecloth spread out on the grass, my father catching me in his arms and laughing when I rolled down a mountain I'd imagined out of a simple slope of highway exit.

My *pays* was a lost country in the distance, a figment of a country—a cuento.

Pablo came in, closing my door behind him. "Hey, Gab."

"Hi." I stared listlessly at his slimy sneakers.

"I'm sorry the old man hit you," he said. "Tía Rita told us."

"Yeah, it's another reason for me to hate this place."

Pablo shook his head. "We don't need any more reasons."

I got up abruptly. "I have to take some aspirin. Tell me about St. Stephen's tomorrow, okay?"

It wasn't the same for Pablo. I was *good*. I hadn't done anything to deserve getting beaten. I always did what our family needed. I was the one who'd completed meaningless puzzles, loyally typed encyclopedias, even tried to make my father's craziness a little less crazy. I'd let myself become enslaved to him so that he wouldn't hurt anyone else. I'd saved him from himself, hadn't I? Did it all count for nothing?

In the bathroom, I swallowed two aspirins.

When I returned to my room, I took out my diary and a pen. Words rushed out in bad penmanship, cluttered like my father's letters with exclamation points.

*PSYCHO!! I'll shove your papers down your throat! Hold you by the neck and SQUEEZE OUT YOUR EYEBALLS, YOUR TONGUE! I'LL KILL YOU!!!!!!!!!!*

As I stared at the words, icy dread crept up my writing hand toward my chest. The craziness had invaded me.

Here was my punishment.

Hadn't I called the police on my own brother? Secretly hoped for my father's arrest? Tried to persuade my mother to let him be deported?

Distraught, I folded the crazy pages over so that I wouldn't have to see them again. Then, closing the diary, I buried it in my cigar box and slid the box under my bed. Like a zombie, I sat waiting. The beating inside me diminished as the aspirin kicked in, but I felt so uncertain about what to do.

Suddenly I freaked: What if someone found my crazy writing? Quickly, I retrieved the diary and tore out the bad pages. But what to do with them?

I stood up to inspect my closet, stuffed with junk: headless dolls Pablo used to take apart, boxes of shoes no one wore, the Important Papers box, our family pictures, my old pink bedspread and the matching vase with the dusty plastic roses, and wads of unattractive fabric Mami was saving to make something out of. She was afraid to give up on anything and throw it away.

I started rabidly pulling things out but she walked in unexpectedly, and I managed to quickly stuff the evil diary pages into my jeans pocket. *Les pages où l'on n'arrive jamais*—the pages no one would ever get to.

"What's this?" As her eyes critiqued the floor, she stooped to lift her Chase Manhattan papers box.

"I'm looking for something," I improvised. "I'll put it all back."

"Why did you take everything out in the first place, mi'ja?" she asked.

"I told you. I need something."

"What are you looking for that you have to make this mess?"

"A box for my old school work. To make room for this year's."

"A box." She left the room but returned moments later with a used UPS box. "Here."

I made a show of transferring notebooks into it, while she stood by with her arms folded like a security guard's and didn't budge. Climbing on the chair, I tried to reload the closet with everything I'd thrown down, but blankets and clothes kept rolling out. Instead of helping, my mother compulsively criticized the way I put everything back. My father's attack on me had barely dislodged her batteries: Here she was again, recharged, with a running commentary on each thing I did wrong. The only faith she had was in her own complaining. I wanted to slam the shoe box right over her mouth. "Mami. Just get out of my room and leave me alone!"

"¿Cómo? ¿Quién te crees?"

*Who did I think I was?* "I'm somebody," I answered evenly in English, "who wouldn't stand around watching my kids get beaten!" I shoved a doll back on the shelf. In English, I could be powerful. In English, I didn't belong to her.

"What did you say? Who did you say stands around doing nothing?"

From the height of my chair, I stared her down. I didn't care what she thought anymore. My chin up, I hopped off, grabbed some pajamas, and headed for the bathroom. Pablo gave me a thumbs-up as I passed him. In the bathroom I locked the door and changed, then crouched under the vanity for my hidden paperback before putting the toilet seat down to read. But all I could do was sit and rub my temples.

Eventually, a tap came. "Coast is clear," Pablo whispered.

In the room, my mother had finished putting everything back pretty close to how it was supposed to be, except that she'd left the UPS box on the floor for me to squeeze up there somehow. I kicked it.

On my bed, the old pink bedspread was folded over the white coverlet. My mother had turned off the harsh overhead light and left my bedside lamp on, a rosy glow in the corner.

My room seemed to have recovered its original identity from when we'd first moved to Miami. After Mami had taken me to Sears for the pink bedspread, she'd sewn the dotted-Swiss curtains and we hung them up and wrapped wire daisies around the panels to let in more light. Together, we'd shaken out the bedspread and made the bed, and then she walked around stretching and smoothing the folds of the cloth. When she'd gotten everything perfect, she stepped back by the door, put her arm around me, and pressed me close. In the curve of her arm, her little girl had rested.


I woke early the next morning and left my house without preparing the café con leche.

Royal Palm was quiet and deserted when I arrived except for a few teachers. I plopped myself on the ground near the dumpsters. The grass was damp, but that was normal. School was normal. No one was trying to kill me or drive me crazy or squish me into the ground like a bug. I took out my excised diary pages and fished around in my pencil case for matches. When I found a broken Newport Menthol, I lit the cigarette and burned holes in the pages. Then I finished smoking the crumb of cigarette and went to throw the burnt sheets into the dumpster.

By first period English, the aspirins had worn off and my headache returned in full force. I told Mrs. Foster I was sick to stop her from hounding me with questions. Fátima really was sick, and I felt lonely without her. I got through the morning thinking that I would find Octavio later and tell him my new cuento, but by lunch, I was too nauseous to talk and asked the cafeteria proctor for a pass instead.

The yard behind our school was a huge field surrounded by a track, the trees leaning over the fence like spectators. As I headed out there, sunlight pummeled my sore head. "¡¿Por qué?! ¡¿Por qué?!" I pressed my fingers into my temples to stop the pounding, but that didn't work. Frustrated and mad, I began to run—first, stomping the ground hard as if to kill my shadow, then crossing the track arbitrarily back and forth. But nothing killed the headache. In desperation, I ran faster, fleeing toward the streets beyond the school grounds.

My head hurt so much, I didn't know what to do, so I kept running through the neighborhood of dogtrot houses until I arrived at a park I'd frequented with David. In the roots of the lone eucalyptus tree, I sat down, protected from the eyes of garbage collectors or retirees who might be wondering why I wasn't in school. Gazing up into the tree's leaves, I felt their darkness swimming toward me and closed my eyes. I imagined my mother in the kitchen, home from the early shift. The washing machine going off. Eventually, she would pick up her dark burden of clothes.

The image of my father, I had to squeeze out. He was a traitor I would never love.

I focused on trying to breathe in the cool air of the tree, and its great shadow contained me. When the beats in my head had finally slowed, I rose cautiously and began the arduous journey back to Royal Palm, with only a brief stop at an air-conditioned convenience store before I headed into the heat again. Florida weighed me down and wore out the last of my energy.

I reported to the school nurse, who looked at my sweaty face and decided to take my temperature. "You're okay," she concluded. "But why don't you lie on the cot until next period?" She gave me an aspirin, but I held up two fingers and she handed me another.

By the end of the day, the headache had finally passed.

At the bus stop, I sat and let 77s and 43s go by. I felt so tired, like I really did want to die.

It was better to be mad. Mad at my mother, mad at my father. Who was worse?

She'd let things get out of hand. It was *her* fault he was so crazy. She was weak, inept. She'd drugged him. Lied to him. Now, she wouldn't stand up for me when it mattered.

And *him*—I'd squashed myself into the ground for him, but he'd crushed me out anyway, as if I were nothing more than a water bug.

A small, hard voice in my brain told me that my father was too crazy to have meant what he did. But in my own crazy heart I believed that he'd hurt me on purpose.

Eventually, because there was nowhere else to go, I forced myself to board a bus and return home. I couldn't bear to use the back door, so I walked around to the front. When I knocked, Manolo gave me a puzzled look before heading off to work.

I went into my room without greeting my parents, then wearily spread my voluminous homework out on the bed. Eleventh grade was going to be no piece of cake. Odd number grades were always the hardest. How I wished I were in an even number. Twelve would be the perfect number to break out of this prison at last.

When Mami came in, I didn't glance up. She kissed my forehead. "Too much homework?" she asked, in a voice fake with sympathy.

I didn't answer.

"Well, come help soon. Don't forget to put that away," she reminded me, indicating the UPS box. After she closed the door, I stared at the box and got up to inspect my mess of a closet again.

How would I squeeze in something extra? I eyed the smaller, water-stained box with our family pictures—maybe I should stick that inside the UPS box?

Climbing on my chair, I pulled down the photo box and couldn't help but grin, despite my dour spirits, at the stiff, colored-over studio portrait on top: Pablo, Manolo, and me, smiling with our fat little hands under our chins. I flipped through a few out-of-focus black-and-white photos under the portrait—my parents on the old Roman bridge in Cartagena; my grandfather and me, holding hands in front of a palm tree with the Caribbean sparkling behind us; blurry people I didn't recognize. Someone—my mother, I guessed—had run out of steam and stopped marking the dates on the back. In one undated photo, she wore dark glasses and a sleeveless dress with big buttons down the front. She was smiling vaguely at some place beyond the camera as if trying to hide her doubts. My father smiled too, his arm around her. He had all his hair then. You got the feeling that the family picture was his idea and that my mother had gone along—as she had with bringing us to the United States, moving us to Florida, treating my father's ideas as if they were normal, and everything else. At different heights in front of them, my brothers and I posed obediently while the sun shot pokers into our eyes.

Under the pictures, I found a pink leather book with "Nuestro Bebé" calligraphied in gold script on the cover. As I opened the baby book, I recognized it as mine. I barely remembered it, though in elementary school, my brothers and I used to go through our childhood mementos constantly while hounding my mother about what we were like when we were small. Had we cried coming out of her? Who was the biggest baby? Whom did she love best?

I love you best, mi'ja, because you're my oldest, she'd said. You, Manolo, because you're my middle child. And you, Pablito, because you're my baby.

How much love could a person give?

The pages of the baby book were embellished with watercolor drawings of storks and flowers. Each page had a gold script title, under which my parents had taken turns filling in information. "Nació" for the date and place of birth and doctor's name. "El bautizo" for the church and time of baptism and the names of my godparents. There was a page with my baby footprint—so tiny and cute! A page for Visitors, one for my Family Tree—my father had laboriously recorded all the way back to my great-great-grandparents on his side and as far as my great-grandparents on my mother's. There was a chart of my monthly growth the first year. My Favorite Toys. My First Word.

I stared at the familiar block letters as my eyes filled with tears.

Papá.

## TWENTY-FOUR

THE SMELL OF MAMI'S ONION, GARLIC, and green pepper sofrito drifted into my room a little later, after I'd finished straightening out the closet and started in on homework. I squared my shoulders, put my pen down, and went to help her.

She was preparing to fry meat, so I pulled the rice pot out of a cabinet, filled the pot with water and set that on the stove to boil. When my father heard me, he scurried in with one of his assignments. "Mi'jita," he said, as if nothing had changed.

I lugged the big rice bag to the sink so I wouldn't have to look at him. Opening the bag, I dumped the grains into a strainer and turned on the faucet.

"Roberto," my mother broke in, while carefully spooning oil into the frying pan.

"¿Sí?" he asked.

"No más." No more.

I stopped washing the rice and let the water run.

"She has too much schoolwork, Roberto. It's too difficult. She needs to concentrate. You want her to do well, don't you?"

"Claro que sí," he answered agreeably.

"Well then, you can't give her any more typing. She has to

concentrate on her studies." Mami lit a match and touched it to the burner.

"Of course," he said, smiling inanely. "I only ask her to help when she's finished."

"No, Roberto," Mami insisted. "You're tiring her out. She can't do all that homework and then work for you too. She's still a child. You'll have to complete your own letters. You have time. I can show you how to use the typewriter."

I was very still, my hands buried in the softened grains under the water.

My father didn't say anything. He gave my mother one of his weird laughs and waited. But when she bustled around without explanation, he simply shuffled back to his room.

That was it. Over. Just like that.

Mami threw the meat into the frying pan. As it sizzled, I slowly carried the bowl of washed rice over and placed it next to her, then grabbed a ripe avocado from the counter. "Should I cut this up?"

She nodded. "Don't throw away the seed," she reminded me, and handed me a jar for the pit.

After I'd cut up the avocado, I stuck the pit in the jar. "What else?" I asked.

"Nothing. Go finish your homework."

In the doorway, I hesitated. The water in the rice pot had come to a boil, and my mother threw the grains in. Her hands were bony like mine, only longer. The wedding rings slipped around on her finger, but she never took them off.

"Gracias, Mami," I said quietly.

"No hay por que agradecer," she answered, waving me away. No reason to thank her.

The porqué of reason, the cause. Only in Spanish could a word mean both why and because.

• • •

Fátima recovered from her flu and returned to school the next day. We couldn't talk much in English class, since Mrs. Foster had assigned passages of *Things Fall Apart* to read aloud, nor at lunch either because too many people were around. Instead, I made plans to stop at her house later, after I was done with work.

As soon as I arrived, she led me into her room by the hand and sat facing me on the bed. "You seem upset, Gabi. What's wrong?"

"I don't know Fátima." I looked away, feeling so alone with my truths. But how could I break down and reveal the very worst truth—the one about my father? "It's just—I'm not sure what to believe in anymore."

"You mean like God? Because of that creepy priest?"

"No . . ." My lip quivered. "It's not that."

"What is it then, Gabi?"

I twisted the handle of my book bag while she waited quietly beside me. She was such a good friend, always kind, always sharing her hope for the future with me. If I couldn't trust her, who would I ever trust again?

"It's everything, Fátima," I blurted out finally, facing her and taking a deep breath. "The thing is," I continued bravely, "my father's gotten to be a big problem. A big problem. And my mother isn't too good at handling things either. So everything's—I don't know—out of control. I don't know what to do anymore."

Fátima's face looked more troubled. "Do you want me to ask my parents for help?"

"No! I mean, thanks, but—see, my father doesn't realize it, when he's being that way."

"What way, Gabi?"

"Like," I swallowed, "hitting people."

"Bad kind of hitting?"

I nodded.

"Like, did he hit you?"

"Yeah." Remembering made my head throb. "He hits every-body."

"¡Ay Gabi!" Fátima's brows furrowed. "Isn't there someone who could talk to him?"

"It's not a talking thing, Fátima. He's—crazy." Once I'd uttered the word, the whole gruesome por qué story spilled out. "It was awful, Fátima, like he was possessed or something. See, he has these delusions, on top of the temper. He thinks we're gonna get millions of dollars from the government, and that everyone's trying to keep him from collecting the money. And I'm all alborotada all the time fearing that he's going to get arrested and lose his green card and we'll end up in some sad life in Colombia with no way back!"

I leaned against her pillow. What a relief it was to finally let the truth out. "We give him these sleeping pills to calm him down and stuff, but sometimes he doesn't take them. I don't trust those pills anyway. He's still crazy underneath. And he could do something horrible too. But all the time, we're like pretending that everything's normal. Only it's not. Nothing in my house is normal. Nothing."

"*You're* normal, Gabi. I swear." Fátima reached over and hugged me.

I broke down and cried. *Philos*—the only kind of love that didn't hurt.


I kept my distance from my father at home in the aftermath of his attack. I didn't kiss him hello or good night. I didn't want to feel anything toward him.

Mami offered him lessons on the typewriter, but he resisted. I figured he might force Pablo to do his dirty work, but my brother shrewdly avoided that by claiming homework the way I used to—although he actually did have a lot to do now. The nuns even gave him free guitar lessons that seemed to be replacing the glue-sniffing hobby.

My father followed Mami around while she cooked or cleaned.

"¡Ay, Roberto!" she complained. "Leave me in peace!"

After a few days of wandering in uncertainty, he decided to write his incomprehensible articles in longhand.

"It's better that way," she confided to me. "He fills more hours in his day." She was meticulous with his pill now and wouldn't leave for work until she saw him swallow it down. Tía Rita and Tío Victor had tried to press upon her the importance of some kind of medical intervention, but my mother clung to her own blind faith in, and loyalty to, my father, come what may.

Although the pill subdued him and writing longhand was laborious, my father acquired new energy for his increasingly strange compositions. Alone, he dismantled whatever feeble dykes we'd once mounted against the vast sea of hypothesis and correlation.

After a few days, it got so he wouldn't come out for dinner.

My mother sent my brothers in there one night to get him.

"I have to work," he said, bent over his scrolls.

I glanced into the room. When he looked up, he didn't really see me. His eyes were filmy, as if with conjunctivitis, and I had the fleeting impression that a person could literally drown in hallucinations, if they were strong enough.

It was only a matter of time, I feared, before that storm finally drowned everybody.


After my confession, Fátima insisted I hang out at her house all that week on the pretext of planning her birthday festivities. I tried to reassure her that my father was absorbed by his elaborate transcriptions, though I was glad she was so concerned. I was also grateful that she didn't try to drag me to church anymore, though she worried aloud about me "losing my way." One morning in English class, she passed me a folded slip of paper, and when I unfolded it cautiously under my textbook I found a holy picture inside. It was the gold-trimmed kind that had been a prize trade back in Catholic school: A beautiful angel with an illuminated face and enormous wings lifted a bouquet of lilies into lazurite blue skies. The caption on the reverse read: St. Gabriel the Archangel, Messenger. Fátima had scribbled, "Do you still believe in angels? XOX, me."

I grinned at her, and she smiled angelically back.


That next weekend was her party. I went over there early, and her father was already roasting a pig in the yard.

In the sisters' bedroom I sat on the floor and helped Fátima blow up balloons. Her sister Rosalía came in, holding a curling iron in her hair, and walked up to the closet. She gestured toward the pink-and-white polka-dot dress on a hanger on the door. "This is it, Gabi," she told me.

"Slinky," I said with an appreciative smile and thanked her for loaning me the dress. It was pretty—so what if it might reveal some curves? I turned to Fátima. "So is your Chemistry friend coming?"

She nodded enthusiastically as she blew up the last balloon and tied it with a white ribbon. Then we grabbed the blown-up balloons and took them outside. After we'd tied them to the fence and festively lined up folding chairs next to each other, we went back inside, stealing a few spoonfuls of black beans from her mother's huge pot. By the time we got ourselves dressed, boisterous relatives had arrived. They were followed by Amy and Octavio, who went to the yard with me to admire the pig (Amy and Octavio) and feel sorry for it (me).

Fátima's heartthrob, Mark, a husky guy with hair shaved short as a soldier's, showed up while we jóvenes were snacking on the

patio and adults danced in the living room. When the doorbell
rang again, I was surprised and glad to see Claudio. His grandfather wasn't doing well, so I hadn't been sure Claudio would come.
In his crisp white shirt, he circled the living room and greeted
every one of Fátima's relatives.

"What a guy," said Octavio.

Claudio joined us outside. There wasn't enough breeze to keep
the balloons in the air, so he helped me tie the floaters closer to
the fence. Some balloons popped, prompting Fátima's cousins to
bring out firecrackers and roman candles. Claudio and I stopped
to watch the spray of comets as they dissolved, leaving in their
wake the golden Arabic moon and its radiant twin star in the
darkness. Adults wandered out, urging us jóvenes inside to take
their places, so we headed indoors and Claudio asked me quietly
in Spanish, "Do you know how to dance to this?"

"More or less," I said with a smile.

He held out his hand. "More or less, I accept."

As he led me out, I looked to Fátima for some moral support,
though I knew Mark didn't dance Latin.

"Come on, Octavio," Fátima said, pulling him by the arm. "We
can't let the old folks defeat us."

Fátima's father lifted a rum drink in the air and cheered us on.
"¡Vamos!"

It was a moderately paced merengue. Claudio held me lightly,
letting me warm up before trying any turns. The cotton fabric of
his shirt was thin, the hard slope of his muscle surprising under
my hand, and suddenly I was happy to be wearing that flirty
pink dress. He pressed my back in for a turn, grinned as we came
together in time, and twirled me again. We picked up the pace
and traded smiles as we slipped through each other's hands. More
young couples joined in, the last of the older folks ceding the room.
As Claudio and I turned one last time, the merengue yielded to

a sentimental bachata, and someone lowered the lights. With his eyes, he asked my permission, then drew my fingers to his chest and pressed me closer. A scent of freshly ironed cotton, rainwater, or something sweeter that I couldn't define filled my face. Into my hair, Claudio breathed the lyrics: *Lloraré*—I will cry for you.

From the yard, men announced the pig-carving, and the dancers released each other. Claudio grazed my cheek with the barest of kisses and said my name once, his voice low. *Gabriela*. We moved to the patio, the air warm between us, my name ringing joyfully inside me.

The next morning, I got an early call—Lara needed babysitting help.

She was unusually energized when I arrived, and I found both girls pink-cheeked and healthy for once.

Luna and Solita played happily while Lara was gone, and I relived my heady feelings of dancing with Claudio. If love could be exhilarating, I fantasized wistfully, wouldn't that be a marriage of *agapé*?

When Lara returned, sooner than expected, she'd brought almond cakes from the Spanish bakery. "We're celebrating your father's return!" she told the girls. Gaily, she escorted Luna and Solita outside to eat, and then came back to prepare our customary coffee.

"Is Walter's work done?" I asked in surprise as I removed two cups from the cabinet.

"Oh no, there's a great deal more." Lara put the cakes on an ivory china plate I'd never seen before that had tiny purple nosegays and a silver edge. "But he can finish here," she added with a smile as she poured the coffee into our cups. "We need him," she said simply, lifting the tray and carrying it to the yard.

As I trailed behind her, I worried vaguely about whether any of the "compromises" Lara had spoken of in the past could be avoided before it was too late. "But, Lara, it doesn't seem like—" I hesitated, struggling to find the right words between honesty and respect, "like when Walter's around, he helps you that much."

"True," she acknowledged, as we claimed the plastic table. "But he does even less thousands of miles away! ¿Sabes qué, Gabi? The problem is that Walter never anticipated a domestic life. He's still—exploring. That makes things difficult for the girls and me." She cast an approving look at Luna and Solita, who'd gotten out the hula hoop. When Lara clapped for them, their round sweaty faces beamed.

"But it doesn't seem fair, Lara," I said dubiously.

"Oh, you're right, my Gabrielita." She offered me the pretty plate with the cakes on it. "But you see, I'm getting a little more time this way."

I tried to return a positive smile. Lara loved Walter, I knew, but the marriage route didn't seem to have provided her with too much freedom even if she did have a lot more independence than Mami. The conversation was disheartening.

After we'd finished our coffees, I went to get Miss McWhorter's brochures and permission forms from my bag. My mother had softened a bit since my father's attack on me, and what did I have to lose by letting Lara try to persuade her about the trip? Lara perused the material curiously, then promised to come by when the girls were napping and Camila could look in on them.


The talk with Mami didn't start out too well.

"A hotel?" my mother exclaimed. "A young girl in a foreign hotel? With strangers?"

"I am sure the program teachers will provide excellent supervision," Lara said. "If you like, I can speak to the counselor for you and investigate the lodgings too. Everything will surely be of the highest quality. It's a school. They're not going to take children anywhere inappropriate."

"Thank you, Lara. It's not necessary. That's too long for Gabriela to be away from her family."

"Not at all, Evi. It's only a semester. I'm sure you've had to be away from your family temporarily."

"Never."

"What about when Tía Julia died, Mami?" I burst in. "You left us for almost two weeks."

My mother shook her head. "It's not the days!" she cried, wringing her hands. "It's just not right!"

I looked at Lara. This was the kind of point that defeated me. I mean, who decided what was right? How could you prove or disprove it?

"Evangelina," Lara said gently. "I know how hard it is. I'm a mother too. But this is a wonderful opportunity for Gabriela. I know you love your daughter. I'm sure you want her to have the best opportunities, the ones you didn't have."

Mami started to cry. "Tú no sabes lo difícil que es..." How difficult it was. "Taking care of a home without help." She cried about how she couldn't manage without me, about struggling to make ends meet, about my father's work problems—and his perplexing illness.

I tried to harden myself, to keep my soul from drowning in hers, but Lara was patient, patting my mother's shoulder and sympathizing with her difficulties. Then Lara gave me a look that meant "go," and I pretended to—turning the corner and leaning against the wall so I could keep listening.

"Roberto was so honorable," Mami said, sobbing. "If you knew, Lara, how hard he worked. After his father died, he was the one who stayed. Even his sisters were gone before him. He wouldn't leave that woman alone. Imagine, Lara. What kind of man does that? *Only* Roberto. *He* was the one who worked the hardest. And had the most hope. When we married and after, when we moved to the refinery, and he was so proud too. Dios mío, I can't explain to myself how this could've happened to him. "

I pictured the young, dark-eyed man standing beside my mother in solemn promise in their wedding picture. The confident father, radiant with hope on our sunny Roman bridge in Cartagena. The stubborn father who'd pressed my wriggling footprint into a pink baby book to immortalize my childhood.

Grief, like a hurricane, struck me. Where was that father now? I cried mutely, doubled over to keep from splitting into a million pieces.

"Ay Lara," I heard Mami mourn behind the wall between us. "I went along with *everything.*" Her voice, full of her own grief and sorrows, righted me—keeping me, as always, a safe distance from my own. "Look what I'm left with now," she added sadly, "no illusions, no hope."

"Hope lives in our children, Evi," Lara told her softly. She complimented Mami over Manolo's industriousness and over her success at getting Pablo into St. Stephen's—and then for the wonderful daughter she'd raised. Slowly, Lara steered the conversation toward my contest victory and the Ambassador trip. Lara asked things like, "You've been to New York, yes?" and got Mami to agree often enough to loosen her fierce grip on "no." Then, somehow, Lara was offering to come over and keep her company on the days I was gone, so that she wouldn't feel so alone.

I couldn't believe it. Waves of gratitude flooded me with more tears, and I stumbled toward my room. I had to stop and lean against the doorway. As I glanced into the room, the planes of elusive light shimmered across my floor, and I felt the first uncertainty. How could I be without my family?

A line strayed out of one of those Leonard Cohen laments from the past and flew around as if lost in my soul—something about the angels who forget to pray for us.

But angels did pray for me: Fátima, Octavio, Lara...and Claudio too.

And my grandfather, the Angel of my Childhood.

So much sentimental feeling inspired me to track down the autobiografía which had earned me the Bellísimo in junior high Spanish. I'd never written to my grandfather, but now as I reread the autobiography, I knew it was the closest thing to a good-bye letter I could compose. Gently, I slipped it into an envelope to send to him.

That evening, long after Lara had gone, I found my permission papers signed on the kitchen counter. But when Mami shuffled in, wearing her reading glasses and carrying the day's bills, she only said, "Ay, mi'ja, make me a tinto, will you?"

I filled the espresso pot and left it brewing to go tuck the forms safely away in my room. When I could smell the Bustelo, I returned and poured my mother her cup of coffee. I hesitated a moment before leaving her. "Thanks, Mami, for letting me go on the trip," I said shyly, kissing her cheek.

She nodded distantly and returned to her bills.

In my room, I hummed the Leonard Cohen tune to myself while I changed my clothes and tried to remember all the verses. But when I lay in the dark with my eyes open, only the words of a question—one of Mami's familiar expressions—floated toward me in a great halo of light. ¿Quién te crees?

Who did I dare to be?

## TWENTY-FIVE

No HURRICANE HAD HIT FLORIDA in more than four years, but one was on its way now. That September, during the gray days of anticipation before the storm, people in my neighborhood came out of their houses to talk about it. Old Mr. Krantz, the only American left on our street, told me that we were lucky to have moved to Miami during the lull. He had lived through the Great Miami Hurricane of 1926, he said, though he was a kid then, of course. Still, he could remember the hollowed-out windows of office buildings and piles of debris that floated down Flagler Street afterward. "That storm left the downtown bank building leaning sideways," he said. "And we heard tell of a piano lifted out of a Miami Beach hotel. Scary stuff," he concluded, shaking his head. "Of course, that was before they gave hurricanes names like they do now."

This one was called Estrella, Star. My science teacher, Mr. Fernández, explained that the Weather Bureau retired the names afterward, so that each hurricane remained unique in history, however mighty or small.

That week, as we waited for our star to fall directly into South Florida, somewhere between Palm Beach and the Keys, Mr. Fernández gave us handouts about the Great Miami Hurricane.

We were to track Estrella's progress across the Atlantic and compare the two storms' post-landfall features. Whereas the 1926 hurricane was a Category 4, Estrella was expected to be a Category 2—not the most dangerous but bad enough to splinter buildings apart and flood the southern coast.

Hurricane frenzy overtook the high school. In English, Mrs. Foster assigned us the Florida chapters of Zora Neale Hurston's *Their Eyes Were Watching God,* up to when the hurricane reaches Janie and Tea Cake. Since I didn't know whether the storm in the book was real or not, I went to ask Mr. Lanham. "Probably the Okeechobee hurricane of 1928," he said, surmising it was named for the enormous Lake Hurston described as a "monster" that woke and grumbled out of its bed. I decided to write my essay on the Seminoles; though they passed so briefly through the novel, they were the only characters with sense enough to head for higher ground before the hurricane hit.

School was canceled the day Estrella was due.

Mami spent most of the day waiting with my brothers and me in front of the TV. Not much else was televised besides weather coverage. Periodically, she got up and went to summarize for my father in the bedroom, though he seemed to have as little interest in this aspect of reality as in any other. Still, she couldn't give up trying to share her anxiety. Each time she left, Pablo unlocked the Florida room door and threw it open. My brothers and I stared at the sky, which was no more gray than when rain is expected. But watching it so intently through the screen made our world feel eerily quiet.

It was 4:17 P.M. when the storm hit the state. Outside, our neighborhood became windy as the newscaster announced Estrella's landfall on Marathon Key. Neighbors who'd stood in doorways went inside. The wind began choking trees and jump-roping through phone lines.

On the TV screen, an anemometer danced in a 90 mile-per-hour gale.

"Lock that door instantly!" my mother ordered.

"The lock doesn't make any difference," I pronounced without looking up. On my worksheet, I recorded the time and wind velocity.

Outside, our street had been deserted.

"The candles!" she exclaimed.

My brothers followed, urging her to find flashlights too.

"There's hours of daylight left," I called, but no one listened. It was more fun to run around in a panic than to sit and wait for Kingdom Come.

The wind increased to 110 mph. Between the Estrella updates, newscasters interviewed people weathered by past hurricanes from Key West to Pensacola. I wished they'd found old Mr. Krantz, with his bushy eyebrows, to talk about the Great Miami Hurricane of 1926. He had such a good memory.

My father finally came out in his mad scientist hairdo and stood tapping a bunch of signature envelopes against his leg. "¿Tienes tarea?" he asked.

Nodding, I pointed at the TV and explained that my homework was related to the hurricane. My father started to unlock the door.

I could hear the fury of the wind outside. "You can't go out there, Papi," I cautioned. Luckily, Mami had double-locked the door.

My father went to get the spare keys.

On TV, they were showing the storm surge at Crandon Park, less than an hour away from us. Waves were nine feet above normal. Now they were labeling the storm Category 3.

My father returned and unlocked the door, but when he opened it the wind came in hot, really hot. I scribbled Estrella notes while repeating the warning that he shouldn't go outside, though my crazy father stepped onto the terrace anyway.

The crazier wind pushed him back.

"Look at the waves," I emphasized, pointing to the screen. "It's a hurricane. Un huracán," I repeated, as if constant repetition might make a dent in his hard head. "You're not supposed to go out in it. It's dangerous. Es peligroso," I repeated loudly, trying to out shout the flapping door.

Mami came running. "Who opened that door?" When she saw him there, she scolded my father. "Roberto!"

My father smiled blithely and stepped out, continuing down our walkway.

"Come back here!" she yelled. As she started to follow him, I rose to help.

"No. You stay here." She pushed me inside and turned, shoving her shoulders forward into the fierce wind.

I braced myself against the door frame and watched her hair and clothes blow every which way. Maybe my father would lose his envelopes and come right back, I thought. Mami should probably leave him be. But she was fussing along behind him, trying to coax him while holding on to her candles for dear life. "Don't you know that everything will be closed?" she screamed.

Our next-door neighbor yelled out through his X-taped window in feeble support, telling my father to be reasonable, hombre, didn't he see that this was no weather to go out in?

When Mami stumbled, my father helped her up. As they struggled to get her upright, and she managed to plant her slippered feet apart for balance, he took off. Aghast, she watched him for a moment, then turned and ran back home. The door swung violently shut behind her.

"¡Pura locura!" she hissed.

Pure craziness was right!

She hesitated over the lock, then decided to leave it alone. "I'm calling Victor," she said.

"He can't do anything, Mami," I told her. "You're not supposed to drive in a hurricane either."

The storm outside was trying to keep up with the one on TV. In the Keys, people who had refused to evacuate were pictured in front of their roofless houses. The announcer interviewed the governor for his grim I-told-you-so. Biscayne Bay was a mess of torn up marina sections and broken boats. There was one report that a stupid University of Miami student had gotten injured while trying to surf "killer" waves.

"Man, he is really crazy," Manolo said when I went to tell him and Pablo about my father's excursion to the post office. "Look at it out there." He and Pablo were standing on Pablo's bed staring out the window as the world went nuts. I was glad my brothers had called a truce after their fight—and the apology letter the probation officer had assigned Pablo to write Manolo.

I climbed up with them, and we watched the wind tear up the neighborhood. I became more nervous about my father—what if he fell? What if the hurricane swept him into the street and a truck hit him? Even if I did hate him, I didn't want him to die. Guiltily, I remembered my furious diary pages and a voodoo horror overcame me. *Oh God, if there is one,* I whispered, *I didn't mean what I wrote. Please don't kill my father.*

"Whoa!" Pablo pointed as a 2-by-4 shot through the heart of Mr. Krantz's royal palm. The limbs of other trees tumbled maniacally through the street. Branches slammed against cars and houses. In awe, we watched an aluminum awning fly, chariot-like, across the sky. Judgment Day had arrived.

"Maybe the old man went inside the 7-Eleven," Manolo said, when he saw my face.

"Or the cops could've picked him up," Pablo added reassuringly.

"We should have stopped him," I said. "We should have stopped him."

I went to go find my mother. "What can we do, Mami?"

Glued to the kitchen window, she ordered me to telephone my uncle. But Tío Victor insisted that someone had surely invited my father in to wait out the storm.

The torrential rains began, and still my father wasn't back. I stayed with Mami at the window, but soon the machine-gun bullets of rain obliterated any view.

After two hours of waiting, my uncle declared that it was time to call the police.


An ambulance picked up my father on Eighth Street after the Santarpio's Sandwich Shop sign went flying and knocked him down. All he got was a broken arm, the uncles told us on the phone later, but the hospital was going to do tests to make sure his head was okay.

When it was safe to drive again, Tío Lucho took Mami to Jackson Memorial.

While we awaited her return, my brothers and I joined people outside inspecting the hurricane damage. A muted sunlight fell through the clouds that hung weakly in the sky. Shaken by Estrella, even the clouds lacked the strength to do their job. Windowpanes had been blown out of our house, and the broken glass shone among chunks of black roofing, garbage, and tree limbs on our lawn. The wind had uprooted our poor tilted street sign. Bent and tangled in phone lines, it lay on the wet gravel, its white "5" and "4" gazing vacantly up.

A felled tree was smashed into the Cabreras' navy blue Chrysler and the car's rear end had been kicked into the air. Down the street, a Venezuelan family who'd been building an improbable two-story in our flat community found their would be hacienda chopped into a pygmy forest of shattered beams. Red tiles that construction workers had covered with plastic were strewn everywhere, the clay fragments transforming our neighborhood into a Spanish ruin.

When she returned from the hospital, Mami told us that my father would remain for a while longer. "He'll be very rested," she said, slumping into a chair. She stared at the empty air as if she were shell-shocked.

Later, she got up and began to inventory the damage. With school and work canceled indefinitely, post-hurricane fix-it jobs like removing junk from our yard and taping up windows went to Manolo and his reluctant assistant, Pablo. Mami also decided that this was a good time to assign major cleaning jobs inside the house to herself and me. But all the fixing and cleaning made me realize what a dump our home had become, and not just because of Estrella. Stationed in the green bathroom one morning, I surveyed the dilapidation: rusted faucets, chipped toilet bowl, a bath curtain that hung unevenly where grommet holes had torn. We'd long ago papered the walls with green trellises, but now the trellises were the paper itself, climbing off the wall as if in a surreal painting.

With a sigh, I finished cleaning and left the pitiful green bathroom for my room. There, on my bed, I found a large box. "Mami!" I yelled. "What's this for?"

Padding over in her chancletas, she held her hands out to one side, her yellow gloves wet. "That's from your father's desk." She frowned at the loaded box. "Why don't you go through it? Save anything important." As she left, she added, "Tú eres la que entiende eso."

*I* was the one who understood it all?

Warily, I eyed my father's junk, oozing out mental cancer. Had typing for him *really* made me understand his craziness? I picked up a sheet of petroleum scribblings and scowled. Crushing the page, I shot it straight into the wastebasket. Then I crumpled another wad, and then another, and on and on until I'd hooped in enough for the wastebasket to overflow and I had to go get shopping bag reinforcements. Then I continued my aggressive crushing of paper until I came upon the beat-up Rickenbacker textbook, *The World We Live In,* decorated with my father's many illogical comments. The world *he* lived in. Plainly, we wouldn't be returning that book, so I threw it into the shopping bag too. When I got to the *Home Mechanics* magazines, though, I stopped. What if my father discovered that it was me who'd thrown out all his stuff? Even on Dalmane, as I knew well, he could get upset.

I jumped up to go find Mami and confer.

In her bathroom, everything gleamed in excess. Tiles, sink, toilet—all were dripping and sparkled, the room redolent of pine cleaner. Hours would be required for all those surfaces to dry.

My mother, at rest in the yard, wore her yellow gloves as she sipped her tinto.

I blocked the sun from my eyes. "Mami. We can't throw out all his stuff."

She gazed vaguely into her coffee. "He isn't going to remember."

"He remembers lots of things."

"Don't worry, it won't matter." She swirled the tinto in her cup and sipped.

Too much Pine-Sol, I thought. Maybe she thinks it will clean out her life so she can start over, but everything is the same, clean or not.

I returned to my appointed chore. If my father freaked out about his missing stuff, I would lie, pretend I had no idea what happened to it. *Maybe the hurricane blew it away, Papi.* Or blame the uncles. *Maybe they brought it to the hospital for you, Papi.* By then, a squad of garbage collectors would have taken away the loose-leaf sheets of mad writing with its excess of majuscules and dark, inky exclamation points.

Something fluttered suddenly in my chest. My father had pummeled me with both fists, tried to strangle his own wife, gone blithely strolling in a hurricane. What was next? If only his madness could be manifested peacefully, I wished forlornly, like that of harmless Teddy who thought he was President Roosevelt in the Cary Grant movie, *Arsenic and Old Lace.* But my father wasn't like harmless Teddy, not at all.

When I reached my old retyped entries from the *World Book Encyclopedia,* the weight of all my sadness made it hard for me to pick up the pages. My father had never even noticed the sea of typos I'd left behind after I quit correcting. A pathetic way in which I'd cheated him.

*Why?* Why had his life and mine been reduced to paper lies?

More than anything else, at that moment, I wished for the courage to ask him to stop. *Stop acting crazy, Papi. Please, please just stop.*

My father's recovery lasted as long as Miami's from the hurricane. Weeks passed, and to my surprise, he remained in the hospital. Then one day, Mami starched and ironed my brothers' shirts and told me to put on the ivory dress I'd worn to the bar mitzvah. She was taking us for a visit.

The dress was much tighter in the shoulders and chest, as if my heart had grown from having too many difficult people to care about. If only my heart were a sponge, I thought, and I could squeeze out the unbearable feelings to make room for the good ones—like my pleasure in the dress's gold sparkles or in the world illuminated by the azabache tear of Claudio's eye.

Tío Victor drove us to Jackson Memorial and Mami led us around the L-shaped nurses' station on my father's floor. There he was, propped in a metal bed with his arm in a cast. His hair was pushed back, 1950s movie-star style. Ricardo Montalbán in *My Man and I.*

"Hola, Papi," I said, and in front of Tío Victor and the nurse, I felt obliged to kiss his cheek for the first time since the knuckle-pounding. His skin was cold, and his shoulder bones looked thin. I had the sense of his heart having shrunk just as mine expanded.

"Hola, mi'jita," he replied hoarsely, as if he hadn't talked in a while.

Pablo and Manolo dumped packages onto his bed.

"Not all at once," said Tío Victor, removing the treats to a nearby rolling table. "Even Roberto can't eat everything immediately, eh Roberto?"

My father nodded and smiled.

Mami leaned over, adjusting the strands of his graying hair. "Are you better, mi'jo?"

"Sí, sí," he said, smiling and nodding repeatedly. Fine and dandy. But the ticking hand was shut tight now, as if something—a butterfly maybe—might slip out.

"You want us to sign your cast?" Pablo asked amicably.

"¿Ah?"

"Don't be ridiculous," my mother told Pablo.

"Oh, what's the harm?" said Tío Victor.

My father said sí to that as he did to everything else.

"All right," my mother relented. "Be gentle."

While Pablo went to borrow a nurse's marker, I glanced around at the clashing shades of green throughout the room, from the

Christmassy green of the counters to the faded lime curtains that partially divided my father's half of the room from the other side where an elderly patient slept. There was no chair by the man's bed, but someone had left cookies on his table. I leaned closer and noticed that they were Anisarios. That was strange.

"Is that man Colombian too?" I asked my mother.

"No, gringo," Tío Victor replied. "Evangelina," he told Mami, "I'm going for a smoke, all right?"

"I'll go with you, Tío," Manolo offered.

Nodding, Mami hovered over my father as Pablo elaborated Gothic letters in black marker on my father's cast and filled in the letters with a yellow highlighter. My father smiled away. Despite the agreeable mood, something was off. He wasn't the familiar peppy-happy of an arroz con pollo and sweet plantains dinner. And why was his ticking hand scrunched so tightly?

I glanced at the other bed, my eyes landing on the Anisarios. Now I remembered. Those were my father's cookies. I'd placed them in a bag for Mami's last visit. Tía Consuelo had sent them when her trip got postponed because of the hurricane. With determination, I marched over and picked up the box. The old man didn't stir.

"Whatcha doin', hon?" asked a nurse who came in to take his blood pressure.

"These aren't his," I explained.

"Sure they are, sweetie. Can you please put them back?"

"They're not his. Look." As she wrapped a black strap around the man's arm and pumped, I showed her the place on the box where it said *Hecho en Colombia*.

The old man's eyes fluttered open and shut, open and shut.

"Sorry, I don't know Spanish," said the nurse, scribbling numbers on a clipboard. She smiled at me. "I should."

"It says 'Made in Colombia.'" I pointed to her patient. "He's not Colombian."

"Huh?" She peered at the package. "Oh. I see what you mean. Hmm. Maybe one of the candy stripers moved it over. You go ahead, dear, give it back to your grandfather."

I didn't correct her but brought the cookies triumphantly to my father's side of the room.

My father looked up from examining the tackily decorated cast.

"Papi," I asked, "do you want a cookie?" I held up the box.

"O sí, mi'jita." He reached forward with the broken arm.

"I can do it for you."

He waited patiently as I tore off the plastic, emptied a few cookies on his tray, and moved the tray in front of him. As he tried to pick up an Anisario with the unbroken arm, he had difficulty opening his clenched hand, so I lifted the cookie to his mouth for him to bite into. Through a mouthful of cookie, he mumbled, "Delicioso, mi'jita," and reached for another. Carefully, I pried apart his clenched fingers. No butterfly.

Something squeezed my swollen heart while I watched him chew.

Long ago, when I was little, I'd contracted scarlet fever and my parents had had to leave me in a hospital in New York. Every morning after my father had finished his night shift, he'd come to see me. One time he brought me cookies, but after he left, the nurses opened my box and divided the contents between me and another young girl in the room. I didn't speak English yet, so I couldn't tell the nurses that I didn't want to share. Not the cookies that my father had given me.

On the drive home, I asked my mother and uncle what the doctors had found wrong. Mami extracted a hankie from the venerated leather bag Tía Consuelo had once given her. Tío Victor waited another second before turning toward us. "Schizophrenia, mi'ja. They gave your father medicine."

"That's different personalities, right?" asked Pablo. "Like that movie. First she's a slut, then she's a mother, and then—"

"*The Three Faces of Eve*," Manolo remembered.

Pablo nodded. "Yeah. Papi switches from being an old man to a little kid."

I edged forward. "Is that true, Tío? Does Papi have different personalities?"

"I don't think so, mi'ja. This isn't a movie, it's an illness." My uncle lit a cigarette and smoked deeply. "Incurable."

Schizophrenia. I slid back in my seat. So that meant we couldn't pretend he was normal anymore.

"Then what's the medicine for?" Pablo demanded.

"To keep your father tranquil."

"Right," Manolo muttered in English. "I'll believe it when I see it."

"But then he'll stay sick...*forever*," I blurted, as the gravity of my father's illness dawned on me. "How did Papi get it, Tío? Why?"

"Who knows, mi'ja? Who knows?" My uncle finished his cigarette and rolled down the window to let out the stale air.

Incurable. We'd called it nervios. Phantom sickness, voodoo. We'd even given my father fake medicine: sleeping pills! But his sickness was *real*. Sunlight pierced through the car windows, and my face felt flushed. "Is it hereditary?" I asked suddenly.

My uncle gave me a wry smile in the mirror. "No te veo cara de loquita," no crazy little girl's face there, he teased as he turned the corner toward our house. "Here we go."

After he'd dropped us off, my mother retreated to the yard with a drink and a fotonovela.

I changed into my worn Cartagena de Indias T-shirt and heard Pablo practicing his new guitar from St. Stephen's. It was amazing how well Pablo was adapting to Catholic school, I had to admit, as I walked into his room and stood by the window to listen. Though Miami's undaunted sunlight blazed through the sky, the afternoon felt oddly finished. Maybe the end of the world was in broad daylight, I reflected, not in the tempest-tossed darkness I'd always imagined.

Pablo strummed the E minor chord. "It's the sad chord," he said, his bright eyes belying the words.

But I believed in the sadness, in everything that broke your heart. Like the things you couldn't fix, like torn photographs and ruined family mementos scattered across Miami by the hurricane... or like my father's crippled hand, forever clenched around the handle of an invisible suitcase as he fled a storm that wouldn't end.

For the next few days Pablo's persistent references to *The Three Faces of Eve* forced me to dwell on the disappearance of my father's previous personality. Were our problems really and truly cured? Or could the madman personality return? I broke down in front of the dreaded *World Book Encyclopedia* one morning and dragged the S volume into Pablo's room to read the schizophrenia entry aloud with him.

"You see?" I concluded, closing the book. "It doesn't say you get multiple personalities."

"It doesn't say you don't," he replied.

I decided I'd better talk things over with Lara.

When I went over there later that day, she sent the girls out to play and we sat down in her living room. "I had no idea it was schizophrenia, Gabi. I'm so sorry. How tragic."

"I didn't either," I blurted. "We just thought he was kind of crazy."

"You poor girl." She folded me into her arms. "Can Walter and I help?"

I shook my head. "But Lara, do you think it gives people split personalities? Like—personalities that come back sometimes?"

"I think what actually splits is the mind. I suppose it's more like a confusion, between what a person believes and what is real, objectively."

"Isn't that true for everyone's mind?"

"Not exactly. You and I know that the difference is there. We filter reality through our perceptions. Your father's mind doesn't see the difference."

"But how clear *is* the difference?" I asked ruefully. After all, I believed in lots of unreal things, such as leaving home, becoming a mightier person. Were there degrees of schizophrenia? Did I have some? I was so obsessed with *thinking*.

Lara brushed the hair back from my forehead. "You must be saddened by this, Gabi, no?"

"I'm kind of used to it," I admitted. "It's like I've been sad and worried my whole life."

"Oh no! You have so much to look forward to!" She hugged me. "You'll have your trip soon. And a good university education ahead of you. You'll be more than fine, Gabi, I promise."

On my way back home, I noticed the extent to which the hurricane had become an excuse for bigger changes. All the old Florida-style aluminum crank-up windows were getting replaced by those wide, modern panes so clear you could see into the houses. No more secrets.


The next day, Tío Victor walked my father into the house as if he were ninety-two years old. The cast was off and his arm was in a sling. Mami propped him on the couch with pillows as my brothers and I stood back. He was skinny, the hair strands combed arbitrarily across his scalp. His clenched hand ticked on the couch, but mostly his eyes were peaceful, as if he'd forgotten all the bad things he'd ever done.

Unfortunately, at dinner he brought up an old favorite: "Many barrels of crude are produced," he began, smiling as he prepared to lecture us across his plátanos.

Pablo threw me a triumphant glance: See? The return of another personality.

"In Barrancabermeja ... ," my father continued, but the words trickled off in mid-sentence.

"Tell your father about your progress with Sister Vincent," my mother ordered Pablo abruptly, though school hadn't yet reopened.

My father blinked twice at Pablo. He asked how old Pablo was.

Pablo grinned and started to tell him, but Mami put her hand over my brother's. "Roberto," she chided, "you know how old your son is."

When my father smiled blankly, she changed the subject to planning for Tía Consuelo's rescheduled trip.

After that, days followed in which my father meandered through the house just listening to the radio. Once, when I sat polishing the dining room table legs, he shuffled into the room and started to whisper-sing a Piero ballad the radio was playing while he peered out through the blinds: "Es un buen tipo mi viejo"—He's a good guy, my old man. The words hurt, and I had to put down my rag to brace myself against the haunting ones that followed: "Anda solo y esperando"—he wanders alone and waiting. Would my father remember that pitiful line? But only his faint "Anda" drifted across the room.

He began to forget. Neighbors' names. Our schools. Trips to his beloved post office. He forgot to go out for fresh air, and we had to remind him.

Mami told my brothers and me that it was because of the Mellaril. Once a month, my father was to return to Jackson Memorial for the psychiatrist to refill a prescription.

"I wonder what those pills do?" Pablo asked the day Mami gave us the lowdown on the medication before going off to clean some more.

"The directions say it's an antipsychotic," I explained. "But Tío Victor told me those drugs are kind of crude, and they make peoples' bodies' stiff and stuff like that."

"At least he doesn't hit," Manolo acknowledged. "That's good."

"Yeah." We nodded in unison.

No more police, no more arrests, no more disappearing green cards, or El Chinos to the rescue. Only my father's ghostly persona. Now my brothers could yell to their hearts' content if they so chose, but they so chose only when too lazy to walk to another room to ask Mami something in person. Occasionally, she yelled at them for dirtying the house; sometimes I yelled along to support her. My father was the only one who didn't yell.

When Mami stopped yelling altogether, I started to worry. Except for fotonovelas, nothing much distracted her anymore. I wished Tía Consuelo would hurry up and get here. I wished my mother's pal Camila, who knew the whole story now, visited more frequently. I wished the hurricane recovery would end so that Mami could return to her crummy but hustle-bustle job. She'd gotten so moribund—her spirit fading loyally with my father's.

The mailman finally brought a letter that shook her from that anomie. "Léete esto, mi'jita," she said curiously, handing me an official-looking envelope. I opened it, skimmed the letter, and extracted a check for my father. The letter promised more disability checks each month.

At last—the Government was sending my father his money.

Donning her reading glasses, Mami marveled. "It might cover our mortgage," she mused hopefully. "Maybe I can go part-time and keep watch on everybody."

She began to plan. Repairs and layaway purchases, long deferred, restored her sense of purpose. I should keep all my earnings now, she insisted to me. "As long as you save. Put some in the bank like your brother. For your college," she added, looking away as she uttered that dreaded word.

What I tried to save were memories. I wanted to remember the father I'd had as a kid, when I loved him the way you were supposed to, whatever that was. *Honor thy father and thy mother.* And though I'd tried to be loyal, in the end loyalty hadn't saved us. Now I had this shadow of a father who was hardly a person. If I could still love him, where was he? The Land of Father, patria, had disappeared into a horizon I would be squinting at long after I'd flown away with my own heavy suitcase of memories.

The day the government check arrived, I left Mami to her planning while I went canvassing the neighborhood one last time for vestiges of hurricane damage—in anticipation of the inevitable catastrophe tale comparisons that would flourish when school reopened the following week. Purposefully, I crossed over toward the recently paved sidewalk on the Cabreras' side of our street, but something compelled me back to our side, the lone holdout with its white gravel pebbles and random reeds poking through. Then I traversed the blocks toward Flagler and soon found myself continuing on to where all the streets yielded to weeds and grass.

Here was the old Miami, with brush fenced back to keep children away from Tamiami Canal. Snakes or a wandering alligator could still surprise you along the rough trail that began where the fence had been torn away by Hurricane Estrella. Slowing my pace,

I followed the overgrown path between shoulder-high clumps of cattails and saw grass. A white heron was fishing on one leg on the opposite bank, and I stopped to watch him, though the wild reeds partially hid him from view. The broad marsh reminded me of a field from one of the poems in my *Solitude* book—a field you couldn't kill, even if its flowers were cut down year after year to sell in towns.

I tore off a blade of grass and thoughtfully skimmed my finger along its edge. Maybe the Miccosukee had made their own paper from these reeds. Maybe the ancient Chibcha, too, had woven paper out of the long fibers of the cartageno trees along the Magdalena. As I gathered more reeds and the heron went on poking the water, my thoughts became as transitory as the fantasy of someone to marry me and take me away from my family. A canoe—my grandfather's—would glide forever across my distant childhood.

I'd told Mr. Lanham that I wanted to study the history of great indigenous civilizations. Lara believed in the greatness of literature, the saints of paper. Across the quiet marsh, the heron's wings flapped and stirred the cattails where he'd stood. I watched him fly up, disappearing into the endless southern sky. Turning, I began to braid the reeds I collected into a long, green *recuerdo de Miami*—a remembrance and a memento that I could carry away.

[ ACKNOWLEDGMENTS ]

I am humbled by all the love, enthusiasm, encouragement, and assistance I've received from so many others on this journey to bring my novel into the world. Among those to whom I owe my gratitude are my editor extraordinaire Selina McLemore, treasure of Grand Central Publishing, and her wonderful team there; Stéphanie Abou, my *simpatiquísima* agent, whose literary and intellectual gifts, cultural sensitivity, and multilingual talents I have been lucky to have guiding me; the incomparable Jenna Blum—special friend, mentor, teacher, and writer who shall live immortal in my heart as the wise and wonderful fairy godmother of *Try to Remember*; my many terrific writer friends who so generously provided their time reading and giving me the best of comments—including Emily Hammond and Steven Schwartz, Sarah Ignatius, Liza Nelson, Randy Susan Meyers, Cecile Corcoran, and my writer-colleagues in the Grub Street, Inc., Master Novelist Council; my daughter and very capable first reader Gabriela Kassel Gomez, my husband, Phil Kassel, who read painstakingly on multiple occasions, and my son Victor Kassel Gomez, who helped me write better because of his kindness to me; Sarah Vázquez, my bilingual editor par excellence; Pauline Adams, who believed in the truth within my story when it was just a speck gleaming from the darkness in my eyes; Hilda Hernández–Gravelle, who believed in the truth within me; Allan Rodgers, whose idealism and flexibility have empowered me and my colleagues at Massachusetts Law Reform Institute to realize and diversify our dreams; my family of birth, my family by marriage, and my family of wonderful friends; and the immigrants who keep on teaching me the virtues of Faith, Courage, and Perseverance.

Grateful acknowledgment is also made to all those, both living and deceased, whose inspiring words, lyrics, and/or music work are briefly referenced, excerpted, and/or adapted here, including: Padraic Colum's poem "Young Girl: Annam" reproduced in full; two lines from e.e. cummings's poem "Tumbling Hair"; a line from the lyrics of Carlos Vives's "19 de noviembre"; a line from the lyrics of Leonard Cohen's "So Long, Marianne"; two lines from the lyrics of Piero's "Mi viejo"; a line from the lyrics of Francisco Gabilondo Soler's "La negrita cucurumbé"; and adaptation of a quote attributed to Wole Soyinka by Derrick Z. Jackson in a *Boston Globe* article; and adaptations of parts of poems written to me personally and to other members of my family by my grandfather, Ricardo Madrid del Risco.

# Reading Group Guide

1. Gabriela, Evi, and Roberto betray one another at pivotal moments throughout this novel. How do these betrayals transform the characters and illuminate the difference between love and loyalty in relationships?

2. At one point in the novel, Gabriela is introduced to the four forms of love—*storge, philos, eros,* and *agape*—in the Greek classification system and later comes to wonder whether the four are equally as important. Is this question ultimately resolved in the novel?

3. Roberto's immigration experience is depicted as more difficult in certain ways than that of other family members. How do his and his family's acculturation difficulties affect their ability to distinguish what is "normal" behavior from what is not when he begins to change?

4. Why do the characters in this family go to such lengths to avoid exposing Roberto's mental illness to the outside world? Are there external social factors that drive some immigrant families to hide their problems and avoid seeking help from institutions designed to help them, such as the police, child protection agencies, and welfare providers?

5. Gabriela's beliefs about adult womanhood are formed in part by her exposure to two significant role models—her traditional mother, Evi, and the nontraditional or "feminist" model, Lara.

What do Gabriela's observations about both of these characters' compromises in relationships with men teach her about her path and choices as a woman?

6. The deportation threat faced by this family of *lawful* immigrants illustrates the fragility of lawful permanent residents' membership in the society that they've ostensibly been permitted to join permanently. Is Gabriela's belief that this is a "double standard" the reason she chooses to disobey some laws later on in the story?

7. South Florida, especially the Miami metropolitan area, undergoes a major transformation during the time frame of the novel (1968–1971). Which of these changes, both positive and negative, affect Gabriela the most and why? What insights does she gain as a result of her interactions with Cuban and Jewish people that help shape her own identity?

8. Gabriela's struggle with her losses launches her on a quest to understand and preserve the cultures of disappearing civilizations throughout the world. What, in the experience of loss, fuels this passion in her?

# Guía para grupos de lectura

1. En algunos momentos claves de esta novela se traicionan Gabriela, Evi, y Roberto el uno contra el otro. ¿De qué manera se transforman los personajes a raíz de ello y se alumbra la diferencia entre el amor y la lealtad en una relación?

2. Hay un momento en que a Gabriela se le informa que hay cuatro tipos de amor según el sistema de clasificación de los griegos —*storge, philos, eros*, y *ágape*— y luego ella se pregunta si los cuatro tienen el mismo valor. ¿Se resuelve esta duda al final de la novela?

3. La experiencia migratoria de Roberto se representa como más difícil que la de sus familiares. ¿Cómo les afectan estas dificultades de asimilación en cuanto a poder distinguir entre un comportamiento "normal" y uno no normal cuando Roberto empieza a cambiar?

4. ¿Por qué luchan tanto los personajes en esta familia para no revelar fuera de ella la enfermedad mental de Roberto? ¿Existen elementos externos en la sociedad que conducen a ciertas familias inmigrantes a ocultar sus problemas y a no pedirle ayuda a las instituciones creadas para proveer asistencia, tal como la policía y las agencias de protección de niños y del bienestar público?

5. Las creencias de Gabriela sobre lo que significa ser una mujer adulta se realizan en parte por ser expuesta a dos importantes modelos a imitar —el papel tradicional de madre que desempeña

Evi y el feminista que desempeña Lara. ¿Qué aprende Gabriela con respecto a su propio camino y sus opciones como mujer cuando observa lo que ambas mujeres han transigido en sus relaciones con sus hombres?

6. El riesgo de la deportación enfrentado por esta familia de inmigrantes *legales* demuestra lo frágil que es ser miembro de una sociedad que supuestamente le permite al inmigrante permanente legal pertenecer permanentemente. ¿Es esta doble moral la razón por la cual Gabriela luego decide desobedecer algunas leyes?

7. Un gran desarrollo ocurre en el sur de la Florida, sobretodo en el área metropolitana de Miami, durante el periodo transcurrido por la novela (1968–1971). ¿Cuáles de estos cambios, tanto positivos como negativos, afectan más a Gabriela y por qué? ¿Qué conocimientos adquiere ella como resultado de sus interacciones con las personas cubanas y judías que le ayudan a formar su propia identidad?

8. La lucha interna de Gabriela en cuanto a sus pérdidas la lanza en una búsqueda mayor de las culturas de aquellas civilizaciones del mundo que van desapareciendo para lograr entender y conservarlas. ¿Qué hay en la experiencia del perder que conmueve esta pasión en ella?

IRIS GOMEZ is an award-winning writer and nationally recognized expert on the rights of immigrants in the United States. She is the author of two poetry collections, *Housicwhissick Blue* (Edwin Mellen Press, 2003) and *When Comets Rained* (Custom-Words, 2005), and the recipient of a prestigious national poetry prize from the University of California. Her work is widely published in a variety of literary magazines and other periodicals.

A respected public interest immigration lawyer and law school lecturer, she has represented civil rights groups and individuals in high impact cases and won professional awards for her accomplishments—including a *Las Primeras* award for Latina trailblazers in Massachusetts. She has frequently been called upon to write and speak on immigration-related topics and has appeared in the media, including on the nationally televised *Cristina* show and Boston's celebrated bilingual late-night radio program *¡Con Salsa!*

An immigrant from Cartagena, Colombia, she spent her formative years in Miami, Florida, and has also lived in New York City, Michigan, and throughout the Pacific Northwest. She and her family now make their home in the Boston area.

*Try to Remember* draws on her personal experiences growing up as a Latina in Miami, during the peak of the Cuban diaspora, as well as on her substantial experiences as an immigration lawyer. Along with her professional work aiding immigrants in improving their legal status in the United States she has had to contend with the difficult issues involved in the deportation of lawful residents from the United States. Often wrenching for the affected families, these deportations have increased dramatically because of changes in laws that have significantly expanded the reasons for which a person might lose his or her legal status and even face permanent exile.

Some of the transcendent themes she explores in *Try to Remember* include the question of what "love" means in a family, and particularly the potential conflicts that may arise for a young woman between the ethic of family loyalty, such as that present in many Latino families, and the ethic of independence perceived as necessary for a woman to achieve career success. *Try to Remember* is also a love story—a story about the power and beauty of love in a Latino family, even though it may be struggling.

If you enjoyed *Try to Remember*, then you're sure to love
these emotional family dramas as well—

# Now available from Grand Central Publishing.

A secret journal threatens to destroy a young
Colombian-American woman as she uncovers
the truth about her mother's past in this stunning debut novel.

Look for future books from
Leila Cobo.

"An intricately woven tale of love and memory
from a deeply talented writer."

—*Booklist*

"López's engaging novel chronicles how four
sisters' lives are shaped by the loss of their
mother and their belief that they were granted
magical abilities."

—*Publishers Weekly*

Look for future books from
Lorraine López.